BEAUTIFUL WOMEN;
UGLY SCENES

BEAUTIFUL WOMEN; UGLY SCENES

C. D. B. BRYAN

DOUBLEDAY & COMPANY, INC.
GARDEN CITY, NEW YORK
1983

All of the characters in this book are fictitious
and any resemblance to persons, living or dead,
is purely coincidental.

Acknowledgments

The author wishes to express his gratitude to the National
Endowment for the Arts, for its support during the writing
of this book.

DESIGNED BY LAURENCE ALEXANDER

Library of Congress Cataloging in Publication Data

Bryan, C. D. B. (Courtlandt Dixon Barnes)
Beautiful women; ugly scenes.

Title.
PS3552.R85B4   1983   813'.54
ISBN: 0-385-17143-9
Library of Congress Catalog Card Number 82-46091
Copyright © 1983 by Courtlandt Dixon Barnes Bryan

For
Monique
as am I

BEAUTIFUL WOMEN;
UGLY SCENES

1

I USED TO THINK I understood women; that I could get along with them reasonably well. Now, I am beginning to realize how many I have infuriated and how, in a sense, I have been at war with women for most of my life.

More than once, during our marriage, Alice accused me of not really liking women. Before she left this time for France, Odette Villars, the woman I am in love with now, told me exactly the same thing.

I protested of course.

I wondered aloud whether instead of my not liking women hadn't she actually meant I did not seem to respect them.

"No, you respect them," Odette said. "You always behave towards women with perfect manners."

" 'Perfect manners,' yes," I said. "But not with the respect that liking them would mean?"

Odette was silent. Silent like a stockpiled bomb.

I do not want to lose this woman. I am afraid she will become so impatient with me she will never want to see me again. We have been through so much together, so many ugly scenes, dinners as tense as a condemned man's last meal; the wrong naked people in the wrong swimming pool; each other's marital battles and infidelities. Small wonder that she is so touchy, filled with resentment and rage! And yet she is also filled with love and thoughtfulness, tenderness and laughter. Most of all Odette is wise. She has a ruthless intelligence which pierces through all the presumptions, excuses, rationalizations, affectations, role-playing I still seem to carry with me like excess baggage into this affair.

I don't want to fight with Odette or with women anymore. We only wound each other, ourselves and those around us. There are too many incidents from these past years of which I am ashamed. I do not want to feel ashamed again.

I don't have many romantic illusions left about men and women. I used to, but that was before I met Odette, and before that dinner, and before our marriages broke apart. Before I found myself in the icy grip of panic, before I really understood how much my unsatisfactory relationships with women were my fault.

Enough time has passed for me to achieve some distance on that period, time enough so that now when I look back on the mess I have

made of my life, when I look back on two ex-wives, two children, two
houses I can no longer afford, it is to see whether I can learn how not
to make the same mistakes with a woman again.

It was Odette who told me a year ago that I could not hope to
understand women without understanding myself. Back then it had not
occurred to me I *didn't* understand myself, although, God knows, there
were clues: Once, for example, when Odette protested, "Would you
want your daughter to be treated by a man the way you treat me?" I
replied with barely a pause, "Hell, yes! I think she'd be very lucky to
find a man as basically decent as I am."

Had we been a vaudeville act she would have hit me with a pig bladder
"upside de head."

Another time she said I was more intent on being loved than I was on
loving—which is why, she added, I was often unlovable myself. I had
no snappy answer for that one. I knew I had always been interested in
the pursuit of beautiful women, yet I had difficulty making a real
connection with a woman, and once I'd made a connection, staying that
way. It also helps explain why I was never able to balance satisfactorily
my yearnings for love, a home, children, sex, success—all those things
other men want, too. I wish I had a better idea what other men want,
what they are like, and how I might be.

Odette has a European woman's unwavering sense of what a man must
be: strong, protective, caring, intensely loyal to his woman, whose well-
being must be his primary concern. (How else, she asks, can a man
expect a woman to provide the same?) And when I fail to live up to her
standards, oh God, she can be cruel! As cruel and as uncompromising,
I have come to learn, as only another woman can be.

Men quarrel like dogs: circling, growling, lunging, snapping, barking;
it is mostly bluff. When one dog gains the upper hand, the other rolls
over onto his back, his hind legs akimbo, exposing his softest, most
vulnerable parts. This is humiliation enough for the victor, who then
walks away.

But women? A woman does not quit until she has torn a man's bowels
from within him and scattered his fragile sense of self to the winds.
Women are so much angrier than men—especially women over thirty-
five! They feel so cheated and betrayed, disappointed and embittered by
their lives, by we men. Can it all be because so little of what they were
educated and trained for, brought up to expect and believe in, has proven
true or even relevant? So many of them seem to feel used and
unappreciated, frustrated intellectually, emotionally and sexually, bored

and lonely, exhausted all the time, isolated with their children and utterly without hope. For the mature woman, these are difficult times indeed.

It has been difficult, too, for men—for me. Difficult to know how to behave toward women. Difficult to know what they wanted. I listened to them, read their books. They said they wanted something more. They wanted equality, self-respect. They wanted to feel close; they wanted to feel passion; they wanted to feel secure; they wanted to feel *whole*.

It did me no good to tell Odette, "I understand." We both knew I didn't. Nor did it do me much good to tell her I loved her; Arthur, her ex-husband, loved her better than I did. He is now loving better Alice, my ex-wife. Several years ago there was a movie, *Bob and Carol and Ted and Alice*, which I never saw. I'm told it was a comedy. But when I look back on that awful night by the swimming pool and that last terrible dinner together—all of which we'll get to—I'll be goddamned if I can see how!

I am alone now. Odette has taken Paul and Vanessa, her children, back for a visit to their grandmother in France, just as she did at exactly this time last year. Although I miss her, I welcome the time her absence has given me to think about men and women, about rage and resentment, about role-playing and the devastating consequences of some of the games people play. Odette's absence gives me time to think, too, about my mother and brother, whose deaths several years ago combined with my deteriorating marriage to precipitate panic. I am trying to understand how my relationships with my family shaped my relationships with women, and why my relationships with women so often resulted in anguish, guilt and pain—not mine, alone, to be sure.

But most of all Odette's absence has given me a chance to think about that last dinner we two married couples shared, about how and why it came to be.

It is difficult to know exactly where to begin.

It all seemed to come to a head just before the twentieth reunion of my college class sixteen months ago. I had been asked to moderate a discussion on "Men's and Women's Interpersonal Relationships During the Midlife Crisis." I was asked to be moderator not because I had even the most tenuous of credentials—I'm a film-maker, not a psychiatrist—but because I was so obviously embroiled in crises of every imaginable kind myself. Seventy or so of my classmates (we were all in our early forties) and their wives attended.

Since I felt that speaking about one's personal problems was rather like talking about one's surgery scars—a subject of consuming interest only to one's self—I intended to open with only a superficial description of the circumstances leading up to the breakup of my second marriage and how the turmoil of that awful period prevented me from ever really feeling I had a true picture of what was going on. But shortly after I began speaking I realized that to try to use a "midlife crisis" as an excuse for what I did was dishonest, and that I had known at that dinner exactly what was going on, but that I had been too frightened to try to stop it.

That dinner had followed a year of grief and loss. The sudden, unexpected deaths of my brother, my mother, my stepfather, an uncle, a close friend occurring, as each had, one right after another in less than twelve months, had filled me with an awful sense of abandonment and the lingering suspicion and fear that Alice, or one of my children, or even myself might be next. The battle I had been fighting during the year leading up to the dinner had been not to save my marriage, but to save myself, because what I felt most of all during that period was afraid.

What was I frightened of?

I stood there that sunny autumnal afternoon in front of my classmates telling them about being afraid of tomorrow, of next month, of next year; I told them of being afraid of ending up old and alone and broke. I told them I knew my fears were silly, that feeling weak and fearful were identifiable symptoms of the "midlife crisis," the chrysalis from which an embryonic and redefined "self" would emerge. "But, oh God," I added, "there is nothing *silly* about the panic when it hits."

No one moved. I could not be sure from their stolid expressions whether my admissions were perplexing or simply embarrassing them. I plunged on.

I told my classmates how the loss of these people had left me feeling isolated and fearful, vulnerable and orphaned, with a terrible longing for reassurance and love. That not finding the companionship and under-standing I needed at home I had gone looking for them in other places, with the predictable result that the woman to whom I had been married for nearly ten years had just the previous month demanded a divorce. "Now when she looks at me in front of our son or speaks to me," I said, "it is as if I, too, were dead."

I started to tell them about the letters I had been receiving from friends over the past few years and how their correspondence had dealt primarily with individual loss: loss of husbands or wives, loss of purpose, of jobs, of relationships, of self-esteem.

At that moment the man who twenty years before had been the editor of one of the undergraduate publications walked stark naked into the meeting room. There was an obvious commotion, some nervous laughter, a joke about my having left out "loss of clothes," quick comparisons of penis size, a "Jesus Christ, Jerry, what are you doing?"

Needless to say, the point (or whatever it was I had been trying to make), too, was lost.

Jerry subsequently gave an extraordinarily articulate speech about the need for world disarmament. "When the last individual has disarmed," he told us, "world disarmament will be complete. I want all people everywhere to present themselves to each other as they really are— naked and without defense . . . P.S.," Jerry added, "I love you." He then sat down and remained seated, his legs rather primly crossed. The meeting broke up soon after.

A few classmates came up to me and talked about having made career changes, of not having felt any great need to get ahead, that they were content to devote their energies to their families. And there was such an obvious air of camaraderie between these husbands and wives that I envied them.

Another classmate, however, said, "I guess we've been able to structure our marriage in such a way as to avoid crises. My job, of course, takes a lot of time, but Beth, here, has been very active in the community. She's on a half-dozen boards: the hospital, the Republican committee, the school, the planning and zoning board, the garden club—did I leave any out? And our two little girls take up what time she has left. But we've been very happy together, haven't we, Beth?"

"Sure," Beth said.

The classmate smiled down at his wife and said, "You don't sound very convinced."

"Drop it," she said.

There was a formal dinner held that night for our class in a hotel. Several of my classmates approached me to say that they, too, had been going through some rough times with their wives. One of them said, "I can't believe how much my wife has changed! She's not anything like the girl I married."

"Haven't you changed, too?" I asked.

"Not at all," he said. "I weigh exactly the same as I did freshman year."

Another said, "For a long time I've been experiencing this turmoil. I have a wife I love, three children, a reasonably rewarding job, a nice house in a nice neighborhood and I keep feeling it's all going to be taken away because I'm an *imposter*. I mean, a guy doesn't earn these sorts of responsibilities until he's an *adult*. All I feel I'm doing is growing *old* without growing *up*."

Late that evening I was standing at the bar and a classmate introduced me to his wife. "Margaret, here," he said, "has always been interested in antiques, she has a very good eye for value. A couple of years ago when our children went away to school, she was rather at loose ends so I helped her open a store. Since Margaret didn't have any previous business experience I had to show her how to set up her books, how to avoid some of the mistakes. But now, for Chrissake, she's netting fifteen—eighteen thousand a year after taxes. It won't be long before she's bringing home more than I do!"

Margaret stared at him. "Don't patronize me," she said.

My classmate looked stricken. "All I meant—"

"I know perfectly well what you meant. The only reason you started me in the antique business is so I'd leave you alone."

"That's not so! You needed something to do!"

"I had plenty to do," she said coldly. "You try running that house for a couple of weeks, cooking dinners, doing laundry, the marketing, and you'll see I didn't need anything more to do. What I needed, what I *wanted* was some time together for us. The children were gone. We were alone. We could travel. See places we'd never been to. But you said you couldn't take the time off from work. So I said, 'Give me one day of the weekend. Just one day for *us*.' "

"We were together. All those weekends, I was home."

"Saturdays you watched football and Sundays, if you didn't take a nap, you watched some other sport. And when I said all I really wanted was a little 'togetherness' suddenly you found time to put me in that store."

"I thought you *wanted* the store."

"By then I did!" she said. "I wanted to see people, to get out of the house. I needed to talk to *someone*, other than the cleaning lady."

"You could have called your friends."

"*My friends?* We've moved so often for your job I haven't made real friends. The women I see are *your* business associates' *wives*. That's why I needed some time with you."

"We're together every night," he said.

"You're too tired to talk to me. You just slump in front of the TV."

"I work hard," he said. "I need time to relax, time to myself, to unwind."

"You get so unwound by ten o'clock you're asleep."

"I work damned hard," he said again.

"So do I!" his wife said. "But I still want, I still *need* to feel close to you."

"You feel any closer, you'll smother me." He turned his back on his wife and walked away. She watched him disappear into the crowd, but made no move to follow him. I stole a glance at my watch; it was a few minutes until midnight. "Margaret," I said, "may I get you a drink?"

She said no thank you, she was going home.

I walked her to the checkroom, then helped her into her Burberry trenchcoat with the woolen liner. "I didn't know you lived near here," I said.

"We don't," she said. She was fishing through her purse for her car keys. "We live in Boston—though it might as well be Cleveland for all I ever see of it. If you run into Bob, tell him I've left."

"For Boston?"

"For Cleveland, for all I care."

When I returned to the bar a classmate standing next to me told me how his eleven-year-old son had fallen out of their car when its door had flown open rounding a curve. The child's head had been crushed flat by the truck following behind. "My wife was driving," he said.

"Is she here with you tonight?" I asked.

"No," he said. He took a sip of his drink. "No, she's not here." He took a deep breath. "She doesn't go anywhere anymore."

"Perhaps she needs more time."

"Eddie died seven years ago," he said. "For the past seven years my wife hasn't left the house. She blames herself for Eddie's death, of course. She barely speaks to anyone. Doesn't even bother to get dressed. She puts a bathrobe on over her nightgown, that's all. Last summer I took a vacation by myself. I had to. It was my first vacation in seven years. I simply had to get away. I met this wonderful, marvelous, happy, understanding woman . . ." He stuck his finger into his drink and twirled the ice. "I couldn't get it up," he said.

The following afternoon Jerry was arrested for taking off his clothes in the end zone of the stadium during that Saturday's football game. I visited him that night in the correctional center where he'd been sent. He regretted nothing but his timing: he had discarded his last piece of clothing at the same instant the spectators' attention was riveted on a scoring attempt at the opposite end of the playing field. He asked that I telephone his mother and if I could bring him a copy of Walt Whitman's *Leaves of Grass* on my next visit, he'd appreciate it very much.

When I telephoned Jerry's mother I told her he was all right, that he was in a very good jail as jails go, and she said, "In *jail?* Don't tell me Jerry's been taking off his clothes again!" There was such a grand mixture of love and concern and resignation in her voice. Evidently, for the past several years, Jerry had been scattering his clothing like confetti from one end of the country to the other.

Late one Sunday morning not long after that college reunion I was sitting at my desk in the small cottage atop the hill in the deep woods to which, because of the terms of the separation agreement with Alice, I had recently moved. My telephone rang. It had been installed only a few days before and I was still unused to its assault upon the stillness surrounding me. The woman caller said I probably wouldn't remember her, but we had spoken briefly at the reunion.

"How are you?" I asked. She had not given me her name.

"I'm in bed with no clothes on," she said. "I've been touching myself. Don't laugh at me, please? I couldn't stand it if you laughed at me."

"I won't laugh," I said.

"And you don't have to say anything," she continued. "I just have to talk to . . . talk to you. Promise me you won't laugh?"

"I won't laugh," I promised again.

"I'm touching myself now," she said after a moment. "It feels nice. It feels good." Her voice was growing lazy. "I hope you're not just being polite. Sometimes I think you are too polite. You use manners to keep people at a distance. Remember what you said at the symposium about being lonely? I'm lonely, too. . . . You have such a sad face. I suppose you've been told that. Except for your mouth. Your lips . . ." There was a pause and then I could hear a sharp intake of breath. "Do you know what I wish you were here to do to me?"

I was trying to figure out who she could be.

"I'm touching my nipples now," she was saying. "I am imagining you are in the room with me, watching me touch myself. My nipples are standing up like little pencil erasers . . ."

Like little pencil erasers. My God, I had used that exact phrase almost thirty years before when I had pretended to have copied a long passage from a dirty book to sell to my classmates at boarding school. I had made up the whole story myself, of course, and was almost immediately found out. My vocabulary had not been up to the fervor of my imagination and my couples kept reaching "incredible organisms." An upperclassman— someone at least sixteen—had pointed out my mistake. Nonetheless he had admired my "like little pencil erasures" simile and that pleased me.

It would be several years before I would see an actual naked breast.

But when the woman on the telephone used that phrase she triggered memories of those mortifying teenage years when I was in love with Janet Ludlow Collins of the very blond hair and the bluest of eyes. Janet had a slight gap between her big, square front teeth and that gap undid me. She wore light summery dresses, delicate flowery pastel prints. And falsies. I loved to watch her move. She had, at thirteen, a dancer's high, rounded bottom and strong, pale, hairless thighs. I had terrible, marvelous, sweaty, sheet-roiling dreams about the slight puffiness of her cotton panties. I never saw them, of course. I never got any farther than kissing her. Janet was in love with the baseball captain; he was the one who told me she wore falsies.

"I wore an IUD for eight years," the woman on the telephone is saying. "It made it too easy to have an affair. Women must be true to themselves. They shouldn't just give their bodies to anyone. It's careless. I don't use birth control anymore because I don't want to be tempted. I'm too vulnerable now. I don't like feeling this way. I'm telling you this because I know you want to understand, because you do understand and because I know you're alone now and I am, too. My husband's downstairs watching some damned football game on TV. . . . . I wish you didn't live so far away. I'd come see you."

"How far away are you?" I asked.

"Shhh," she said. "Don't get tricky. And don't say anything. You don't need to say anything. All you need to do is listen, listen to me and"—there was another sharp intake of breath—"and watch."

Look, but don't touch, she might just as well have said. Wasn't that the unspoken rule which defined the parameters of all my earliest relationships with the opposite sex?

The first girl I fell in love with was Peggy Brown in the second grade. I was seven or eight, several years younger than my son Peter is now. Peggy was in love with Charlie Leonard—all the girls were. During recess when the other boys would tease and chase Peggy as tokens of their love, I would try to save her. I learned she did not always want to be saved.

Once when Charlie was chasing her, I ran in front of him and dropped to my knees so he would trip over me and fall like the bad guys did in the Saturday matinee serials, giving Peggy time to get away. Instead of tripping he simply sat down on me and, after a moment, Peggy stopped running, circled back and sat down on me, too. They both remained there sitting on my back, laughing and catching their breaths, squashing me with their weight. I could imagine the breeze blowing through Peggy's blond, her *very* blond hair, sunlight dancing in her bluest of eyes. I was so humiliated I wanted to run away, but I could not get up.

At fifteen I fell in love with Maureen Nichols. I used to row the width of the lake on which we spent summers just to see her, talk to her, sit by her side. It took me all of June and the first three weeks of July before I gathered enough nerve to tell her I loved her. I caught up with her at the bottom of the steps to the timbered, old lodge dining hall. It was dusk, the mosquitoes had savaged me all the way across the lake; I was covered with little red welts. "Maureen," I said, "Maureen, what would you say if I told you I loved you?"

"Boy! Those mosquitoes really got you, didn't they!"

"Maureen, I—"

"Listen," she said, "I've really got to run. My parents are waiting for me in the dining room. They'll kill me if I'm—"

"Maureen, *please*," I interrupted. "I want to tell you something. I love you."

"Oh," she said.

She looked at me with a mixture of embarrassment and impatience in *her* bluest of eyes. "Well, that's really sweet of you, nice of you, I mean. I mean, thank you, I guess. But, see, I can't really encourage you. I mean, I'm already in love with—"

I pressed my fingertips to her lips, not wanting to hear. I stood before her, heat rising to my face, my nostrils filled with the scent of bug repellent and sweat. She turned away from me and I watched her blond hair bounce as she sprang up the lodge dining hall's steps, then I fled into the woods and threw up.

"Have you ever read Colette?" the woman was saying into the telephone. "No, don't answer me. Don't speak. . . . Every woman needs to find a man she can respond to. Become a part of. Can lose herself in. Can become the whole woman she wants to become: the virgin-whore, the daughter-mother, the child-woman. Before a man can penetrate a woman, he must penetrate her mind. When you spoke at that symposium you gave me goose bumps . . . I'm still touching myself . . . Do you travel very much?"

"I get to Boston more than I do Cleveland," I said.

Margaret was silent for a moment. "How long have you known it was me?"

"Ever since you said your husband was watching the football game on TV."

"Why didn't you tell me you knew? I think I'm going to hang up," she said. "I'm very embarrassed."

"Don't be," I said.

"I've never called anyone like this before."

"I believe you."

"I really never have done anything like this," she said. "I don't know what got into me." Margaret gave a sharp bark of a laugh. "Well, that's part of the problem. Nothing's gotten into me since the first week in September. But I need friendship more than I need sex. I was feeling lonely. I was just lying here in my bed with the Sunday *Times*. I was looking at the advertisements in the magazine, the couples on the beach, and I felt like touching myself. But it was just so lonely, you know what I mean? And then I thought of you."

"I'm very flattered."

"Don't be polite," she said.

"That was nerves, Margaret," I answered. "I didn't know what to say."

"You don't have to say anything. I just felt like talking. You know, maybe I'll call you again sometime. I don't feel so embarrassed now. It was nice talking to you."

"It was nice talking to you, too," I said.

The last time my wife Alice and I made love she said, "The reason why you don't turn me on is because you're too sweet and you talk too much." I had rolled over onto my back and lay there, hurt and angry and incapable of remembering a single word I had said.

When months later I happened to tell Odette about the telephone call we were lying on my bed in the cottage, with the woodpecker we'd nicknamed "Coitus Interruptus" hammering away at a wood shingle on the roof of the house.

"Are you going to meet her?" she asked.

"Of course not."

"But you're friends with her husband."

"Until the reunion I hadn't seen him for twenty years. There's no reason to start seeing each other now."

"Of course there is," Odette said. "His wife."

I rolled over onto my side and touched her naked hip. "What do I need to do to convince you that I've changed? That I no longer feel compelled to go to bed with every woman I see?"

"You need only stop taking such obvious pleasure in telling me about the women who call."

It wasn't my pleasure that made me tell Odette about the women who called, it was my surprise. For the first twenty years of my life no woman had ever called me first. No woman I had wanted had ever wanted me. And so I spent the next twenty years getting even, hurting back, wounding the women I cared about before they could wound me. I had never been faithful because I was afraid that as soon as a "Charlie Leonard" came along the woman I was with would as inevitably as had Peggy Brown circle back to sit on me.

I had been a virgin until the afternoon of the Homecoming game, the fall of my college junior year. I was twenty years old and in love with Hope Bromley, who was a virgin, too, and a sophomore at a college nearby. For months we had held back, not "gone all the way"—a phrase which, it seemed to me, should be written with little stars inserted between each letter for emphasis like Leo Rosten's H*Y*M*A*N K*A*P*L*A*N.

Hope and I would lie naked in my college bedroom surrounded by bookcases filled with blue-bound Oxford University Press onionskin-paged volumes of British poets watched over by a slightly ratty stuffed Great Horned Owl. I was wonderstruck by Hope's body, the velvety texture of her rose-petal skin, the sweet, womanly curve of her hip, the fullness, the weight of her breasts, the seeming brittleness of her blond pubic hair.

No mystery has ever been greater or more exciting to me than that of a woman's body seen and explored for the first time. I could not keep away from Hope, could not stop touching her even for an instant. I was obsessed. "Well, look, if I just put it in you a little . . ." I would shamelessly say. "Not all the way, I promise, just a bit of the head . . . I won't move. I promise. See? You can trust me. I won't push. Doesn't that feel good? Maybe just a little more now, another fraction of an inch. Ah, God, Hope, why don't we just—" and POW! Her body would suddenly materialize across the bed away from me and I would be left twanging and vibrating like a piano string.

I'm not sure why it was the afternoon of the Homecoming game that Hope gave in. Perhaps she was like Napoleon's army responding to Moscow's winters and I had simply worn down her will to fight; but I think Hope, too, felt it was time. Virginity had become almost a burden, a barrier to her becoming the woman she felt emotionally she already was. And so that afternoon she didn't pull away; instead she held me to her and she was as trembly and eager as I was. Afterward, when *It* had finally happened, we felt no disappointment, not one shred of regret. Our first attempt at making love had proved totally joyful, an event filled with laughter and awe, tenderness and relief, and a passion that took both of us by surprise. More than twenty years have passed and I still look back on that first afternoon with gratitude and love.

Those initial shy explorations could have gone so badly! I wanted so much to be a good lover: strong but tender, thoughtful though sure—a Gary Cooper or a Jimmy Stewart instead of a Clark Gable or John Wayne. My sense of masculinity was so fragile and shaky—why did it take me so long to understand that a woman felt the same way? At twenty it seemed to me that everyone in the world had made love except me—and well. I worried that if I bungled it Hope would end up disappointed, hating me, think me a fool; I worried she would feel dirty somehow, used. Instead, it was marvelous. We were marvelous, like puppies. We loved making love and couldn't wait to do it again. We were together every weekend until I graduated, went into the Army, and was sent overseas. Hope married someone else while I was away; the marriage lasted four years. She was divorced a little less than two years after I returned. She married a second time several years later and divorced again about six months before my second wife and I separated.

A year ago last September—early in that same month before my twentieth college reunion, when my second wife would ask me for a divorce—the month of that terrible dinner—I was sitting in my nearly empty office behind the house we still lived in then. The telephone rang. I had been looking out the window at the sun trying to break through the clouds.

"This is your third wife," a woman said.

I could not place the voice. At first I thought she might be one of Alice's New York City friends; there seemed to be a slight hardness to her "r's," a trace of the Bronx.

"Who?" I asked.

"It's Hope!" she laughed. "Who else are you planning to have as a 'third wife'?"

The third wife business had been a joke between us that had gone sour not long after our first divorces. We had exchanged occasional Christmas cards, irregularly written. At the time of this phone call, I had not seen or spoken to Hope for over ten years.

"I'm going to be in New York next weekend," she said. "I hear you're celebrating your twentieth reunion next month and, well, I was thinking isn't it about time we celebrated our own?"

The sun suddenly broke through the clouds bathing my office in light.

"You're not saying anything," Hope said.

I told her I was smiling.

"Well, will you come see me in New York?"

"You know I will," I said.

I met Hope for lunch at the Biltmore—it seemed like an appropriate place. We were both somewhat nervous; I was, I know. In the back of my mind was the unresolved question: could we have saved each other any of the anguish of the previous years if we had married each other, if I had not fled? We could have married after college; I would have had to go into the Army, but I could have requested an assignment to a Stateside post. Instead I had volunteered for an overseas assignment to give myself some time to think about my future and Hope had made plans of her own.

Hope had changed little in the ten years since I had seen her—a certain thickening about the waist that was not unpleasant. She was an utterly beautiful woman, even more beautiful now that she was mature. Men looked up at her from behind their newspapers and magazines as she passed. Hope's hair was still very blond, but there existed now just the slightest edge of terror in her, yes, bluest of eyes.

When I had met Hope in the lobby and we had kissed (a bit awkwardly, bumping our cheekbones too hard), we had stood there for a moment just looking at each other, our eyes swiftly cataloguing the changes, noting them with kindness, affection, the sort of look brothers and sisters exchange after a separation of years.

"Come on," I said, "I'll get us a drink."

"Can we eat? I'm starving," she said.

"We can go directly to the dining room and have a drink and order."

"You look thinner," she said.

"Not 'thinner.' More lithe. Like a cat," I said. "I now move like an old and somewhat battered cat."

We held hands all the way to the dining room.

After our drinks arrived and while we waited for lunch, Hope and I talked about how the last time we had seen each other ten years ago we had been in New York City, too. I had taken her then to Allen's, a dark wood-paneled and brass-railed white-collar bar on the East Side in the Seventies that has since gone under. There, over hamburgers and home fries and beer, she had told me how she was deeply in love with the Washington correspondent of a Belgian newspaper who was either unable or unwilling to get a divorce. She had smiled rather ruefully, I remember, as she said she always seemed to be falling in love with the wrong man.

Her first husband, she told me, liked to call her "Mommy" and wanted her to make love with him outside in the garden of their New York brownstone, while their neighbors were holding a cocktail party just on the other side of the high wall. She wouldn't. (He since gave up his law practice and now operates a sports parachute center in New England.) After dinner we had gone to a movie and later she had firmly kissed me good night at her hotel elevator's door. I had told her I would like to come up, but she said no, we shouldn't, she couldn't, not while she was so in love with her Belgian correspondent. I did not argue with her although I did not understand why she should feel that way.

I would not understand until Odette.

During lunch that afternoon at the Biltmore, Hope told me about the life she was making for herself in California, that she had gone back to school to get her graduate degree and discovered she had a natural affinity for economics and had already been offered an excellent job with one of the development agencies within the UN—hence her visit to New York.

I did not ask, nor did Hope offer the reasons for her second divorce; she told me, instead, about her vacation in Rio de Janeiro and of her affair with a German architect there.

During the next thirty minutes she must have related the details of at least a half-dozen other affairs. She told me about them with a certain amount of bravado, but it was clear that none of them had left her any happier than had mine.

And then Hope asked me why I had stayed married to my second wife for so long.

"Oh, Hope, you know all the reasons why people stay married: children, routine, money, weakness, cynicism . . ."

"Those aren't the real reasons. Not yours."

"I love having my children around me. I love having a home. I *need* a solid base."

"Why? Why when you're unhappy?"

"You wouldn't believe me."

"Try me."

I shook my head. "No, you don't know—you can't know what it's been like this past year or so."

"What do you mean?"

"I mean I thought I was going crazy."

I can see Hope's warm, open, caring expression now as clearly as if that lunch had taken place today instead of over sixteen months ago. I remember the way the waiters drifted past our table overlooking the street. I can remember the softness of the worn white linen tablecloth, the china, the heavy silverware, the businessmen all about us, the deep thrum of their voices. I looked up at Hope, my first lover, my friend.

"You know, the last three producers I worked with died. The first in a car crash, the second was killed by a mugger while jogging in Central Park, the third made a joking reference within my hearing about my being the Angel of Death and two weeks after the film was in the can he dropped dead on a tennis court. He was twenty-eight years old. Not one of them reached forty-five."

"But you can't believe you're responsible for their deaths!" Hope protested.

"Normally I wouldn't. But it hasn't been—*I* haven't been normal. Things started coming apart a year and a half ago when the airline commissioned me to do a Hawaii promo. I took it because it gave me a chance to visit my brother Carter, who'd been living out there for about fourteen years. He was helping me film a night-surfing sequence. We had all these kids with torches riding the waves in and one of them was struck by another's surfboard and washed up dead at our feet. About a month after I left Hawaii my brother disappeared in the ocean . . ."

"Carter? Was he ever found?"

"No," I said. "That was a year ago last June. Two months later, in August, my uncle died just a day after he and I had had lunch. And three weeks after that, in September, my stepfather died. People I cared about just kept *dying*. Harry Pelman, who produced my film about the 'Moonies' in Gloucester, was killed jogging that same summer. My friend Roy Fredericks—"

"I remember him," Hope said.

"—was killed filming an automobile race in the South of France in October, last year. It just wouldn't *end!* And then the Christmas before last my mother . . ."

"I never wrote you. I wanted to," Hope said, "but what is there to say?" She shrugged helplessly.

"I was driving back from the airport. I'd put Alice on the plane and Peter and I were on the way home when I suddenly found myself saying a prayer for my mother. The telephone was ringing when I reached the house. My mother had had a massive coronary. Never knew what hit her. . . . I didn't know what was happening, why it was happening. Everyone was dying and all I could think of was my producer's line about my being the Angel of Death. I was scared to talk to people, to answer the phone. I worried about who would be next. Alice? One of the children? I kept thinking somehow it was *my fault!*"

"Had your mother had any history of heart problems?" Hope asked.

"No. Nothing. The last time I saw her was a couple of weeks before she died. She came to visit and we were sitting up late together talking, Alice had gone to bed, and my mother said, 'Promise me if I have a stroke, if I turn into a vegetable and am put on some machine, promise me you'll pull the plug.' I had never heard her talk that way before. She had always been the most vibrant, alive, *determined* to live woman. But after my brother's death, Uncle Paul's—he was my mother's older brother, only brother—and my stepfather's death all happening in the space of three months she had suddenly seemed gutted and tired, terribly alone."

"Her son, her brother, her husband," Hope said. "It must have been awful for her."

"I remember her face the next morning as we said good-bye. How could I not have sensed it was for the last time? She was standing next to the open door of her car. I have no idea what she said. I recall only the expression on her face: a little lost, wide-eyed, frightened of I didn't know what. Two weeks later she was dead and six weeks after that I was living alone in an apartment in Leadville, Colorado, frightened and worried about who would die next.

"That was the winter before last," I told Hope.

I had run out of money and had taken a job as a visiting professor at a college on the east slope of the Rockies. The cancer documentary I had started in 1976 was taking me twice, three times as long to edit as I had thought it would. For the past two years I had spent all my working days immersed in death, in the terrible anguish and loss and rage cancer caused. I had become as obsessed by the mystery of the disease as the researchers I had filmed. I could not talk about, write about, think about anything else.

What money I had left had been invested in a Canadian petroleum stock, which had suddenly and inexplicably been suspended from trading on the New York Stock Exchange. My funds were therefore locked out of reach. I had borrowed seven thousand dollars. I was taking Valium.

I bought life insurance, made out a will, got Blue Cross health insurance, took a physical, quit smoking dope, and took vitamins instead. I tried transcendental meditation, yoga, took long walks in the cool, high altitude air.

When I wasn't editing or teaching I was in the college library investigating angels. I had come to believe that God in His infinite mercy might not want His angels to be aware of their true purpose on earth, that if one knew one was an Angel of Death, could one still perform such a task? In rabbinic writings I discovered references to more than a dozen different Angels of Death and in my craziness I could find reason to believe I might be any one of these.

I had even begun to wonder whether I had ever actually existed as a child. During that long, last evening with my mother I recalled asking her what I had been like as a young boy. It had been a question asked in utter innocence; I was trying to relate some of my experiences to those of my son in order to better understand him. My mother looked at me for a moment and said she couldn't really remember. And later, when I had played that scene over and over again in my mind, I found myself wondering whether there hadn't been something strange and evasive about the look she had given me. Was she afraid because I was coming too close to the truth? Was that why she was killed?

I did not tell Hope that I had even come to suspect that Janet Ludlow Collins and her falsies, Peggy Brown and Charlie Leonard of the second grade, Maureen Nichols rushing up to meet her parents in the dining lodge, none of them had ever really existed. That the photographs in the family albums were nothing more than clever fakes. What I did tell her was that I had eventually come to my senses, that I had learned to live with the loss. In a curious way the deaths of my mother and brother, stepfather, and uncle had made it impossibly hard to recall my past with any clarity. I remembered episodes, yes; little *tableaux vivants* in which the dead members of my family seemed almost charmingly posed. But these episodes seemed strange and artificial, again clever fakes. It was nonsense, I now realized, to think myself an Angel of Death. As I told Hope, I could just as easily have come to believe I was Anastasia, say, or Peter Pan. But it was not nonsense to me then, nor when I spoke to Hope was I certain that my calling it nonsense was anything more than bravely whistling in the dark. The day before I had met Hope in New York I had had to take Peter, my then eight-year-old son in for his annual physical. When he had lain stripped to his underpants on the examining table, rigid with apprehension and pluck, I saw him suddenly as a corpse.

I had to touch him, speak to him, make Peter move before my eyes and only then did my terror dissipate.

What makes me so sure it is nonsense now? I'm not. It's only that nobody close to me has recently died. Still, a couple of weeks ago when I returned to the cottage, I discovered that a photograph of Odette I'd hung had fallen off the wall. The glass had shattered across her chest. As casually as I could, I telephoned Odette to see if she were all right.

After our lunch at the Biltmore, Hope and I went to some art galleries and then to her hotel room and bed.

"Your technique has improved," she told me. "But some of your youthful impulsiveness is gone."

I kissed her on the throat.

And much later, during dinner, she reached across the table and took my hand. "Are you going to spend the night with me?" she asked.

"I'd like to," I said.

"Yes, please do," Hope said. "I can't stand sleeping alone." She looked at me a little embarrassed. "It's the nights I hate." Her fingers fluttered nervously within my grasp. "The nights and the early mornings—those hours before the dawn when everything looks so black." She forced herself to smile. "I still like the afternoons," she said. "And evenings. Especially evenings like this . . ." Her smile suddenly crumpled. "But, oh God, the nights can get me. I just can't stand being alone."

We sat up together in her hotel bed watching the Home Box Office movie, her feet all curled up in mine. And later, when her head drooped against my shoulder, and still I could not sleep, I watched the second feature alone. Several times Hope cried out in her dreams; I could not make out what she said. I could only hold her, fold my arms around her until her body would relax and I could feel the tension leave her. She would roll against me then, nuzzle her nose into my neck, her lips making little kissing sounds.

At about four that morning I awoke with that sudden stab of anguish I'd grown almost accustomed to. Hope wasn't in the bed. I saw her sitting in a chair next to the open window. The curtains had been drawn back and the shade raised. She was hugging her knees to her chest.

"Hope, are you all right?" I asked. I got out of bed and walked to her side.

"When do you have to leave?"

"Later. This afternoon. Are you all right?"

"I was worrying about this coming night," she said. "I know it's silly, that I'll be back in California the day after and I'll be fine. But I was worrying about being alone in the city tonight and what I would do."

"You still have friends in the city, don't you?" I asked. "Someone you could see?"

"I suppose so," she said. "There must be someone . . ."

"I won't leave you until you've got your evening set."

Hope came back to bed then and we knew it would be the last time we would be together for a long time. And yes, it was still marvelous making love, and we said things like why had we waited so long. But we knew why. We needed one another more now as friends than as lovers.

We had been lying together silently for what seemed like a long time when Hope asked if I was still awake.

"Yes," I said.

"What are you thinking about?"

"How glad I am to have seen you again. That I wish I knew how to help you more."

Hope gave a hollow little laugh. "I was thinking I wouldn't mind at all if you really were the Angel of Death."

That afternoon in the train taking me back to that dinner and my angry wife a small newspaper item caught my eye. It was an Associated Press filler out of Belgrade:

This Little Piggy Went Home
BELGRADE, Yugoslavia (AP)—
A homesick pig walked more than forty miles to the farm of his former owner, the newspaper *Politka Express*, reported. The pig had been sold the day before.

I remember thinking, "Ah, you poor doomed sweet pig, I know exactly how you feel."

I tore the story out of the paper and I must have tucked it away when I got home because I found the clipping again about three weeks ago when I was cleaning out my desk. Rereading it now sixteen months later makes me realize I could not then have understood the humiliations the pig and I would so willingly undergo, nor could I foresee how weak and spineless we would come to feel. I could plead now in the pig's defense that it could not anticipate what was in store. I would have defended myself, too, with that argument a year ago. But not anymore.

Back *then*, continually confronted by the hostility and resentment of my wife, the lack of intimacy with my daughter, my dissatisfaction with my work, my feelings of isolation, vulnerability, confusion, my loss of purpose, self-esteem, and self-control, my terrible battles against anxiety and mortal fear that I had somehow become an Angel of Death . . . then, I could not understand how or why these crises were happening to me.

Now, I understand that some of them were quite normal and inevitable, but the rest of them—especially those having to do with my relationship with women—I see I brought upon myself.

That evening after I had left Hope in New York, the garbage and dirty kitty litter box had been left out for me like storm warning flags at the back door to our house. And when Odette Villars and her psychiatrist husband Arthur arrived for dinner and I saw the quick little looks exchanged by Arthur and my wife and the studied indifference with which Odette looked at me, I think I knew then what was coming. All four of us did. But not one of us, not Alice, nor Arthur, not Odette, nor I—not one of us made any move to stop it.

Several years ago a Jesuit priest in the Bedford-Stuyvesant ghetto of New York published a little book for the children of his community in an attempt to interest and engage them in their lives. "Every man has the challenge to name life," the priest wrote, "not to label it with the easy slogan or cliché, but to tell it like it is . . . To name life means looking at life, tasting it, letting it crash through our defenses so that we become vulnerable in the face of life's many experiences. Every man's choice of life depends upon his discovering and naming of its rhythms, shapes and themes. Every man lives to name life, and if I name life I must risk my word, my tears, my laughter and dancing—my*self*, in putting a name to this experience called living."

What follows now is my attempt to name life—and if there is any dancing that I risk, then I hope it will be neither waltz nor disco, but something rather like a gavotte, which my old dictionary defines as "a dance of French origin, somewhat resembling the minuet, remarkable for its combination of vivacity and dignity." I will attempt to perform it, however, with a certain amount of raising and stomping of feet.

I used to think I understood women.

They used to think they understood me.

2

IT IS DIFFICULT for me to recognize what is true between a married couple. By that I mean, what is real, what is *fact*, and not just what one or the other perceives is going on. I also find it hard, following some awful marital crisis or confrontation, to understand and especially to admit the reasons behind what was said or done. During our marriage Alice and I operated within such a labyrinth of rages, sensitivities, disappointments, confusions, and imagined slights that it is virtually impossible for me to assert with any certainty that either of us understood or appreciated each other's motives at any time.

At some point we must have been decent persons, basically thoughtful and respectful of each other's feelings. But that all changed, and changed partly because we each made certain basic assumptions about how the other was to behave as the "husband" and as the "wife." And those roles one of us *expected* the other to play led predictably to resentment, defensiveness, an unwillingness to compromise, guilt, and finally an abdication of responsibility. We didn't care. Too often what one of us took for anger was the other's cry for help. Understanding—when and if it came at all—arrived too late. Our marriage developed into an adversary relationship, that of a handball-to-wall, until eventually in the course of several long late summer evenings, culminating in that dinner with the Villars at our house, our marriage—and the marriage of Arthur and Odette—broke apart, out of loneliness, desperation, boredom, sexual curiosity, and a desire to punish our spouses.

Julio Cortázar, an Argentine writer for whom I have the deepest admiration, wrote in his novel *Hopscotch:* "If the volume or the tone of the work can lead one to believe that the author is attempting a sum, hasten to point out to him that he is face to face with the opposite attempt, that of an implacable *subtraction*."

I think what Cortázar means is that writing is and must be a form of distillation, an attempt to extract the essence of the characters, their relationships, mood, behavior, the scene, the story. (There is also that sense of Hemingway's dictum of what is important about a story is what is left out; but I believe that the key word is distillation, not omission.) Memory serves much the same function. That dinner took place over a year and a half ago and my recollections of what went on that night are

necessarily colored by my own bias and interpretation of the events, and
by the fact that during that period I was quite crazy. Everyone, including
Odette, agrees with me about that. Nevertheless I find that as much out
of shame and embarrassment as of the passage of time I have determinedly
attempted not only to "subtract" but to *erase* that dinner's more painful
details, to blot them out of my mind. I have not been entirely successful,
for even now as I try to reconstruct that evening my memories are so
crowded with a desire to make excuses, to explain, to justify why I
behaved the way I did that I feel out of fairness to the others that I
should simply *report* that evening with the nonjudgmental detachment
of a motion picture camera's eye. If, however, in doing so, the direction
seems at times a bit one-sided, blame it not on the cast that was
assembled, but on the inevitable subjectivity of any documentary film-
maker's point of view.

That dinner.

It was the last meal we ate together, "we" being Odette and Arthur,
Alice and me. Another couple was present—that is, another male and
female. Philippe, the third man, was a houseguest of Arthur and Odette's,
a friend of theirs from France. The third woman was Alice's cousin
Barbara T. (so-called to differentiate her from Barbara T.'s mother, Alice's
aunt, known as Barbara S.). Barbara T. was also Alice's best friend. I
make the distinction about Philippe and Barbara T. not being a "couple"
because by the time of that dinner, Barbara T. had asked us to make
certain she did not get stuck alone with Philippe.

The guest list is the "Cast" of course.

FADE IN:

*1. EXTERIOR: PRINCETON RAILROAD STATION PLATFORM. LATE
SUMMER. 4:05 P.M.*
A LONG SHOT as the 3:05 train from Pennsylvania Station in New York
approaches the station.

*2. EXTERIOR: ANOTHER ANGLE—FROM THE PLATFORM AS TRAIN
COMES TO HALT.*
Passengers step out onto the platform, about an equal mix of college
students, commuters, women who have been shopping in New York.
The camera closes in on me disembarking and stays with me as I head
across the platform until I disappear among the other passengers.

CUT TO:

3. INTERIOR: OLD STONE FARMHOUSE. 4:06 P.M.
It is Alice's and my house, an old pre-Revolutionary War stone farmhouse,

formerly owned by an architect who had added a glass and fieldstone open-to-the-ceiling, one-story addition. The rest of the house retains its exposed beams and wide-plank flooring.

ALICE is arranging a cold pork roast on a serving platter in the kitchen, which looks out upon the addition. BARBARA T. is standing at a counter next to her polishing silver. The radio is playing.

CUT TO:

4. *EXTERIOR: TWO-LANE HARD-TOP COUNTRY ROAD. 4:15* P.M.

Camera picks up a dark green Peugeot station wagon heading north, then tracks with the Peugeot as it passes through the farmland.

5. *INTERIOR: PEUGEOT.*

I am driving. I reach down and tune radio and stop at station playing Elton John's "Mama Can't Buy You Love."

CUT TO:

6. *INTERIOR: OLD STONE FARMHOUSE. 4:15* P.M.

We hear the same Elton John record on the radio in the house. ALICE is fixing two vodka tonics. She carries them into the dining room and hands one to BARBARA T., then stands examining the room with a critical eye. The table has been set. ALICE picks up one of the crystal wineglasses by the stem and holds it to the light, rotating the glass gently to check for spots. ALICE goes from glass to glass while BARBARA T. is arranging the silver salt and pepper shakers and ashtrays she had been polishing. Two vases of low, fresh-cut flowers stand on either side of a silver Tiffany bowl filled with fresh fruit. ALICE takes one of the vases and moves it to the sideboard. She removes the silver bowl, too, and carries it into the kitchen. BARBARA T. is placing small glass cigarette boxes between every other place setting. ALICE returns with four silver candlesticks, which she places on either side of the remaining vase of flowers, two at the head of the table, two at the foot. ALICE then again stands back and examines the room.

CUT TO:

7. *EXTERIOR: OLD STONE FARMHOUSE. 4:25* P.M.

My green Peugeot station wagon turns into the driveway and parks. I step out and walk toward the back door of the house.

CUT TO:

8. *POINT OF VIEW (POV) MYSELF. 4:26* P.M.

I approach the house and see the dirty kitty litter box and bags of garbage waiting for me at the backdoor. The camera remains over my shoulder as I open the door and enter the house.

CUT TO:

9. *INTERIOR: OLD STONE FARMHOUSE. KITCHEN.* 4:26 P.M.

BARBARA T. is closing the dining room door, "sealing-off" that room until the dinner party begins, as ALICE turns toward me, her face angry.

ALICE

Where the hell have you been?

MYSELF

New York.

ALICE

You said you'd be coming back this morning.

MYSELF

I had lunch with a friend from the *Village Voice* and caught the 3:05. Hi, Barbara T. How's your foot?

BARBARA T.

Fine.

No, wait. CUT.

I've got to stop here for a minute while I explain the business about Barbara T.'s foot. And the tone of her "Fine."

The day before I'd gone into New York to meet Hope, Barbara T. had come to stay with us. (She had been spending at least two or three weekends with us out of each month while she was looking for a job in New York.) Alice had gone off shopping, Barbara T. was upstairs taking a shower. I had come into the house from my office in the garage for some coffee when I heard a crash like broken glass coming from the shower and a little yelp of pain. I went upstairs and stood by the bathroom door and called, "Barbara T.? Are you all right?"

"I've cut my foot," she replied, then after a moment added, "Come in." She was sitting wrapped in a towel, on the edge of the tub, her foot resting inside it on the porcelain. The bathroom was hot, filled with steam. A light dribble of blood was flowing down toward the drain. The ceramic soap dish had come out of the wall and shattered in the bottom of the tub.

"How badly did you cut yourself?" I asked.

"It's on the bottom of my foot. I can't see it well enough to tell. It doesn't hurt really."

I turned the water on and had her stand while I rinsed the blood off her foot. Although the cut was clean, it looked quite deep. She was balancing herself on one foot while I knelt before her. Her towel came undone and fell to the floor. She made no move to retrieve it; instead, she leaned closer to me.

"That's not fair," I said.

Her body was humid, pink from the shower. I could feel the heat radiating from her hip inches from my brow, a heat that beat at me in waves. Barbara T. loosened her grip on my shoulder and bent forward to pick up her towel. Her naked breasts loomed before me. "I've got to sit down," she said.

She swung around on her good foot and neatly folded her towel, then placed it on the toilet seat lid. She turned back again as she sat facing me resting her cut foot on its heel. I wrapped a hand towel around it; the bleeding had all but stopped.

I was still kneeling. Barbara T., sitting with her legs slightly parted, did not speak. On the wall, over Barbara T.'s shoulder, hung an antique china plate with a Cyclopean eye centered within the legend "Thou God See'st Me." There was a light sheen of moisture between her breasts, a scent of shampoo and conditioner and perfumed soap. I had to touch her.

When my hands rose to the insides of her thighs, her legs opened, her knees brushed my hips.

"You are so beautiful," I said.

"I've been in an absolute sexual haze for you for three days."

I lightly touched her nipples and ran my fingers down her stomach to the beginning of her pubic hair. Contractions rippled through her belly.

"Oh God," she said. "Oh God."

"Let's," I said. I stood up and began to remove my clothes.

"What if Alice returns?"

"We'll hear the car."

"I'm scared," she said. But she did not move away when I knelt back before her open thighs. "This is so crazy," she said. "We're so crazy!"

When I entered her, she gripped my shoulders tightly, her fingernails dug into my skin. We began to move slowly together.

"You're so wet!" I said.

"I love the feel of you inside me."

I was holding her by her hips.

"Touch my breasts, my nipples," she said. "Yes, there. Like that," she said, "just like that." She was lightly biting her lower lip, her eyes almost closed. "It feels so good," she said. "Why does it have to feel so good?" She opened her eyes and watched the way our bodies merged and fell apart. "Can you come quickly?"

"I don't want to," I said.

"I do," she said. "I'm going to," she said. "Jesus, I'm going to." A red flush suffused her breasts, rose up her throat and to her cheeks. "I'm going to! I'm going to come now," she said. "Right *now!* I'm coming *now!*" she said. Her body began to jerk, to snap as if she were receiving electric shocks. Her jaw muscles were rigid, her teeth clenched, her eyes screwed tightly shut. She was still coming; her body bucking. Her thighs, her knees clamped about my hips, pinned me, pulled me to her, gripped me tight. I did not, could not move.

By the time Alice returned the bathroom had been cleaned up, the broken pieces of soap dish removed. I had left a note explaining Barbara T.'s accident and that I was taking her to the doctor in case she needed stitches in her foot. She didn't.

There is just one more point I want to cover before returning to the "movie." One can now see that my question to Barbara T. about her foot was less innocent than it was meant to appear. In those days, it seemed to me, the majority of everyone's conversations were like that: their meanings had little to do with what was being said. For "How's your foot?" read: "You and I have a secret. I loved what we did!"

Barbara T.'s response, "Fine," contained only caution. It was noncommittal to an extreme. But so was Barbara T. That was part of what fascinated me about her. I never heard her express a strong opinion, never saw her take sides. At that time I probably saw her more often than any woman other than my wife and yet I don't think I knew her any better after three years than I did after three weeks. I don't even know what there was to know.

"How's your foot?" I had asked.

"Fine," she had said, watching Alice out of the corner of her eye.

Barbara T. was like one of those mysterious, celestial "Black Holes," into which everything disappeared and from which nothing returned. Except while making love, she gave off no light, no heat, no radiation, no sound. I often had a sense that all my words, thoughts, actions, my *self* would spiral slowly about her, that bit by bit, infinitesimally, gradually, the spiral would accelerate as I was being pulled toward her, then faster and faster until, caught in her field of sexuality, I would be sucked inside and disappear only to reappear, be spat out, ejected almost immediately at some other, far distant point as if I had never existed at all. Nor had what we had done. It couldn't have. And to look at her one would believe that it hadn't. Barbara T.'s surface was unruffled, unchanged, undisturbed. Everything was calm. And everything about her would remain so—until she was caught in the throes of passion again.

It was only then that she seemed alive. Her face flushed, her lips twisted, a low almost painful sound came from deep within her throat. Her eyes would focus and unfocus, her fingers grip and tear, her body shudder, thrash, and pitch. All the barriers seemed to be lowered and I felt I was reaching the real Barbara T.

I'm not sure that I ever let her reach me.

I was never in love with Barbara T. But I was desperately lonely and starved for the affection she showed me, and occasionally she seemed as desperate and as lonely as I. A couple of times Barbara T. said she loved me, but those were times when we were in bed together and always just after she'd come.

About two weeks after that dinner (which I soon will get to) Barbara T. and I met in New York. It would be the last time we'd ever make love. Barbara T. was talking about our afternoon together in the shower and the times we'd made love during the month before. "I loved the recklessness of it," she said. "All the places. And that afternoon after the pool party, I must have come ten times."

That conversation took place on the afternoon Alice was supposed to be spending with Barbara T. in the city. And when I returned to New Jersey that evening, that was where Alice said she had been. She had been, but she had spent the majority of that afternoon with Arthur, of course.

I never did confront Alice with the truth. I never wanted to for a reason whose charity could perhaps be understood only by another man: I would rather my wife get away with an affair than know she had been betrayed by her best friend. My liking to make love with Barbara T. had absolutely nothing to do with Alice's finding out.

On the train that afternoon coming out of the city I read an Associated Press filler, this time out of South Africa:

The End of a Friend
JOHANNESBURG, South Africa (AP)—The *Sunday Express* reported that a woman accused her husband of having an affair with her best friend. The other woman did not deny the affair, only that she was the best friend, the newspaper said.

It was not something I later read aloud to my wife.

Would someone get the lights, please?

FADE IN:

*10. INTERIOR: OLD STONE FARMHOUSE. LIVING ROOM. 7:15
P.M.*

ARTHUR and PHILIPPE arrive early and let themselves in through the back door. ALICE has not yet finished making up her face. There is a certain amount of calling back and forth between ARTHUR and ALICE, from the master bedroom above the stairway leading down to the living room. It is curiously lighthearted and intimate bantering, far more friendly than she has been with me. ALICE is wearing a Ralph Lauren dress bought on one of her trips to New York. It looks very good on her with her summer tan. ARTHUR is wearing a necktie, something he rarely wears. He is of the turtleneck school of psychiatry.

11. INTERIOR: LIBRARY.

I have taken their drink orders and am in the library rummaging through the liquor cabinet. I am wearing my "Lord Vère de Vère at Home" costume: a blue blazer over soft white linen trousers. A light blue shirt with thin candy-red stripes and a dark blue silk bow tie with white polka dots. I am kneeling before the open cabinet doors searching through the bottles in the back for a vaguely remembered fifth of Campari for PHILIPPE.

BARBARA T. enters the library and stands slightly behind my shoulder. She is wearing a loose-fitting dark burgundy dress. When she leans forward to touch my cheekbone with her fingertip, the dress falls slightly away and I can see her breasts, bare beneath the cotton, the nipples pink and slightly pinched. She runs her fingertip lightly across my lips and I touch BARBARA T.'s fingertip with my tongue.

BARBARA T.

We're so *bad!*

(Not until we hear ALICE descending the stairs do we move apart.)

12. INTERIOR: LIVING ROOM. TEN MINUTES LATER.

ALICE is at the kitchen counter, which separates the kitchen from the open living room. She is standing behind the twin stainless steel sinks and dishwasher like a captain on the bridge of his ship. BARBARA T. is beside her, drying a glass. PHILIPPE walks into the library to join me. ARTHUR is reading on the couch. There is a knock on the back door. BARBARA T. starts to move around ALICE to answer the door, but ALICE shoots her a look and BARBARA T. goes back to drying the glass.

MYSELF

(Calls from library:)

Isn't anyone going to answer the door?

(ODETTE opens the back door herself and enters. She has driven down from her house alone.)

ODETTE

Hello? Am I too early? Too late?

ALICE

Your timing, as usual, is perfect.

ODETTE

(Seeing ARTHUR reading a magazine and wanting him to show good manners mouths:)

Don't read.

ARTHUR

(Mouths back:)

Fuck you.

ODETTE

(Wheels away from him to face ALICE and BARBARA T.:)

Incroyable!

(ALICE shrugs. ODETTE leaves the living room and joins me in the library. From where ALICE and BARBARA T. are standing they can both see me kiss ODETTE warmly on the cheek.)

CUT.

Something has to be pointed out here and now. We were not—we *are* not—terrible people. We were behaving terribly, yes; but we had reached that dreadful stage through the attrition of our marriages, the deterioration of our emotional well-being and our perceptions of ourselves.

If I were to have to describe my own behavior that evening, it was as though I were a visitor in my own house. And yet, I know within me there was utter turmoil. I was like a nuclear reactor seething and bubbling away and barely in control. I had clamped down my wall of defenses and was incapable of relating—Arthur's favorite word—to anything that was going on. Even the breakdown of my marriage engaged me more as an observer than it disturbed me as a participant, as a man. Alice used to say that I was devious and manipulative (for all I know she still does), but I don't really think that is true since it would imply a far more reasoned and deliberate behavior than I then was capable of.

Odette was the only one among us who seemed entirely sane. It could have been the more solid structure of her European upbringing that gave her her self-control: She usually gave an impression of relaxation and serenity in social situations, an effortlessness and familiarity with entertaining, a casual elegance not unlike the way she wore her clothes. (Odette could throw anything on, mix colors and fabrics and styles with abandon, and still look as if she had stepped from the pages of the European edition of *Vogue*.) But the night of that dinner, Odette seemed cautious, edgy, impatient even with me. She had a sixth sense about my attraction to Barbara T. But there was another reason for her impatience that I was not yet aware of: I did not know how hard she was hoping Alice and Arthur would get along, how much Odette thought she wanted to be free.

Arthur believed he knew exactly what was going on. He had that infuriating smugness that so many psychiatrists seem to have. It has always struck me as being similar to the sort of self-assurance the very best simultaneous-translators achieve. Their ability to listen in one language and explain it in another was what Arthur felt he shared with them and it was what would give him such confidence that when the rest of us said something, he alone knew what we really meant.

Barbara T. was, as I've said, a "Black Hole." And Philippe was the "guest," the *voyeur* watching very closely everything and everyone. He was a rather straight, moralistic French family man plunked down among the savages. After that dinner when he drove Odette back home much later that night, he told her, "Either you stop seeing this couple now, or you're headed for a divorce."

"Would that be so bad?" Odette asked. "I care for Arthur. I will always care for him, but I was suffocating. I think my life would be better if we *were* divorced."

"You don't know what you're talking about!" Philippe replied.

And, of course, as Odette admitted later, she didn't. No one does really understand divorce who hasn't been through one.

I am aware that I have not dealt with my feelings about Odette at this point, nor have I provided much about Alice. I'll get to it all later. It's time now to reassemble the cast for the next scene.

Places everybody!

FADE IN:

13. INTERIOR: DINING ROOM. 8:30 P.M.

The dining room is bathed in the soft glow of candlelight and wall sconces with low wattage candle bulbs on a turned-down dimmer switch. There are small oil paintings in carved and gilded wooden frames, mid to late

nineteenth-century pastoral scenes of cows grazing, a pasture bordered
by woods, a surprisingly detailed portrait of an angry pig. The dining
room table, an antique tavern table with a heavy wooded plank top, is
the same color as the room's exposed corner and ceiling beams. The
long-stemmed crystal wineglasses sparkle, the silverware shines. I am
seated at one end of the narrow table, the end farthest from the dining
room door. ODETTE is on my right, BARBARA T. on my left. PHILIPPE
is seated on ODETTE's right. He will be on ALICE's left when she sits;
ARTHUR, who is standing next to her at the sideboard, will be on her
right.

ALICE is serving; ARTHUR is handing her plates. Everyone is "dressed
up." There is a curious sense of artificiality to the evening, of children
pretending to be adults. ALICE is telling ARTHUR which plate to give
to whom.

ALICE
(As she's handing ARTHUR his plate:)
I have saved the end piece you like so much for you.
(ODETTE looks over at me. I know what she is thinking; they are
behaving like husband and wife. BARBARA T.'s foot nudges mine. I
return the pressure. ODETTE, in reaching for the silver salt shaker,
knocks her wineglass flying. The crystal shatters, the red wine soaks into
my lap. ODETTE looks stricken.)

ARTHUR
(As napkins are passed up my way:)
Odette, Jesus Christ, you're such a klutz!

ALICE
Not the linen napkins! I'll get paper towels.

MYSELF
(Rising:)
It's nothing to worry about. I'll just quickly change.
(I look down at my pants. The brilliant red wine covering the crotch of
my white trousers makes me appear to have been gored, disemboweled:)
I think I must have worked that bull a bit too close!

BARBARA T.
(Picking pieces of broken glass off my plate:)
When you take your pants off soak them in cold water in the sink.
(I touch ODETTE's shoulder as I leave; ALICE, seeing this as she
returns from the kitchen with paper towels, accidentally-on-purpose
bumps me as we pass each other at the door.)

CUT TO:

14. INTERIOR: DINING ROOM. ABOUT TEN MINUTES LATER.
As I return to dining room, now wearing a pair of blue jeans under my
blazer, we hear BARBARA T. saying:

BARBARA T.

—are certain advantages. For example, there are times when I like
it if someone comes fast.

(There is a moment of silence during which nobody looks at anybody
else, except for PHILIPPE, whose glance flits from face to face.)

MYSELF

(Sitting and turning to ODETTE:)
Have I missed something?

ODETTE

Probably not.

ARTHUR

Odette, like most women, does not like to be rushed.

ODETTE

I don't like to be pushed either.

MYSELF

According to the mimeographed sheet, I thought our dinner discussion was scheduled to be on "Man's Role in Society."

PHILIPPE

A man's role is to take care of his woman. His family. I do not
understand why American men feel compelled to make it more
complicated than that.

MYSELF

Because it has *become* more complicated. The roles—the *rules* are
changing.

ARTHUR

We must redefine our interpretation of what it means to be a
"husband," a "wife."

ODETTE

How would you know?

MYSELF

(Raising wineglass:)
This seems like an appropriate time to show our appreciation to
Alice for this lovely dinner . . .

CUT.

Odette tells me I was very busy being amusing that night. That I was
filling the air with social chitchat, that whenever I said anything it was

preceded by a credit line such as, "Well, as my great-uncle Burton used to say . . ." or, "One of the issues the *Times* raised was . . ." And that I never let anyone in on what I was thinking myself. She must have been right because when Odette and I were at dinner the other night with two of my oldest friends, a couple who had moved into our old Mercer County town at approximately the same time as Alice and I had in 1970, the man said he felt for the first time he was getting to know *me* and not the various images of myself I had tended in the past to project. I could argue, I suppose, that any one of those images was legitimate since during that period I never had the foggiest idea of what I was thinking or who I was.

Sometimes I was playing "Lord Vère de Vère," sometimes the politically concerned citizen-cinematographer, sometimes the aging hippy freak, sometimes the overly protective and responsible parent, the dutiful though misunderstood and unappreciated husband, sometimes the Perfect Lover, always the loyal and generous friend, eventually the cad, the whimperer, the bore.

I felt that every woman I knew during this period was trying to take great bites out of me, that they wanted more of me than I was able, much less willing, to give. And what I wanted from them, for the most part, was to be left alone—alone, that is, after the hunt and chase, pursuit and conquest. For the only activity in the world that I truly loved at that time was the courtship and seduction of beautiful women.

I used to love to hunt birds, too—earlier in my life. (I am aware of the irony here.) I loved the setting—the woods and open fields; the dogs—Labradors and springer spaniels, pointers every now and then. I loved the clothing—the slightly stiff, canvas-fronted brier-proof field pants, the soft and aged hunting boots, the faded old flannel shirts, an autumn-colored deep-pocketed tweed. The leather bag for the shells, the gun itself: a 20-gauge Parker I'd bought used and had had fitted to me at Abercrombie & Fitch. I loved, too, the men with whom I used to hunt: my stepfather, my cousin Tom, Roy Palmer, a Nebraska farmer whose cornfields bordered the tenant farmhouse I had rented while making a film. Roy and I hunted together the last time either of us would ever hunt. Both of us had come, by then, to hate the killing more than we loved the hunt.

I was to quit screwing around for much the same reason. I loved the hunt of women, but I hated the guilt. And what was so odd, so strange and sad, was that even though I was going to bed with all these different women as often as I could, I very rarely had an orgasm. I practically never came—unless I masturbated, with them or alone.

I don't think I'm really ready to talk about this yet.

And I don't want to go back to that "movie" either. It angers and . . .
and it *tires* me. I'd like to just cover the rest of that evening as quickly
as possible.

After dinner we moved into the library—my favorite room in the
house.

It really *was* a library, with two walls of floor-to-ceiling bookcases filled
with books. At night, after Alice had gone to bed, I would stand before
the shelves reading the titles, remembering passages and characters like
old friends. Occasionally I would pull out a book thinking I would read
only a paragraph or so and end up reading through the night. The books
are all in cartons now in storage. I don't have room in my cottage for
bookcases. I hate that. I don't feel complete unless I have my books
around me.

Well, that night after dinner, we all moved into the library. Brandy
was offered, a joint passed around. Alice put the new Donna Summer
album on the stereo, then turned and held out her arms to Arthur to
dance. I danced first with Odette while Philippe danced with Barbara
T. The library is a small room and occasionally we bumped into one
another. It was I, usually, who bumped into someone else. I am not a
very good dancer, not good at all.

Alice loved to dance and she was extraordinarily good: fluid, showy,
sexy, jivey. She had all the steps, all the moves. (The year I went to
dancing school I was instructed in the fox-trot and the waltz and in
something, if I remember right, called "The Shag." Alice, therefore,
rarely danced with me.) That evening, Alice didn't really dance *with*
Arthur either since, no matter who her partner was, Alice seemed to
dance alone. But that was the fashion in dancing then. The only time
partners danced cheek to cheek was when their bottoms touched.

I don't mean to imply that Alice lost herself in her dancing; she didn't.
She was always acutely aware of whose eyes were on her and whose
were not. I wish I could simply say that she was a terrific dancer and
leave it at that, but there was something more to her dancing that I
thought I recognized, a desperateness that left me feeling sad.

I didn't think she needed to work at it so hard.

Alice, I now know, wasn't working hard. Dancing was an escape for
her, her way of having fun.

I, too, danced with Alice that night. And I danced with Barbara T.
But I remember best dancing with Odette and how well we seemed to
fit. It was only the second time we had danced together and yet—and I

know how corny this sounds—it was as though we had danced together all our lives. What is curious is that Odette says I danced with, looked at, and held her exactly the same way I danced with, looked at, and held Alice and Barbara T. As though, in Odette's words, "Each of them was the only woman in the world."

By midnight when Barbara T. went up to bed, Arthur and Alice had already spent an hour in the kitchen by themselves. When I had gone in there to get more ice I found Arthur comforting Alice, who was in tears. I don't know why she was crying. There was nothing about the situation that encouraged me to ask.

Philippe and Odette and I stayed up talking in the library until Odette said she was tired and Philippe drove her home. That must have been around one o'clock. I went up to bed then myself. The stairs creaked loudly in the old house and I saw Barbara T.'s light go off in the guest bedroom at the top of the stairs just as I reached eye level with the bottom of her door. I tapped lightly on her door as I passed and called, "Good night," but there was no answer.

Arthur and Alice were still talking when I fell asleep. Odette later told me that Arthur did not return home until six that morning. She also told me that Alice had visited her the next afternoon saying she had to talk to Odette. I only learned this part of the conversation a month ago, over a year and a half after this talk took place.

Odette had poured Alice and herself a couple of beers and suggested they talk in the garden.

Alice followed Odette outside and held the glasses while Odette wrestled a couple of deck chairs into the sun. The two of them sat for a few minutes talking about the weather, the garden, the children, with Alice all the time closely watching Odette's face and with Odette being careful not to give any hint that she was aware of what had happened between Arthur and Alice the night before.

Alice then said that she had been so glad when Odette and Arthur had moved to the town, that Odette was the kind of person Alice had been looking for for years, someone "young and pretty, who dressed well, and would be fun to have lunch with. But now," Alice added, "now I wish you were old and fat and ugly so that I could hate you."

"Hate me? Why?"

"Because of Arthur," Alice said. "If I could hate you everything would be so easy—so much easier. But because you and Arthur have been in love with each other, were in love, in a way you always will be, too. And I cannot fight that."

Odette asked Alice if she had not at one time been in love with me, too?

"I have never loved him," Alice said. "I have never been in love with him."

"Then why did you marry him?"

"It was timing. It was just the right time." Alice then told Odette how I had "fucked a coed" six months after she and I were married and that she had never forgiven me for that, never trusted me again. She told how I had "thrown" my child on her the Christmas we were married, that we'd never gone away on a honeymoon.

"But didn't he love you?" Odette asked.

"He said he did. And he was very sweet. A good man. Generous. If I'd been nicer to him I could have had anything I wanted. But he did not excite me. Did you know he made me go to a psychiatrist with him a couple of years ago? We went together and he asked the psychiatrist if he thought I might be a lesbian. I'm not, of course."

"Why would he think that?"

"Because I can't bear him physically."

"Why not?" Odette asked. "He seems—"

"—Oh, he's a very sensuous man, thoughtful in bed," Alice said. "But I'm not in love with him. He doesn't excite me. And when he touches me . . . I just turn off."

"Are you in love with Arthur?"

Alice looked at Odette closely, uncertain how far she should go. "He's the first man who's ever excited me. Who has ever really turned me on. We cannot even look at each other without . . ." Her voice trailed off.

"Is Arthur in love with you?"

"I don't know. He hasn't said."

Odette's laughter startled Alice. "That's so typical of him!"

"It doesn't matter anyway," Alice said. "I wouldn't break up my marriage just for love alone. Never. There has to be something more. Security. Stability."

"Well, Arthur's a doctor."

"I know and, see, this might be my only chance. I'm thirty-four and Arthur is the first man I've ever felt this way about."

"And what do you want from me?" Odette asked.

"Nothing. I just thought we ought to talk."

They were both silent for a moment. Odette was lighting a cigarette, Alice was sipping her beer. And then, totally out of the blue, Alice said:

"If you keep your married name it's going to cause a real screw-up on the credit cards."

Where was I during all this?

I had gone up to check on the much larger and grander house I had bought with Alice just two months before. By then we had already knocked out the bigger house's walls, torn up its plumbing and wiring and gutted its kitchen. It would be another eight months before the house could be lived in—or put back on the market.

I never did live in that house. Arthur and Alice did, the next summer, when we were all in the process of getting divorced. I didn't really care.

By then Odette and I and all of our children were living in a rented beach cottage out at Bradley Beach. What I did really care about was learning how to truly *love* Odette, to love a *woman*. Because I felt that once I understood *that*, I would understand how we had all managed to get "there" from "here" and understanding that I could, as I've said earlier, avoid making those same mistakes again.

3

I THINK, in some ways, events began to build toward that dinner as early as two and a half years before—in May 1978—when I visited my brother Carter in Hawaii. It was on that trip that the first of what was to become a series of deaths occurred. And although my brother insisted that there was no reason for me to feel responsible, I knew that the young man would not have been killed had I not been trying to film the torchlit night-surfing sequence for the airline promo.

The night-surfing scene was a stupid idea to begin with, but Bernie Wooten, the airline representative who had come out to Hawaii with my soundman Harry Abbott and me, had done an Alpine promo containing a sequence of torch-carrying skiers winding down a nighttime mountainside for the same airline the year before. The shot had gone over very big with the vice-president in charge of production, Bernie's boss, and as Bernie had told Harry, Carter and me over lunch at the Ilikai Hotel, "My boss does not believe you can repeat too much of a good thing."

"But Bernie," I said, "water has a markedly different effect on fire than air does. How are the surfers going to keep those torches from going out?"

"They hold them up out of the water," Bernie said.

My brother lightly punched my arm. "How come you didn't think of that?"

"What's to think about?" Bernie asked. "All we do is round up a bunch of kids, get them standing on their surfboards holding torches over their heads, then film them riding the big waves in."

"The torches are still going to get wet," Carter said.

"So, we'll get torches that don't mind getting wet," Bernie said. He adjusted his prescription dark glasses so he could better see the young bikini-clad woman approaching our table. "What do deep-sea divers use?" Bernie asked. "Those underwater torches that Captain Nemo's divers used in the *20,000 Leagues Under the Sea* movie."

"How come you didn't think of that, Carter?" I laughed.

"I only read the book," he said.

"Well, whaddya think?" Bernie asked. "Can you get the shot?"

"If Carter can round up the surfers and you can get the torches and Harry can get the lights, I can get the shot."

The young woman pulled a chair up to our table and sat down between Carter and myself.

"I'm Bernie Wooten," the airline rep said, holding out his hand to her. "How would you like to be a movie star?"

"Nora Rosenthal-Gribbs," she said. "I already am."

Bernie looked questioningly at me.

Carter had introduced me to Nora the day after I had arrived in Hawaii on this trip. "You've got to see her," he had said. "When she's wearing her bikini she is—next to Diamond Head—the biggest tourist attraction on Waikiki Beach." Nora stood at least five feet ten, with broad shoulders, huge breasts, a tiny waist, flaring hips, and long, firm-muscled legs. She had graduated summa cum laude from a university in Washington state the year before, where she had rowed on its undefeated women's crew. She had married a law student her senior year and left him behind on the mainland to study for his exams. Ostensibly, Nora was attending the University of Hawaii's summer session to earn credit toward a master's degree in English, but she spent most of her days on the beach and a lot of her nights at Carter's apartment, where I, too, was staying.

"Will someone please tell me what this lady means?" Bernie asked.

"I used Nora yesterday in the Beautiful-Young-Girl-Washing-Her-Hair-in-the-Waterfall shot," I replied.

"Why wasn't I along on that?" Bernie asked.

"You weren't invited," Harry said.

At 10 P.M. that night Carter and I were standing knee-deep in the water. I was carrying my new Cinema Products-16 35mm camera on my shoulder and standing as close as I dared to the inrushing waves without risking having the saltwater splash on the Angenieux 10- to 150-mm zoom lense. Carter was next to me, a battery-powered bullhorn in his hand. Harry Abbott was back on the beach doubling as the lighting gaffer for this shot. We had rigged rented 1,000-watt quartz Tota-Lites on lighting stands twenty-five feet apart for about fifty yards down the beach. When we turned them on they threw enough light to illuminate the dozen or so young men sitting astride their surfboards about thirty yards out.

"That's the seventh wave," Carter told me. "They'll try to get up on the ninth."

"I hope they're counting the same as you," I said.

"GET READY, BRUDDAHS!" He had to shout into the bullhorn to

be heard over the noise of the gasoline-powered lighting generator. "KEEP THOSE TORCHES UP!"

I called to the beach, *"Hit the lights, Harry!"* then turned back quickly to avoid being blinded. The quartz lights slammed into the night. The eighth wave broke and rushed in toward our feet.

"Take forty-three," Carter mumbled.

The ninth wave surged. The surfers were trying to paddle with one hand, holding up their torches with the other. Surfboards skewed about in little quarter-circles. One surfer got up, then another, and a third; they rushed to the front of their boards. The CP-16 whirred next to my ear. The three surfers were too far apart to frame in the same shot, so I zoomed in on the two closest together. The spray of the breaking wave sparkled in the lights. The surfer on the right dropped his torch. I released the trigger on the handgrip. The whirring stopped. I looked at Carter. "There went another fifty feet of film," I said.

"It's never going to work. You've already used a thousand feet trying to get this shot."

"Any ideas?"

He shook his head. "I really don't think it can be done. In surfing, you need both hands free to paddle to catch the wave right. That's why only a couple of them are lucky enough to get up at the same time."

I turned back to the beach. "BERNIE?" The lights were blinding.

"Back here!" Bernie called.

Harry killed the lights. I still could not see a thing. I waded back toward Bernie's voice. He met me at the edge of the beach. "It's not working," I told him. "The kids need both hands free to get up on their boards."

Carter splashed back to join us. "Does it need to be surfers?"

"Whaddya mean?" Bernie asked.

"What if we get a bunch of Hawaiians carrying torches in outrigger canoes and have them surf the outriggers in?"

"You don't think that would be too much like 'Hawaii Five-O'?" I asked.

One of the kids carrying his surfboard under his arm came up to us. "Fuck it, man," he said. "It's dangerous out there. I mean you keep burning yourself with those fuckin' torches and those lights are so fuckin' bright, you can't see a fuckin' thing."

"We only need about eight seconds at the most," Bernie said.

"Eight *good* seconds," I said. I turned back to look at the surfers. One kid was lying flat on his board paddling back out to join the others.

Beyond him a wave surged and two surfers got up. They were both holding their torches. Harry saw them at the same time and flipped on the Tota-Lites. I quick-focused the camera and began to shoot, counting the seconds under my breath. *One-one hundred, two-one hundred, three-one hundred* . . . It was unbelievable! They were doing it! The two of them filled my viewfinder. If they could only hold it, it would be a beautiful shot. *Six-one hundred, seven-one hundred, eight-one hundred, nine-one hundred.* The surfer on the left lost his balance, wobbled, recovered, then fell. The breaking wave caught his board and catapulted it high into the air. "LOOK OUT!" I heard Carter scream. I continued to film, pulling back on the zoom to keep the arcing board in view. The surfboard began to drop tail first. The kid who'd been paddling out looked up just as the surfboard's tail fin hit him.

"Holy Christ!" Bernie said. Carter was already racing down the beach. *"Get an ambulance!"* Carter was yelling. *"Get a doctor out here!"*

I saw people running up the beach toward the hotels and handed Harry the CP-16.

"Did you get it? The board hitting the kid?" he asked. (Back in New York Harry free-lanced for Channel 7 news.)

I looked at him and nodded. I knew what he was thinking. We could probably sell the footage to a station in Hawaii. I reached my brother just as the boy's lifeless body washed up at his feet. Carter pulled the boy up the beach and turned him onto his back. "Oh, Jesus," Carter said. The boy looked as though he had been hit in the face with an ax. His nose and lower jaw were gone and one eye hung loose from its crushed socket. Someone behind us spun away and threw up.

"Does anyone know the boy's name?" I asked.

"I do," Carter said quietly. "I know his mother. She owns a flower shop in town."

The other surfers were coming in. We could hear sirens. Someone placed a beach towel over the boy's shattered face.

My brother was looking over at me. "Are you all right?" he asked.

"Do you mean am I going to be sick?"

"No, I mean are you *all right*? Or are you, as usual, going to find some way to blame this all on yourself?"

I turned away from the dead boy's body. "The boy wouldn't be lying here if we hadn't been trying to film that shot."

Carter took my arm and walked me down the beach. "When are you going to quit taking responsibility for things in life you can't change?"

"When I quit feeling they were my fault."

"This wasn't your fault!" Carter said impatiently. "You've only made two big mistakes I know of in your life that you can take the blame for."

"Only two?" I asked. "What were they?"

"Getting married."

Carter had been best man at my wedding to my first wife Maggie fifteen years before. He and I had shared a room in the Hilltop Motor Inn overlooking Adams Lake not far from Litchfield, Connecticut, where Maggie and I were to be married the next day. I could remember that night Carter asking me, "But why are you marrying her? Why not some other girl? Any other girl."

"Because Maggie loves me," I had said. "And she needs me."

"Do you love and need her?"

"Sure, I do," I said. "Of course I do."

"I think you're making a big mistake."

I suppose I knew that, too, but I was too caught up in the wedding machinery to have the courage to stop it.

The afternoon following the wedding my mother drove my brother back down to Stamford, where he could catch a train back to New York, and she continued on into Greenwich, where she and my stepfather lived. About three months later Carter telephoned me from the airport. He had decided to move to Hawaii and was calling to say goodbye before boarding his flight. It was the last time I heard his voice until the summer of 1969 when I flew out to Hawaii to spend a month with him. On my way out I was to stop off in Mexico to get a divorce.

During the first years of my marriage with Maggie I think we were both trying to make a go of a bad thing. We busied ourselves so that we would not have too much time alone. To my astonishment my first documentary was selected by the Lincoln Film Society for inclusion in their "New Director Series," screened at the Museum of Modern Art. The film was about a small settlement of descendants of Hessian deserters and runaway slaves who had hidden themselves away in the Ramapo Mountains north of New York and whose inbreeding for generations had caused genetic ravages. The film was shown on Public Broadcasting and later bought for a showing on network television, where it subsequently led to an appallingly successful comedy series starring "Pickles" Jackson and "Buggsy" Brown. That one film and its spin-offs supported Maggie and me for the three years we lived in Europe. During those years I doubt if Carter and I exchanged five letters.

I shot my next two documentaries while Maggie and I were abroad.

The first on the fate of babies fathered by black GIs and born to German women, had been bought by the BBC and Public Television. And I was still editing the second, a film on Madrid's Prado Museum, when Maggie became pregnant and we decided to return to New York for the birth of our daughter Joan in the summer of 1966. The sale of the Prado documentary occurred shortly after Joan was born. Life should have been sweet, but it wasn't.

Maggie was depressed and irritable all the time and instead of being supportive and understanding I was impatient and sought escape in my work until, one night, Maggie angrily shouted at me, "You're such a goddam bore! All you ever think about are your stupid little films!"

"It's my 'stupid little films,' as you call them, that make it possible for you to live as well as you do," I replied.

"You call this *living?*" she asked.

We stuck it out together for another two years until Maggie couldn't stand me any longer. We separated in the summer of 1968. Maggie took Joan to live with her in Oregon and I found a one-room apartment on Fourteenth Street at a rent low enough for me to afford retaining a base in New York. I went to the University of Montana in the winter of 1969 to be a visiting lecturer in their communications department. That was when I wrote my brother Carter asking if I might visit him in Hawaii that summer. He wrote back immediately, insisting I come. I arrived early in June.

Carter always seemed so much more sophisticated and intelligent than me. Perhaps that was because he was five years older, and a younger brother tends to hold his older brother in awe. But his life seemed to run so much more smoothly than mine. He had never married. We had both inherited the same amount from our grandparents—enough to provide an income of about $350.00 a month, but through shrewd investments he had managed to triple his inheritance, whereas I had had to invade mine for the down payment on Maggie's and my house, and what was left would all be going to her in the divorce. He did not need much money to live in Hawaii and when he did need extra cash he would take a short-time job at the Alawai Boat Yard, or teach yoga at a convent, or free-lance for a newspaper, or tend bar in a hotel. In 1969 when I first went to visit him in Hawaii he was taking out a different girl every night, was into Krishnamurti, Meher Baba, oneness with God, vegetarianism, and LSD. I hadn't been there more than a couple of days when he asked me to take acid with him. "Look, pal," he said, "it's going to be a beautiful experience, a profound experience, one you'll never forget."

"I don't know," I said. "The idea kind of scares me."

"Of course it does, the first time. But you shouldn't worry. No one is more stable than you are."

No one is more stable than you are.

In 1969, when he said that, it was as though he had told me I was a bore. Ten years later, if anyone had called me stable I would have kissed them on the lips.

When I look back on that first visit to Hawaii I remember being astonished at how many friends Carter had: all the Hawaiians, the resident haoles, the Portuguese, Samoans, Chinese, Japanese, and Filipinos he knew who worked on the island, all the beach boys, the waiters, the black coral divers, boat builders, store owners, the people who worked in the hotels. He and I would walk together down to the beach and almost instantly be surrounded by his friends. He would introduce me to them saying, "This is my best friend and, incidentally, my brother."

"You bruddah? No kiddin'?" the beach boys would ask. They would look at our difference in height (Carter was five inches shorter than me) and they'd laugh and punch him on the shoulder. "Hey, bruh', wha'hoppen to you, eh?"

Because I was Carter's brother people were always offering me free surfing lessons, skin-diving trips, rides on the catamarans or outrigger canoes. If they saw me by myself on the beach, they'd flop down beside me to talk. They'd all be so *nice!*

Carter's friends would tell me how much he had been looking forward to my visit, how often he'd spoken about me, how proud of me he was that my films had done well. "It's a beautiful thing to see two brothers as close as you are," they would say.

I believe we were close. I don't think I'm kidding myself that he loved me as I loved him.

And, oh God, he made me laugh. The first time he showed me his apartment above Honolulu he pointed out the fishnet canopy he'd hung over his bed. "I used to take out a girl who was terrified when I brought her up here that a lizard would drop on her in the middle of the night. I put the net up to soothe her," he explained. "Actually, I think the lizards got to really dig the net. They'd run across the ceiling to where the net hung beneath them, then close their eyes and let go. There was one Gekko who got so he could do a one-and-a-half back somersault before he'd hit. I gave him a 'seven' on that," he said, then added, "Out of a possible degree of difficulty 'eight.' "

"What happened to the girl?" I asked.

"She got a 'five.' "

I loved the way his mind worked, the way he could be both enmeshed in and detached from a situation at the same time, always distant enough to laugh at himself, at what he was saying or doing.

"The mosquitoes were so bad in Raiatéa," he told me one afternoon when we were sitting in his Volkswagen watching a sunset, "they'd bite me on the fingers while I was playing the guitar." There was about a two-beat pause, and then he said, "By the way, that's a pretty fair indication of how well I play the guitar."

When I think back on that first visit to Hawaii I remember, too, how hard Carter tried to work me out of my depression over having gotten a divorce. I knew the failure of a marriage wasn't the end of the world, but I felt guilty and hurt and despaired over how little I would see my daughter Joan. To cheer me up Carter was constantly introducing me to girls he knew and urging me to take them out. They were all college students—"Beach Bunnies" he called them—all tanned, with trim figures, sun-bleached hair, and half his age. Occasionally Carter and I did go out with girls together, but I felt inhibited, shy with them and him. I never knew what to say to those girls. It wasn't just that I felt I had lost the knack for small talk or that even when they were being serious about something, it was never anything I could get serious about. I just felt too old for them, stodgy somehow, and never as good company as Carter. As a result, I wasn't good company; and inevitably the girls would end up being entertained by him.

My heart just wasn't in it. One reason was that I knew any girl I saw in Hawaii the odds were that I would not see her again.

But there was another reason.

When I was a sophomore at college nearly eleven years before, I had brought a Christmas vacation date back to my brother's New York apartment. I had been trying for most of that fall semester's weekends to lure her into bed with me without any success whatsoever. That evening in New York I had been drinking the way sophomores do who don't have any sense and not long after we had arrived at my brother's steam-heated apartment I passed out. At about two in the morning when I awoke I heard my brother and my date making love. I felt angry and betrayed, yes, but most of all I felt hurt and humiliated at how eagerly she had gone to bed with him. In Hawaii, that visit, I was unwilling to risk that same anguish again. If I had had but little self-confidence in my relationships with women prior to Maggie's and my divorce, I had even less afterward.

I think I envied Carter's freedom with women, his irresponsibility, his ability to stay uninvolved and to break clean. All I could think about was how my relationship with Maggie had ended up with her living in Oregon with our daughter and with me standing in a Juarez courtroom with a dozen or so other uncomprehending Americans while a Mexican judge spoke to us in Spanish and a little boy tried to sell us Chiclets whenever the judge paused for breath. I didn't think that even Maggie's and my marriage, as sad as it was, deserved as depressing an ending as that. I wanted to put it all as far behind me as fast as I could. I had hoped that month I spent in Hawaii that first visit would do it. But I left after only three weeks because a call came for me to film a "love-in" being staged in a Los Angeles park, and it was there at that "love-in" two days after I had left Carter in Hawaii that I had met Alice, who six months later became my second wife.

I was squinting through the viewfinder of the rented Arriflex I had mounted on a heavy tripod and was shooting all the young people in their flowery costumes and beads. Girls with long hair and headbands and peace buttons were passing out apples and rubber-stamping the backs of peoples' hands with "Peace" and "Love." Two electronically amplified rock bands were blasting out music from opposite ends of the open field. And somewhere in the middle a Vietnam veteran was making a speech against the war.

It was an odd gathering, schizophrenic, really, in that it was neither the true "love-in" of the early sixties nor the sort of hard antiwar rally that one had started to see from the mid-sixties on. Perhaps the confusion was a result of the summer weather, the California attitude, the rally's promotion as "The Last Great Love-in," I really don't know. I had been holding a tight shot on the angry veteran's face and then was slowly pulling back so that as his image receded, the frame included more and more of these young California girls who weren't listening to him at all, when a young man near me said, "Oh, wow, if only life could be this groovy forever!" and I heard a young woman reply, "What's so groovy about this bullshit, I'd like to know!"

I had to look at her.

The big voice belonged to a small woman with remarkable green eyes, false eyelashes, and strawberry blond hair cut short like a boy's. She was wearing a pair of loosely fitting gray walking shorts belted at the waist with a silk scarf, a white cotton halter top with no bra underneath, and a battered New York Mets baseball cap on the back of her head. Looking at her it was difficult to know how old she might be, anywhere between nineteen and twenty-nine was my best guess. I later learned she was twenty-four. The young man she had been with had wandered off and she remained standing next to me with one hand on her hip, a tightly rolled marijuana cigarette in the fingers of her other hand. She took a hit and passed the joint to me saying, "Here, sport, fold your lip over this and see if it improves your focus."

I had to laugh. Her cockiness, her New York accent, her ballsiness seduced me.

"This is the second of these overindulged flower children's gatherings I've been to this week," she said. "It's all such bullshit, really. They go around passing out peace buttons and flowers and poor quality dope, they embrace each other and say how terrible the war is and how all you need is love. Then they climb into their Corvettes and Dodge Chargers bought by their daddys and won't give anyone a ride home. My cousin and I waited for two hours for a ride after the last one. Finally got picked up by a Mexican in a truck carrying fresh figs . . ." She cocked her head to one side and gave me a sassy look. "You planning to Bogart my joint or would you care to share it with me."

I apologized and passed her back her marijuana.

"I wasn't worried," she said. "I saw it had gone out." She held the joint to her lips and waited for me to relight it for her.

Alice and I had dinner together that night at a Mexican restaurant, went bar-hopping after that, and spent the night in the apartment of a friend. The next morning when I awoke she was sitting up in bed groaning. "Tequilas . . . margaritas," she was saying. "Jesus, I should know better than that!" She covered her eyes with her hand and cautiously slid out from under the covers then put her feet on the floor. "I don't remember where the bathroom is," she said.

"Second door on the right."

She nodded and stood up, took two steps, then screamed and began stamping her foot on the wood floor.

I rushed out of bed. "What is it?"

"Spider!" she cried. "It bit my foot!"

I knelt on the floor next to her and gingerly picked up the remains of what she had crushed. I looked at it for a moment, then held it in my open palm for her to examine.

"*Ugh!*" she said, making a face. "What *is* it?"

"Your false eyelash," I said.

Six months later, as I've said, Alice and I were married.

I think I loved Alice, I really do. She was so different from Maggie—from *me!* She was gregarious, self-confident, opinionated, fun. She was like a New York street kid: brassy, quick to size a person up, street-wise, always looking for a bargain, and utterly fearless. We spent two wonderful months together in my Fourteenth Street apartment while she dragged me out to movies, museums, galleries, favorite spots, and then we moved together that fall to a small, rented, tenant farmhouse along the Platte River northwest of Omaha, Nebraska, because I'd received a grant to do a film on the yearly cycle of a small Midwestern farm.

It was just the two of us on that prairie land. Alice made it fun. On days I didn't film we would drive around the countryside together in my old Volkswagen bus. We bought a Newfoundland puppy and named him "Burp," and Alice and I and Burp would take long walks. I loved being with her out there, loved the land, the open sky, the weather, the little towns where Alice found primitive antiques, quilts, a rolltop desk. I think, at first, she loved being out there, too. She started wearing bluejean jackets and flannel shirts. She got a pair of workboots with sturdy rubber soles and brass eyelets for the laces that went above her ankles. She wore men's soft felt hats. She began to look like a boy, except for her incredible green eyes. Roy Palmer, the farmer I hunted pheasant with and whose farm I was filming, began referring to Alice as "The Kid." His wife, Louella, called her "Honey."

I don't think I could have stood that year in Nebraska without Alice; I would have been too lonely. I didn't realize how lonely it was for her.

Just before Christmas Alice and I flew back to New York. We were married standing in front of a bricked-in fireplace in the living room of her mother and father's Upper West Side apartment. We had two nights at the Plaza Hotel, then returned to Nebraska in time to pick up my daughter Joan, then three, at the airport in Omaha. It was my turn to have Joan for Christmas.

I was so happy to see Joan that I didn't realize how thoughtless I was being to Alice. *Now*, of course, I can understand how Alice might have resented spending our first Christmas together with a child of mine by a previous marriage. *Then* I thought only of how lucky and grateful I felt to be able to share Christmas with them both.

Joan spent two weeks with us, then I put her on a plane back to

Oregon and her mother. In January and February the snowdrifts and arctic winds kept Alice and me inside the house. When she saw that the filming had ground to a halt she said we "should get the hell out of" there and go someplace warm. I told her I couldn't.

I explained that if a real blizzard came it was important that I be there to film its effects, and besides, I added, we didn't have the money.

"You had the money to fly a three-year-old back and forth," she said quietly.

Ice and snow gave way to mud. I was given an appointment to teach at the University of Nebraska, one course a week, and I took Alice with me most of the time to the Lincoln campus. We made friends with people who worked at the public television station there and Alice, at last, had some people to talk to. One afternoon that summer, this would have been the summer of 1970, I had Joan again for the month of June and she and I were returning from the cornfields when I saw an unfamiliar car next to our farmhouse. My brother Carter had suddenly turned up.

His sudden, unexpected appearance in our small, two-bedroom farmhouse made Alice tense, she made me tense, I made Joan tense, Alice and I and Joan made Carter tense.

"How long is he staying?" Alice asked me the second night of Carter's visit. We were sitting up in bed.

"I don't think more than a week."

She was silent.

"Let's get a baby-sitter and drive into Omaha for dinner and a movie tomorrow night."

"Why can't Carter sit?" Alice asked.

"But I thought the three of us could go together."

"You don't think he'd like the opportunity to spend a quiet evening with his niece?"

"He's with her all day. Joan's only four years old. She's in bed by eight-thirty . . . I can't just leave him behind, not after how good he was to me when I stayed with him in Hawaii."

She rolled over in the bed so that her back was to me. After a moment she said, "Then why don't the two of you just go in together?"

"But I want you there, too!"

"Why?"

"Because you're my wife." I rested my hand on her hip. "I was hoping the three of us could get away from the farm, have dinner in town, and have a good time."

"The two of you are good at having a good time without me."

"Oh, Alice, please? He's only going to be here a short time. He's my brother. You're my wife. I want you to be friends, together."

"We're together—*all* of us—twenty-four hours a day. I want to be alone with you."

Carter and I did go to Omaha together for dinner the next night; Alice stayed home. It was her decision, and although Carter and I pleaded with her, she said she'd rather watch TV with Joan.

"But does she make you happy?" Carter asked me during the drive.

"She's never been married before," I said. "She doesn't understand the compromises a marriage takes."

"She doesn't seem very affectionate toward you."

"She's been upset, that's why."

"Because I'm here?" Carter asked.

"Because of you. Joan. Me. Nebraska. It wasn't what she expected. She's used to being a single girl in New York and she thought she was marrying a New York film-maker. Instead she finds herself in the middle of cornfields with a husband, a four-year-old who isn't hers, a brother-in-law she's never met. . . . It's funny," I said, "I was so looking forward to the two of you meeting, of getting to know each other and becoming friends. I was so *sure* that she'd—that you'd both really like each other. . . . I guess you both need a little more time, that and a different set of circumstances."

"People who can love are easy to get to know," Carter said. "Those who can't take a lot longer."

"I guess I'm not terrific at it, myself," I said.

"No, you're not. And Alice looks like the sort of person who needs a lot of love."

"Who doesn't?" I flared. I was angry that he had agreed with my self-estimate so swiftly.

"Maybe if you gave her more love you'd get back more in return."

"I'm *trying!*"

"Don't just try, do it."

We drove the rest of the way into Omaha in silence.

During dinner Carter spoke to me about his search for happiness, about how changes were taking place in him over which he had limited control. "There are only two ways to cure the deep unhappiness," he was saying, "self-knowledge or self-oblivion. Since I am basically a lazy, passive person I can see why back in New York I chose self-oblivion as the easier path. But now, through meditation and yoga, I can . . ."

I wasn't really listening. I was thinking about Alice. I was wishing she had come with us, that I felt guilty to have gone without her, that I resented feeling guilty, that it was her own damned fault, that she'd probably be angry when we got back, that I wasn't going to let her spoil my dinner with my brother. . . . But still, I wished she had come.

". . . It's difficult to cling to nothing at first," Carter was saying. "You have that feeling of having partially outgrown and partially rejected a former consciousness, that *persona* by which you defined yourself. But ultimately, you let go of it. Like the way a butterfly lets go of its old cocoon: slowly, with tentative flutterings, gaining strength from the sun until it starts to soar—"

"—into the beak of some giant bird," I interrupted and immediately wondered why I felt the need to wisecrack whenever he talked like that.

"Or into the arms of God," he said.

"Oh shit, I'm sorry. I always get nervous when you start talking to me about God."

"God shouldn't make you nervous," he said. "It's people who should. That's why I went to Hawaii. I think what attracted me was that these were the happiest people I ever saw in my life and I must have suspected somehow that if there was any key to my happiness, that it must lie there with them. After that, it was just a question of being with people who were progressively happier and happier until I started to meet the angels."

"*Angels?* What are you talking about?" I asked. "Do you mean the kind who 'do God's work?' "

"Look, if a man thinks he's doing God's work, he probably is whether he knows it or not."

"Who are these angels?"

"They're just ordinary people—that is, they *seem* just like ordinary people until you get to know them, or they feel they can trust and relate to you."

"Can someone *become* an angel?" I asked. "Is that what you're trying to tell me, that it's a state of enlightenment?"

"Someone either is an angel or isn't," he said. "And there are a lot of angels I'm not yet privileged enough to see. I'm still a beginner."

"If *you're* a beginner, then what am I?"

"I'm not sure," he said. "Sometimes I think you might be an angel, yourself, although I can't yet figure out what kind. That's partly because I don't think you know yet what purpose you serve. Your task might simply be to witness, but I may be wrong. You do have a different kind of power than I. I do know that."

"Power? What kind of power?"

"I can't tell you what it is," he said. "You'll have to find it out for yourself."

The waiter came by to take our dessert order and after he'd gone Carter didn't want to talk about angels or power anymore. Nor did he ever talk to me about it again. I never forgot that conversation though. It came back to haunt me when I began to worry that I was an Angel of Death.

Carter left our Nebraska farm two days early and I did not see him again for nine years, not until I went back out to Hawaii to shoot that airline promo.

I would have loved to have taken Alice and the children on the trip to Hawaii, but we could not afford it. The yearly cycle of the farm film had led to a film on the Chicago commodities exchange. Alice wanted to put down roots back east and, thinking my income would grow, that it would keep up with inflation and expenses, I had gone heavily in debt to buy an old stone house in New Jersey. Our optimism had been unfounded. The market for documentaries, for *independent* documentaries, was shrinking and with it my bank balance. I was worrying about money all the time. Alice had said she didn't want to go to Hawaii anyway. "It's not a vacation," she said. "You're going to be working or with your brother all the time. Thanks, but no thanks."

"Then with the money I make from the promo you and I will take a trip, just you and me together," I said. "Choose a spot. We'll get someone to stay with Peter."

"I'll believe it when I see it," Alice said. We'd been married, by then, for eight years. She had good reason to be cynical.

The attendants were loading the dead surfer's body into the back of the ambulance and Carter and I were answering the police officer's questions. Bernie Wooten had shown the officer our permit to film, but the officer seemed more disturbed by the gasoline-powered lighting generator than by the surfer's death. A moment later the doors slammed on the ambulance and it was moving slowly up the beach to the access road between the hotels. Harry Abbott was dismantling the lighting stands, packing up the Tota-Lites. Carter and I walked down to help roll the cables and put away the rest of the equipment. We were just finishing up when Bernie joined us. "I think everything's cool now," he said.

"What do you mean?" I asked.

"The police realize it was an accident," he said.

"Shouldn't someone see his mother? Tell her?"

"She knows already," Carter said.

"Someone told her?" I asked.

"She just knows," Carter said. "You don't understand these people like I do. She'll be told by someone of her own family. She has a brother on the police force, another is a fireman. The best thing we can do is to stop by her store in a day or so and tell her how sorry we are."

"What about the funeral?" I asked. "Shouldn't we help out there? Don't we have some responsibility?"

"*Don't say that!*" Bernie whispered harshly. "We're *not* responsible! It was an accident. They all signed waivers. It was nobody's fault. You start talking responsibility, then you open yourself up to a lawsuit. It was nobody's fault. I don't want to hear about fault. Let's just pack up and get out of here. The torch shot was a lousy idea to begin with."

I spent one more night with Carter before leaving the next morning. That night Carter invited Nora to join us and the three of us ate at a Chinese restaurant. When we cracked open our fortune cookies mine said, "You are domestically inclined and will be happily married."

Carter's was, "You never worry about the future."

Nora opened hers last, guffawed, then handed it to Carter, who passed it to me. Nora's fortune read, "You may attend a party where strange customs prevail."

"I wonder what kind of party they had in mind?" she asked.

"Probably a hotel luau," Carter said. He pushed his chair back and stood up. "Shall we go back to my place?"

"I think you'd better drop me at my apartment on the way," Nora said.

"Don't you want to stay with us?" Carter asked.

"Thanks for including me in your dinner, but I think the two of you should spend your last night together alone."

I did not protest.

Carter looked at me and then at Nora. "Whatever you'd prefer," he said. "But you may be missing out on a party where strange customs prevail."

Carter and I dropped Nora off then drove on up the hill to his little house overlooking the city. He rolled us a joint while I opened the bottle of good wine we'd been saving for this, our last night. He put some music on while I poured two glasses, then we sat back for a moment not speaking.

Finally Carter said, "It was fun working with you on this film. I'd really like to do something with you again."

"I would, too. Maybe after I finish this goddam cancer documentary we could do something together."

"How's it coming?"

"Slowly." I lapsed into silence.

"What are you thinking about?"

"The boy last night. It was terrible. It was the first time I've ever seen anyone killed. It was so sudden. So unexpected. It scares me."

"Scares you?"

"There was no chance to get ready for it. At least while I've been doing this cancer documentary I've *known* some of the people were going to die. I *knew* they were terminal. *They* knew they were terminal. But that boy last night. . . . It just seemed so random and violent and awful."

"It could happen to any of us," Carter said. "We could be crossing a street . . ."

"Cheery thought," I said.

"Cheery conversation," he replied. "Change the subject. Are you looking forward to going home?"

"I guess so," I said. I thought for a moment, "I'm ready for it now."

"Do you have to steel yourself? Is it that bad?"

I laughed. "No, it's not like that. It's just the return to the 'real world,' the world of mortgages and Alice and bills."

"It's real here, too."

"Not to me."

"I don't ever want to go back. I love these islands, the people," he said. "I'm simply trying to live a life of truth. I'm trying not to delude myself. I want to see the universe face to face and to understand its nature . . . I do my five meditations, my yoga . . . I fast . . ." Carter laughed suddenly, "And I look forward to menopause."

"Menopause? Why?"

"If I could rid myself of sexual desire, then I would be free. According to Buddhist teaching, Desire, Hatred, and Illusion are the three things at the root of evil. Freedom from Desire, from Illusion, from Hatred are at the root of good. . . . I don't think I have many illusions and I don't hate anyone, but when you're living in a place where all you see are beautiful young girls squeezed into tiny bikinis, it's hard to attain Nirvana since, in my case, ultimate happiness becomes the desire to throw my bones on every single one of them I can."

"Perhaps that is your karma," I said. "To bring happiness to the women."

"No, pal," he said, shaking his head. "I don't bring them happiness, nothing real that lasts."

"God knows I don't seem to be able to bring that to Alice either."

"Do you want to?"

"Of course I do. My fortune cookie was my secret desire: to be happily married, and to have enough money to live in a nice house and be able to provide properly for my kids."

"What would make Alice happy?"

"For me to quit fucking around."

"How much do you do?"

"An occasional lonely wife . . . I hate it. I hate it. I hate the subterfuge, the guilt, the . . . the *reality* of it."

"So why not stop? Why continue doing it?"

"Because it makes me feel a little less lonely."

"Not happy, though?"

"No."

Carter took a sip of his wine. "A celestial diva once asked Buddha what the most horrible pain was. The Buddha answered, 'A bad conscience.' Maybe you'd feel better if you quit."

I had no answer.

"Well," Carter said, "it's something to think about."

I left Hawaii the next morning and a couple of weeks later Carter moved to a small house on the island of Maui on Makena Beach. He wrote that he was happier now than he had ever been.

On Friday, June 16, 1978, just about a month after we had finished shooting the airline promo and I had left Hawaii, Alice and I had come into New York City to have dinner with my mother and spend the night. My stepfather no longer felt well enough to attend the theater and so at least once every couple of months my mother, who loved the theater, would invite Alice and me to go to a play with her. What play we saw never mattered so much as the excuse the invitation gave us to be together.

When I think about my mother—and I do, still, a lot—I think about her understanding, her capacity to accept human frailty without being either gullible or overly solicitous. She had great warmth, love, and generosity. She was very wise, but not an intellectual. (She had never aspired to a college education, and therefore never attended college.) She was a superb reader and brought to her reading and to her theater-going as much critical acumen as anyone I've ever known. Her intellectuality, achieved through experience and an openness to sensation, was visceral and intuitive; it was also, however, always solidly based upon reality. And yet she had her blind spots: she knew and cared next to nothing about art, cared little for music other than a few readily recognizable classics and Bing Crosby's recordings, rarely attended a movie, and except for news programs, was utterly bored by TV. I think this was because her intellect was so thoroughly rooted in practicality and common sense.

My mother was wonderful company. She had an extraordinary talent for making her companion feel just a little bit more witty, intelligent, charming, and handsome than, perhaps, he really was. I'm not sure how she did this. She didn't flatter. I know she had little patience with any of the social poses. I think she brought out the best in people simply by expecting the best of them. She was articulate, amusing, quick to laugh, and quicker with the wisecrack if an ego needed deflating.

Alice and I were looking forward to that evening and the theater with my mother. I don't remember what play we were going to see because we never saw it.

Alice was in the bathroom when the telephone rang. It was a friend of Carter's calling from Maui. Our baby-sitter had given him the number of the hotel where Alice and I were staying. Carter and another friend, he told me, had left at about eleven the morning before for a sail around Molokini, a tiny island about a mile off Makena Beach. A storm had come up and when, by 5 P.M., Carter and the friend had still not returned, the Coast Guard had been notified.

I don't remember feeling anything but businesslike. I asked the caller for as many details about the boat, their sailing plan, how good a sailor the friend was, their physical condition—were they high? What had the storm been like? The caller did not know very much, only that Carter and his friend had gone out on a Hobie Cat, a small sailing catamaran, that it had been painted yellow, that he thought the friend, like Carter, was a good swimmer, that a Hobie Cat was easy to sail. "I really don't have much information, I'm sorry," he apologized. "But I thought you ought to know."

I thanked him and telephoned the Coast Guard in Hawaii.

The Coast Guard duty officer told me they had not been notified that Carter was missing until after dark, but two helicopters, five Civil Air

Patrol planes, and a Coast Guard cutter had been searching since two in the morning and would continue, he said, until dark, "which will be about seven hours from now." There had been no storms since the one Carter's boat had disappeared into. The Coast Guard was aware that the boat was a Hobie Cat and that although the yellow paint was supposedly faded it should still be highly visible since Hobie Cats do not sink. "On the other hand," the duty officer said, "you should be aware that if the boat overturned it floats with near-negative buoyancy."

"What does that mean?" I asked.

"It means very little of your brother's boat would be visible above the water." He also said the water was warm and that they had fished people out of the ocean after three days with no serious effects.

"I was told they were planning to sail around Molokini," I said.

"The search planes have covered that. Molokini's just a little volcanic cone that sticks up out of the water. If they'd been on it, they'd have been visible. Frankly, we don't believe they're in the water," he said. "They may have reached one of the other islands. Kahoolawe, perhaps."

"Isn't that the one the Navy uses for bombing practice?"

"All practice has been suspended for the duration of the search." He paused for a moment. "I'm sorry, there's nothing more we can tell you at this time. We'll contact you as soon as we have any news."

I gave him a series of phone numbers where either myself or my mother could be reached, thanked him, and hung up. By this time Alice was dressed.

"What was that all about?" she asked.

"Carter's missing," I said. "He went out on a sailboat yesterday and hasn't been seen since."

"Do you think he's drowned?"

"I don't know," I said. "I don't know what to think."

Alice sat down on the side of the bed next to me and took my hand. "Are you going to tell your mother?"

"Yes."

"He's going to be all right. You'll see."

"Jesus, I hope so," I said. I kissed Alice on the cheek. "I'd better try to call Ma."

She was not at the club where she was staying; they thought she had already left for the restaurant.

"You go on ahead," Alice told me. "I'll meet you there."

The restaurant was two blocks from the hotel. My mother was sitting alone at a table. "Where's Alice?" she asked when I sat down.

"She'll be along in a minute," I said. "She wanted to give us a few minutes alone."

My mother looked at me quizzically.

I had thought on the walk over how best to break the news. I knew that I shouldn't attempt to keep anything back. I felt that if I properly marshaled all the facts I could still present a reasonably hopeful and still realistic picture.

"Ma," I said, "I just got a phone call from a friend of Carter's in Hawaii. Carter and another guy went out on a sailboat yesterday morning and—" I might just as well have stopped there. I saw from the expression on her face that she knew Carter was dead.

Still I told her everything I knew. I explained about the current being of tidal influence so that the net transfer of water was twelve hours one way, twelve hours the next; that the water was warm; that the Coast Guard was still searching; and that there were at least six more hours of daylight in Hawaii; that the Coast Guard did not believe they were still in the water; that they may have taken shelter or could have sailed to any one of the neighboring islands: Kahoolawe, Molokai, or Lanai.

"He's dead," my mother said.

I went back out to Hawaii to see if there was anything I could do, to try to get the Coast Guard to extend their search. But there was nothing anyone could do. Carter had disappeared and was presumed dead. On the airplane returning home I read through some of Carter's notebooks and journals with the hope that I could piece together something that could be published in his memory. In the back of one of his small spiral jotting pads there appeared the following note: "My brother thinks he has a heart, but he does not know how to love."

A small memorial service was held for Carter in the cemetery just outside of New York City where my father was buried. He had died when I was a child. My mother and stepfather, my uncle and aunt, and Alice and I attended.

Within six months of that service my uncle, my stepfather and my mother, too, were dead. And I was feeling afraid and isolated and vulnerable and out of control and I was on my way to Leadville on the east slope of the Rockies to be a visiting professor in the Communications Department of Rocky Mountain State.

I knew when I left home that my marriage was shaky—that *I* was shaky, that I was leaving behind my wife, my children, my home, my*self*, and I wasn't sure what or who would be left when I got back.

I had been able to cope with my brother's death, my stepfather's, the uncle I had loved. But the death of my mother destroyed what stamina I had left. I felt orphaned. Terribly alone.

My relationship with Alice had deteriorated to the point where only the barest civilities were exchanged. This was largely my fault. I was tense all the time, felt the constant pressure of worrying about money and not having completed the film. I was locked into depression and could not break out. I was always tired and awakened unrefreshed from what little sleep I was able to get. I would try to calm myself, talk to myself, ask myself why I was in such a state. But I *did not know* why. I could not understand what was happening to me. I knew only that I was alone and that no one could help me; and I believed that even if I were to find such a person, he or she would eventually abandon me, too.

I did not eat. I could not concentrate. I hardly spoke. I was frightened all the time. Alice, alarmed by the sudden precariousness of my emotional state, did not know how to respond. She tried giving me peptalks; we would end up enraged.

Three weeks after we had buried my mother Alice told me she thought it might help if I went back to work on the cancer film. "You haven't touched it at all," she said. "Is it because of Ma's death?"

"Do you mean am I using Ma's death as an excuse?"

"I didn't say that."

"I can't look at it!" I cried. "Goddam it, Alice, can't you understand? Everyone in it is dying too!"

"You've got to finish it. We need the money."

"*Don't you think I know that?*" I shouted. "Why the hell else do you think I've taken that job at Rocky Mountain State?" I stormed out of the room.

Two minutes later, ashamed of my outburst, I walked back in to Alice and found her crying. "I'm sorry, Alice, I didn't mean to get so mad."

"I loved your mother. I miss her, too," Alice said. "And no matter what you think I even liked your brother. But you can't just give up."

"I haven't given up!" I said, fighting down the anger I felt rising again. "I just need a little more time to get myself straightened—"

"We haven't got time," she said impatiently, brushing her hand through the pile of envelopes on the table. "How are we going to pay all these bills?"

"In two weeks I'll be in Colorado on salary. I'll be earning enough to get these bills paid. Bear with me, Alice. Be patient, *please?*"

At that moment Joan came down from her bedroom. "What's for dinner?" she said.

"Chicken," Alice said.

"*Again?*" Joan made a face and went back upstairs.

"That child!" Alice said. "I don't suppose you'd care to take her out to Colorado with you?"

"I can't, you know that."

"Because she'd get in your way."

"For the same reason we talked about you not coming with me. It would mean pulling the children out of school, renting a big place, uprooting the family. We decided there was no sense in doing that—"

"You and she decided that."

"Alice, you and I decided that. Joan was there, that's all. We agreed. We all said we'd simply try to get through the winter as best we could. The point was for us to earn some money, save it, and not spend it on flying back and forth for visits until the spring break. I'll only be gone one semester. I'll be there for seven weeks and return for two weeks in March, then go back to Colorado for seven weeks more. It's going to be difficult—"

"What's going to be difficult for *you?* You've only got yourself to take care of. Get your act together and it won't seem so hard."

"Get your act together" was a favorite expression of Alice's during that time. I wished to God I could. But I needed someone or something solidly rooted to cling to, someone or something safe and familiar to deflect the unrelenting anxiety I felt. Alice, sensing my panic, would withdraw from me as if my fears were contagious, a disease virulent enough to destroy her as well.

When I tried to speak with Alice about my anxiety, she did not want to hear. I needed her support; she needed me to be strong and resolute. Any sign of weakness or uncertainty on my part scared her. If I were unsure of myself, of what I was doing, where I was going, whether we were going to make it—and that, in this case, meant being able to pay our bills—Alice became frightened of what would happen to her. She depended upon my stability. And I had been stable until my mother's death. Suddenly I wasn't anymore.

Now, of course, I know that the inner turmoil, the breakdown of relationships, the terrible loneliness, the deepening and seemingly irreversible depressions, the diminishing physical powers, the awesome feelings of loss, the sense of being constantly enmeshed in crises without knowing how or why they'd come about, *now* I know these are all symptoms of a midlife crisis. But *then?* In those days none of us knew what a "midlife crisis" was. I was the first kid on our block to have gotten one.

On the flight out to Denver I was thinking of Alice's line, "Get your act together."

Get my act together? What does one wear to play the *Madwoman of Chaillot?*

Basic black with pearls, of course.

4

I BEGAN TO COME "unglued" that semester in Leadville nearly three years ago.

I know how flip, facetious even, that expression sounds, but no other word seems quite so appropriate for how I perceived my state of impending fragmentation. I was not yet "going to pieces" or even "falling apart." Instead, like the cheap laminated plywood dresser with its curled-up edges that sat in the windowless bedroom of the dismal apartment located for me by Rocky Mountain State's Communications Department for my semester as visiting professor, I was simply and terrifyingly coming unglued. I had thought that when I settled into the apartment in Leadville, had unpacked my clothes, photographs of the family, books, personal things, that the uneasiness would go away. But the apartment in Leadville—one of those single-bedroom units in a small, gray cinder-block post-World War II building about a mile from the campus—only depressed me more.

The living room contained a Danish modern couch and two Danish modern chairs, one of which the landlord had warned me not to sit in. A Danish modern coffee table wobbled upon an orange and blue motel-shag rug. The couch and chairs were covered with a worn lime-green tweed fabric interwoven with red thread. The walls, too, were light green except for the trim of the picture window looking out on the Texaco station across the street. The trim was a Chinese lacquer red. At night, sitting on the couch with both the lamp atop the two-tiered table and the bare ceiling light turned on, I felt like Jonah sitting inside the whale's stomach—a feeling enhanced by the view across to the aluminum and Formica dining table beached in the middle of the sand-colored spattered linoleum floor. From that angle, the scene was duodenal—if not, in fact, upper intestinal tract.

I spent the majority of my daylight hours working in the freshly painted white kitchen, the only bright room in the place. There, at the small kitchen table butted up against the wall, I wrote, cut, rewrote, and edited the cancer documentary script that I had by then been working on for three years. I sat facing a double electric wall socket above which I had taped a photograph of the New Jersey house. Alone at night I would look up between bites of chicken pot pie and imagine myself walking from room to room, pausing here and there to talk with a child.

Sometimes I would pretend I was in the library with Alice, a fire crackling in the old stone fireplace as we watched the evening news. I was overcome with homesickness.

I also missed terribly all the trappings of being a father, a husband, a member of a family—of still *having* a family, a mother, a stepfather, an older brother alive.

I missed sitting in the library and having Peter, our eight-year-old, fold himself over the arm of my chair with his latest drawing of a cat. I missed the sudden, crackling burst of sillies that Joan, by then a huge-footed twelve-year-old would get for no apparent reason at all—no reason, that is, apparent to me. I even missed having my lap used as a Handi-wipe by Burp, our enormous slobbering, shedding Newfoundland dog.

I have always been sentimental about family life, dressed it in ermines it did not always deserve. The photograph albums I so faithfully kept recorded a myth as dangerously deceptive as "The Brady Bunch."

As soon as my telephone was installed I called home. It must have been around 7 P.M. their time. Alice answered and in the background I could hear the canary singing along with the television, the children's laughter, a car honking as it passed outside.

I said things were fine, that I was a little lonely, but that in the past three days I had already met some people I thought I would like.

"What am I going to do about the bills?" Alice asked.

I told her she would have to hold off paying some of them until I had received my first check from the university in another eight to ten days. The lawyers handling the settlement of my mother's estate would lend us some money should we really get short, I said, but that I hoped that wouldn't be necessary. Even though I was worried about money at the moment, I was sure the pressure would be off when I turned in the film.

She said, "Can't you just put all this in a letter to me?"

"Well, sure," I said. "I already have. But I thought it would be good to talk."

"All I need to know is how much and when the money will come," she said.

"That's what I'm trying to tell you. I'm not sure when it will arrive. It'll be at least another eight to ten days, maybe as long as two weeks."

Alice was silent and I could tell from the background noises they were all watching "Let's Make a Deal." Then she said, "Your cat has diarrhea all the time."

"Tallulah's very old." (I had had Tallulah since Maggie and I were married. Maggie sent Tallulah back to me with my daughter Joan.)

"I know how old Tallulah is."

"Tell the children not to let her drink the milk they leave in their cereal bowls. That's what causes it. . . . How are things otherwise?" I asked. "How are you and the kids?"

"Fine. We're all fine," she said. "You know we all get along much better when you're not around."

When I didn't—couldn't—speak, Alice went on.

"Was there something else you wanted to talk to me about?"

"No." I had wanted her to say she loved me, missed me, that they all missed me. I felt as if I'd been hit.

"Okay, fine, then," she said. "The children send their love." I could tell from the flatness of her tone that her eyes were once again fixed on the TV. "We miss you. G'bye." She hung up.

I sat next to the dead telephone feeling sick to my stomach.

You know we all get along much better when you're not around.

When Alice and I had married we had no way of knowing that Joan would eventually live with us, too. Maggie, my first wife, and I were married for just over five years. Joan was two when her mother and I separated, three when we were divorced. Alice and I were married while Joan was living with her mother in Oregon. Maggie remarried out there, but it lasted less than six months; her husband walked out on her. And then, several years later—this would have been the summer of 1974—a friend returning from Portland told me he had seen Maggie working nights as a waitress in a cowboy bar.

I felt sad and telephoned to see whether there was anything I could do to help her out.

"I don't know what's happening to me," she said, bursting into tears. "I just can't seem to get it together. I'm making such a fucking *mess* of my life! Sometimes I just feel like . . ." Her voice trailed off.

"Like what?" I asked, alarmed.

"Don't worry, I'm not going to kill myself!" she said, then added, "Jesus, why do men always think women are going to kill themselves? I don't want to die, I want to *live!*"

There was silence for a moment and I could hear Maggie blow her nose. I said, "Maggie, would it help if I took Joan to live with Alice and me for a while?"

"You want to take my child away from me? Why? Do you think I'm a bad mother?" There was the edge of anger in her voice.

"Oh, Maggie, no," I said. "I asked because I thought you might like a break. If Joan were with me you'd have more time to concentrate on yourself, to find yourself a better job."

"You want custody of her?"

"No, no custody. Let's keep the lawyers the hell out of this! It would be an agreement, an arrangement between us, that's all. And when you felt good again, good about yourself, your life, she'd come back out to stay with you."

"My life's fine!" she said. "Joan is all I've got."

Joan then would have been just under eight years old.

I continued to see Joan on alternate Christmases and Thanksgivings and a month or two during the summer for another two years and then toward the end of May 1976 I was working in my office behind the house one afternoon when the telephone rang. It was Maggie.

"How would you like to keep Joan with you for the next year?"

"For the year?" I asked. "Why?"

"I've been offered a pretty good job but it would mean I'd have to travel, be away from home for long periods of time."

"Doing what?"

"I'm not sure. Sort of a secretary, sales representative with a small company out here that makes wood stoves."

"Wood stoves?"

"Everyone out here is very energy-conscious and I've met this wonderful man and he has a small foundry. He's been casting wood stoves for the last year or so and he can't keep up with the orders. So he's expanding and . . . well, I like him very much. We get along very well and he wants me to work for him—*with* him—and it could be my chance."

I was silent.

"You told me a couple of years ago, you offered to take Joanie and I was hoping you might still want her. She's—"

"—Of course I *want* her, Maggie. It's all so sudden! I need a little time to think."

"She's at an age now where she needs a father . . ."

"I'll have to talk to Alice," I said.

"Can you let me know as soon as possible?" Maggie asked.

"Of course I will," I said.

"Joan wants to speak to you."

"Put her on," I said.

There was a moment's delay and then Joan came on the phone. "Hi, Daddy."

"Hello, honey, how are you?"

"Okay. Am I really going to come live with you and Alice?"

"I hope so," I said. "Would you like that?"

"Sure," she said. "It'd be okay."

"You could go to school here, see your friends . . ."

"I don't have any friends there."

"Of course you do," I said.

"Who?"

"Jesus, honey, I can't think of all their names right now. There's Jennifer and Wendy—"

"Wendy's a twit. And Jennifer's so stuck up she pretended last summer she'd never met me before."

"Well, you can make new ones."

"I'm no good at making friends."

"Nonsense," I said. "How are you otherwise? How's school? Is there anything you need?"

"Is there anything I need?" Joan repeated, then said, "Mommy wants to talk to you."

"Hello?" Maggie said. "Listen, Joan's going to need braces. Maybe they could be started there?"

"How much is left in Joanie's trust?"

"Nothing," she said. "I had to use it to make the down payment on this house."

"Maggie, damn it all, braces will cost a couple of thousand dollars! Can't you contribute to some of those dental bills? I mean I set up Joan's trust to take care of that sort of thing. You got your own settlement to put into a house."

"I needed Joan's, too," she said. "You wouldn't have wanted her to live in any of those houses at the sort of price I could afford."

"But didn't your husband, what's his name—"

"His name was Walter," Maggie calmly said.

"Didn't Walter leave you anything?"

"Nothing an abortion couldn't take care of."

"You were *pregnant?*" I asked. "And he *left?*"

"No, I wasn't pregnant. I was making a joke."

"Oh," I said.

"Look, please, if you can take Joan for a year or so—"

"—Or so?"

"For a year. If you can take Joan for a year it would really help me out. It may be my only chance to get out of this rut. I think it's a good company. It will get bigger. It's my big chance."

"Okay, Maggie, I'll talk to Alice."

"Joan sends her love."

"My love to her, too."

"And thanks, honey," Maggie said.

Honey? "Okay, Maggie. I'll let you know."

"I don't want her," Alice said.

"But, Alice. We have plenty of room. There's a good school, which she'll be in all day. I'll do everything I can to make it easy on you. I'll get her breakfast, her lunch, make sure she cleans up her room. I'll take care of her—"

"I don't *want* her." Alice said.

"But, Alice, please, Joanie's—"

"No!" she said. "Don't do this to me."

"Alice, I—"

"No! Damn you! No!"

"But I'm her *father*."

"Then you deal with it. It's your problem. Yours and Maggie's. It's not mine. I can take it a month or two during the summer but not all year round. If Maggie's job is so good, why can't she get a sitter? Someone to stay with Joan while she's gone?"

"It wouldn't be the same. Joanie's almost ten. She needs a parent around."

"Well, I can't—I *won't* take her for an entire year."

Ultimately, I did not give Alice a choice. I didn't feel I had one either—other than to ignore the welfare of my child. And as much as I felt it was unfair to Alice I also felt Maggie deserved a chance to straighten out her life.

That conversation with Maggie and later with Alice took place, as I've said, in May 1976. Joan came to live with Alice and me that summer; she was then ten years old. With the exception of alternate Christmases and Thanksgivings and a month or two in the summer, Joan has lived with me ever since. Just over a year ago when I was discussing all this with Odette, she first mentioned that conversation that had taken place between her and Alice the day after that dinner party when Alice had come to Odette's garden.

"Alice told me that your daughter came to live with you the day after you were married," Odette said.

"She didn't come to live with us," I said. "She spent that Christmas with us. It was my turn to have her. Alice knew about the visitation clauses when we started living together."

"She told me you threw your daughter on her the day after you were married. That it was a surprise."

"No . . . no," I said, shaking my head. "How could that be? Alice was there when all the arrangements were made. Maggie was still living in Oregon then, so Alice and I had had to go through that whole rigamarole of finding a nonstop flight—only one came into Omaha—the unaccompanied-child forms, meeting planes, phone calls . . . We picked up Joan when we returned to Nebraska. She spent two weeks with us at the farm, then went back to her mother in Oregon. We didn't see Joan again until the next summer and—"

"But she *was* with you when you got married."

"For the first two weeks."

"If Arthur had had children by a previous marriage I wouldn't have wanted them on our honeymoon."

"But it wasn't a 'honeymoon' *per se*," I said. "Alice and I never really had a honeymoon except for a couple of nights in the Plaza Hotel. Nebraska had been our honeymoon. We'd been living together about six months before we decided to get married and we were alone again for six months after Joan left. So that first year, with the exception of about two weeks, we—but, no, Odette, I know what you're saying. I see your point. I should have had her for Thanksgiving and left Christmas for the wedding and ourselves—"

"Or scheduled the wedding for when Joan wasn't around."

"Or that. But the reason why I didn't was that it would have meant not having my daughter for three Christmases in a row. And she was still so young then, and Christmas with young kids . . ."

"There are do's and dont's as far as a woman is concerned," Odette said. "You don't take kids along on a honeymoon. Mothers either."

"But there are honeymoons and there are honeymoons! It wasn't as though Alice and I were taking Joanie with us to Paris, or to some tropical paradise. Alice and I got married over Christmas because it was when I had a break from the filming and we decided to get married in New York."

"Why didn't you take a honeymoon?"

"I had to be back in Nebraska for the film."

"And then Joan came to live—"

"That was seven years later."

"—and as you said, you didn't give Alice much choice."

"Odette, what was *my* choice? I was the child's father. I didn't want her raised by a live-in sitter."

"She would have survived. Children are tough. Your first loyalty was to Alice."

"My first loyalty was to all my family."

"And yourself."

"My 'self' as a husband and a father. I didn't just dump my daughter in Alice's lap and say, 'Okay, you cope. You do all the work.'"

"Who did the laundry?"

"Alice."

"The marketing?"

"Alice."

"The cooking?"

"Alice. One dinner a day. But all right, I admit, it was still a load to dump on her. Jesus, Odette, I know how much help she gave me, that she made it possible for me to have Joan. At the same time, I don't see where I had any choice."

"It wasn't Alice's problem," Odette said. "It was your problem."

"Why wasn't it *our* problem? Why wasn't it the sort of problem a married couple shares? Why didn't she try to understand what I was up against instead of resenting me and my kid?"

"I would have resented it, too," Odette said. "You were always willing to do your best, give your best for your children. Why weren't you willing to do the same for your wife?"

"I was. I *did*. At first. But I quit trying so hard when there wasn't anything coming back but anger and resentment. Even then, but even then I think I made it possible for Alice to have a pretty damned good life."

"Measured by material things."

"That's the only goddam thing she was interested in!" I was surprised by how swiftly the anger resurfaced. "Don't think she didn't make us aware of her feelings! Don't think a day went by when she didn't make her resentment known!"

When I went off to Leadville that winter semester, Alice's resentment was palpable. And had we not needed the money so desperately, I certainly would not have gone. I knew Alice thought I was trying to escape, running off like Captain Video to some space adventure while she was stuck on planet earth with my kid, whose mother was making a new life for herself in Oregon. I *had* stuck her with an extra child but I was not, as she believed, having a marvelous time.

I was not, as I've said, because I was coming unglued.

I spent my days with a red balloon of anxiety inside my head. It would suddenly inflate, burn my temples, push the bones of my skull apart. As the anxiety increased, the pressure built, expanded within me, threatened to blow me apart. The attacks would strike without warning, I would have to remain absolutely still, force myself to breathe regularly and deeply until they would pass. The fiercest attacks occurred early in the morning—at three or four, rarely as late as five—and I would be jolted awake in the bedroom with no idea where I was.

I would fumble for the light switch, a lamp, find none in a familiar place, and, panicked, knock my wristwatch off the night table, sometimes a filled ashtray, the clock, an empty glass of milk. Everything would crash and clatter to the floor and I would freeze, seated bolt upright in the bed, a hand, my own, clutching my throat.

Oh God, how I hated those attacks! Hated my powerlessness to control them. They frightened me, stripped me, made me feel out of control, *weak.* I would try to diminish the attacks when they hit, cope with them by making them seem common, silly, benign. I called them "the morning dreadfuls" in the hopes that by belittling them I could make them, like nightmares, disappear.

But the attacks wouldn't disappear. Even though I could make them recede the cancer film *still* wasn't finished; there were *still* bills to be paid; my brother, my stepfather, my uncle, my mother—they were *still* dead.

I would get out of bed, clean up the spilled ashtray, pick up the glass, the alarm clock, whatever else I'd knocked to the floor. I'd busy myself in the kitchen, make myself a cup of instant coffee, smoke a cigarette, read a book of Zen *koans*, write a letter, masturbate, anything to get back to sleep. But there were all those predawn mornings when nothing worked, when I'd lie awake with my temples burning, thinking oh-my-God, oh-my-God, what-am-I-going-to-do? and see the sun come up.

There were so many moments when I would reach for the telephone to speak to Alice, but would never complete the call. I knew that no matter what I tried to tell her she would hear only that I was afraid.

You know how much better we all get along when you're not around.

She was probably right.

Because I was aware of Alice's resentment toward my daughter's presence I was overly protective of Joan; and aware, too, of the demands upon Alice that Joan's presence made, I would overreact when she was inconsiderate or overly boisterous if Alice were home. I was constantly trying to placate the warring sides. And since Joan was not above playing one of us off against the other, my absence no doubt did make life easier. I understood, too, why Alice would think I was just running off to another "adventure," why she would think I was having such a good time. I knew she believed I would immediately go to bed with some other woman. I always had.

There is a joke about a monstrous tidal wave that devastates the entire East Coast of the United States. Millions are wiped out. All these people are waiting in line for processing and admission through the Gates of Heaven. Two guys way back in the line are worriedly shifting from foot to foot, discussing their chances of getting in, when suddenly at the head of the line a great shout of joy can be heard. Hats, confetti, whatnot, are flung happily into the air, and as the cheering continues and rolls on back through the line toward them the two guys ask, "What's going on? What's going on?" The answer finally reaches them: *"They're not counting adultery!"*

Well, I didn't count adultery either. I never felt I was betraying Alice by giving another woman what Alice had made so clear she did not want herself. She wanted my fidelity, sure. But she didn't want me.

The reason why you don't turn me on is because you're too sweet and you talk too much.

A man with any sensitivity wants to give his woman pleasure in bed. A man wants to believe if he is open and loving and tender his woman will respond. I could bring Alice to orgasm, that was nothing more than technique, but I never felt I could make her *respond*. In the nearly eleven years we were married Alice never once initiated a sexual act. And, dear God, why was I so incapable of showing her the joy, the excitement, the laughter and sharing that making love could be? I tried. At least I believe I did.

"Why do you insist on romanticizing it by calling it 'making love'?" she would taunt me. "It's *fucking*, that's *all* it is."

And when I came to feel that nothing would change her mind, a feeling exacerbated by the delight she took in her attractiveness to other men, I came to feel less of a man myself.

Why did I marry Alice? Because she was fun. She was good company, provocative, opinionated. Even when it became clear that what I had mistaken for strength was only bravado, she was fun. Her irreverence, ballsiness, pushiness, appealed to something I felt lacking in me. Opposites attract. Neither of us any longer pretended to be in love— though I had loved her in the very beginning. I don't think that Alice ever said to me, "I love you." Not even in the beginning. She did once write "I love you" on a card attached to a Christmas present. I saved the card for years. She loved my blue blazer; I loved her tank tops with no bra. She loved my being so tall; I loved her being so short. She loved my being a film-maker; I loved her being a street-wise New York City kid. We got married because of timing; we were both lonely. Our marriage failed because we wanted to be loved more than we wanted to love.

And so as I've said, the vicious circle began: Because I wasn't getting tenderness and affection at home, I went looking for it elsewhere. Because I went looking for it elsewhere, I wasn't getting any at home. And all right, yes, I did go to bed with a coed a year (not six months) after Alice and I were married.

Alice was away; we had had a terrible quarrel and she had left our Nebraska tenant farmhouse for a weekend in New York. I have no real excuse other than the fact that I spent my teaching days surrounded by nubile, hard-bodied, corn-fed, nineteen-year-old farm girls in class after class. As I would stand at the lectern they would cross and uncross their legs, stretch, lick their lips, flutter their eyelashes, lightly touch their breasts. Musk would roll up at me like fog in a valley and it was already obvious that Alice felt making love to me was a chore.

"Can't you come more quickly?" she would say.

I *love* making love. I *hate* to hurry. And after that coed, I was not unfaithful again for years. Three.

My fifth night in Leadville the telephone rang just as I was sliding my Swanson's "Hungry Man" TV turkey dinner into the oven. The graduate teaching assistants were holding a party and would I come? "Yes," I told the caller. Yes. Yes. Yes. I did not want to be alone.

The party was held in a steamy little apartment only a few blocks from where I lived. The living room was crowded with young men and women dressed exactly alike in flannel shirts, down vests, blue jeans, hiking boots. I had introduced myself to the hostess, a young woman with long, unwashed black hair and rough, chapped hands, who led me into the kitchen where the bar had been set up. I was pouring myself a glass of red wine when I felt a hand on my ass. I turned around and it was Nora Rosenthal-Gribbs.

"Hello, bruddah," she said. She leaned forward and kissed me on the lips.

"You know each other?" the hostess asked, surprised.

"This man has made me a movie star," Nora said.

"If there is a surge in the tourist population of Hawaii," I said, "Nora will be responsible."

"How *are* you?" Nora asked. "How's Carter?"

"Let's find a place to sit," I said. I took her arm and guided her through the standees in the kitchen until we found an unoccupied couple of chairs in the living room.

Just as we were sitting down she pointed to a man standing not far from us in the living room. "Do you see that man over there? The one with the beard and the pipe?" (Three quarters of the men in the room had beards, but only one of them had a pipe. Practically no one in Leadville smoked.)

"The one with the red hair?"

"His name's Abner Locke. He's an associate professor," Nora said. "Last semester I was talking to him in the faculty lounge and I quoted the opening of Kubla Khan: 'In Xanadu did Kubla Khan / A stately pleasure-dome decree . . .' and Locke interrupted to say Keats had always been one of his favorite poets. When I pointed out that 'Kubla Khan' was written by Coleridge, not Keats, he only smiled and said, 'Ah, well, yes, of course. I knew it started with a "K".'"

"Was he serious?"

"Probably. The majority of the people in the English Department are more interested in skiing and hiking than literature. That's why they've come out here, anyway."

"What are you doing here?" I asked.

"I'm still going after my master's. When I heard you were coming I couldn't believe it! All we need now is to get Carter here and we—"

"Carter's dead, Nora," I said. "He drowned last June."

"Oh, shit." Nora said. She sat looking down at her hands. "How'd it happen?"

I started to tell her when a young man drifted over to join us. Nora introduced him as her husband and sent him away immediately to fetch her a drink.

I told Nora about the Hobie Cat and the storm and the Coast Guard search. And then I told her about my mother and uncle and stepfather. I couldn't help myself. I had to talk about it to someone and Nora was the only one there I knew. And besides, she had *known* Carter. She had seen him *alive*.

"I miss him so much!" I said.

"Of course you do," she said. She saw her husband approaching.

"Listen, I can't really talk about Carter in front of my husband. I'll come over to your place tomorrow around two-thirty. Will you be there?"

"Probably. I teach in the mornings, but I'm usually back at my apartment by early afternoon."

"I'll bring some wine," she said. "And I've even got some pretty good grass. We'll smoke a bit, toast Carter, and talk."

"Good," I said. "Let's do it."

"How do you like Leadville?" Nora's husband asked.

I don't know that I ever really intended to have an affair with Nora. I certainly did not open my door to her the following afternoon with that in mind. But then she said she thought we ought to talk in the bedroom so nobody walking on the sidewalk outside my apartment would know she was there.

We lay back together on the bed, smoked some dope, drank some wine. We talked about her husband, who had transferred to the law school and how she couldn't smoke grass in her apartment because if they got caught it was a felony and he wouldn't be able to practice law. And then she said, "Look, while we're here we might as well fuck."

I must have hesitated for a moment because she quickly added, "Unless you don't feel like it, of course. It isn't because of Carter, is it? I think he'd really like us to."

"I'm not so sure," I said.

"Well, I'd like to," she said. "I've never fucked brothers before."

I hesitated no longer. Nora was available and willing. And I, ever since I was nine years old and discovered Carter's incomplete but mesmerizing deck of pornographic playing cards, have, as must now be obvious, been totally dazzled by sex. Besides, what rowing had done to Nora's pectoral muscles made them impossible to resist. Nora didn't just have breasts, she had *tits:* full, heavy, meaty, firm, with great rose-tinted aueroles surrounding her nipples. I don't know which one of us, Nora or myself, liked her breasts more. When we made love they would flow, crest upward, break across her chest like waves, like surf. She loved to have me play with them, to lightly crush them. Take them into my mouth.

"Carter liked them, too," she said. She was kneeling astride me and she leaned forward to gently brush them back and forth across my lips. "I think the two of you were maybe weaned too soon—ow! Naughty! Mustn't bite!"

When she would begin to come, she would rear back, cup and squeeze her breasts, a red blush would suffuse her chest, her throat; a high, keening *oh-h-h-h* would escape her lips, she would pinch her nipples and then her whole body would go rigid, shudder once, twice, a third time. She would clamp her thighs about me and then suddenly collapse on my chest.

The first time we made love with Nora on top I remembered her telling my brother how she preferred that position and his laughing response that since she was so much stronger than him, she could pretty much secure whichever position she demanded. I didn't want to think about my brother just then. If I started thinking about Nora and my brother the room would soon be filled with ghosts. And so I lay there beneath Nora, my arms around her, and I talked to her. But almost immediately she sprinted out of my arms and off the bed. She dressed hurriedly, tucked in, bound, covered up those incredible breasts, talking all the while about James Joyce, her master's thesis, English Department politics, the flower imagery in Hamlet, God only knows what. She pulled on a pair of blue jeans, a dark green cotton turtleneck and a thick flannel shirt, heavy woolen socks, and hiking boots. "Ultimately what I came to realize," she said, "is that the whole New Criticism school was obsolete. That instead of making me appreciate literature, these critics were ruining it for me."

I was still in bed covered by a sheet. "Nora . . . ?"

"Of course I'm aware that that whole southern school of critics, Red Warren, Cleanth Brooks, and the like—"

"Nora?"

"—had enormous influence in the thirties and really through the fifties—"

"—*Nora?*"

"—when you were in college. But today, most critics . . ." She paused. "What?" she asked, looking at me for the first time since she'd gotten out of bed.

"Do you really respect me, or are you just using my body?"

"That's *exactly* the sort of thing Carter would say!" She was already scooping up her books. "The two of you are alike in many ways. And I don't just mean your humor," she giggled. "Listen, I've really got to run. Will you be here tomorrow? Can I come by at about the same time?"

If Nora had had any sense of humor, any ability to laugh at herself, I never saw it. I ordered for her a tight T-shirt with the legend LOVE ME FOR MY MIND. She was not amused; had she been, I know I would have liked her more. What Nora and I shared was only a desire for sex. Still, I was in no shape to handle a relationship with a woman that was any more complicated than that. And clinging to her body I was able to ride out those psychic storms and even, upon occasion, reach safe harbor, sanctuary, or whatever private cove one can associate with momentary peace of mind. Nevertheless, sometimes, though seldom intentionally, she did make me laugh. Just before Nora would climb onto my bed and just after she had removed her last article of clothing (a pair of white cotton J. C. Penney panties as a rule), she would unlatch the thin gold necklace from which a small gold Star of David hung suspended in the deep valley between her breasts. She would then neatly coil the chain upon my plywood dresser. The first time she did this I thought it was out of religious delicacy, but when she saw me watching her she explained, "It gets in the way when I give head."

Years ago when the first commercially successful homosexual novel was published I remember my mother asking me what it was about. I told her it was about "blow-jobs in movie balconies," a literary evaluation which did that book a great disservice when I later got around to reading it.

" 'Blow-jobs'?" my mother asked. "What is that?"

"Fellatio?" I said, searching for the word that would make the meaning clear.

My mother looked blank.

I tried again. "Oral intercourse . . . ?"

"Oh-h-h!" she exclaimed. "You mean cock-sucking."

I had been in Leadville about a month when I got a telephone call from Alice saying Burp, our Newfoundland, had run away.

"How long has he been gone?" I asked.

"Two days," she said, then added, "This isn't the first time either. He's been crazy ever since you left. He keeps waiting for you to come back. He's been spending all day by the gate whining. Then sometimes he manages to get out. Joan leaves the gate open or Peter does by mistake and he runs off. But this is the first time he's been gone this long."

"Did you call the dog warden?"

"Of course I did. First thing. Joan's got Peter all upset. Peter left the gate open this time and Joan told him that Burp had taken off for Colorado to find you. She's been reading *Lassie* to him."

"Oh God," I said. "Why do you suppose he's been running off?"

"I told you. He's been crazy since you left."

"Well, he'll probably turn up. Maybe someone took him in. Has he still got his collar and ID?"

"Unless he managed to lose it on this trip."

"Then he'll be back or someone will call to say they have him. . . . How are things otherwise? Did you get the paycheck?"

"It wasn't as much as you said it would be."

"I know. I'm working on that. They deducted more than they were supposed to. The next check will be bigger."

"I hope so. The heating bill was enormous for last month."

"How are the children?"

"They're fine."

"Can I speak to them?"

"Joan is on an overnight and Peter's asleep."

"Well, give them my love," I said.

"I will."

"And you're all right?"

"I'm fine."

"Good," I said. "Well, I'm sorry Burp's run off."

"He wouldn't have if you'd been here."

"But, I couldn't be, Alice. I can't be. You know that."

"All I know is I'm stuck here taking care of everybody and everything while you're out there fucking coeds," she said, and hung up before I could respond.

I had never cared much for dogs before Burp. I had grown up with cats. I had, as I've said, bought Burp for Alice when we were living in Nebraska. He had been but a six-week-old cube of black fur. But even though I gave Burp to Alice, the dog claimed me. Perhaps this was because I took him for walks. Or perhaps it was simply because I was the one who fed him his meals.

Back in Nebraska, as I've mentioned, we owned a Volkswagen bus. Burp loved riding in it more than anything in the world. When I'd go for a drive across those gently rolling hills, Burp would leap into the bus with me and plant himself in the gap between the two front seats. He would stand with his head level with my shoulders, his huge front paws spread and braced, anchored like Ahab's on the *Pequod*'s heaving deck, his drool webbing the gearshift knob. If, as would often happen, I'd think of something while driving I wanted to tell him or I'd point out something in a field as we'd pass, he would roll his great whale eyes back at me and his tail would thrash like a giant fluke until overcome by the attention he'd give me a tremendous lick on my cheek.

Later, when we had moved to New Jersey, he would sit with me all day in my office, or be waiting at the gate for me when I came home from New York. He loved me, I loved him. It was as simple as that.

Alice's phone call had come on a Wednesday. Burp, she'd said, had already been gone two days by then. I did not hear from her again until late Sunday afternoon. I was just getting ready to go over to Nora and her husband's apartment for dinner and TV.

"Burp's dead," Alice cried. "Some sonuvabitch shot him. He was found in the woods about six miles west of here."

"Shot him? Who?"

"Probably some goddam dentist from New York with a high-powered rifle who thought Burp was a bear."

Alice and I spoke for about twenty minutes, she weeping and I trying to reassure her that it had happened very fast, that if the hunter had been a good shot Burp hadn't felt a thing.

"How could he be a good shot if he was so stupid as to think Burp was a bear? How many wild bears do you think are in New Jersey?"

"I don't know," I said.

"And besides Burp was shot in the stomach not the head."

"How do you know that?"

"The warden told me Burp had left a trail of blood through the woods. That's how they found him. He bled to death."

"Have you told the children?"

"I told them Burp was killed by a car. I didn't want—"

"I know. You did the right thing. Jesus, I'm so sorry. Did they—do you know how long he was alive after he was shot?"

"A long time," Alice said. "He walked nearly a mile before he fell. He was coming back here. To us."

I could not speak.

"What gets me," Alice said, "is that Burp died *all alone*."

After the phone call I walked into the bedroom and stayed there for a long time. Despite my sorrow over Burp's death I did not, could not, cry. I just sat there on the bed and took deep breaths and tried to control the hot band of pain in my temples. I was still sitting there when the telephone rang again. It was Nora wondering where I was. They were waiting dinner for me.

"You all right?" she asked.

"Yes, I'm sorry," I said. "I lost track of the time."

"You coming over?"

"Yes," I said. "I'll be there in about fifteen minutes."

"You creative types are pretty flaky," she said.

I broke off with Nora soon after that evening. For the past two weeks she had begun appearing too often, wanting more from me than just sex. "I'm beginning to fall in like with you," she said. It got so I did not feel very good about myself. I began to remind myself of another film-maker I had admired until he made a cruel, unspeakably patronizing comment concerning a woman he'd been involved with, a remark that made me lose all my admiration for him on the spot. "She was having an affair with me," he had said, "but I was just fucking her."

I knew the woman he was referring to, had been friends with her for years, and liked her. And since I liked Nora, too, but no more, probably, than that film-maker had liked my friend, I was quickly losing what little respect I had for myself. It wasn't only that I felt guilty, I just didn't feel very *nice*. Not nice at all. And being nice, in those days, meant keeping out of trouble; being nice meant not creating any additional strain.

I left a couple of lights on in my apartment so it wouldn't seem so desolate when I returned, and walked to Nora's.

On several successive Sundays I had had dinner at Nora's house to watch a televised series on PBS. I did not have a television set and Nora's father-in-law had given them a giant Zenith color TV. Nora would sit between her husband and me on their rock-hard tufted Victorian sofa surrounded by heavy stripped oak tables and chairs. There were fake antique brass student lamps with green glass shades and Kulich framed posters from the Supremes and Rolling Stones concerts. There was also a large rectangular college banner on one wall and above it, suspended from the ceiling, hung Nora's highly polished and quite beautiful varsity crew oar.

We would sip Gallo Hearty Burgundy and watch TV. I had no difficulty dealing with the husband; he was a nice, simple guy. I was even able to convince myself that going to bed with his wife had nothing to do with him. I don't deny that such a rationalization is utterly ridiculous. It does, however, accurately reflect how I felt then. As for Nora, she got a kick out of the intrigue.

At one point during that Sunday evening at Nora's following Alice's phone call about Burp, Nora's husband left us to get himself a beer. Nora immediately dropped her hand onto my crotch and gave me a squeeze.

"I just love knowing I'm fucking both men in this room," she said. I didn't like her comment. It was the sort of thing a man would say. That *I* might have said.

It was snowing when Alice telephoned me again the following afternoon. Peter was so upset over Burp's death that she had kept him out of school.

"How's Joanie taking it?" I asked.

"It doesn't seem to bother her at all," Alice said. "But then she never cried over Ma's death either."

"She holds everything in. I wish I were there to talk to her."

"Why? What good would it do?"

"I could maybe help her express her feelings."

"Well, Peter and I had a good cry and we both feel better now. In fact he's gone off to play with a friend."

"Tell him I love him and miss him—and the same goes for Joanie and you."

"We miss you, too," Alice said.

I had barely hung up the telephone when Nora arrived. Instead of feeling happy to see her I felt hassled, crowded. The prospect of having to make love to her did not excite me at all. I did not care if I ever went to bed with her again.

5

NORA SHUCKED OFF HER DOWN jacket and her hiking boots and without saying a word proceeded past me in my living room where I was sitting on the couch with papers scattered across the coffee table and on the floor around my feet. She went into the kitchen, poured herself a glass of red wine, and returned a moment later saying, "I haven't got much time today. I've got a student meeting me in my office at four o'clock."

She put down her wineglass, crossed to the big window looking out on the Texaco station and the now snow-covered Fremont Street and pulled the curtains, plunging the room into darkness. I reached across to the two-tiered table and turned on the light. Nora was already unbuttoning her flannel shirt. Her blue jeans followed and her heavy brass belt buckle fell on the edge of the coffee table with a *clunk*.

"Aren't you going to get undressed?" Nora asked. She stood before me in her white cotton panties, long underwear shirt, bare-legged except for a pair of Ragg wool socks.

"I think we need to talk," I said.

"Can't we talk in bed?"

"It might be more difficult."

"Oh-oh," Nora said. "It's going to be one of those talks, is it? Shall I put my clothes back on?"

I did not answer.

"Then I know what this talk is all about, don't I?" she said. "You want to stop seeing me. Why?" She stepped back into her blue jeans. "Have you found somebody else?"

"Somebody else?" I asked, surprised. "No, of course not. There isn't anyone else I see here."

"Then why do you want to stop?"

"I just haven't felt very good about it lately."

"Because you haven't been coming?" Nora saw the look on my face. "It's nothing to worry about," she said. "I haven't minded—except when you've tried to fake it a couple of times. Is there something you'd like to do in bed that we haven't been doing? Do I bore you?"

"No, no," I said. "It's nothing like that."

"Then what is it?" Nora was buttoning her shirt.

"I just don't think we ought to go to bed with each other. It's more than I can handle."

"*Why?*"

"It just is, Nora. Things get in the way."

"What sort of things?" When I didn't answer she finished dressing and sat down beside me on the couch. "You said things get in the way. Do you mean Carter?"

I nodded. "Among others."

"Because I fucked him, too?" Nora asked. "Does that bother you? You never talked about it. You never asked me what he was like."

I shrugged. "What was there to ask?"

"If someone . . . if I was balling someone who'd made love to my sister, I think I'd want to know what she was like. It's only natural."

"I'm sure Carter was very good. He—"

"He was," Nora said. "Different from you, though."

I did not speak.

"You will notice I did not say better. I said *different*. I know how fragile men's egos are. He was more *care*free. It was always a game with him. And he was more spontaneous, more passionate in a way. But I sometimes got the feeling that it didn't really need to be me. But with you . . . ? It's different. I can't explain it. It's as though you always want it to be something special. Something it cannot always be."

"My wife says I romanticize it."

"She's probably right," Nora said, then added, "But maybe you need that. It's part of your kick. That's what I meant about you and Carter being different. Maybe you have to be in love with the person, or *think* you are for it to be good."

"I just don't want it to be complicated."

"Who makes it that way? Me? You?"

"Not you, Nora," I said. "It's something that's happening to me."

"It's the altitude," Nora said. "Leadville's at seventy-five hundred feet. Everyone feels disoriented, tired at first."

"It's *not* the altitude," I said. "Jesus, if it were just the altitude I could understand it!"

"Understand what?"

"Whatever this is I seem to be going through."

"But what does it have to do with you and me?" Nora asked.

"It doesn't have anything to do with you, Nora."

"So why can't we keep seeing each other like we have been?"

Speak with any man who has passed through what has become popularly known as the "midlife crisis" and he has only a limited capacity to describe the upheaval that occurred. He might say—as I have—that he felt "crazy" or "frightened." Or he might speak of having been in some rudderless limbo; that it was a very difficult period. But beyond this there is not much he can or will say. There are some things men and women can't explain to each other.

During that semester in Leadville and throughout the year that followed, the year during which the most intense feelings of panic took place, I kept believing if only I'd be good enough, strong enough, brave enough, etc., the nightmare would go away. I felt if only I could find the right person, the anxiety would fade. But in Leadville, held as I was by that inner-turmoil's grip, it was difficult for me even to determine where I could go for help.

I tried to keep busy. I worked hard on the film, prepared for and taught my classes. I took yoga three evenings a week. I attended transcendental meditation classes. I wrote letter after letter to Alice and the children, even to friends I hadn't corresponded with in years. ("Hello? Hello? Is anyone there?") I was desperate to maintain some sense of continuity with my former life—the life I'd led before everyone had died.

Initially, I think, my affair with Nora had been based as much upon her association with my brother as it had been based upon sex. She was continuity; seeing her I saw my brother. But as the affair progressed, the association changed. It became increasingly difficult to think of her as the Nora of Carter and Hawaii. She became the Nora of Rocky Mountain State—someone who now wanted more from me than I could give.

Nora could not help me. I knew that. Nor could I think of anyone who could. The week before I had left for Leadville I had bought myself a new address book. I entered into it the addresses and telephone numbers of my mother and brother despite their deaths. I did it for what seemed to be at the time a perfectly good reason: a sentimental denial of their absence. But in Leadville, whenever I saw their listings, I would feel only the most terrible jolt of anguish that I had no way of talking with them anymore. Still, more than once that winter, I thought of dialing my mother's telephone number. I remember thinking it was not yet entirely inconceivable that she wouldn't somehow answer the phone. We have all been taught the inevitability of death, but we do not believe it. Not until someone close to us dies; and, really, maybe not even then. Maybe not even until Death beckons to ourselves.

"If you don't want to go to bed with me now," Nora was saying, "why did you ever begin?"

"I wanted to then," I said.

"Why?"

"I liked being with you—I still do. But it's gotten more complicated now. I thought you could help me—"

"—And I don't help?" she asked.

"You *can't* help, Nora. That's the point."

Nora stood up impatiently. "I wish I knew what the fuck was going on!" she said.

"I wish I did, too," I said miserably. I stood up to go to her and suddenly felt so dizzy I had to sit back down.

After my brother's and stepfather's deaths my mother would fall down. Her way of coping with grief had been to keep busy, too, and she had burned herself out. For the first weeks after my stepfather died she would restlessly pace from room to room, tidying a table that didn't need to be touched, rearranging the silver-framed photographs she loved, moving flower vases about, then suddenly there would be a *thump* and Alice and I would rush in and find her sitting, dazed, on the rug.

"I don't know what happened," she'd say. "I just fell down."

We'd help her to the sofa and make her sit, talk to her, try to make her rest. Instead she'd get up and start wandering around again. There were evenings when we might have a couple of cocktails, a bottle of wine with the meal and she'd be fine. The next evening she might have no cocktails and but one glass of wine and she'd fall down. My mother was not sleeping well and so some nights she and I would sit up and talk. She would tell me about her childhood, about growing up with her brother, my uncle Paul. She would talk about the early years of her marriage to my father, the parties they attended, their friends. She talked about my stepfather, my brother. And I would tell her how Carter and I had talked about her all the time, how we had loved the CALL ME IF YOU DONT RECEIVE THIS telegram she had sent us in Hawaii.

We did not speak about their deaths.

God never entered into these discussions. I knew better than that. After my brother drowned she had told me a story about a friend whose husband and three children had been killed in a terrible automobile accident. In that one instant her entire family had been wiped out. After the funeral service the well-meaning minister had begun speaking to my mother's friend about it being "God's will." The woman had looked at the minister and replied, "Fuck God."

About six weeks after my stepfather's death my mother entered a hospital for a rest and to see if there was any medical reason for her fainting spells. At the Admissions Desk the nurse filling out my mother's form turned to my mother and asked, "Next of kin?"

My mother and I looked at each other somewhat startled. The question was so sudden and awful and brutal we burst out laughing. I was the only one left.

That winter in Leadville I received a letter from a woman I had known for years in New York. She and I had had a brief affair during my marriage to Maggie, but even after it had ended we continued to be friends. I had once taken her to lunch with my mother in New York and afterward, on the way back to her apartment, she said she had been very relieved when the lunch was over. "I felt jealous," she explained.

"Jealous?" I asked. "Why?"

"Because the two of you are the perfect couple. You and your mother even flirt with each other. You really do! Trading stories, bantering back and forth, teasing each other, catching nuances I never could. No matter how much you included me, pushed me into the conversation, cued me with stories you wanted me to tell, I still felt out of place, unsophisticated by comparison, unclean—"

"Unclean?"

"As if bits of the children's spilled orange juice still clung to my dress."

I hugged her and dismissed it from my mind. My friend, however, did not. Ten years later when she wrote me in Leadville to say she had heard about my mother's death, she referred back to that lunch with my mother and her feelings of jealousy and then went on to say:

"The only reason I was able to give you up was by convincing myself it was your mother's heart you were chasing, that you were looking for someone the equal of your mother to whom you could give your love. There was always a vast loneliness in you, a great empty space waiting to be filled. Sometimes I'd get impatient because I'd see your body, your face, your hands in bed next to me but *you* weren't really there. I hated those moments after we had made love when I could feel you pull away. I always felt a chill. That's why I'd quickly dress and leave. I wanted warmth, love, affection. I couldn't stand the cold.

"Maybe that is what makes you irresistible to women. Each one of us believes she will be the only one finally to touch your heart. It's the challenge, isn't it? It's also why I've never felt jealous of either of your wives. They have never had your heart and they must know that. It's terrible to know. Perhaps, too, that's why you pursue woman after woman searching for the one to take the chill away. But of course no one can— certainly no one has, yet.

"I'm sorry, truly sorry about your mother's death," her letter concluded, "I know how much you meant to each other."

Frankly my friend's letter pissed me off. I sat there alone in Leadville, her letter in my hand. I was thinking what a stupid thing it had been for her to write that I had been always chasing my mother's heart. What my friend had witnessed had been nothing more than the classic interplay between a mother and her grown-up son. Why did she have to make it any more complicated than that? Why does a woman feel threatened by a man's love for his mother. Isn't that what each of them wants from her own sons?

How much of my love for my mother was Oedipal I neither know nor care. During the first five years of my life my mother either had or was recovering from tuberculosis. She was isolated at one of the TB sanitoriums in the Adirondacks for at least two years, then confined to bed when she returned home. One afternoon in Hawaii Carter and I discussed our inability to remember ever being held by her as children; I'm not sure she was allowed to. Tuberculosis was very scary then. She had been out of bed for less than a year when Pearl Harbor was attacked; six months later my father left for the war.

I was sent away to boarding schools when I was nine. Three years later, my father was dead. I was away from home at summer jobs from the time I was fourteen on. I did not see my mother except for school holidays at Christmas, Easter, and Thanksgiving and for a couple weeks at either end of the summer. I did not feel deprived nor a "banished child." I had a secure base.

Watch any young child's behavior with his mother: he will crawl away from her, halt, turn back to reestablish contact with his mother's eyes, then, after a reassuring word or glance, the infant will crawl farther away—perhaps even far enough to leave the room. The infant might explore on his own for a moment, but soon he will crawl back to where his mother is in view. Eventually the infant becomes the child, the child the young boy, the young boy a young man who no longer needs to *see* his mother to know she is there.

When I needed my mother she was there. And later, when she needed me, I was there, too. She was my mother, I was her son; it was no more complicated than that. My aunt Bea, on the other hand . . .

Aunt Bea, my uncle Paul's wife, had occupied such a rich space in my youthful fantasy life—Carter's, too, I discovered—that I'm surprised she didn't break out in a nervous rash whenever her two nephews were about.

No older woman ever seduced me—though a *seduction* would hardly have been necessary had one happened by. No boarding school corridor master's wife ever for me unbuttoned her blouse. No red-lipped friend of my mother's ever asked me to rub sköl suntan lotion on the backs of her thighs. No classmate's mother rustled her silken legs together and gave me meaningful looks when I spent a weekend at his house. "When you talk about this, and you will, be kind . . ."

Be *kind?* Jesus, I would have been munificent, lavish in my praise! I would have babbled my gratitude for so long that, like some stultifyingly unfunny baggy-pants comedian, they would have had to come after me with the hook.

I'm getting away from the point: I missed my mother very much. She had been my secure base, a base that meant as much to me at eight as it did at thirty-eight. As I have said, her death, more than any other single incident, triggered the anxiety attacks in Leadville, the terrible sense I was coming "unglued."

"No one ever told me that grief is so like fear . . ." C. S. Lewis wrote in his diary in 1961, "the same fluttering in the stomach, the same restlessness, the yawning. I keep on swallowing." Lewis wrote this shortly after the death of his wife, but the loss of any person one cares about deeply can cause a grief more akin to terror than to woe.

Death confronts us with the uncertainty of all relationships. (No one will stay with me forever. No one can help keep me safe.) If my mother's death had not come after all the others, it might have affected me differently, I don't know. But coming as it had on top of all the other griefs and losses I had suffered through that year, I found myself desperately searching for continuity, some meaningful, comforting attachment that had survived.

Except for Alice and the children, there was none; and, as had been made clear, they all got along much better when I wasn't around. So I created an attachment with Nora. I constructed an impossible role for Nora to play, and when she was not up to the part, when instead of providing comfort she reminded me of what I least liked in myself and what I had lost, I told her I did not want to see her anymore.

"You don't think you're overreacting?" Nora asked.

"I probably am," I said.

"So what are we going to do?"

"We're going to be friends who don't happen to go to bed with each other."

"Jesus," Nora said.

I stood up carefully, then walked to the window overlooking Fremont Street and pulled open the curtains. It was snowing harder now and as I stood there looking out at the street Nora came up behind me and touched my neck. I turned slightly and put my arm around her waist and Nora laid her head against my shoulder. We were standing there in front of the window when Fred Noonan walked by, looked up at us, and waved. Without thinking, Nora and I both waved back. "Oh, shit," Nora said. "Now he'll come in."

Noonan was a shaggy-haired, thin-faced, untenured assistant professor of English about my age. Like myself he had been divorced once and married again. His second wife was a potter and taught at the college, too. The Noonans lived in an apartment a block further up Fremont Street, so he and I often found ourselves walking to and from the campus together.

I heard him scraping his boots outside and I opened the door for him. He was shaking the snow off his duffle coat. He nodded at me, peeked in at Nora, then looked back over his shoulder as a pair of coeds cross-country skied up the deserted street. "Winter sports," he said.

It wasn't clear whether he was referring to the skiers or Nora and me. "Am I interrupting something?" Noonan asked as he entered the room. When neither Nora nor I answered he said, "Ever since prostitution was declared illegal humans have been left with no recourse but affairs or one's fevered imagination. I think the two of you are very healthy. You're externalizing. The rest of us are left simply with the internalization of our fantasies. We're being driven to private booths in porno halls . . . May I use your phone?"

I pointed to the telephone next to the coffee table. "Would you like some coffee? A glass of wine?" I said.

"Coffee, if you've got some." He was dialing as I left for the kitchen and then I could hear him saying, "Hello, my little dove, my sweet-lips, my—yes, well, I've stopped off at our distinguished film-maker neighbor's for a cup of coffee and some mind-bending hallucinogenic drugs—I'm kidding, oh, light of my life . . ."

Nora joined me in the kitchen. "I'm going to ask a favor of you," she said.

"Sure. What is it?"

"I want one last time with you," she said.

"But . . . ?" I gestured with my head toward Noonan's voice.

"Not today. I've got that student coming in a little while anyway. Can we make it tomorrow?"

I looked at her and nodded. "Of course we can. There's no need for it to end ugly."

"Ugly? It won't end ugly," Nora said. "I don't mean to be patronizing, but I don't think you could handle that."

I looked at her for a moment. In the silence between us we could hear Noonan still on the phone: "Yes, my sweet," he was saying. "I won't forget. I know I forgot yesterday, but—yes, and the day before, but I won't forget today . . . No, I don't actually have it with me at the moment, but I will be sure to stop and pick one up . . ."

Nora stood on tiptoes and kissed me on the lips.

"I'm sorry, Nora."

"Don't be. I'm leaving. I'll see you tomorrow. Two-thirty, okay?"

"Okay," I said. I poured Noonan's coffee and Nora and I walked back into the living room together. Noonan was still on the phone, an expression of anguish on his face. I helped Nora into her coat and she blew Noonan a kiss as she went out the door. "Tomorrow," she whispered.

I nodded, yes.

I watched her walk up the street, then went back inside my apartment and closed the door. Noonan was slumped dejectedly on the couch. He did not look up until I sat down opposite him, then he asked, "Have I ever discussed with you my 'Dagwood Theory'?"

"I don't think so."

"Its basic premise is that all women consider men nincompoops," he said. "My wife Gloria, for example—that was Gloria, obviously, on the phone—Gloria considers me an incompetent because for the past two nights I have forgotten to pick up a *TV Guide*. She needs it so she can plan in advance what dreadful TV movie she will sit slack-jawed and insensate in front of. And so my sweet-lips, my little turtle dove—I call her such endearments in an attempt to disarm her, to blunt her attacks— my little flower thinks me a ninny because I have failed to bring home a *TV Guide*. Women tend to link everything together," Noonan continued. "If you break a dish, you're inept in bed. If *A*, then *B*. *Quod erat demonstrandum*. And then, and then! When women beat on men, call us nincompoops or what have you, we men 'assume the position.' Bend forward and grab our ankles because consciously or not we believe the beating, the abuse, is deserved."

"We do? Why?" I asked.

"Because we know we're wrong. It's not just that any man with even the minimum degree of sensitivity realizes the essential validity of women's rights, but he realizes, too, the essential wrongness of man's domination over women in all areas: the economic, the political, the home. For years women have been denigrating themselves, feeling inferior as women, and miserable as a result—"

"They've been helped along in those feelings by men."

"Of course they have! Of course they have. We've been doing it to them for generations."

"But it was the way we were brought up," I said. "We were taught that women were different from men—and not only did we men think that, but so did the women. And by 'different' there was also the suggested meaning 'not as good.' This couldn't all have been an illusion. Men were expected to take care of women, not simply because the women wanted to be taken care of, but because they *needed* to be taken care of. They were fragile. Men were supposed to protect their women—"

"Now the women get angry if you offer to help. Women are asserting their independence and it's very threatening because we men no longer feel necessary and so now, *now* we've begun putting ourselves down as men. They don't even want us for sex, they can do it better themselves. Jesus, did you, speaking of which, read the lesbian manifesto that the undergraduate gay rights group published in the campus newspaper? Men were referred to as 'potential donors' throughout."

"Donors?"

"Seed donors—as in, 'This is my mother and donor'—it's a lovely extra-galactic matriarchal phrase, no? It even has a hint of breeding farms. And so no wonder we men, we husbands, are suffering from terrible self-doubts," Noonan said. "We question our worthiness, whether or not we are essential, needed, or even wanted. So we seek our wives' approval, and when we don't get it—which is constant—"

"What is constant?"

"Our wives' disapproval," he said. "When all we get from them is their beating on us, we fight back. But what is curious about these terrible fights that ensue is that someone, someone is receiving a very strange form of gratification. The role of 'mother' is in there somewhere." Noonan was silent for a moment, then he said, "Why do we manipulate our wives into mothers?"

Noonan's question startled me. I told him that that was the sort of thing I had always thought my wives had tried to do with me, to manipulate me into the role of father. "I would be the person who would tell them what to do, who would take responsibility for the decisions that needed to be made, who would give or withhold permission—"

"Permission?" he asked.

"When they would ask for something they knew we could not afford, but they wanted me to be the one to deny them the pleasure of having it so they would have an excuse to be angry, so I would be the 'heavy.' "

"Ah, yes," Noonan said. "That's the 'You never let me have any fun' variation. I know it well."

"Maggie, my first wife, so totally relied on me that she drove me to despair. She was afraid to make a phone call, an appointment, to make a choice . . . If we went out to dinner she'd ask me what she should eat. I've been wondering lately whether I had done that to her, had I somehow cowed her, rendered her so insecure she was incapable of expressing opinions on her own."

"Ah!" Noonan said, wagging his finger at me, "See how swiftly we accept the blame? Why do you think it was your fault? Isn't it more likely that that had been her pattern all her life?"

"I don't think so," I said. "I don't know. I was such a novice husband. . . . I didn't know what being a 'husband' meant. I believed that all I had to do was work hard, be a responsible husband and father, and I would have the love and respect of my family. At issue here is the assumption of predictability, the reliability of—to use your word—the pattern: if A, then B. If A and B, then C, and so on. I had expected life to follow a mathematical formula. And the funny thing is that for a while the formula even proved true. I worked hard, I married a beautiful woman with whom I had a beautiful—well, I think she will be beautiful— daughter. My first film brought me a certain amount of recognition, if not fame, and some money. We traveled, lived abroad, found a lovely old house in a lovely old community when we returned. . . . And I kept asking myself why was Maggie always in tears?"

"Maybe she was a manic depressive like Gloria," Noonan said, and shrugged. "Except I can't remember when was the last time my little turtle dove was on a high."

"No, I don't think so, that's too easy," I said. "It had to do with what I've already said. I didn't know what being a husband meant. I had no role-model, no example to follow, I never had a father around."

I was six when my father went to war, nine when he returned. He died when I was twelve. I told Noonan one of the strongest memories I had of him was the day he came home from the war. We were living on the farm and the ancient hot water heater had sprung a leak the night before, flooding the basement. My brother and I had painted a "WEL-COME HOME DAD" sign, which we'd hung on the door. We were disappointed that he had not worn his uniform home. He had to step over my bicycle to reach the front door. Once he was inside the house he said to my mother, "Jesus Christ, how could you let this place get so run down?" To my brother and me he said: "Don't come back inside until all your junk and the dog bones are picked up off the yard." My brother and I started cleaning up, and my mother, instead of calling the plumber, disappeared into the basement and fixed the leak herself. "A point I'm trying to make here," I told Noonan, "is that the Second World War had as liberating an effect on our mothers' generation as the women's movement has had on their daughters'. My mother, during the war, had become a more than adequate electrician, plumber, mechanic. . . . My father had become an accomplished planner of amphibious invasions. . . . As my wife said to me the other day, 'We all get along much better when you're not around.' "

"And you questioned your worthiness, right?" he asked. "You were probably even a little hurt. But what you should have felt instead was happy at how independent you've made your family."

"If they were any more independent, they'd be collecting my life insurance."

Noonan and I talked and talked, about our wives, the war between the sexes, affairs, passive dependency, guilt.

"Nora doesn't seem to feel any guilt at all," I said.

"I know. That's one of the more interesting aspects of the changes that have been taking place in women," Noonan said. "Women are far more capable of having sex without guilt now than men are—and, worse, they want it *all* the time!"

There was a sudden banging at my front door. "*Noonan?*" a woman shouted. "I know you're in there!"

"Ah, busted," Noonan said, rising majestically to his feet. "That must be my little turtle dove. I'll let her in."

Noonan opened the door and a woman bundled up in layers of scarves pushed past him and into the room, then spun about to face him. "Goddam you, Noonan!" she said. "Do you have any idea what time it is?"

Noonan pushed back his sweater sleeve; his wrist was bare. "I'm sorry, my pet, but I seem not to be wearing my watch."

"It's six-thirty!" she said. "I've been waiting dinner for you the past half-hour!" She turned to me. "Hello, how are you? I'm Gloria Noonan. We've never met," she said, and stuck out a sandpapery hand.

"Would you like a drink? Some wine? Coffee? Whiskey?" I asked.

"I've come to take this worthless man I'm married to home," she said.

"She talks like that," Noonan said, "to mask her deep love for me."

Gloria Noonan paused for a moment and looked at her husband, then turned back to me. "Maybe I will have a drink. Do you have any Bourbon?"

"I'm relieved that our dinner can wait a bit more," Noonan said.

Gloria paused midway through unwrapping one of her scarves. "Noonan . . . ?" she said warningly.

He raised his hands as if to ward off a blow.

"On the rocks?" I asked.

"The drinks or our marriage?" Gloria said. "I'll take a little water."

The Noonans invited me back to their place for a chili dinner that night. Their bickering was nonstop. The most innocent or seemingly innocent comment from one would lead to an uproar in the other.

"Your chili was very good tonight, my sweet," Noonan said.

"It wasn't too spicy?" Gloria asked.

"I thought it was delicious," I said.

"Not as good as Wendy's though," Gloria said. "Noonan's first wife."

"Wendy did make good chili," Noonan agreed.

"Then why did you divorce her?" Gloria flared.

"Because she also made one of my graduate teaching assistants."

"I wonder why," Gloria said.

I left them that evening feeling even more lonely than I had before. They reminded me of Alice and myself.

Alice and I couldn't talk either. Usually I didn't want to talk.

Other men with whom I have discussed marriage have told me they had much the same feelings. And it is here that we get into why our wives are so angry with us so much of the time.

One of Alice's major complaints was that after dinner all I wanted to do was sit down with the afternoon newspaper or a book or watch TV, that I didn't want to talk to her about her problems, *our* problems.

She was right.

I would have spent all day working on a film, trying to get the correct pacing, coordinate the movement, the images, to make the words exactly right. It was difficult for Alice to understand the intensity of the concentration, the pressure that was involved. It is difficult for anybody

to comprehend the efforts of another, especially if one is not in the same
field oneself. I would return from the office with a headache, a belly full
of frustration if the work had not gone well. I would want only to unwind,
hide. . . . Alice would want to talk.

"Not now," I'd say.

"When then?"

"Some other time."

"*When?*" Alice would ask.

"Tomorrow?"

And the battle would begin.

I would not have given Alice what she needed: appreciation, companionship, a sympathetic ear, my *attention*. It didn't really matter what her
complaint might have been. (I had not, as I had promised, made Joan's
dentist appointment, fixed the garage door, the screen in the bathroom,
helped enough with the household chores . . .) Her complaint only
seemed one more problem, more pressure. And so I would retreat, grow
silent, distant, focused even more on things external to her, on the TV.

Alice would become furious, more demanding that we talk. I would
withdraw even more. Alice would become strident, abusive, venomous
with rage. I would be angry, too, but careful not to let it show; I would
not give her the satisfaction of knowing she had gotten to me.

We were like children: if you're not nice to me, I'll bug you until you
are.

Alice and I could have avoided many of these fights had I been more
conscious and considerate of her needs—needs which though directly
opposed to mine could have been resolved through compromise. And
these needs, as I have discovered again through conversation with
married friends, constitute one of those basic differences between
housewives and husbands.

When a husband comes home from work he wants to *relax*.

When a woman in the home finishes her day, she wants to *relate*.

From the moment Alice arose she would be busy with household tasks,
running to the market, taking children to meetings, doing the hundred
big and little things that keep a house and family afloat. There was no
progress, only repetition. The beds would have to be made again, the
laundry run through the next day once more. More meals would have
to be cooked. The endless repetition of these tasks made her feel a
servant in her own house, trapped and abused. She needed a sympathetic
ear. And since she could not talk to me, she would telephone someone
like Barbara T.

They would talk long distance for over an hour and I would get crazy about the size of the bill. But I knew how important these phone calls were to Alice, how her cousin, Barbara T., and her other women friends provided her with the companionship, the support, the sympathy, and approval she was not but should have been getting from me.

Alice needed to feel good about herself. I needed that, too, but whereas I could achieve some measure of self-respect from my work, Alice could get it only from others, her friends, the majority of whom felt just as trapped and isolated and resentful as Alice did. Why was this so? Their marriages were just as barren as ours, their husbands as unsympathetic as I.

If, like Prufrock, we were measuring out our lives with coffee spoons, our wives were measuring theirs buying wicker and stripping and refinishing chairs. The irony is that when we husbands were together our complaints were virtually indistinguishable from those of our wives. We all felt unloved and unrespected, misunderstood, and resented by our selfish and uncaring mates.

Each of us had wanted to get married; none of us wanted to be a husband or wife. A good marriage demands that one's first priority be one's partner; it cannot exist for us whose first priority was ourselves.

"I've tried to be a good husband," I told Alice. "Why won't you try to be a good wife?"

And just what did I mean by "a good wife"?

Someone who appreciated and loved me, who alleviated the loneliness I felt. Someone who wasn't always angry and resentful, who didn't always create pressure, make demands, who wasn't always wanting *something more.* Someone selfless and comforting, who didn't keep score.

I can just hear Alice: "Someone like *Mom?*"

Yes, goddam it! Why not?

Isn't that what we all want? To be joined with another, to recapture that childhood intimacy and familiarity one had with one's mother? There one's life had that perfect symmetry of absolute peace and harmony and safety and limitless time.

"Why do we manipulate our wives into mothers?" Noonan had asked. I think the answer lies less in our wanting to "assume the position" than in our longing to be safe.

This is all much more difficult than I thought. You cannot expect someone who suffers from vertigo to lean over a very high cliff and describe with any objectivity what he sees. It is the same with trying to articulate my confusion and panic over what was happening to me that

winter after my mother's death. I am still not so distant from the emotional
chaos of that semester in Leadville that I do not feel the pull of the pit
from which I've emerged. I do not yet feel entirely safe.

I did not have a class the day after I had had dinner with the Noonans
and was able to work in the film editing room in the basement of the
Communications Department until I finally got the scene right; I'd been
working on it for the past several days:

A middle-aged man had developed a cough and, unable to shake it,
finally went to his doctor, who took a chest x-ray. The x-ray revealed a
mass in his lung and he was admitted to the hospital for an evaluation.

A pulmonary physician and an oncologist were brought in to see him.
The pulmonary physician performed a bronchoscopy, inserting a fiber-
optical tube down the patient's trachea and taking a biopsy, which
revealed the man had a form of lung cancer called small cell, or oat cell
cancer.

The oncologist did a bone marrow biopsy, which indicated that the
patient's cancer had already metastacized, disseminated into the bones.
This meant that there was no way to cut the tumor out; it was inoperable.
The only hope was chemotherapy and radiation.

The particular scene I had been trying to edit had been filmed with
two cameras in the oncologist's office the morning he had brought the
patient and his wife in to discuss the results of the laboratory tests and
their findings. The narration leading up to this scene has made it clear
that once small cell carcinoma enters the bone it is deadly and that when
a patient's disease is this serious, an oncologist brings in both the patient
and the spouse because the doctor does not want one spouse trying to
hide it from the other. One camera was on the patient and his wife, the
other on the doctor. Both cameras were hidden behind one-way glass.
We see the patient and his wife come into the doctor's office and sit.
The oncologist greets them and the husband begins telling about the
difficulty they had finding a parking space. The doctor listens patiently.
The wife places her hand on top of her husband's and the man's voice
falters, then stops. The doctor immediately begins explaining the results
of the tests. The wife's hand tightens and the husband covers her hand
with his so that her hand is now sandwiched between both of his.

"We will not be operating," the oncologist tells the husband.

The man pats his wife's hand saying, "That's a relief."

"Instead you will be given chemotherapy and radiation."

"I see," the man says. The camera holds on his face for a moment and then he asks, "Does this mean I have to give up smoking?"

There is a series of lightning-quick cuts between the faces of the man, his wife, the oncologist. The doctor, who had pretty much seen and heard everything by then, showed no expression, but the patient's wife looked surprised. The husband awaits the doctor's answer.

"Quitting smoking would be helpful," the doctor says, "but it won't make much difference."

"Oh, that's *very* good news!" the man says; he wipes his palms.

The doctor turns to the patient's wife and meets her look. Her hand flutters to her mouth, then immediately drops back to her lap. She looks down and then back up at the doctor. He continues to look directly at her until she turns away from him and stares out the window. We see she is biting her lip. She has understood immediately that her husband's not having to give up smoking is the worst possible news. We know that, too. We know that even if he responds to radiation and chemotherapy he has less than twenty-four months to live. The patient's wife turns back from the window and again takes her husband's hand.

The whole scene takes less than one minute on the screen but there were over twenty cuts. The wife's pain and courage suffused the scene; I felt the editing had turned out well.

I walked from the Communications Department building across the campus to my apartment, let myself in, took two Bufferin, and sat down on the couch. I was thinking how compared to that poor man with the inoperable cancer my troubles were peanuts. I had but to finish the film. *Finish the film . . . ?* I could feel the panic begin. There was a slight prickle, a warmth in my temples that spread gradually until it met in a knot across my brows. "Not now!" I said aloud. "Not now!"

It infuriated me how these attacks would hit without warning, how I could be joyous one moment, in despair the next. I tried to concentrate on a memory that made me happy. It was the only way I could block out those other images—images that burned into my head like meteorites too fast to identify but for their heat. I tried to think about my childhood on the farm surrounded by woods. It was idyllic. I was happy then.

It is hot and dry beneath the trees. I remember exactly the feel of the moss and fallen leaves so spongy underfoot, and the fierce sexual energy and excitement with which I remove my clothes: a striped T-shirt, tan hand-me-down corduroys, sneakers, socks that forever disappeared beneath my heels. I am eight years old and amazed by my body. The air is warm and soft upon my skin. I remove my underpants and drop them on my pile of clothes. Naked now I stand perfectly still. The trees are tall and unthreatening, light and shadow dapple the ground. A crow calls. I hear the jays respond, the deep *thrum-thrum-thrum* of a tractor far away. I stand in a patch of sunlight, dust motes drift about. I look at the fine silver blond hairs on my arms, my thighs. A tingle begins in my groin. My testicles tighten. A light surge of blood enters my cock. It begins to throb, blush red. It's such an amazing sight! Mesmerized, I watch but dare not move. I have not yet made the connection between touching my penis and it feeling good. I am aroused, but do not know it as such. I will not have a label for this strange mood I am in for several more years. It is only a curious red excitement still, recognizably different from the blues and yellows and greens of my other summer moods. The agitation grows within me as my penis expands. I begin to run.

I race naked along deer paths from sunbeam to sunbeam, until panting and exhausted I collapse onto the soft ground and, with a mixture of awe and intoxication, look down at my jutting, boyish erection as if it could, itself, reveal the mystery from which it has sprung.

There is no sense of time. Not until the dinner bell rings will I be expected to turn back, to come home to my mother—

[Your mother is dead.]

—to my brother—

[Your brother is dead.]

—To my family with whom I feel safe, where tomorrows stretch for as far as I can see in perfect harmony.

[Concentrate upon the woods!]

The woods. I was always careful to remember where I had left my clothing in the woods. By the time the dinner bell rings I am dressed and on the dirt road back to the house. After dinner my brother and I do the dishes. He washes, I dry and put away. Usually we listen to a radio show. It is Sunday and one of my favorites: Edgar Bergen and Charlie McCarthy.

"Where were you all day?" my mother asks me.

My brother says, "If it's still light enough outside when we finish, let's play some catch."

We are outside. Fingers raw from gripping the baseball's stitching. He is trying to throw a decent breaking curve. I have bone bruises in my palm from the thin catcher's mitt. "Chuck to me, babe!" I call. "Chuck to me!" I throw back grounders, fly balls that arch upward into the darkening summer sky. Inside the house I can hear the telephone ring.

[The connection is surprisingly clear. "I think you ought to know your brother and his friend went out yesterday morning in a Hobie Cat and they aren't back yet."]

"C'mon, babe, chuck to me!"

The telephone is ringing.

We were supposed to grow old together! Goddam you, why did you die? Why did you leave me alone, too!

The telephone continues to ring. It is Nora. "I'll be there in about ten minutes," she says.

I think about the small boy in the woods with his erection. I was free then, not bound up by the sexual guilts and insecurities and expectations I felt now. I thought about Maggie and Alice and all the women in between whom I had loved and hated, threatened and felt threatened by, whom I had hurt and who struck back at me.

"I'll be here, Nora," I say.

Nora arrived with a bottle of champagne in one hand and a small paper bag in the other. She put the champagne down on the coffee table. "If I'm going to have my swan song," she said, reaching into the paper bag, "I want to go out in style." She pulled out a small package of frozen strawberries. "It's the best I could do," she explained. "There aren't any fresh strawberries around here this time of year."

"It's a lovely idea," I said.

"Do you have something I can put them in?"

"In the kitchen. I'll get some bowls," I said.

"No, I'll get them. You open the champagne."

I picked up the champagne bottle and tore off the foil. "I should have brought you some flowers."

"That would have been nice," Nora said.

Was there a slight edge to her voice?

A moment later Nora returned from the kitchen with two cereal bowls filled with strawberries. "Shall we have our picnic here, or shall we have it in the bedroom?"

"Whichever you'd prefer," I said.

"Which would *you* prefer?" she asked.

I hesitated. "Why don't we start here," I said, "and work our way into the bedroom when we're ready."

"In other words you're not ready now," Nora said. She put the strawberries down on the coffee table. When she straightened up I hugged her saying, "You know that isn't what I meant. You've just arrived. We aren't in any hurry, are we?"

"I'm not."

"Then why don't we sit down and relax with our champagne and strawberries. It's nice to see you again."

Nora pulled away from me. "Yesterday you told me you didn't want to see me any more."

"I know," I said.

"Do you?" She looked at me, then reluctantly came back into my arms. "I'm sorry," she said. "I promised myself I wouldn't turn bitchy."

"You haven't."

Nora lifted her champagne glass and toasted me. "Here's to you," she said. "I hope all your dreams come true."

We touched glasses and I thanked her. I was thinking that I didn't have any dreams, I wasn't able to see that far ahead yet. We sat down on the couch together and ate our strawberries.

"I care a lot for you," Nora said, "I really do. And I have no doubt your life will straighten out. I know your film will be marvelous and you will make another and another marvelous film . . ."

"I'd settle at the moment for just finishing this one."

"How's it coming?"

"I think I'll have the rough cut done in time for the spring break next week."

"Will you take it to New York?"

I took a sip of my champagne and nodded yes.

"Then we should toast your film, too," Nora said, and she again touched the rim of my glass with hers. "Good luck."

"Thanks," I said. I could feel the distance growing between us, but I couldn't help it.

"Shall we take our champagne into the bedroom?" Nora asked.

"I've rolled us a little something, too," I said.

"Well," Nora said, "if we're going to do it for the last time, we might as well do it well."

"Might as well," I said, and smiled, but the smile did not hold. I just wanted to get it over with.

The next afternoon when I returned to my apartment after classes I found a note Nora had slipped under my door:

Dear Man, there is everything to say but nothing that would make any difference. As I told you yesterday afternoon before we went to bed, I truly care for you and will do everything I can to help. If that means staying away from you, then that is what I will do. I am therefore setting you free.

Don't feel badly—if, in fact, you do at all. It's very simple: I chose you and you chose to be free. There is nothing I can do about that. It's a no-win situation for me. And, frankly, I'm having some difficulty dealing with your rejection—the brutality of which I think you have little sense of. I want you to know I come away from this experience with a part of me gone. But I will not backslide. I will not attempt to call you or see you alone.

I think I handled my closing scene quite well. I exited with my head high, without recriminations or angry words, all the while sensing your mounting relief that it was ending, watching you get farther and farther away, withdrawing into yourself more and more—and saddest of all, after having had sex, not making love.

And so *aloha, bruddah*. I wish you all the luck in the world and the same goes for whomever you choose next.

Nora signed her note with her initial "N" and just beneath her initial she had drawn a little angel. It was supposed to represent the archangel Michael, the role I had performed several weeks earlier in a passion play staged as part of the English Department's Elizabethan Pageant.

What Nora and the other members of the English Department had not known was that my interest in Michael arose because he is represented among Christians as St. Michael, the benevolent Angel of Death who led the souls of the faithful into the eternal light. It had required a certain amount of bravado on my part to accept a role like that. I wasn't sure I might not be tempting fate. I could not escape my lingering sense of foreboding, my anxiety over what disaster might occur within my family next. I still did not have any feeling of control over my life. The orderly progression of "if A, then B" had given way to if A, then why not X or a squiggle, a nonsense series of numbers and symbols, the drowning of a brother, the death of my mother, an uncle, the shooting of a beloved pet. If there was a pattern, I could not discern it.

Unless I was an Angel of Death.

Still, when the English Department asked me to play Michael I had agreed. Someone constructed a huge set of cardboard angel wings and covered them with gold glitter. Someone else made me a long white robe to wear.

I wanted to stand in costume on the lip of one of those granite cliffs overlooking the interstate brandishing my sword at truckers and tourists as they wheeled on by. But the winds were so strong along that slope of the Rockies and my glitter-wings so large, I feared I would be lofted skyward like a kite. I settled for the cast photograph instead.

I sat posed in costume before a film-editing machine surrounded by satin-clothed coed "Devilettes" and the top-hatted and white-tied professor of medieval history, who stood behind my right wing, his red trident-forked tail satanically draped across my shoulder. I sent a copy to my soundman friend Harry Abbott in New York with the caption "Am concentrating hard on finishing the film despite, as you can see, strong temptations and near impossible odds."

The prettiest coed in the photograph was a "Born Again" nineteen-year-old with a young, hard, swimmer's body. She took my class. "When you talk to us about film-making," she told me early in the semester, "I get dry-mouthed."

A week later she came up to my desk after class with a loaf of bread. "When I bake," she said, "I feel like Mary Magdalene." Her loaf was heavy enough to have sealed Christ's tomb.

I was sitting on my couch with Nora's note and drawing of an angel when the coed showed up at my apartment door. I let her in and she said, "God told me I shouldn't come to your place today." She strode about my small living room, picking up books and photographs as she spoke. "I said, 'God,' " she continued, " 'God, if you don't want me to go to his apartment just make sure I get lost.' And the next thing I knew I was on a street I'd never seen before." There was about a two-beat pause and then she brushed her hair back from her brow and smiled brightly and said, "But, I found you anyway!" She turned the photograph she was holding toward me. "Who's this?" she asked.

"My brother," I said.

"He's fantastic-looking! Where does he live?"

"That was taken in Hawaii. He died there about nine months ago."

"Unkk!" she said, making a funny little half-embarrassed sound in the back of her throat. She held up a second photograph.

"That's my mother," I said.

"Don't you have any pictures of your wife?"

"They're in the bedroom."

"May I see them?" she asked, heading for the bedroom door.

"I'll get them," I said.

Both photographs were over a year old. The first, taken at a party at a friend's house, was of Alice gesturing animatedly, her head turned to show her left profile, which she considered her most attractive side. The other photograph was of Alice holding Peter. Her head was turned to her right in that photograph, too.

"Your wife is very pretty," my student said. She stood before the couch holding the two Lucite-framed photographs in her hands. "I didn't think your wife would look like this. I mean, I imagined her being taller somehow, dark-haired, more refined."

"Refined?" I asked, puzzled. I moved next to her to look at the pictures.

"Ethereal, less of this world. . . . How tall is she?"

"About five feet three."

"It must be neat being married to you," she said. "Your wife must really miss you alot!"

I sat down quickly.

"Are you all right?" she asked me. "Sometimes the altitude—people don't realize—"

"It's not the altitude," I said. A rush had hit without warning again.

"Was it something I said?" She leaned forward, looking at me worriedly. I tried not to peek down her blouse. "Boy," she said. "I just know I shouldn't have bothered you." She straightened up and sat down next to me on the couch.

I told her she wasn't bothering me, that I was glad she had come. I asked her about her Bible-reading group. If I could get her talking I could stall the anxiety attack.

"Are you all right?" she asked me again. "Would you like to pray?"

"*Pray?*"

She began to slide from the sofa to her knees. Her skirt rode midway up her smooth taut thighs. I could not tear my eyes away. The farther down she slid, the higher up her skirt rose until she was kneeling next to the coffee table with the back of her skirt rucked up behind her panties. Her legs were bare all the way up to her ass. I couldn't believe she was unaware of that and yet there she was with her hands clasped together saying the Lord's Prayer.

Our Father who art in Heaven, Harold be thy name, prayed Long Island school kids according to the New York *Herald-Tribune* years ago. *Lead us not into Penn Station,* they prayed. *Give us this day our jelly bread . . .*

The telephone rang, shocking the coed to her feet. It was Alice. She had paid all the bills with the last university check I had sent her and had only two hundred dollars for the rest of the month.

"I'll be paid before I come home next week," I said, "I'll bring that check with me." The coed was moving toward the door and I gestured to her that she didn't have to go.

"Is there someone with you?" Alice asked. "There is, isn't there! You've got some fucking coed in your room!"

The coed opened the door. I cupped my hand over the mouthpiece and told her to stay if she'd like.

"Answer me you sonuvabitch!" Alice was shouting into the phone. "You were fucking some coed when I called!"

"No, I wasn't, Alice. I was just saying good-bye to one of my students," I said.

"God be with you," the student said.

Alice was swearing at me still.

6

THE TWO-WEEK MIDSEMESTER break at Rocky Mountain State began on the twelfth of March and lasted until the twenty-fifth. I stepped off the plane at Newark Airport expecting to be met by Alice and the children and was surprised to find that Alice had sent her cousin Barbara T. to meet me instead. Alone.

I liked Barbara T.—although at this time it still bothered me that I couldn't seem to get to know her very well. I had first met her when she came east to stay with Alice and me about a month after Carter's death. I knew only that she and Alice had grown up next door to each other on the West Side of New York and that they had attended the same schools through junior high until Barbara T.'s mother had divorced her father and left for California. I couldn't get to know Barbara T. because she never said anything personal to me, ever.

Ostensibly Barbara T. had come to spend weekends with us while she looked for a job and an apartment in New York. I say "ostensibly" because I never had the impression she was looking very hard. Had she been serious she could have stayed with her sister in the city, or she could even have stayed with Alice's parents on the West Side. But then, Barbara T. did not *need* to work. Unlike Alice, Barbara T.'s side of the family had money—not millions, certainly, but enough to provide her with a livable income. And besides, Alice and I liked having Barbara T. around. She was easy to be with.

I had been a little apprehensive at first, especially when I realized how many weekends Barbara T. intended to stay. I was worried that she and Alice would form an alliance against me. But, as became evident, Barbara T. did not form alliances. Alliances implied commitment. I don't think Barbara T. was committed to anyone, not even herself. There was something missing in her. What it was, I do not know. I always felt that she was marking time.

Having Barbara T. around was like living with a cloud—not a storm cloud, mind you, nothing that would cause any concern—just a pretty white cloud which moved about depending upon the winds. When Alice blew, Barbara T. moved away from her; when I blew, she moved away from me. The result was rather calming in a way. She was wonderful with the children, had endless patience for their games—ours, too, it came to seem.

While I was waiting for my luggage, I asked Barbara T. how things were at home.

"We'll talk on the way down," she said, then added, "You look awful. Have you been sick?"

So much for the immediate benefits of meditation and yoga.

During the drive, Barbara T. told me that my daughter Joan had been driving Alice crazy, that Joan expected Alice to pick up after her like a maid, Joan never cleaned her room, that her school reports said she "was just putting in her time rather than making any effort," that she was "turning in her homework late, she was daydreaming, her papers marred by careless mistakes."

"Well," I said, "I don't think there's a student in Leadville I couldn't say the same thing about."

"Alice was so angry with Joan the other day that she was going to put her on a plane back to her mother that afternoon. It was Valentine's Day and she'd found Joan a big card saying 'I love you!' Alice gave it to Joan at breakfast. Joan just ripped it open, glanced at it, and said, 'Yeah, thanks.' And that was it. She hadn't even bothered to get Alice a card and never said anything nice about the one Alice had found her. Alice was so hurt and angry she wanted to slap her on an afternoon plane."

"I know," I said. "Alice called me in Leadville."

"Alice was so upset, she was in tears!"

"I spoke to Joan. Chewed her out, but I don't know if it did any good. She's almost thirteen and all teenaged girls are in worlds of their own. I'm not sure she knew how to respond to Alice's card. She's never been good at expressing her feelings. She was probably shy . . . I don't mean to be making excuses for her. Her not helping Alice, her irresponsibility and laziness have to stop. I'll keep a close eye on her while I'm home. . . . How are things otherwise?"

"Fine. Good."

"Is Alice having any fun?"

"Not much."

"Have you been able to get out at all?"

"Do you mean Alice and me?" Barbara T. asked. "We had that weekend in Stowe."

"Stowe? What weekend in Stowe?"

"Didn't Alice tell you?"

"She never mentioned it on the phone."

"The trip was on me," Barbara T. said. "A dividend check came that was a complete surprise so I decided to spend it."

"That was nice, Barbara T."

"Well, you've been very generous about letting me stay with you."

"Alice must have loved getting away. Did the children have a good time?"

"We didn't take the children."

"Ah," I said. "When did you go?"

"Last weekend," she said. "We decided to go after Alice called you in Leadville and you had some girl in your room."

"That was my Born Again coed. Alice, of course, assumed I was balling the girl."

"Look, it doesn't matter to me what you do," she said. "It's between you and Alice."

"Did you have a good time at Stowe?"

"Depends what you mean by 'a good time.' "

"Well, I was talking about the skiing."

"The skiing was fun, too."

It was not an opening I wanted to pursue.

One could argue, I suppose, that if one truly loved another, one would wish for that person whatever brought him or her joy. I remember the obsessive permissiveness of the 1960s, how everyone was supposed to love, love, love everyone else. But I was never able to reach that stage of enlightenment where I could or would want to know my wife had been with another man.

"How's your film coming?" Barbara T. asked.

"Pretty good, I think."

"Is PBS going to take it?"

"I hope so. I should probably hear next week."

"What if they don't take it?" Barbara T. asked. "What will you do?"

"Slit my wrists," I said.

I had mailed the cans containing the rough cut of the film to George Mason, my producer in New York, just before I left Leadville. Mason would look at it over the weekend and then show it to the appropriate people at PBS at the beginning of the week. If PBS decided to take it, that would provide enough money to pay for the final cut, the print, the sound . . . if not, there was little hope that a commercial network would become involved.

Commercial network documentaries were now almost exclusively made by their network news staff and their whole attitude about how to use their film footage was a denigration of what I felt a documentary should be. Too many commercial network documentaries have degenerated into illustrated lectures by some blow-dried "correspondent" who not only tells us what we're looking at and why it should upset us, but also that there's nothing we can do about it even if it *does* make us mad. I still believe a good film speaks for itself and that an audience is intelligent enough to form its own opinion on what it is seeing.

Barbara T. and I arrived at the farmhouse a little before 10 P.M. No huge, slobbering black Newfoundland rushed out to greet me; Burp was really dead.

"So you're back," was the first thing Alice said when she saw me. The second was, "Peter was tired so I put him to bed." Third: "The children's toilet is broken and probably needs to be replaced." And finally, "I've got a terrible cold. I'm going to bed."

"I'll be up soon," I said. "I just want to talk to Joan."

"Stay as long as you want," Alice said.

Barbara T. followed Alice upstairs.

Joan poured herself a glass of milk, and I made myself a drink. We sat down together in the library. I was touched that she had waited up to see me. As exasperated as she often made me, I enjoyed the moments we had alone. She told me that she was trying to help Alice more, that she was making an effort to clean up her room but it was hard because of all the papers she had from school, that when they started to pile up Alice would simply throw them away.

"Alice threw out my entire Egyptian project I'd been working on for three weeks," she said. "That's why I missed some of my homework assignments this term."

"Why'd she throw it out?"

"I don't know," Joan said.

"I'm sure Alice didn't mean to. She probably didn't realize it was important. What you have to do is make sure the papers you're working on are always in a safe place on your desk."

"I don't have any room on my desk," she said. "And if I put anything on the floor she throws it away."

"Okay, we'll get a box. Something you can put your papers in so they won't get lost."

Joan sat opposite me wringing her hands.

"Is something wrong?"

"Am I going to spend the summer with Mommy?"

"Of course. Why?"

"When will I go?"

"As soon as school lets out."

Joanie took a sip of milk and looked up at me with a faint white mustache coating her upper lip. "Daddy . . . I've been thinking about going back to live with Mommy next year . . ."

I felt a sinking sensation in my stomach. "Is that what you'd like to do?"

"Yes. I think so."

"Have you talked with your mother about this?"

"She says the schools in Oregon are very good."

"But did you tell her you wanted to live with her again?"

Joan nodded yes.

"And what did your mother say?"

"She said she wanted me home."

"Home?"

"With Mommy."

"And what has Alice said?"

"I haven't said anything to her. I haven't talked to her about it."

I glanced down at my watch. It was ten-thirty. "You'd better go to bed now, Joan," I said. "We can talk about this in the morning."

"Can't I watch a little TV?"

"Not tonight. You've got school tomorrow. You go on to bed."

"Alice lets me watch as late as I want."

"Good *night*, Joan," I said. She did not move, so I pulled her out of her chair and hugged her. When I started to relax my hold, she pushed herself against me and I held her tightly in my arms some more. "You're getting very tall," I said.

"I'm taller than most of the boys in my class."

When we went upstairs I followed her into the bathroom to look at the toilet.

"It keeps running after you flush," Joan explained.

I lifted the lid and looked inside. The float was riding too high. As a result the intake valve never shut and water continually ran into the overflow pipe. I had Joan take a look. "All you need to do is bend the float rod down an inch or so," I said. "Give it a try."

The moment she bent the rod down the flow of water stopped. I flushed the toilet and let it refill. The toilet worked perfectly. "Welcome to the wonderful world of plumbing," I said.

"You mean I *fixed* it?" she asked, surprised.

"Yep." I patted her on the back. "Now was there something else Alice said needed fixing?"

Joanie giggled, "Probably only me."

"That we can take care of by you going to bed and getting some sleep. I'll come up and check on you, okay?"

"Okay, Daddy," she said, and impulsively hugged me. "I love you," she said. "I'm so happy you're home."

"Me too, kiddo. I'm sorry only that it's for such a short time."

"I know," Joan said. "That's why I think it would be better if I were with Mom."

I looked at my daughter. Why hadn't I understood that Joan wasn't choosing her mother over me? *I* hadn't been around! She was choosing her mother over Alice. That's all it was.

I returned to the library and sat down. I could hear Joan in the bathroom brushing her teeth. I was trying to remember what Alice had said needed fixing other than the toilet. I drew a blank.

Along with the vast swings in mood, the insomnia, the anxiety attacks, I had become increasingly disturbed by my inability to remember what people had told me or even what I had done the day before. As a result of this short-term memory loss I would squirrel away in my pockets lists of appointments and notes on what people had said to me that I thought might be important at the time. I also kept a fairly concise daily journal containing phrases I hoped would later trigger the full memory of what had occurred. Unfortunately, when I would read the entries containing phrases such as, "failure to keep a low profile when everything cries out for the opposite," or "like a child shouting in an empty house to keep his spirits up," I would have no idea what they meant. I also had problems remembering where I had left my lists. It was the old joke:

PATIENT: The reason why I've come to see you, Doctor, is because I'm having a real problem with my memory.

PSYCHIATRIST: How long have you had this problem?

PATIENT: *(Pause)* What problem was that?

I recently spoke with a doctor friend of mine who had passed through a midlife crisis at about the same time as I had and he said loss of short-term memory was the result of anxiety producing adrenaline which in turn chemically reacted with something or other that affected one's memory. I carefully wrote down what he said, but—you guessed it—I can't remember what I did with those notes.

Peter was sound asleep in his bed with Tallulah, the old cat, curled up on his feet. He was sharing his pillow with a battered stuffed bear, a flop-eared dog, and an earless-tailless-eyeless something-or-other. I stood in his bedroom looking down at his head pressed into the pillow, kissed him lightly on the cheek, and crept back out. Joan's light was still on and I went up to her room and kissed her good night. When I came back down I saw that Alice had turned off our bedroom lights. I undressed in the dark and slid into bed. I lay there, my eyes wide open, feeling Alice's heat beside me. It was only eight at night, Leadville time, and in the thick sea-level air, my red corpuscles seemed charged with electricity. I wasn't tired in the least. I listened to Alice's breathing, but couldn't tell whether she was asleep or not.

"Are you awake?" I whispered.

There was no answer. When, however, I rolled toward Alice and lightly touched her hip, she jerked out from beneath my hand with such savagery I was stunned. I lay back again feeling a sudden chill in the air surrounding me. I had not touched her as a prelude to making love, I had only wanted to make contact. It would have been nice if we had held each other, shared a moment.

I got back out of bed and put on a pair of pajamas, a bathrobe, and went downstairs. As I passed the guest room door I saw that Barbara T.'s light was still on.

I made myself a fresh drink and carried it into the library and sat with it in my chair next to the fireplace. On the table beside me were Lucite-framed photographs of the children wrapped in beach towels by the pool, a small snapshot of my mother taken years before. It was quiet in the library, the only sound coming from the occasional automobile passing on the street outside.

I'm not sure what sort of "homecoming" I had anticipated. Alice's coldness could not have been all that unexpected; it was no different from being greeted with the garbage and dirty kitty litter box when I would return from New York. But Joan's desire to go back to her mother had taken me by surprise, and as I sat alone in the library I tried to sort out my thoughts.

There was a sound on the stairway behind me and a moment later Barbara T. appeared. She was wearing a long, white nylon nightgown that left her arms bare.

"Couldn't you sleep either?" I asked. "Would you like a drink?"

"What are you having?" she asked.

"A Bourbon. What would you like?"

"Anything. Vodka. Vodka tonic."

She tucked the nightgown under her legs as she curled up in the stuffed chair opposite mine. I mixed her a drink, passed it to her, and sat back down.

"Cheers," I said.

Barbara T. smiled at me over her glass.

Her smile utterly undid me: soft, affectionate, tender, comforting, understanding—at least, I perceived it as such. Barbara T.'s smile had the impact of a totally unexpected gift. I was wonder-struck at the swiftness of my change of mood: despair one moment, euphoria the next. I was amazed, too, at how vulnerable this indicated I had become.

I wanted to bury my head in her lap. I wanted to feel her skin next to mine, her cheek, her hand. I felt such a rush of longing for her that tears sprang to the corners of my eyes and my throat became rough. I took a sip of my drink, another, forced the whiskey down. When I looked up at Barbara T. again the smile was gone. Her expression had lapsed back into that unruffled surface calm I had seen so many times before; the fire, or whatever it might have been, seemed to have gone out.

She shifted in her seat to put her drink on the table over her shoulder and her nightgown grew skin-taut across her bosom and thighs, clothed her nipples like a light snowdrift, took on a faint, creamy translucence where it curled tightly around her belly. I could not look away. I was hypnotized by the outline of her body, suddenly so electrifyingly aroused I didn't even care if I were caught. She had held that position for no more than an instant, but for that instant she had seemed almost nude. And when she turned back and the nightgown fell slack across her bosom and her thighs I felt vaguely ashamed, embarrassed by the urgency with which I had looked, and still, I admit, vaguely aroused. I did not know where to look or what to think and rather than say anything, I finished my drink. When I dared look at Barbara T. again she was smiling once more, an odd half-smile, half-bite of her lower lip.

"Would you rather look at TV?" she asked.

Had she meant rather than looking at her body?

"Instead of sitting here with me," she added.

"No, no, I like sitting here with you," I said. "I like the quiet. I was just getting used to being home."

Barbara T. rose from her chair and reached for my empty glass. The lamp behind her silhouetted her body, naked beneath the gown. She was standing with her legs slightly apart less than eighteen inches from me. I was aware of a myriad-fold pattern of whites, of shadows, of flesh, the scent of bath oils, warm skin, the long, slender muscles of her thighs, the creamy swelling of the sides of her breasts, her utter femininity, the drape of the gown over every womanly curve and hollow. A wildness was growing within me. Her body, so close to my hands, had a sheen, a mother-of-pearl luster, a hint not so much of rosiness, warmth, and life as of silver, chalk, and frost. The excitement that rose within me was like the coiling of a spring, a bowstring pulling back. I have no idea how long the moment lasted, whether Barbara T. had simply risen and taken the empty whiskey glass from my hand, or whether she had been transfixed, rooted to one spot by the fearful, hungry longing of my gaze. Whichever it was, the instant was an epiphany: I sensed with an instantaneous animal certainty that Barbara T. had felt it, too, and what is more, *what is more*, the two children and her cousin asleep overhead acted not as a deterrent but as a powerful stimulant.

And yet, when she had made my drink and sat back down opposite me again, her face was once more composed, her gown slack about her bosom, a pool across her thighs. I do not think we spoke for quite a while. The silence grew around us, the air became thick and charged with the electricity that presages a storm. My mouth felt dry. Barbara T. shifted her position again so that she was sitting cross-legged in the armchair, the nightgown collected in one fluid, practiced motion like a diaper at the top of her smooth, alabaster thighs. One of Barbara T.'s hands pressed the gathered nightgown to her lap, the other dropped to a mole high up on the inside of her right thigh. The mole, a small, brown beauty spot, snagged my eye; I could not look away. When she touched it lightly, smoothed it, circled it, laved it with her fingertip like a tongue, I was mesmerized. Not until she lifted her hand did the spell break. When I looked into her eyes once again nothing was there.

I could not understand it. Had she come downstairs to torment me? To frustrate me by first offering and then withdrawing what I could not get from my wife? There were simply too many conflicting signals for me to feel certain I had any idea of what was going on. Was she unconscious of what she showed? Was I supposed, like some eunuch, not to respond? Had she known I had come downstairs feeling rebuffed and joined me to double the rejection by first arousing me and then disowning any responsibility for what she had done?

Barbara T. slowly lifted her right knee and tucked it under her chin. "I've missed you," she said. The nightgown, collected between her legs, left the entire underside of her right thigh exposed. The white flesh, the silk, the nakedness of the soft inner part of her thighs, the curve of her buttock were all the more devastating because of the veil.

"I've missed you, too," I said. I wanted to go to her, kneel before her chair, lift her nightgown above her breasts. Instead I asked her if she'd like another drink. She said she didn't think so, that she was going to go to bed.

"I guess it is about that time," I said.

I followed her up the stairs where she paused, one hand on the guest room door, the other lifted to lightly touch my cheek. "Good night," she said. "Sweet dreams."

Sweet dreams indeed.

As I stood in the bathroom brushing my teeth I remember being surprised by my expression in the mirror: it was anger. I looked, in fact, as sore as hell.

The next morning Barbara T. and Alice went into Princeton to go shopping and I drove Joan and Peter to Philadelphia to visit the Franklin Institute, one of my favorite museums. By the time we returned home Barbara T. had gone, left for Massachusetts to spend the weekend with her grandparents.

On Monday morning George Mason, my producer, called me from New York and said, "I feel almost certain PBS will take your film."

I was speechless for a moment. "You are? They will?" I blurted. "You had a chance to see the whole thing?"

"Yes," he said. "It's very powerful. Very strong. I've already shown it to McHenry at WNET. He wants to see you. Perhaps we could meet at his office to talk."

"Certainly," I said. "I could be there by midafternoon."

"How would Friday be, then? Around three?"

"Friday at three. Fine," I said. But Friday was such a long way off!

"Okay, I'll set it up and get back to you."

"I'll be here," I said.

After we'd hung up I wrote down what George Mason had said. He had been "almost certain." He'd found it "very powerful. Very strong," but he hadn't said "PBS is going to buy it. Yes." And yet McHenry had seen it and he was high up in the Channel 13 hierarchy. I telephoned a friend who had been with Channel 13 for years and repeated the conversation I had had with my producer and asked if McHenry had said anything.

"McHenry's said more already about this film than any documentary we've got scheduled for this year," my friend said. "He has all the brass

in the screening room watching it now. It's the most exciting thing to
happen in this office in forty-eight months."

"What do you *mean?*"

"Everybody's talking about it. Everyone's giving up smoking. You've
made a helluva film."

"I *have?*" I asked.

"Of course! It's marvelous."

"It needs to be cut," I said. "It's 'fat' now . . . Jesus, do you really
think WNET's going to buy it?"

"I don't know," my friend said. "All I can tell you is that McHenry
wants to."

I would have to wait until Friday, then, before I'd know.

When I came into the house from my office in the garage and told
Alice about the telephone calls, how excited I was by the news, she said,
"Your cat had diarrhea in the dining room."

"But isn't that good news about the film?"

Alice was standing at the sink with her back to me. "We can celebrate
after they send you the check."

"Ohhh, Alice," I said. "Why are you being like this?"

"Like what?"

"So hard. Why can't you share my excitement at this news about the
film?"

"Because I hate your film," she said, turning to face me now. "I hate
it for having taken so long, for what it's done to our marriage—it's all
you've talked about or thought about for the past three years. It's such
a depressing, boring goddam thing. It's as though it's given *us* cancer,
too. And when you finally finish it—if you ever do—you'll just start
another film and go off to some college to fuck coeds again."

"No I won't."

"You *will!* Even *I* understand that it's impossible to make a decent
living as a documentary film-maker. There's no market for them anymore.
There's no general audience, no means to distribute them. You used to
be able to sell them to film libraries, to schools. The grants are drying
up. You spent almost as much time trying to raise the money for this
film as you did shooting it. The foreign market is paying less and less
. . . You're in the wrong business and you don't have the sense to
recognize it."

"Things will get better. With the cable network expansion there'll be
more of a demand for these films."

"Cable will show old movies and reruns," Alice said. "Look at your friends in the business! How many are left? All of you upper middle class socially motivated graduates of the fifties and sixties wanting to do something important with your lives, wanting to make films that will change the status quo . . . the only thing you've changed is *your* status quo."

"But when PBS takes this film . . ." I said.

"You'll make, what? What do they pay now?"

"About two hundred dollars per minute. From ten to twelve thousand for an hour film."

"On which you'll have spent three years. So your income averages out to around three thousand dollars a year—and you don't even qualify for food stamps."

"No film-maker lives on what PBS pays, Alice," I said. "That's why one applies for grants! I applied for grants from everybody but the American Tobacco Institute for this one."

"Well, it's scary," she said. "You're so irresponsible about money it terrifies me. I hate to say this but it's a good thing your mother died and is leaving you some money or I don't know how we'd eat."

"The money hasn't come in yet," I said.

"Don't you think *I* know that?" she asked. "When will it be settled, by the way?"

"I don't know. Another few months, I guess."

Alice turned back to the sink. "How much do you think this house is worth now?" she asked.

"Ours?"

"The one we're living in."

"Maybe a hundred thousand."

"So if we sold this house you'd have assets of about a hundred thousand."

"Sold this house?" I asked. "Why? I thought you loved it here."

"*You* love it here," Alice said. "The house is too small. Too old. Nothing works."

"But where would we go?"

"Anywhere but New Jersey."

"Do you have some place in mind?" I asked.

"Stowe's nice," Alice said.

"I wouldn't know."

I was thinking about Barbara T.'s line. "The skiing was fun, *too.*"

I left Alice in the kitchen and went back out to my office to be alone. Alice's idea of selling our old house, moving again, was almost more than

I could bear. Didn't she understand how much this house meant to us— to me? How could she suggest such a thing? It would be like selling a member of the family! How could we leave the room Peter was practically born in, the room in which I'd read him bedtime stories night after night: *Good Night Moon; Little Toot; Frog and Toad; George and Martha; Stuart Little . . .* How could we leave the library with bookshelves we'd put in, painted, and filled with friends? Leave the dining room with its memories of family dinners, parties, Christmas turkeys past? Leave all those beams and mantels and doors we'd scraped and sanded and oiled to restore the old wood? The rough plaster walls we'd replastered and painted over and over again? Didn't Alice understand that that old house was our *glue?* It was what held us together! It was practically all we had left—other than Peter—to show for all those years of bickering and betrayal.

I took the train into New York City on Friday. I had slept very little the night before, woken up at four, tossed and turned in bed before going downstairs to smoke cigarettes and read in the library. If PBS did not accept the film I did not know what I would do. When I reached Grand Central I called George Mason. My producer said he would not be able to attend the meeting with McHenry at WNET and that I should go there alone.

I went to WNET's offices and was ushered down a long corridor, zigzagged into a labyrinthian passageway through a secretary's office and finally into Mr. McHenry's. My only impression of that trip was that I would never be able to find my way out by myself and that we had encountered, it seemed, an undue number of unnecessary doors.

Mr. McHenry began by asking me about Colorado, how I liked Leadville, teaching, what the students were like; he was obviously trying to put me at ease—was he also trying to break the bad news? I told him the one anecdote I thought might amuse him, about how I had met an old rancher out there who had told me he had "run eight hunnert head of buffalo" on the grazing lands between Fort Collins and Centennial, a tiny town about twenty-five miles to its north, and that when I had asked the man how he "ran that many buffalo" he had replied, "Wa'al, you don't try to turn them none."

My mind seemed suspended over my voice like a balloon. I was hearing myself tell the story, but watching Mr. McHenry's face. I felt I was going on too long, that if Elliot McHenry were to tell the same story, he could cut it by two thirds. When the anecdote ground clanking and shuffling to a halt he smiled as if there might be something essential to the story that I'd left out, and then he began to talk about my film.

He started by probing gently here and there, always asking questions that required thought: "Were you intending to give the impression of such-and-such when you showed so-and-so?" "Could there have been any other interpretation for the government's failure to support research into this-or-that?"

I tried to answer his questions as best I could.

And then Mr. McHenry said, "I see only one problem about your film—it's really more our problem than yours—"

Oh God, I thought, *here it comes.*

"The film runs about two and a half hours now," McHenry said. "That's a bit long, of course."

"Yes, I know," I said. "I want to cut it down."

McHenry made a few notes on his pad, then he looked up at me. "You don't anticipate any major problems in editing?"

"No more than usual."

"It's the sort of subject that demands a full examination. Will two hours be enough?"

"*Two* hours?" I said. "You'll let me keep it that long?"

"I don't see how you can do it justice with any less."

"Two hours would be wonderful. That will let me keep so much of what I was afraid I'd lose."

"I think then you should consider it settled."

"Sir?"

"We'd like to run it as a two-hour special next fall."

Had I not been aware of how grievously uncomfortable it would have made Mr. McHenry, I think I would have burst into tears.

The next thing I remember is walking on the sidewalk down Fifth Avenue. I don't recall what more Mr. McHenry and I had said, how I made my way back to the elevators and out of the building. I recall only passing the windows of Bergdorf-Goodman with my insides exploding with joy. I tried to telephone Alice from a public phone on the corner. Nobody was home.

It must have been the next day or the day after that I met Odette Villars for the first time.

I had walked up to Brandon's Market, about a block from our house, to pick up a half-gallon of milk and was standing near the front of the store when Odette came in. She and her husband had bought the gray Federal house further up the street near the corner and although I had seen her walking with her two young children (her eldest, a daughter, was about Peter's age) or her husband here and there around the town, I had never spoken to her.

I had, of course, noticed how attractive she was, that she was tall (five feet ten) and graceful and recognizably different from all the other women one saw about the town. She always appeared elegantly dressed whether she was in blue jeans and a down vest or a huge woolly sweater and corduroy slacks. There was never anything ostentatious about her dress, just good materials and perfect tailoring. She had a fur jacket, too, one of the most handsome I had ever seen (a Canadian silver fox, I later learned), which she would fling on over her French blue jeans. Odette, I have discovered, has an uncanny ability to anticipate styles; what she picks up at a handicraft fair this summer will almost certainly appear as the height of fashion in next year's *Harper's Bazaar* and *Vogue*.

Anyway, despite never having spoken to Odette, I had learned a few things about her, the sort of things one quickly learns in a small town: She was French, married to an American psychiatrist, and was considered somewhat aloof.

I was standing near the vegetables, talking with the market owner's son, when Odette entered, smoothly swept a shopping cart out of the stack by the door, and with her eyes on the display to her right, drove her cart squarely into a tower of grape soda. There was a terrible crash, grape soda cans teetered, toppled, fell, bounced, caromed, rolled all over the store. At least a dozen cans fell into Odette's cart.

There was that moment of stunned silence that always follows a calamity of this kind and I found myself smiling. I could not help it. And when Odette's eyes met mine and she saw me grinning, a hint of a smile came into her eyes, too. Charlie Brandon, the owner's son, looked down at Odette's cart with its dozen or so cans and asked, "Will you be wanting all of these, Mrs. Villars?"

"No, she said, "I do not care for grape soda drink at all."

I don't know if we introduced ourselves—certainly Odette would not have initiated an introduction with a strange man at this or any other time. Nor do I remember what if anything else we said. Odette and Charlie and I gathered up the cans into the semblance of a stack and we, the three of us, must have talked a little bit. I suppose I asked Odette how she liked living in our town and where she had moved from. What I primarily remember are her large brown eyes and that she looked so pale and unhappy. I remember also that the instant after she had smashed into the pile of cans and had seen me smiling, her eyes had registered surprise. Had she, I wondered, expected to be yelled at?

When one first looks at Odette one knows immediately that she is a European; I'm not exactly sure why. I do know it has nothing to do with fashion; it must be her extraordinarily expressive features. Europeans have a language articulated solely through the vocabulary of an eyebrow, a pursing of the mouth, a sidelong glance, a finger to the forehead, the biting of a lip. If I were to try to describe her face, several of its features press instantly forward, demanding to be noticed first: her deep brown eyes; her thin, knife-straight nose and full sensuous nostrils; her wide mouth with its faintly pouting lower lip. When she asks me, as upon occasion all women ask their men, "Do you think I'm beautiful?" I invariably hesitate because "beauty" has so little to do with what mesmerizes me about her face. Fashion models on magazine covers are beautiful but there often seems to be nothing happening behind their eyes. Odette's face is so *alive!* It is the face not of a Cheryl Tiegs but of a young Jeanne Moreau. It is a face with features assembled so uncompromisingly that she cannot disguise what she feels; she cannot hide her moods.

When we lie together nude I cannot turn away. I have to look, have to touch, know, inhale her body, the scent high on the back of her neck, behind her ear, beneath her jaw, the hollow of her throat. I need to taste her skin, her lips, her mouth, her tongue. Always I caress her body with wonder at how such soft and gently swelling curves could emerge so subtly from such finely chiseled lines and planes. I have to trace her tear-drop breasts, the premenstrual buoyancy of her belly, the taut muscle bands along her upper thighs. I have to touch her ears, her cheekbones, kiss the sides of her nose, her wide, smooth, unmarked forehead, the delicate web of wrinkles at the corners of her eyes.

After we have made love and are lying quietly together the brown of her eyes becomes so dark her pupils almost disappear. It is then that the most lovely shades of magenta, rose, and lavender appear beneath her drowsy eyes, spread down to her high cheekbone ridge. Little beads of perspiration cling to the side of her temples, her lips are slightly parted, a wispy strand of hair curls across the corner of her mouth.

"Do you think I'm beautiful?" she asks. It seems so inadequate to answer only, "Yes."

It does not surprise me that when the teenage daughters of our friends need advice they consistently seek out Odette. She is compassionate and wise and uncompromisingly honest with them. She knows there is no need to remind them that they are still children and have much to learn. She speaks to them as one woman to another and they love her for that. And because she is so secure now in her own skin as a woman, she is more of a woman than any I've known.

She has also made me feel like a man.

But I am getting ahead of myself. I did not, could not, of course, have known or even sensed any of this that day I met Odette at Brandon's Market.

I knew only that an attractive woman had suffered a comic mishap and that despite the tremulous sweetness of her smile, her large brown eyes seemed, for reasons I had no way at that time of understanding, ineffably, utterly sad. Once the scattered cans had been collected, Odette went her way and I, after picking up my half-gallon of milk, went mine.

Two days after my encounter with Odette, Alice drove me to Newark, where I boarded a nonstop flight for Denver and the final six weeks of teaching at Rocky Mountain State. Fred Noonan met the plane and we drove up to Leadville through a blizzard with winds gusting to fifty miles an hour, blowing the snow from Wyoming or Kansas or God knows where. It didn't matter where the blizzard came from, I had the sale of my movie to PBS to keep me warm. I didn't give Odette Villars another thought.

7

BY THE END OF THE second week in May I had finished both the cutting of the film and my teaching job at Rocky Mountain State and I was free to return home.

Neither Alice nor the two children could disguise their embarrassment at having me enter the Newark terminal wearing my students' parting gift: a Dakota-style, sage-colored cowboy hat. Twelve-year-old Joan emitted a great honk of laughter upon seeing me; eight-year-old Peter pointedly turned and wandered far enough away so that no one would mistake him for someone related to me. And as for thirty-three-year-old Alice . . . when I leaned forward to kiss her, the hat's stiff brim struck her in the eye. The hat was not a success.

In the dark green Peugeot station wagon on the drive back to our old stone house Peter leaned forward from the back seat to ask, "Daddy, are you glad to be home?"

"Yes," I said. "I've missed all of you."

Alice shot me a look, but I ignored it. I *was* glad to be home. I was returning to them determined to make up for my absence by being a good husband, a good father, a loving and responsible, healthy and caring man. I wanted us to be a family again.

Peter was still leaning forward. "Can we have some ice cream when we get home?"

"Have you had dinner?" I asked.

"I fed them at the airport." Alice said.

"Can we?" Peter asked.

"I don't want any," Joan said. "I'm on a diet."

"A diet? Why?" I asked.

"She thinks her ass is too big," Peter said. "Will someone—*ow!*" he cried. "Joan hit me!"

"He deserved it," Joan said.

"I did not. All I said was—*ow!*" Peter yelped. "She hit me again!"

"I'm going to keep hitting you until you quit bugging me."

"Will someone please answer my question," Peter said. "Can I have some ice cream when we get home?"

"Yes, yes, yes, you can have ice cream," Alice said impatiently. "You can have anything you want!"

Peter sat back silently; Joan was staring sullenly out of the side window; Alice was looking stonily ahead. I tried to think of something lighthearted to say, but my throat had turned to stone. Why, I wondered, was the *idea* of a family always so much better than the reality?

We rode the rest of the way home in silence.

By a quarter to ten that night Peter had had his ice cream and was in bed. Joan had gone up to Alice's and my bedroom to watch TV. I put some ice in two glasses and carried them into the library where Alice was sitting. I fixed us each a drink from the library liquor cabinet, then sank down in the chair opposite her. "Cheers," I said, raising my glass. "I'm glad to be home."

"Cheers," Alice said, sounding tired.

"Thanks for meeting me at the airport," I said. "I know it's a lousy drive."

"I'm going back tomorrow."

"To the airport?" I asked. "Why?"

"Barbara T. is meeting me there," she said. "We're flying out of Newark to spend a week in Puerto Rico."

"You're leaving *tomorrow?*" I asked, suddenly sitting forward. "To *Puerto Rico?* When did you decide this?"

"Three weeks ago when I deposited your last paycheck from the university."

I sat back dumbfounded.

"Uncle Norman—Barbara T.'s father—has a condo, so it will cost us practically nothing. And besides," she added, her tone sodden with sarcasm, "it will give you an opportunity to become reacquainted with your children."

"What about *us?*" I asked.

"You and me? We'll go on as usual."

"How can we do that if you leave the day after I return? Why are you leaving right now?"

"Because Barbara T.'s father wasn't using the condo. He invited her and she invited me."

"Is this the only time you and Barbara T. could use it?"

"I don't know. Barbara T. invited me for now and I couldn't very well suggest a different time. And since you'd be home to cope with the children I didn't see any reason why I shouldn't go."

"Did you tell Barbara T. I'd be just getting back?"

"What difference does that make?"

"The difference is that it would be nice if you and I could have a little time to get reacquainted, too. Jesus, Alice, we haven't seen each other but for two weeks since the beginning of the year. Don't you think we ought to spend a little time together before we split up again?"

"I'll only be gone a week or so."

" 'Or so'?"

"Uncle Norman wasn't sure when he'd be getting back," she said. "We might even be able to stay there an extra week."

"So you might be gone two weeks?"

"Don't you think I deserve a break?"

"Of course you do. It's just the way you've gone about it that strikes me as odd."

"Odd? In what way?"

"You haven't given me much warning."

"Why do you need a warning?"

"I was planning to go to New York to meet with McHenry and Mason. We still have to lay in the final sound track."

"So what? Joan's almost *thirteen*," Alice said. "She can take care of Peter and herself. They don't need you to be here all day. They can ride the bus to school and back. You can get them some TV dinners if you're going to get home late. Joan, for God's sake, could even get off her ass and cook a meal. So what's the problem?"

"The problem is I'm left with the feeling you can't wait to get away from me."

"I need a break."

"I understand that," I said.

"And since you won't take me on vacations, unless I go now I don't know when I'll get the opportunity again."

Alice started telling me all the reasons why we never took vacations together, listing the excuses I would give—that I was too busy, too poor, the children—and I couldn't help wondering *who* is *this woman who* resents me so much!

Marriage can blur and confuse one's understanding of one's self. A husband and wife can become a "couple," a new organism that makes each part unsure of how well he or she could function without the other, unsure of what one's *self* is, or has become. The semester I had just finished in Leadville had given me the opportunity to gain some perspective about myself, Alice, and our relationship. I had certainly come to appreciate better what she had been doing for me all along— the boring household chores whose completion I had taken for granted.

I had tried to tell Alice this, through letters; I had written her of my gratitude for putting up with the children while I was gone. I wrote that I knew I could not have taken the Leadville job without her, that she had had the most difficult part, and that I recognized how tiresome it had been—all of which was true and, of course, easy to write but meaningless unless backed up by thought and deed.

". . . There was always some reason," Alice was saying, "some excuse why we couldn't get away." Would I have packed Alice off for a vacation if she were not already taking one? Since I had not made any plans to do so, in all honesty, the answer presumably is no. But spring and summer were the best seasons to be around our old farmhouse and I would not have wanted to leave until winter in any case. I certainly wouldn't have wanted her to go—with me or without me—the day after I returned. Be that as it may, Alice's own message had come through loud and clear: she was in no mood to forgive me for sticking her with the children, and she was taking off for Puerto Rico whether I liked it or not. If I really wanted, as I had told her, things to be different— meaning, simply, wanting Alice and me to get along—then I would have to accept that Alice deserved and needed a break and ignore the trip's timing.

"As for our getting reacquainted," Alice was saying, "we'll be together when I get back. In the meantime there are several problems around here that need to be taken care of."

"Like what?" I asked.

Alice then launched upon what amounted to a "Damage Control Officer's report" on the house, the car, the garage. It went like this:

1. The mortar holding the stones together on the north side of the house was coming loose; water was leaking in around the window frames and the plaster wall in Peter's room was crumbling onto his floor.

2. The Peugeot was burning oil and there was a "clunking" sound in the transmission.

3. The furnace man did not think our hot air furnace would last another winter; it was beginning to throw smoke into the house.

4. The roof on the garage was leaking and at least half of it would need to be replaced. Also, clapboards were rotten on the office east wall.

As she related the problems I could feel the panic beginning. I closed my eyes and massaged my temples.

"Don't blame me!" Alice said loudly. "It's not *my* fault."

"I wasn't blaming you, Alice. I was worried about the money, that's all."

"There's the money from your mother's estate. There's PBS and your final paycheck from the college. It doesn't all have to be done at once. Incidentally, I charged my airline ticket to Visa so you can pay it off a little at a time. It was three-eighty something, round trip." She sat across from me, daring me to protest. When I didn't say anything she pointed to the ceiling above the bookcase. "See that stain there? That's water damage. Joan let her bath overflow. The whole ceiling needs to be repainted . . . and while we're at it we might as well repaint the rest of the room. I've always hated this color," she said.

She had asked me to pick the library's colors.

The ceiling was white; the bookcases that covered two walls of the room, the fireplace and mantel and the wood-paneled fourth wall were a pale colonial gray.

"What color do you want?" I asked.

"Something brighter, more cheerful. This room is always so depressing and dark."

"We don't get direct sunlight because of the hedges and trees."

I had planted the hedges and let them grow up.

"Yellow might be nice. A creamy yellow," she said.

"Yellow's the hardest of all colors to paint," I protested. "Even if I base-coat and put on two coats of paint, the yellow will look gray."

"Not if you do it right," she said. "We should probably think of new slipcovers, too."

I could hear Joan flush the toilet upstairs. I closed my eyes again.

"Your cat has clawed them."

"What?" I asked, opening my eyes.

"The slipcovers," Alice said. "Your cat has clawed the slipcovers."

I got up and went out to the kitchen for some ice cubes and stood before the refrigerator looking at Peter's school drawings, the announcements, phone numbers, and schedules taped to the door. I was thinking of Alice's litany of troubles, of how she managed to make me feel that the difficulties of owning an old house were my fault. I put some ice cubes in my glass and walked back into the library. Alice was smoking a cigarette. The children's toilet was still running.

"There's something seriously wrong with that toilet," Alice said.

"I'll take a look at it."

"And some of the tiles are loose in our shower."

"Is there anything else you can think of that's wrong?"

Alice looked at my expression. "I told you, don't blame *me*. It's the house *you* wanted to buy."

"You said you liked it."

"I said it was 'all right.' "

I held up my hand. "Look, let's drop it. We own the house, it's where we live, I'll see what I can do about the things that need to be fixed. I don't want to get into a quarrel my first night home."

"I'm not quarreling," Alice said. "I'm only telling you what needs to be done."

"All right, Alice," I said. "Why don't we just relax for a while, not discuss problems, give ourselves a rest."

Alice stood up. "Since you don't want to talk anymore, I'm going to bed."

"I just don't want to talk about problems," I said.

"You never do."

After Alice left, I sat with my drink until I heard her close the door to our bathroom. Then I went up and fixed the children's toilet, came back downstairs, and finished my drink.

I don't believe that that evening I had any illusions that Alice and I would ever be happily married. I hoped only to be left free to live in relative peace, to be able to continue with my work, to provide a comparatively stable home environment for my wife and children. If I was going to accept responsibility for the problems with the house, then I was, in Noonan's terms, "assuming the position." If I was the one to have decided to buy the house it was because Alice had been unwilling to take part in the decision herself. It was a tactic I was used to. We'd be driving along a country road and Alice would say, "Let's get something to eat."

"Fine," I'd say. "Where do you want to stop?"

"Anywhere," she'd say. "You decide."

I'd drive until I'd find a place that looked reasonably clean, which might have decent food. "This place look all right to you?" I'd ask.

She'd shrug her shoulders. "I don't care."

Afterward I'd get, "Why'd you pick a crummy place like that?"

Or Variation Number 2: "Why'd you think I'd like *that* movie?"

Or Variation Number 3: "I hate this dress! Why'd you tell me to buy it?"

The advantage Alice gave herself by refusing to make decisions was that she forced me to be the one to choose. And no matter what I chose, of course, the decision could later be used against me. By abdicating any responsibility for such decisions Alice manipulated me into becoming the heavy no matter how well-meaning my intentions. Maggie had done it to me, too.

"Do what you want," Maggie said, "you always do."

"Don't blame me," Alice said. "It's the house you wanted to buy."

Why did I let her get away with it? Because had I called her on it, we would have ended up in a fight. And what would we have gained? I hate fights. I would probably have reinforced her rage and resentment against me and all we'd have to show for it was another ugly scene.

I waited until I could hear Alice was finished in the bathroom, then I turned off the lights in the library and went upstairs. Alice was in bed watching Johnny Carson on the little bedside TV.

"I think I'll take a quick shower," I said.

Alice did not look up from the TV. She said, "You'll see for yourself the loose tiles."

As I stand beneath the hot spray soaping myself I think about Nora's breasts, their fullness, their creaminess, the nipples pink and hard, the way when she bends forward their roundness fills my eyes. I imagine Alice tied down on the bed while I fuck Nora beside her: In slow motion, like divers underwater, Nora and I tumble from position to position while Alice watches, unable to stop us. She strains against the straps holding her legs and arms widespread. We can hear her protesting. I am kneeling behind Nora, my hands guiding her hips back to me. I watch as Nora's hand slides up Alice's body to her breast. Nora's hand cups Alice's breast, her thumb moves back and forth across Alice's nipple. Alice's body stiffens, she thrashes and jerks back and forth, trying to escape Nora's caress. But Nora persists, supports herself on her knees and elbows so that her hands are free. She squeezes both of Alice's breasts now, touches both of Alice's nipples. Despite herself Alice is becoming excited. I begin to quicken my thrusts into Nora, bend over her to hold her breasts. She is making little moaning sounds. "Oh yes," she is saying, "do me like th—"

The bathroom door opened. I heard the toilet lid go up, a moment later the rattle of the toilet roll. Then Alice flushed the toilet and I was hit by a jet of hot shower water.

"Hey! Jesus!" I protested.

"Sorry," Alice said.

When I joined Alice in bed ten minutes or so later she had turned out the lights in the bedroom but she was still watching TV. She lay on her side with her back to me.

The last time I had made love had been with Nora over two months before. I lightly touched Alice's hip; this time she did not jerk away. I continued to caress Alice through her nightgown, massaging the small of her back until she rolled over onto her belly, her eyes never leaving the TV. I put my hand under her nightgown, moved up the back of her thighs, her buttocks, to the small of her back again. She did not protest. In fact, when my hand moved down over her buttocks I felt her thighs move slightly apart. She was lying now on her stomach, her head cradled on her arms, her eyes open watching some stand-up comedian making Los Angeles freeway jokes. I continued to caress her back, her buttocks, her thighs. When my hand dipped between her thighs to touch her she stiffened only slightly and then relaxed; her legs remained apart. I was wearing an old nightshirt and I lifted it above my hips so that, like Alice, I was naked from the waist down. I was still on my side and when I moved toward Alice my erect penis brushed against her hip. The stand-up comic was prattling on. I sensed that if I asked Alice to turn the TV off she would have to face what was happening to her. Sex, with Alice— when it occurred at all—had to take place almost in secret, as if it were coming to pass without her knowing. Usually she insisted the lights be off; I was surprised therefore that she was permitting what little light came from the TV screen. I wondered whether it didn't mean that she *liked* being touched while watching TV, that she was, somehow, turned on by it, that in fact the TV was in some way responsible for her arousal. Was she fantasizing that it was all happening to her in front of an audience? Would that be the sort of thing to excite her? Was that her "Secret Garden"?

I had by now insinuated my hand entirely between her legs and she was beginning to respond. Her hips were moving ever so slightly, just a tensing of her muscles to meet my touch. I caressed her a moment longer, then removed my hand.

"Roll over," I whispered. "Lie on your back."

Alice hesitated, then rolled over. I let my hand drift up her stomach, her rib cage, to her breast, enfolding it gently, never quite touching the nipple. Her head was still turned toward the TV. The comic finished, and a commercial came on. Alice's head rolled toward me.

"I have to go to the bathroom again," Alice said. She brushed the covers aside and quickly went into the bathroom. Ed McMahon was holding a can of dog food next to his cheek and pointing to the label. I heard the toilet flush, then Alice running some water.

She made it back to bed in time for the resumption of the show. Alice lay back down beside me, first on her side, curled toward the TV, then when I touched her on the hip, she rolled onto her back again. My erection, in the meantime, had wilted.

"My turn," I said, getting out of bed. I picked up my pack of cigarettes and carried it into the bathroom. Back among the cigarettes was a joint. I lit it and took a couple of hits while I let the water run. Then I put it out, leaned forward, and looked at my wrinkles in the mirror over the sink. I was wondering whether I should offer Alice some of the dope. She would probably say something like, "Why? Do you think I need it?" or she'd ask me why *I* needed it and it would be one long, drawn-out boring hassle. On the other hand, if she did take some, and she loosened up a bit . . . She used to smoke it with me all the time. But it never really loosened her up. She only withdrew further into herself.

I turned off the water, flushed the toilet, and came back to bed.

She looked away from me and back at the TV. She was no longer wearing her nightgown.

I began again to caress her. She lay on her back, her head turned away toward the TV, her eyes half-open. Was it my imagination, or had she turned down the sound? I did not touch her belly until the camera panned across the audience. Her eyes opened wide with their applause, then immediately closed. As if to freeze that image in her brain? I pulled off my nightshirt and threw the covers back and I continued to caress her until her breathing changed and she was ready. I mounted her and began to move inside her, gently at first, gradually with increasing force. Her eyes remained tightly closed, her head still turned toward the TV. She was responding now, raising her hips to meet my thrusts. Her breath was coming faster. I waited, held back, watching the TV out of the corner of my eye. Then, when the moment was right I told Alice, "Now! Open your eyes!"

The audience was applauding again. She was staring into a hundred faces, who were staring back at her.

Her orgasm was immediate and powerful. When it was over she would not look at me. And a little later, when I reached across her to turn off the television, I saw she was crying. I lay beside her, tried to find out why she was crying, but she would not speak. She would not tell me why.

Alice left for her flight to Puerto Rico at ten the next morning. At breakfast she reminded me of the children's appointments. Other than that we hardly spoke. I wasn't sure whether she was angry at me or

herself. The tension was so great that when she pulled out of the driveway
I felt relieved.

The relief did not last.

True, there was no more open conflict with Alice; we couldn't fight if
she wasn't there. But the daily hassle of coping with the children made
me realize how inadequate had been my appreciation of what she had
done. *They always needed something:* meals, snacks, school lunches, help
with their homework, individual attention at odd moments. They needed
to be driven to doctor's appointments, friends' houses, back to school for
sports. They needed clean laundry, sheets changed on their beds. They
needed to be told over and over again to quit fighting, to quit shouting,
to get their feet off the furniture. They had to be told to wipe up their
messes, feed the cat, put the food they'd removed from the refrigerator
back inside.

Joan, especially, left a trail of books, clothing, barrettes, junk, behind
her, like cookie crumbs through some enchanted woods. In the evening
she would examine the meal with suspicion and disdain.

It occurred to me one of the major reasons for the diminishing birthrate
in this country was that more and more fathers were coping with the
children at home.

Still, since the children were in school from eight in the morning until
half-past two, I could get some work done.

I had Burt Taylor, my architect friend, come by after work for drinks
one afternoon to take a look at the garage clapboards and roof and the
north side of the house. He gave me the name of a stone mason who
would patch up the crumbling mortar and showed me where the asbestos
shingles on the garage were shot. Then we walked around to the side.

"I'm not busy at the moment," Burt said. "I could reroof that whole
side of the roof for around four hundred dollars."

"You'd take on a job like that?"

"It will keep me out of my house."

"You and Nancy having at each other again?"

"I can't stand the fucking bitch!"

He had said it so angrily I couldn't help but laugh.

"It's not funny," Burt said, but he was smiling, too. "I can't help it.
She's driving me crazy! She harbors grudges, stores them up all day,
then empties them on me at night. I spend more time calming Nancy
down than I do talking with the children . . ." He was testing one of the
clapboards, pressing a knife blade into the wood to see how soft it was.

"You might be able to get away with replacing only this section here. Higher up the clapboards look good. I'll know better when I get up to them."

"You want to do the clapboards, too?"

"Why not?" he shrugged. "Like I said I'm not busy now. . . . How long is Alice gone for?"

"A week. Maybe two."

"You want to go to a movie one of these nights?"

"Sure," I said. "You have one in mind?"

"The only thing I have in mind these days is keeping the hell away from my wife!" Burt punched one of the clapboards so hard it split beneath his fist.

"Jesus," I said. "Let's get a drink before you destroy the place."

Burt and I carried our beers into the library and sat down. We could hear Peter and Joan arguing upstairs; but they had not yet reached a savage enough stage for me to intervene.

"How's your daughter?" I asked Burt.

"Anna?" He made a face. "It seems like only yesterday she had braces and zits and it was reasonably tranquil around the house, but now . . . now she has tits, the braces have come off, and our house is filled with drooling teenaged boys. There's one in particular she favors, I think, only because she knows he bugs me. I can't go into the living room without finding the two of them glued together on the couch or climbing into each other's mouths. Jesus, it's disgusting! And when the little prick isn't trying to get Anna to perform some unspeakable act he's in the refrigerator eating my lunch. 'Oh, hi, Mr. Taylor,' " Burt said, imitating a young boy's falsetto, " ' I just saw this sandwich in here going to waste and . . .' I'd like to 'waste' him!"

I sat there grinning at my friend.

Burt shook his head. "The thing is, I *understand* it. I *remember* what it was like. Anna brought home a girl friend of hers from school the other day, some fifteen-year-old who's in her gymnastics class. They were trying on some new leotards and tights and this fifteen-year-old comes to me in her leotard with nothing on underneath and she's all tits and ass, and she asks me what I think. If I'd *told* her what I thought I would have gone to prison! It's not fair! I tell you, I'm so horny I can't stand it! Did you know they've opened a massage parlor on the road to Trenton? You have any interest in going?"

"To a massage parlor? No, I don't think so."

"Why not? You might enjoy it."

"I doubt it," I said. "My sex life is lonely enough without having to pay an absolute stranger."

"Strangers are the best kind. You don't have to talk to them afterwards."

"I *like* to talk afterwards!" I said. "At least for a little while."

"Afterwards I'm always starving," Burt said. "I want to get something to eat."

"Me, too!" I laughed. "I can't help it, I almost immediately start thinking about food."

"And Nancy wants me to hold her."

"Ah!" I said, smiling. "The legendary after-glow!"

"Last sighted by a Swedish shepherd girl northeast of Gothenburg," Burt added.

"—in the late seventeenth century, then lost until ceded in error by the Treaty of Nystad to Russia—"

"—along with all of the Swedish possessions of the eastern Baltic—"

"—except Finland," I said. "Whereupon the after-glow was enjoyed by Catherine the Great innumerable times—"

"—until she had it encased in a Fabergé egg," Burt said.

"Didn't Fabergé come after Catherine the Great?" I asked.

"Who didn't?" Burt laughed.

We were like school kids sneaking a conversation while the teacher was out of the room: faintly naughty and daring, worried a little about getting caught.

"Another beer?" I asked, pushing myself up out of my chair.

"Why not," Burt said. He followed me into the kitchen. "Whatever happened to the old 'wham-bang-thank you, ma'am'?"

"It went out with premature ejaculation."

"With *premature ejaculation?*" Burt laughed. "Jesus, when was the last time you had a premature ejaculation?"

"Nineteen fifty-seven," I said.

"There was a girl named Becky Katz—Pussy Katz we called her—I *ruined* her dress the night of my high school senior prom. . . . We had snuck out to the parking lot during intermission. Harry Dalrymple, I remember, had lent me his car. I had barely climbed into the back seat with Pussy and she whipped it out of my pants. 'Oh, Burt,' she said, 'is this all for me?' and . . ." His eyes misted over with what I mistook for nostalgia. "And now," he continued, "I have trouble getting it up."

I passed a can of beer over to my friend. His expression was so serious and sad. "I have that problem, too," I said.

"You do?" he asked, sounding hopeful.

"Sure," I smiled. "Sometimes after making love I can't get it up again for ten, fifteen minutes at a stretch."

Burt laughed despite himself. "You sonuvabitch! I'm *serious!*"

"I know you are. And you probably think you have some terminal disease."

"Maybe I do," he said.

"Maybe you're just not turned on."

"It's happened not only with Nancy."

For the next twenty minutes Burt and I talked about sex in general and the problems we were experiencing in particular. The basic area of agreement between us was that it wasn't as good now as it used to be, that it lacked the excitement, the frenzy we used to feel. That, for the most part, the sexual act—even with a new partner—rarely lived up to the anticipation, and that even though it felt good, the orgasm was never as sharp as that which we could give ourselves.

"And the thing is," Burt said, "Nancy wants it *all* the time."

"Every day?" I asked.

"No, but if we don't make it at least once every three days she starts turning mean. And the meaner she gets the less turned on I get."

"Well, that's not the problem I have with Alice," I said. "She *never* wants it."

"Never? But I thought she . . . I mean, she gives the impression that she is a very sexy lady."

"I know."

"So what do you do?"

"Daddy?"

I turned around. Joan was standing in the doorway.

"When are we going to have dinner?" she asked.

Burt looked at his watch. "I've got to be going," he said. "Call me if you'd like to hit a movie."

The following morning I had an appointment with Mr. Beckwith, the furnace man, and we spent twenty minutes on our backs in the basement crawl space while he showed me where the heat exchange at the top of the furnace had rusted out.

"You could get a new heat exchange from the factory," he said, "but by the time it's installed and adjusted you'll have spent almost as much as you would for a new furnace. And the new furnaces are much more efficient. You're going to have to do something. Your furnace is going to soot up the house. It's just a matter of time."

After Mr. Beckwith left I poured myself a cup of coffee and took it outside the front door facing the street. I sat down on the steps figuring that with the new furnace, the new side of the house, the new car, the new garage roof, I could expect to spend around ten thousand dollars— money I did not have.

But I knew, as I sipped my coffee, that I would have a check coming in soon from PBS and that eventually my mother's estate would be settled and I would own the house free and clear of debt. I realized that I did not need to panic. Everything was going to be all right.

That is why when Odette Villars approached on the sidewalk I was smiling. She was wearing washed-out old blue jeans, a cotton flannel shirt beneath her husband's cardigan.

"*Allo, ça va?*" I asked.

"*Oui,*" Odette replied. "*Et vous?*"

"*Tout va bien.*"

She then rattled off something in such rapid French that I was totally lost.

"I'm sorry," I said, "but if you are to speak with me in French you must speak slowly, as if to a child." I suddenly found myself laughing. "That sounded like Hemingway dialogue: 'The bridge is terminated. I was thinking of thee, Maria, and of a hotel in Madrid where I know some Russians, and of a book I will write sometime . . .' "

"Do you like Hemingway?"

"I think he is truly good. Would thee like some coffee? I've got to cut that out right now!"

"I don't think I want any coffee," Odette said, "but I'll sit here in the sun and have a cigarette with you."

"We could go inside," I said.

"No, I like the sun."

I made room for Odette on the steps of the house and she sat down next to me, turning her face up to the sun. She looked like an entirely different woman from when I had seen her last. The dark circles under her eyes that had made her look tired were gone, there was color in her cheeks, her hair shone.

"I have been taking advantage of the sun," she said. "I try to sit outside for an hour or so in the afternoon before the children return from school."

"How are your children?" I asked.

And so it all started, innocently enough. It always does.

Odette and I had a cigarette together; we talked about books and movies, our children and ourselves. She told me that after she had met me at Brandon's Market the afternoon she had crashed into the tower of grape soda cans she thought I had been so nice to her, and "not at all the sort of man" she had expected to find there, that she had asked who I was.

"They told me you were a *metteur en scène*," Odette said, "but no one had ever seen any of your films. You must be very intellectual, yes?"

"You mean because nobody has seen my films? I don't do the sort of movies you're thinking of. I do documentaries. For television. They aren't shown in theaters. And I do things that are crap, too. For money."

"Why not?" Odette asked. "One has to eat. There is a difference between what an *artiste* does for himself and what he does for money. . . . It is delicious here in the sun." She unbuttoned the cardigan sweater and when she shrugged it back from her shoulders I could not help but notice she was not wearing a bra and I forced myself not to look at her nipples pressing against the cotton of her shirt and the outline of her small breasts. But when she leaned back on her elbows to return her face to the sun and closed her eyes I stole another look. I thought she was utterly beautiful.

While Alice was in Puerto Rico, Odette and I met three or four times. We would have a cup of coffee together; I would drop by her house on the way to the market or the mailbox on the corner, stay fifteen minutes, then flee out of nerves or guilt at talking with another woman while my wife was away. Alice had done that to me.

No—I had done that to myself.

Odette's daughter, Vanessa, was almost Peter's age and her son, Paul, was younger by two years. Her children would drift down the street in the late afternoon to play and either Odette would pick them up at my house, or I would walk them home to hers. They were perfectly capable of making the walk by themselves, but the children gave Odette and me a chance to talk. By the end of that first week the Villars children and mine had become friends. So had their mother and I. Paul would tag along after Peter like a small terrier at his heels. Vanessa would sit for hours braiding Joan's hair. Odette and I would sit on the lawn and laugh and talk. That first Sunday afternoon Odette brought her husband Arthur down for a drink. "I've been wanting to meet you," he said. "Odette talks about you all the time."

It seemed a benign enough comment.

Alice's "week or so" in Puerto Rico turned out to be ten days. Burt Taylor had replaced most of the rotten clapboards by the time she got home. A stone mason had come and begun pointing up the fieldstone where the house leaked. I was busy working either in my office or outside. The temperature had risen enough to open the swimming pool, and once I got the residual water pumped out, I spent my late afternoons cleaning and painting the bottom. I did not see Odette at all during this period and I was surprised by how much I missed her. I made excuses to walk up to the market just on the chance that I might run into her. On a couple of occasions I drove by her house. But her car wasn't there and I assumed she had gone away.

And then about two weeks after Alice had returned Odette telephoned to invite Alice and me to dinner. Alice was out marketing so I was the one to answer the phone.

"Have you been away?" I asked.

"Arthur's had a series of meetings in New York so we've been in and out. I went to Southampton for a week, too, to stay with a friend."

"Are you tanned and beautiful?" I asked.

"Well, I'm tanned . . ." Odette said, and laughed.

"I missed you," I said.

There was silence.

"I don't mean to embarrass you," I told her. "I just meant to tell you I liked seeing you around."

"Well we'll be here for a while now. Can you and Alice come to dinner the twenty-sixth? We'd both like to meet your wife."

"The twenty-sixth? What day is that?" I asked.

"This Saturday night."

"I don't see why not," I said. "What time?"

When Alice returned from the market and I told her about the invitation she asked why we had been invited.

"I saw Odette several times when you were away. I think the two of you will like each other."

Alice looked at me curiously. "When did you see her?"

"I met her first at the market over the spring break and then she walked by one afternoon while I was sitting outside and we talked. She has two children about Peter's age and they came over here a couple of times to play. So we—Odette and I—saw each other then. She's very nice, really. I think you'll like her."

"What's her husband like?"

"Arthur? He's a psychiatrist. He seems nice. I've only met him once."

"Where do they live?"

"They bought the Kelloggs' house."

The Villars were the third couple to have owned the gray Federal house two blocks up from Brandon's Market since Alice and I had moved to town. Each of the men who had lived there had been psychiatrists. The first had abandoned Jung for Krishnamurti and vegetarianism and had been divorced almost immediately by his wife. The second couple were both child psychologists—well, she was a psychologist, he a psychiatrist—and had painted the downstairs rooms in bright primary colors. They had also covered the beautiful old wide chestnut floors with speckled linoleum and let the house deteriorate badly. They stayed four years, then moved to Texas to accept positions with a juvenile detention home.

The Villars had spent their first six months in the house ripping up the linoleum, scraping, painting, refinishing, and scrubbing. The toilets, evidently, had not been cleaned in years. That is why, or partially why, Odette had looked so tired when I first saw her.

That first night we had dinner with Arthur and Odette, Alice and I brought a couple of bottles of French wine, which Arthur accepted saying: "You know you can get a California Burgundy at the bottle shop that is even better than this and it costs a dollar and a half less."

"I wish I'd known that," I said.

Alice and Odette seemed to get along well, each of them at one point expressing her pleasure at discovering a "friend" on the same street. Odette said it had been the worst winter of her life, that she had been very lonely, felt very much the foreigner and had wanted to go back to France.

Alice said everyone felt the same way when they first moved here.

"And during the winter months," I said, "people don't entertain much. Everyone stays pretty close to home."

"That's not so," Alice said. "Everyone takes off for a vacation in February—everyone," she added, "but us."

I left the kitchen and went outside to join Arthur. We stood there over the barbecue speaking about the things men talk about who are thrown together without knowing each other well: sports, the economy, house repairs, the real estate market, automobiles, town politics, the sort of topics one can skip in and out of without too much trouble. A couple of times I felt I had said something relatively amusing, funny enough to have warranted a polite laugh. Arthur, I discovered, did not have the same sense of humor.

When we walked back into the house Alice was sitting at the kitchen table with Odette. "Women power!" Alice was saying. She waved her fist in the air. "The revolution is coming. Things are going to change!" Alice looked up at me and repeated, "Things are going to change."

"Down, Fang," I said.

Odette laughed.

"Things are changing, *have* changed," Arthur said. "The women's movement has already had enormous impact on men's consciousness. We are all trying to break through that male-female role-playing, which is so dangerous and has created such resentments. Emotions were considered feminine; rational thinking and problem-solving were considered masculine. Now we understand men have feelings and women are in decision-making positions. We are forced to confront one another on a person-to-person rather than gender-to-gender basis. It is the movement that has made women confident enough to be self-assertive. To go after what they want."

"What *do* they want?" I asked.

"Women want *wives!*" Alice said. "Someone to do the shopping, the laundry, the meals, to clean up after the kids. Why should women always be the ones to have to do these things?" Alice asked.

"Because traditionally women tended the campfires while men hunted the meat," I said.

"When was the last time you went out to hunt meat?" Alice asked.

"The day before you returned from Puerto Rico," I said. "Armed only with a tattered ten-dollar bill I fought my way up to Brandon's Market past cunning bicyclists, giant pickups, sullen suburban matrons in station wagons, where I killed some savage freshly ground top sirloin for the kids."

"You bought ground top *sirloin* for the kids?" Alice asked.

"Alice," I said, "the point I was trying to make is that the majority of men are still away from the cave all day at jobs while the women are tending the fires at home."

"What about women who have jobs?" Odette asked.

"Then the work should be shared," I said.

"Don't you share the work now?" she asked, surprised.

"Of course we do," I said. "We—"

"—We don't." Alice interrupted.

"We may not do the same jobs," I said, "but we share the load."

"I cook, he eats," Alice said.

"That's not fair, Alice!" I protested.

"You're right. It isn't," she said.

"You make dinner. I make the breakfasts and lunches," I said.

"I don't eat breakfast or lunch," Alice said.

"The children do," I said.

"But you get up with them," Alice said. "Why shouldn't you make their breakfasts? They're your children, too."

"I know, I know," I said. "I don't mind doing it. I only—"

"Why should you *mind* doing it?" Alice demanded.

"Alice, I thought we were talking about the feminist movement," I said, glancing over at Arthur and Odette. "I don't want to get into an argument with you over who does what for the children."

"Who does what for the children is at the *root* of the feminist movement," Alice said.

"No, it isn't," I said. "The root of the feminist movement is economic. That's what the Equal Rights Amendment is all about. Equal pay for equal work. As it now stands the average woman is paid—"

"—fifty-nine cents for doing the same work a man gets paid a dollar for. I know that!" Alice said. "That's not what I'm talking about. I'm talking about women being treated like second-class citizens in their own homes."

"Do you think I treat you like a second-class citizen?" I asked.

"Who's talking about *you?*" Alice asked. "Why is it whenever I talk about men in general you take it personally?"

"I suppose because since I'm the man you've lived with for the past ten years, I'm the one with whom you have the most experience and I assume you're basing your opinions on personal experience."

"You're not the only man I know," she said. "Not every man is like you."

"Dinner's ready," Arthur said.

I hated these conversations with Alice. I never could understand why she became so angry so swiftly. I complimented Arthur on his wine, Odette on her *gratin de pommes de terre à la dauphinoise,* said the dinner was delicious. I tried not to say anything that would fuel Alice's rage, but still it was difficult to ignore the tensions between us. She was so touchy that even the most innocuous comment would anger her and I was seldom aware of what specifically had set her off.

Was I a male chauvinist pig? In Alice's eyes, yes. To say that it was not deliberate—of course, that only made my attitude all the more infuriating. I was a natural. By which, I mean, I acted the way I had been brought up to act. I didn't think I was behaving any differently from other men my age I knew. The roles had been established long before I joined the cast; I was only following the script: A man works to make life possible, a woman to make it pleasurable, or something like that.

Problems occur in a marriage when a couple begins keeping score. When the woman one marries doesn't want to be a wife and the man doesn't want to be a husband. For what are a husband and wife but a couple who want to make life better for each other? It's easy when a couple is in love. But Alice and I had not even really liked each other for some time—*nor had we met any other couples who did!* We were all so caught up in resenting our spouses for real and imagined sins that I had come to believe there wasn't any such thing as a happy marriage, that it could not exist. It certainly didn't exist among the couples Alice and I saw. Somewhere along the line each of those marriages had contracted a disease, in many cases one which was terminal, and one sensed the couples were simply waiting for the marriage to die. They had started out healthily enough; in some of their houses wedding photographs were still on display: the young bride and bridegroom smiling out from under now-bizarre haircuts and hairdos, grinning at the photographer with that confidence one has at having successfully climbed up one more step on the ladder of the American dream.

What happy, humming domesticity we envisioned. What fun it had been to select our costumes, houses, dogs, for our roles.

But then what had been fun became commonplace, and what had been mildly amusing in the other became aggravating: the husband's habit of hanging his trousers by their cuffs clamped in the top bureau drawer; the wife's little pile of crumpled Kleenex on the bedside table, the husband leaving the toilet seat up after taking a leak, the wife's leaving the automobile with an empty gas tank before the morning station commute—the hundred little acts or habits then become magnified into deliberately thoughtless provocations so that when one next saw the other a battle would break out—or worse, one faced the other's sodden, interminable sulk.

"Darling? Is there something wrong?"

"Fuck off."

Somewhere along the line we forgot how to be friends. We forgot how to have fun together, to play, to make the effort, to care. We forgot to encourage and compliment each other, to flirt, to surprise, to gift. The bright shiny child's toy that once was our marriage had become bent, battered, and chipped. And rather than try to revive its luster, to repair it, we cast about for something or someone new.

We accepted that passion would die; we were resigned to that. But we expected something deeper automatically to take its place: a companionship, a closeness that would illume us as a couple, suffuse our faces— our *beings*—much as faith lent translucence to the martyr's skins. When this didn't happen, we felt disappointed, even betrayed.

Where had we picked up such romantic ideas?

In books. Movies. Fairy tales. From our own secret longings.

I don't remember seeing during my childhood such a companionship at home. (I was seldom there; and even when I was home one parent or the other would be away.) Did I think, in the absence of myself and my brother, that my parents were deeply in love? No. But *their* parents— my grandparents—were.

Or were they?

My grandparents had been married to one another until they were separated by death. But that might be attributable to the fact that divorce for their generation was unthinkable. Accommodations, compromises, were made.

Alice and I made compromises, too. "Trade-offs" might be a more accurate word since we kept score. And since a score is important only when one is competing, it follows that we must have been engaged in some sort of contest short of war. But the difficulty I had with the game Alice and I were playing was that either she or the times we were living in kept rewriting the rules. That is why that night at dinner with Arthur and Odette, when the topic of men and women arose, I could not hide the apprehension I felt.

"Why do men feel so threatened," Alice was saying, "when all we women ask is to be treated as equals?"

"Do you feel you're not being treated equally?" I asked her.

"Equal to what?" she asked. "I'm treated like a housemaid except that I don't get paid for it."

"Oh, for Chrissake, Alice!" I said impatiently.

"What is our alternative?" Odette asked. "That is the issue. If we leave our homes for a job, hire someone to take care of our children and do our housework . . . what job can we get that pays us as much as we pay those we've hired? We'd all be getting minimum wage."

"Unless," Arthur said, "you had a trade or provided a service there is a demand for."

"But I *did* have," Odette said. "And I quit my job when we had Vanessa because you didn't want me to work. So I stayed *home* and worked. I kept our house, raised our children, paid our bills, while you

got through your residency, began your practice. Now *you're* all set and
I'm ten years out of the job market."

"What did you do?" I asked her.

"I was a brain surgeon," Odette said.

There was a moment of stunned silence.

Arthur said, "Odette was a linguist, she—"

"I was with an import-export firm," Odette interrupted. "I was in their
market-research department . . ." She explained that her official title
was "executive bilingual secretary," and that she translated the paperwork
from English into French, French into English, did research on European
products, looked after the Europeans when they came to New York. But
I was listening with only one ear.

I was still thinking of her "I was a brain surgeon" reply, that it was
the sort of off-the-wall comment Carter would have made and loved.

". . . I was beginning to get somewhere," Odette was saying, "I *was*,"
she said, looking defensively at Arthur, "and I gave it all up."

"And now," Alice said, looking at Odette, "the two of us are dependent
for money upon them." She waved her hand at Arthur and me. "It's
degrading! You yourself," Alice said, pointing at me, "said the root of
the feminist movement is economic. So is the relationship between a
husband and wife. The wife works in the home. Why isn't she paid?"

"She *is*," I said. "Although a salary may not be paid, she has access to
his salary, she is protected, taken care of, sheltered, clothed. His
retirement, life insurance, *et cetera*, provides a pension plan. . . . Again,
you have to return—symbolically, anyway—to the campfire and the cave
and traditional roles. The man brought home the meat, the woman
cooked it."

"We've come a long way, baby," Alice said.

I ignored the sarcasm. "Odette made a very interesting point," I said,
"and that is the 'Catch 22' of the women's movement. These women who
left the job market to raise families cannot readily reenter the market
when their children are grown. What kind of a job can a thirty-five to
forty-five-year-old woman get whose job credentials for the previous
fifteen to twenty years were those of a house mop?"

"Cleaning lady," Alice said.

"A waitress," Odette said.

"A lot of women seem to go into real estate," Arthur said. Then he
added, "But Alice had a good point, too. The economic dependence of
wives upon their husbands is degrading."

"Being poor is degrading," I said. "I listen to women saying how much they hate to cook, to clean, to do housework, and I can sympathize with them, but how many men do you think enjoy their jobs? What percentage of American males is fulfilled by their work? Five percent?"

"What has that got to do with anything?" Alice asked.

"The point is most men don't like what they're doing *either*," I said. "In addition they have the terror of growing older, of being replaced by younger men, of being cast out of the companies for which they've worked for twenty years with little hope of reemployment after the age of forty-five, at the same time as their family's demanding a greater income to meet college expenses . . ."

"That is why so many women are now going to work," Odette said. "But when they come home they're still expected to cook dinner, do the house cleaning and laundry, take time off to drive the children to their dentist appointments. . . . A woman who works outside the home is still considered by her husband—and her community—to be working 'part time.' Somehow her job isn't as *serious* as her husband's. A man wonders why a woman can't be fulfilled and be married, too, and some women *can*. Some women *are*. It depends on the woman, on the marriage. But for the majority of women, there is no fulfillment in doing the same tasks over and over again. There is no satisfaction in doing the laundry, mopping the kitchen floor, scrubbing the bathtub well. It's just going to have to be done all over again."

"So what is the answer?" I asked.

"The answer is to pay the wife what you would have to pay someone to do those tasks for you," Alice said.

"How do you feel about that?" Arthur asked me.

"I think that what Alice is talking about here is not a marital relationship but a business relationship. And if that's so, should the husband then charge rent if he owns the house? Should he deduct the cost of her food, the use of the company car, health insurance? Does he have the right to fire? To hire? Should there be separate checking and savings accounts? Do they share the children's expenses? Medical bills, tuition, clothing? If a couple bill each other for the services they render one another why be married at all?"

"Why *be* married?" Arthur asked me.

"Jesus, Arthur," I said. "You're doing a psychiatrist number on me. You answer one question with another."

"See?" Alice said. "He feels threatened."

"Not 'threatened,' " I said. "Impatient."

"Why?" Arthur asked.

In exasperation I glanced over at Odette. "Why does anyone get married?" I asked. "It's a matter of choice. One chooses to marry instead of choosing to live alone."

"But people live together without marrying," Arthur said. "The reason people marry is generally because they want to raise a family, have children. If you don't want children, why marry?"

"To make that commitment," I said. "I married because I wanted to marry. Because I was ready for that commitment."

"I don't want to make this personal," Arthur said. "I'm not asking you why you married Alice. I'm asking you why if you were not married now you would choose to marry again?"

"I don't know that I would marry again," I said. "I don't think I would unless . . . unless I met a woman I was so utterly in love with that I knew I never wanted to live without her. Marriage should be more than a convenience, an exchange of services. A marriage should be the merging of two souls. The combining of a man and a woman's spirit and strength, their determination to succeed with one another against all the outside opposing forces."

"You seem very idealistic," Arthur said.

"Whatever that means," I said.

"Arthur," Odette said, "do you think women are more idealistic than men?"

"I suppose," Arthur said, "we must define what one means by 'idealistic.' If you mean—"

"I mean, Arthur, less realistic," Odette said. "Less practical, governed more by their emotions than men."

"Then we're not talking about 'idealism' at all, are we?" he said. "You're asking me if I think women are less realistic."

"That's what I just said," Odette replied.

"In some ways I would have to say 'yes,' in other areas 'no,' " Arthur said. "Generalities are always dangerous." He pushed himself away from the table. "Shall we have coffee in the garden?"

"Isn't there also the suggestion that to be idealistic is the opposite of being cynical?" I asked.

"*Nobody's* more cynical than women!" Alice said. "We've seen it all. We've heard all the lies, faced all the disappointments, cleaned up the mess you men have made of our lives, and now we're saying, *enough!* We've had enough!" Alice stood up next to Arthur. She waved her fist in the air again. "The revolution is coming!"

"Every revolution is based on ideals, Alice," I said.

"Bullshit!" she replied. "Revolutions occur because the poor and oppressed aren't willing to tolerate the injustices and repression of the ruling class!"

"What ruling class?" I asked as I stood up. "We men? Your husbands? Jesus, Alice, the vast majority of men haven't got the *energy* to repress women. For Chrissake, we're just trying to do our jobs, to get along, to survive!"

"Your fly's open," she said, and taking advantage of my embarrassment and confusion, she took Arthur's arm and walked with him out of the kitchen into the garden.

I was still standing behind my chair, Odette was standing behind hers. I zipped up my fly, then started stacking the plates to carry them over to the sink.

"Leave them," Odette said, "we'll do it all later."

"Why don't I just clear the table?"

"I'll do it," she said.

"No, you make some coffee and while you do that I'll get this done."

Odette and I worked silently together. We could hear Arthur and Alice laughing in the garden. I was scraping the plates into the garbage. "Your dinner was delicious, Odette."

"You enjoyed it?"

"I regret only that Alice and I always seem to act out our psychodramas in front of others."

"I did not understand her anger. I am not a feminist, I think, like she is. But perhaps it is not the same. I have not had the reason. Arthur and I always shared the housework, the children, the cooking. Evidently you do not."

"I don't know how to cook very well."

"You could learn," she said.

"I suppose so," I said uncertainly.

"You don't sound convinced."

"I'm aware of my limitations," I said.

Odette placed a pot of coffee on a tray and surrounded it with cups and spoons. I picked up the tray and followed her out to the small garden behind the house.

Alice smiled brightly at Odette. "Arthur tells me the two of you are leaving for France in a couple of weeks."

"As soon as the children are out of school," Odette said. "We like to go back at least once a year so that I can see my family. The children can retain their French, their *grand'maman* can see them."

"I've never been to France," Alice said.

"But that is deplorable," Odette said, turning to me. "You must really go together. Just the two of you."

Alice simply looked at me and laughed.

Later on that evening as Alice and I walked home I asked her how she had liked the Villars.

"They seem nice," she said.

"You seemed to get along well with Odette. It would be nice if you two could be friends."

"Why shouldn't we be?" she asked.

"There's no reason why you shouldn't be. I was saying only that it would be nice if you had a friend close by. . . . How did you like Arthur?"

"He's very handsome."

"Do you think so, really?"

"You don't?" she asked.

"I hadn't given it much thought," I said. "He doesn't strike me as having much of a sense of humor. Otherwise he seems a nice guy. . . . A bit of a wine bore, perhaps. But that seems to be the fashion among doctors. I don't think I ever caught what kind of a psychiatrist he is. Does he see private patients?"

"Of course he does."

"But not at the house, right?"

"He has an office in Princeton. He's connected with the university. And twice a week he goes to his office in New York."

"New York, too? He must keep busy."

"There are a lot of fucked-up people around here," Alice said.

"Not just around here, I suspect."

We were at our property line now, passing the tall hedges that blocked the view into our garden. A light was on in the library. Joan was probably watching TV.

"Have you made Joan's plane reservations yet?" Alice asked.

"No, not yet. I'll call tomorrow."

"Tomorrow's Sunday," Alice said. "The travel agency will be closed Monday Memorial Day, too."

Joan was waiting up for us when we walked in. "Daddy, Harry Abbott called. He said he wants you to call him as soon as you came in. He says it's important."

"Didn't you give him the number of where we were?"

"He said he tried to call you at the Villars' but their phone was off the hook."

I recognized the telephone number Joanie gave me as that of ABC News. It took a little while for me to get through to Harry. "Are you doing anything tomorrow?" Harry asked.

"Not that I know of, why?"

"Two of the news cameramen have called in sick. Hedley wants some footage of a Memorial Day ceremony in a small town and I thought maybe you could shoot the film. I'd do the sound for you and they'll send out one of their asshole correspondents to do the narration. What do you think?"

"Sure. There's one at Rosemont about eight miles from here that would be just right."

"Meet you at your house?"

"It will start at eleven," I said, "better be here by ten."

"That means leaving the city by eight," Harry said, "Wonder-boy will love that."

"See you then, Harry," I said and hung up.

Rosemont is a little town down the road with a population of under two hundred. I thought their Memorial Day ceremony would be good because a new monument was being dedicated to the Rosemont men who had served during the Korean and Vietnam wars. I asked Alice if she would like to go with me. She did not. Nor did Joan. Joan preferred to go into Princeton where she might run into a friend. Peter would want to go with Joan because there would be a marching band.

That night in bed next to Alice I thought about Odette, how easy it had been to talk with her, how nice it was to find a female friend. The last thing I thought about before I fell asleep was to ask Odette if she and her children would like to go to the Rosemont Memorial Day ceremony with the ABC crew and me. I would call her in the morning.

Again, I think it's important to say that it all started out innocently enough. By that, I mean, if I was aware that I was taking a big step by calling Odette, I suppressed it at the time. Instead I convinced myself that calling her was more a "neighborly gesture" than a means of being with her. And, yes, I suppose it was a chance to show off a little, too. Odette had never seen me at work with my camera.

At breakfast I asked Alice again if she wanted to go to Rosemont with me and when she said she didn't, I said, "Maybe I'll call Odette."

"Odette? Why?"

"She's probably never been to a Memorial Day service in a small town. It might be interesting for her to watch how it's covered by a news team."

"Will you take the children?"

"Joan and Peter don't want to go."

"Her children," Alice said.

"Sure, if they want to come."

When I telephoned Odette she said Arthur was taking Vanessa and Paul to a miniature golf course, but that she thought it would be fun to come.

"You'll come? Really?" I asked. I could not hide the pleasure in my voice.

"Of course I will," she said. "Alice and I can chat while you work."

"Alice isn't coming," I said. "It will just be you and me—and ABC News."

There was a slight pause and then Odette said, "Should I come down to your house or will you pick me up?"

"I'll pick you up," I said.

When I told Alice that Odette would go with me she said, "That's ducky."

Harry Abbott arrived with Brad Edwards, the ABC News correspondent, a little after ten. They parked the white station wagon with its black ABC News logo on the roof and doors near the garage so I could load my camera, lenses, film, and cartridges into it. Alice, wearing a pair of faded cotton cut-offs and a tank top, came outside with me to greet them.

"Hello, Alice," Harry said, "you're looking good." And he kissed her on the cheek.

Brad Edwards climbed out of the car and introduced himself to Alice and me. He was young, not yet thirty, and handsome in that inoffensive way TV newscasters sometimes have. "It's a great pleasure to meet you both," Edwards said.

Alice and I were so startled by the resonance of his network voice that neither of us responded. And in the silence Edwards glanced about at the garage, the high fence and hedges around the house, then said, "You have a lovely place."

"You can't really see much of it from here," Alice said. "Would you like to come inside?"

Edwards glanced at Harry Abbott. "Do we have time?"

"Go ahead," I said. "I still have to load my gear."

"I've always been interested in old houses," Edwards said.

"Well, this is an old house, all right," Alice said.

Harry gave me a hand with my stuff. "How's it going with you?" he asked. "I hear the cancer film's terrific."

"It's in New York. They're laying in the sound now."

"You know I saw the Hawaii promo on TV the other night."

"You saw it? How?"

"Apparently they've cut it up into a commercial. You'll be interested to know they kept the torch-surfing sequence in. It runs about two seconds, but it's there. So is Nora in the waterfall. They gave her a good five seconds."

"I saw a lot of Nora this winter. She was at the same college I was teaching at."

"Oh yeah?" Harry asked. "How was she?"

"Fine," I said.

"I'll bet," he said, and laughed.

The gate opened and Alice and Brad Edwards reappeared. "We all set?" Edwards asked.

"We have to make one stop on the way," I said. "I told a friend we'd pick her up."

"A friend?" Harry asked.

"Odette Villars. She lives up the street."

" 'Odette . . .' " Edwards said. "She must be French."

Harry rolled his eyes at me. "Did you see how quick 'Scoop' here picked up on that? You just can't beat a keen newscaster's mind."

Edwards looked a bit embarrassedly at Alice, then back at Harry. "C'mon, Abbott, will you? Give me a break."

"I'll get in the back," I said.

Edwards turned to Alice. "You're not coming?"

Alice shook her head. "No, I'm going into Princeton with the kids."

I was relieved she hadn't changed her mind. I didn't want to be with Alice; I wanted to be with Odette.

Odette was waiting for us in front of her house. She was wearing her French jeans, a silk blouse with a tweed jacket on top. I got out of the car and opened the door for her. "Good morning," I said, and kissed her on the cheek. She slid into the back seat beside me and I introduced her around. "Harry will do the sound and Brad the narration," I explained.

"What am I going to say?" Edwards asked. "Maybe you ought to give me a little background on this town. They're dedicating a new monument, is that right?"

"That's right," I said. "It's to the town's Korean and Vietnam veterans."

"So we'll want to say something about that . . ." Edwards said, and he made a note. He twisted in the front seat to look back at me. "Rosemont, I gather, was your idea. What was your thinking behind that?"

My thinking at the moment was how nice it was to feel the pressure of Odette's shoulder and her long legs next to mine. "It's a very small town," I said. "And a very small town will sometimes project a truer image of how people really feel. Small-town speakers say what they think, not what they think should be said—"

"Hey, that's terrific," Edwards said. "I want to write it down just like that . . . 'Say what they think, not what they think should be said . . .' "

"The speaker will be a man named MacKenzie," I continued. "He owns the local hardware store. He was instrumental in having the new monument put up. The Vietnam veterans asked him to say something at its dedication, so he will."

"What about the visuals?"

"It'll be pretty straightforward stuff. Dedication of the monument, parade to the cemetery, 'Taps,' a chaplain."

"Parade, eh?" Edwards said. "A marching band?"

"Fife and drums," I said.

"Outta sight!" Edwards said.

"John Denver lives!" Harry muttered from the front seat.

"So it starts with the new monument dedication," Edwards said, "then there's a parade—where is the monument? In the cemetery or in town?"

"On the town green," I said. "It's not much of a 'green' though. More a little park. It's not but about ten yards square."

We drove on in silence for several minutes and then I leaned forward. "Bear right at this fork, Harry," I told him. "We'll be there in just a few more miles." I looked at my watch. It was almost ten-thirty.

"A few more *miles?*" Edwards said, alarmed. "Jesus, what am I going to say? You guys have got to help me out."

"I don't think you'll have to say very much," I told him. "What we can do is shoot the dedication, some of the parade, the ceremony at the cemetery, and we can write a voice-over afterwards."

The narrow two-lane highway twisted down a steep, curving hill and the little town of Rosemont lay ahead. The Fife and Drum Corps was already milling about the sides of the main street. They were dressed in their handsome Revolutionary War uniforms and the corps's younger members wore their long hair pulled neatly back and tied with ribbons.

There was an honor guard from a local VFW post carrying the thirteen-starred colonial flag and the 1775 flag—the red-and-white-striped flag with a Union Jack in the upper left-hand corner—they also carried the current fifty-starred flag, too. Harry parked off to the side and Odette and I got out and went around to the back of the station wagon to unload the gear. Edwards remained in the front seat. He had adjusted the rearview mirror so that he could see in it to comb his hair.

Harry was leaning into the open back of the station wagon. "You forgot your tripod," he told me.

"I'm not going to be using the Arriflex," I said. "I brought the CP-16. I like it better."

Odette was standing off to one side. I gave her the Angenieux lens in its case to hold, then slid the camera out of the back and tightened the shoulder grip. I took the lens back from Odette and mounted it on the camera.

"Can I help?" Odette asked.

"Can you hand me the film cartridge? It's that gray boxy thing near the seat."

Odette bent forward to reach into the back of the station wagon, then turned to ask me if what she had her hand on was what I meant, but instead she caught me admiring the curve of her ass. I smiled sheepishly and she smiled, also, and gave her rear such a joyful wiggle that I laughed out loud and she did, too.

"You've got it," I said.

"What?" she asked.

"The film cartridge," I said, then laughed again. "Among other things." I took the cartridge from her and slipped it into the camera. Harry Abbott had unpacked the Nagra 4.2 tape recorder, and as I raised the 35-mm camera to my shoulder, Harry lifted out the recorder. "Odette," he said, "can you get the Sennheiser for me?"

"It's the shotgun microphone on the floor there," I said.

Odette bent over again to reach into the back of the station wagon. This time I caught Harry giving her an admiring look. She pulled out the microphone and straightened up. "Is there anything else you need?"

Harry plucked his watch off his wrist and tossed it far into the back. "I seem to have left my watch somewhere in there," he said.

Odette just smiled.

We could hear the snare drummers practicing riffs and a few of the fife players doing trills. I looked at my watch. "It should begin in another ten minutes," I said. We walked across the road to the small green and the townspeople moved away to give us room. I spotted Mr. MacKenzie in the crowd and waved to him. He came over and I introduced him to Odette and Harry and explained what we were doing there. Edwards ambled over and I introduced MacKenzie to him, too.

"I don't want you to be nervous," Edwards told MacKenzie.

"Why should I be nervous?" MacKenzie asked. "I live here."

"Fine," Edwards said.

"Mr. MacKenzie," I said, "where will you be standing when you dedicate the monument?"

MacKenzie walked over to the new granite monument. "I'll be right here. But Tom Mahoney and the priest come before me."

"What will they do?" I asked.

"Father Solowinski will say a prayer. And Tom Mahoney, he served in Vietnam with the 3rd Marine Brigade—he's standing over there in the dress blues—will read the names of those on the new monument, and I'll make a short speech, then the parade to the cemetery begins."

I took up a position on the edge of the green and framed my shot. I could pull in close on the speakers if I needed to, otherwise I could keep the whole green with the Rosemont Fife and Drum Corps lined up in the background. "Will we be in the way if we film from here?" I asked.

"Suit yourself," MacKenzie said.

Harry Abbott had set up the Nagra and he came over to MacKenzie and me. "I wonder if I might get a sound-level reading from you," he said. "Would you mind just standing where you'll give your talk and say a few words?"

"What should I say?" MacKenzie asked.

"Doesn't matter," Harry said. "Anything."

I looked around for Odette. She was standing with Brad Edwards on the other side of the green. When she saw me looking at her she came over.

"He's adorable," she said. "He really is! He's so young and he wants so much to be good. He's over there all worried about what he's going to say. He thinks you're marvelous."

"Me? Why?"

"Because you've helped him out. He says usually the cameramen treat him like he was dirt."

I looked over at Brad. He was nervously adjusting his tie. I beckoned him over. "You okay?" I asked him.

Edwards nodded.

"I think we can let the ceremony tell its own story," I said. "We'll shoot it and then come back and you can fill in the blanks, okay?"

"Should I do an intro?"

"If we need one we'll shoot it later," I said.

There was a drum roll. The Rosemont Fife and Drum Corps assembled into two orderly ranks. Father Solowinski said a short prayer, then the Vietnam vet came forward to read the names of the men on the new monument. I had fortunately pulled back far enough so that when Mahoney walked into the shot it was possible to see from his limp that he wore an artificial leg.

Odette, standing next to me, whispered, "He's so young!"

Forty-five minutes later we were packing the equipment back into the station wagon. We had filmed an introduction and a closing: "This is Brad Edwards in Rosemont, New Jersey, for ABC News." MacKenzie invited us back to the firehouse for a beer and he told Odette he knew her house well, that it had belonged to his grandparents and that it should last another two hundred years. Two pretty teenaged girls asked Edwards for his autograph and he was happy.

On the drive back home Odette and Harry sat together in the front seat while in the back I worked with Edwards on the script for a voice-over narration he could tape at the studio when he returned to New York. At Odette's house she and I got out together. Even Harry got out to kiss her good-bye.

"I had so much fun!" Odette told him. "It was nice of you to include me."

"Any time, *any* time," Harry said. "It was a pleasure to have you along."

Brad Edwards stuck his head out the window and told Odette to call him if she was ever in New York. "You, too," he added, looking at me. "I wish you worked with us at ABC."

"Sometimes I wish I did, too," I said. I turned to Odette. "I'll call you when I get home. I just want to unload my gear, then why don't you come down?"

When Harry dropped me at my house I told him his film was in the back seat and to telephone me if there were any problems, then I went into the yard. Vanessa and Paul were playing with Peter beside the pool. Joan was keeping an eye on them.

"Where's Alice?" I asked her.

"She went off with Mr. Villars," Joan said. "I don't know where they went."

I telephoned Odette to tell her her children were at my house.

"I wasn't worried," she said.

"And Alice is off with Arthur somewhere."

"That doesn't worry me either."

"*That's savoir-faire!*" I said.

"What?"

"It's just the punch line of an old joke."

She did not say anything.

"Would you like to come down for a swim?"

"Thank you, no. I think I'm going to take advantage of the peace and quiet."

"How 'bout a drink later on?"

"We'll see," she said. "Send the children back if you get tired of them."

"No," I said. "They're fine. They entertain each other."

"Maybe I'll see you later, then."

"I hope so."

I did not see Odette again that day; in fact, I saw her only once briefly during the next week because I had to work on the cancer film in New York. She was at the check-out counter of Brandon's Market when I stopped in to buy a six-pack of tonic. We had little opportunity to talk.

Both Peter and Joan finished school at the end of the first week in June and the Villars left for France. I telephoned Odette the afternoon before they left to wish her *bon voyage*. I'm not sure it was the right thing to have done. I sensed that she was a little surprised I had called. There was a somewhat uneasy silence, which I filled by blurting out an invitation to her to come down for a swim.

"Arthur won't be back much before five-thirty," she said.

"Leave him a note telling him to come when he gets back."

"Well, all right . . ." she said.

When I went back into the house to tell Alice I had invited the Villars down for a swim she surprised me by not seeming the least upset.

Odette and her two children arrived at about four, Arthur at about a quarter to six. We ended up barbecuing hamburgers. Arthur spoke mostly with Alice, and I with Odette. There was nothing special about that evening as I recall. The Villars left reasonably early because they wanted the children to get a good night's sleep before the trip and Odette wanted to pack.

I was sorry to see her go and told her.

A week or so later I drove Joan to Newark to catch her flight to Oregon where she was to spend the summer and, ostensibly, the next year with her mother.

Joan has no memory whatsoever of her mother and me living together; she does remember my leaving, though. When her mother and I separated and Maggie moved away, I saw my daughter only on vacations. Along with the physical distance came an emotional distance as well. We drifted apart until 1976 when Joan came back to live with me. By then she was ten and she had learned to hold her emotions in. She didn't smile much; she didn't really expose her inner thoughts at all. She had become distant with me, aloof, both untouchable and untouched.

I knew she was jealous of the attention Peter, the youngest, got. I tried to diminish Joan's resentment by being consistent in my treatment of them both. But the age difference made equality impossible.

She did not like me to hug her, to express affection in front of others. It embarrassed her if I put my arm around her shoulder. I don't know why. Alice didn't like me to hug her either, but it was hardly the same situation. That first night I came back from Leadville I remember how surprised I was when Joan hugged me and said that she loved me and was happy I was home. It was the first outward sign of affection she had shown me in a long time. I glanced at my daughter sitting silently next to me in my old Peugeot. I wondered what she was thinking.

Joan did not like me to question her too closely about her feelings or what she wanted to do. She had said she wanted to be a photographer and I bought her a camera and offered to give her lessons. She left the camera behind when she went out to her mother's. She said she wanted to play the guitar, but never expressed any desire for lessons. I wished I knew what was to become of her. I was thinking about all this during the drive to the airport because Joan and I hardly spoke.

"Write me, will you?" I said as she boarded the plane.

"I will."

"And let me know if there's anything you need."

"Okay."

"Have a good summer."

"You, too."

"I'm going to miss you," I said. "A year is a long, long time."

When I returned home I had to begin preparing the library for its new coat of paint.

All the books needed to be taken off the shelves and moved into another room, a job that should not have taken too long, except that I kept discovering books I'd forgotten I had and I'd have to dip into them and read a little bit here and there.

Barbara T. arrived to help Alice choose new slipcovers and a paint color and the two of them were gone the majority of the first few mornings

but spent their afternoons in the sun around the pool. Once I started
prime-coating the library they would occasionally come in, shining with
perspiration and suntan oils and stand around in their bikinis inspecting
the progress.

At night with Alice asleep beside me I would think of Barbara T. in
the guest bed next door, how she had brushed against me that afternoon
or lightly touched my arm. I would lie in bed next to Alice imagining
how Barbara T.'s breasts would feel in my hands, my mouth. I would
imagine her thighs opening, her mouth twisting, her head lolling back.
I would toss and turn all night, roiling the sheets about me so that by
morning I would have to fight my way free.

I finished base-coating the library early in the afternoon of the first
really hot day in June, then went upstairs to shower and clean off the
paint. I looked out the bathroom window to where Alice and Barbara T.
were sitting side by side in tilted-back deck chairs next to the pool. They
had both removed their bikini tops and I just stood there at the window
for a moment admiring their bodies, their breasts.

Because of the thick privet hedges, the fence, and the hemlocks that
surrounded the property, the pool was invisible from the street. Our
driveway was gravel so one could hear an automobile approach. Alice
and I had often sunbathed nude or skinny-dipped, and on a couple of
occasions late at night had been joined by other naked couples in the
pool. It had never been anything extraordinary, there were no stupid
comments, no too-lingering looks.

But that afternoon standing at the bathroom window I looked at Alice
and Barbara T. for a long time. Their bodies were so lovely, so nice.
Their eyes were closed, their heads back, the long line of their throats
curving gently down. I was admiring their breasts, their weight, their
arc as they flowed in a giant teardrop around their rib cages and then
disappeared under their arms. I loved, too, the slight dip of their
sternums, the rib cage separations and the way that line melted into the
puddly warmth of their stomachs. I watched Barbara T. spread more oil
upon her belly, then smooth it upward to her breasts. Her hands covered
her bosom, gently rubbing in the oil. She turned to say something to
Alice and Alice laughed; I was too far away to hear what was said. Then
Alice squeezed some lotion into her own hand and rubbed her palms
together and began applying the suntan oil to her breasts. Both of the
women were lying there, their heads back, their eyes closed, their hands
moving on their breasts. Alice said something to Barbara T., who laughed,
then stretched, raising her arms over her head, arching her back,

thrusting her breasts up at the sun. Alice was watching, too. But then suddenly Barbara T.'s body slammed back down into the deck chair and they were both looking up at the bathroom window where I stood. Instinctively ducking back into the bedroom, burning with shame, I sat on the edge of the bed, my face in my hands, feeling . . . *dirty*. Like a little boy caught.

And then I felt angry. I had only been looking out the window and admiring the attractive, healthy, half-nude bodies of my wife and Barbara T. If *they* wanted to try to turn it into something dirty, it was up to them. I got back off the bed and went into the bathroom again. Alice and Barbara T. were now both in the pool, their bikini tops on their deck chairs and their bikini bottoms, too. They stood close together midway down the length of the pool, water lapping underneath their chins.

The next day I received a check from the lawyers for my inheritance from my mother's estate, with a note that I could expect a second check for approximately the same amount in another six months to a year when the estate was finally settled.

And two weeks after that Alice persuaded me to make a down payment on a new, grander house. That took place just after I had spent a night in New York with Barbara T.

8

THAT JUNE I SPENT three or four days a week in New York City finishing the film. Usually I would take the train back to New Jersey at the end of the day; but occasionally, because of the sound technicians' schedules, I would have to work late, and then I'd spend the night in town. I didn't mind. I liked having a free evening and, as it turned out, it gave me a perfect alibi for the night I spent with Barbara T.

During the days I did not commute to New York I continued to work on painting the library and, as I've said, Barbara T. and Alice would drift in and out. Sometimes Barbara T. would stay to talk to me while I painted. If Alice were around, Barbara T. would throw on a light cotton bathrobe over her bikini; if Alice were not, Barbara T. would remain uncovered. During one of those visits I told Barbara T. that I would have to work the following day in New York.

"I have to be in New York, too," she said.

I put down my paintbrush and turned to look at her. "Will you be staying the night?"

"I could," she said.

"Um," I said.

"Uh-huh," Barbara T. said. And she *smiled!*

And so, without further ado, if someone will please get the lights . . .
FADE IN:
137. INTERIOR: LOBBY, MIDTOWN NEW YORK CITY HOTEL. 4:30
P.M. *MID-JUNE.*
While BARBARA T. stands slightly to my left and a couple of steps behind me I sign the guest register and put down the pen as the RESERVATIONS CLERK taps the bell and I turn to BARBARA T., who is biting her lower lip.
138. POINT OF VIEW (POV) BARBARA T.
The BELLBOY approaches over my shoulder and stops to pick up two obviously mismatched pieces of luggage. As the BELLBOY lifts the suitcases he glances up at BARBARA T. and me . . .
139. POV MYSELF.
We see BARBARA T.'s eyes skid away from the BELLBOY, then uncertainly meet mine.

165

CUT TO:

140. INTERIOR: LOBBY SHOWING ELEVATOR ENTRANCE.

BARBARA T. and I follow the BELLBOY to the elevator, whose doors
are open revealing a late-middle-aged couple already standing within.
The BELLBOY steps aside to allow BARBARA T. and MYSELF to pass.
As BARBARA T. enters the OLDER MAN removes his hat; his WIFE
shoots him a look. I join BARBARA T. and we both face front as the
BELLBOY enters, turns, and punches our floor button. As the doors
slide slowly closed we see BARBARA T. and me not speaking, facing
front as the WIFE has removed her compact from purse to examine her
face in the mirror.

CUT TO:

141. INTERIOR: HOTEL ROOM. MOMENTS LATER.

We hear the sound of a key being inserted in the lock, the door swings
open, BARBARA T. enters followed by MYSELF and the BELLBOY
with our two suitcases. As the BELLBOY performs his routine room
check, BARBARA T. and I stand silently by.

BELLBOY

(Turning toward me:)

The bathroom is here. The light switch is next to the door. If you
need anything my name is Albert.

MYSELF

(Handing the BELLBOY a tip:)

Everything looks fine, Albert.

BELLBOY

(Pockets the tip:)

Thank you, sir.

(He backs out of the room pulling door closed behind him. As I move to
place the DO NOT DISTURB sign on the doorknob and lock the door,
BARBARA T. looks about the room, which is dominated by a large bed
with a plain wooden headboard and nubby magenta bedspread. Above
the bed hangs a watercolor reproduction of a midtown Manhattan street
on a rainy night. Directly opposite the bed is a low combination chest
of drawers, vanity table, and writing desk, above which hangs a large
mirror. There are bedside tables with not unattractive lamps, a pedestal-
mounted color TV set with a placard advertising several R-rated movies
on the order of, say, *Emmanuelle in Bangkok*, two comfortable stuffed
chairs with a low table and standing lamp between them.)

BARBARA T.

(Moves to curtained windows:)

This is crazy. I'm so nervous!

MYSELF

Don't be.

BARBARA T.

(Has pulled the curtain aside to look out:)
But what if someone should see us?

MYSELF

(Moves to her side:)
We're on the fifteenth floor.

BARBARA T.

(Lets the curtain drop:)
I didn't mean from the *street!*

MYSELF

(Hugs Barbara T:)
I've been coming to this hotel off and on for fifteen years and I've
never yet run into anyone I've ever seen before—including the
people at the desk.

BARBARA T.

But still, what if we do?

MYSELF

(Gently massages the back of BARBARA T.'s neck:)
Shhh . . . It's all right. Don't worry.

BARBARA T.

I can't help it.

MYSELF

Everything's fine now. Really. The door is locked. No one can come
in. No one can see us. No one knows we're here. We're perfectly
safe.

BARBARA T.

(Crosses to the bed and sits down:)
It's so quiet!

MYSELF

Would you like some music?
(Fiddles with the TV set:)
It has an FM radio.

BARBARA T.

(She reaches inside a tin cigarette case and removes a carefully rolled
joint:)
I don't do this very often.
(She lights the marijuana cigarette and inhales deeply.)

MYSELF

(Finds appropriate music and turns back to Barbara T.:)
    Do what very often?

BARBARA T.

(Exhales slowly:)
    Go to hotel rooms with men.

MYSELF

    I don't either . . . I let them buy me lunch occasionally, but I draw
    the line at going to their rooms.

BARBARA T.

(Passes me the joint. She has not smiled:)
    Would you like some of this?

MYSELF

(Inhales and holds it down, then exhales slowly:)
    Don't be nervous. It's nice just to be together. I've been wanting
    to be alone with you for so long! We've got all the time in the world.
    Nobody's going to interrupt us. We can do whatever we want.

BARBARA T.

    The only thing I think I want right now is a hot bath.

CUT TO:

142. INTERIOR: HOTEL BATHROOM. SOMEWHAT LATER.

BARBARA T. is immersed in the hot bath water up to her chin. An
ashtray rests on the side of the tub. She is pinching the last bit of the
joint between her fingers as she inhales. I am standing in front of the
sink shaving, wearing only a hotel towel.

BARBARA T.

(Her voice is more languid; she has relaxed:)
    I wonder what Alice would say if she saw us now.

MYSELF

    She'd tell me I was leaving a mess in the sink.

BARBARA T.

    She did say something odd to me once.

MYSELF

    What? . . . Oh, *damn!*
(I have cut myself shaving.)

BARBARA T.

    Well, when she and I were in Puerto Rico I said it was a shame that
    you couldn't be there with us, that it was the sort of place where all
    one wanted to do was lie on the beach or go back to the room and
    fuck.

MYSELF

(I am applying a piece of tissue to the reddening stain on my chin:)
And what did Alice say to that?

BARBARA T.

She just laughed and made some comment about you and me that
I immediately blocked.

MYSELF

What did she say?

BARBARA T.

I can't remember exactly. But she sort of hinted that she wouldn't
mind my going to bed with you.

MYSELF

She said *what?*
(She has my full attention now:)
How did she put it?

BARBARA T.

(Begins soaping her arms:)
That's the thing. I can't remember. It came as such a shock I simply
blocked it out.

MYSELF

Well, she certainly never said anything like that to *me*.
(I look at myself in the mirror and pull off the bloody tissue. The cut is
still open and more blood appears:)
If the bleeding keeps up at this rate I should be dead in about
seventy-two hours.
(Looking away from the mirror to BARBARA T., who is now sitting up
in the tub soaping her breasts:)
You're lovely. You really are.
(Crossing to toilet and sitting down on closed seat:)
Do you remember that night I came back from Leadville and you
sat up with me in the library? You were so beautiful in that nightgown.
God, I wanted you so much.

BARBARA T.

I know.
(She sinks back down in the tub until the water is lapping her chin.)

MYSELF

(Looking down at the towel in my lap:)
I feel the same way now.

BARBARA T.

(Sits up in tub again:)

Show me.

                    CUT TO:

143. INTERIOR: HOTEL ROOM.

It is much later. The heavy hotel curtains have been pulled aside leaving only the white gauze curtains closed, through which the city's night-time lights are visible. BARBARA T. and I are in bed. She is resting on one elbow facing me, I am on my back. We are sharing a cigarette, which she passes me, then leans forward to kiss my shoulder.

                    BARBARA T.

We're so bad.

                    MYSELF

I know. That's what made it so good.

                    BARBARA T.

I want to suck you.

                    MYSELF

I love it when you talk like that.

                    BARBARA T.

I love it when you *are* like that.

(I stub the cigarette out in the ashtray and kiss her neck.)

I love your cock. I do. Really. It's so beautiful. So smooth . . . It likes it when I touch it. See?

(She lifts the sheet:)

Look what's happening.

                    MYSELF

I don't have to look.

                    BARBARA T.

It's getting so hard . . .

(Her head dips beneath the covers.)

                    MYSELF

You're so good.

                    BARBARA T.

(Emerges back above the sheet:)

I want you to come.

                    MYSELF

(Slight hint of panic in eyes:)

No, not yet. We've got all night.

                    BARBARA T.

(Sitting up suddenly:)

All night? Jesus, what time is it? I was supposed to call Dorothy at six-thirty.

(BARBARA T. pulls herself up on the bed until she can reach her wristwatch:)

Almost seven-thirty!

MYSELF

Who's Dorothy?

BARBARA T.

(She is now leaning over the side of the bed rummaging through her pocketbook:)

My ex-college roommate. I was supposed to be staying at my sister's tonight, but I told my sister I was staying with Dorothy—what *did* I do with her number?—and I need to call Dorothy so she can cover for me—*ah!* Here it is!

(She comes back up onto the bed with a scrap of paper in her hand, then wriggles on her stomach far enough up on the bed to reach the telephone:)

What do I have to do to get an outside line?

MYSELF

Dial nine if it's a local call.

BARBARA T.

(Dials:)

I hope she's there . . .

(I am sitting up in bed now, BARBARA T.'s body is stretched out. As BARBARA T. talks, the camera cuts back and forth between my POV and medium close-ups of the two of us:)

Hello, Dorothy? Hi, it's me . . . Fine. Wonderful. And you? . . . No, I'm in New York . . . No, I can't. That's why I'm calling . . .

(We see the slope of BARBARA T.'s back, her shoulders hunched as she rests on her elbows speaking into the telephone. I am admiring the curve of her spine, the swell of her hips, the twin mounds of her buttocks. As BARBARA T. talks I reach over and run my hand gently down her back to the end of her spine, massaging the muscles, then my hand moves to her buttocks:)

. . . I'm supposed to be staying with my sister Helen and she thinks I'm staying with you. So can you cover for me?

(My hand moves to the backs of her thighs and then I touch her more boldly. One hears the sharp intake of BARBARA T.'s breath:)

Nothing. I just thought I was going to sneeze.

(BARBARA T. smiles over her shoulder at me and at the same time parts her thighs. I begin to caress the insides of her thighs, the soft tender skin excites me. BARBARA T. is telling her friend about a sale at

Bloomingdale's; her tone is soft, dreamy. Her thighs open further. My thumb goes into her:)

It's a very good sale. Maybe we can—oh!—go tomorrow . . .

(BARBARA T. squirms and lifts herself up against my hand:)

There are some Halston slacks that are to die over . . .

(I kneel between her open thighs, my hands on her hips. I raise her hips until she, too, is kneeling and her bottom rocks back against me. BARBARA T. continues talking on the telephone when I enter her. I move very slowly with just the tip of my penis nudging into her. BARBARA T. is still talking about the Bloomingdale's sale as she pushes back against me. I hold her away with my hands:)

. . . and I *want* to go to *Saks* tomorrow *too*. They're al*so* holding a *sum*mer sale . . .

(I can tell she is enjoying it, that she is excited by the idea of getting fucked while talking to her ex-college roommate on the phone:)

Oh, *guess* who I saw the *other* day! Do you re*member* Paula *Turn*bull who lived *down* the hall *from us* junior year?

(A craziness begins to grow within me. She is deliberately prolonging the conversation. I want to break through her control, to make her moan into the telephone. I grab her hips and thrust into her until I can feel the entrance to her womb. I plunge into her again and again until she begins to tremble and I can feel the muscles tightening in the backs of her thighs. She rocks back against me harder and harder, impaling herself on my cock:)

Oh, my *God!* Oh, my *God!* No, I'm all *right!* You *won't* be*lieve* this. You *won't* be*lieve* what's *happening* now . . . No, *I'm* all *right* . . . I've *got* to go! I'm *hanging* up! I'm *hanging* up! . . .

(BARBARA T. fumbles with the telephone button, presses it down, tries to replace the receiver, drops it on the cradle, and twists back over her shoulder to look at me:)

You're unbelievable! What are you doing to me?

(I feel BARBARA T.'s hand snake between her thighs to touch herself. Her whole body begins to buck uncontrollably. Her face is pushed into the pillow. I can tell she is close and I reach between us to pull her hand away.)

MYSELF

Not yet. I don't want you to come yet.

BARBARA T.

Unfair!

(She is at the very edge of orgasm. I am moving very gently, slowly, teasing her, not moving either hard or fast enough to make her come. I am riding the curl of the wave as it builds. The first tendrils of surf, little silver slivers of pleasure dart between us. Her hand lifts to touch herself again. I do not stop her. I can feel her fingers move lightly, sweetly. She is moaning softly.)

MYSELF

Do you want to come now?

BARBARA T.

Yes-s-s . . . Please, I want to come.

MYSELF

Maybe wait a little longer?

(I break the rhythm, move more slowly still. BARBARA T.'s hand drops away.)

BARBARA T.

What are you doing to me?

MYSELF

What you want.

BARBARA T.

Oh God.

(I build the wave back up again, move into her more powerfully, increase the speed:)

Not fair! Not fair!

(Her mouth is twisted, her brow damp, hair sticks to her temples. She pushes herself back at me hard now:)

Don't stop this time! You mustn't stop!

(Her fingers lift to touch herself again. Her body begins to shudder. Her eyes squeeze tightly shut:)

Don't stop! Don't! I'm coming!

(The wave breaks. BARBARA T.'s head thrashes back and forth on the pillow, her body jerks out of control. I concentrate on not slipping out of her and when she collapses forward on the bed and lies there, limp, I am still inside her and do not withdraw until her breathing and mine return to normal:)

You really are a sonuvabitch.

MYSELF

(Rolling off to one side:)

I know.

BARBARA T.

I think that's what turns me on about you.

(BARBARA T. turns over until she is sprawled on her back, her arms and legs slack, one foot touching mine. She turns her head to face me:)

Did you come?

MYSELF

Not yet.

(I touch her body gently, her stomach, the ridge of her hip bone, slide my palm gently up the swell of her bosom, bend forward to lightly kiss her breast. Her hand presses my mouth to her, her fingers twist in my hair. I can hear her steady heartbeat and lie with my cheek on her breast. We remain like that until BARBARA T. pushes my head away and sits up.)

BARBARA T.

I've got to pee.

(BARBARA T. swings her legs over the side of the bed and stands. She walks a bit unsteadily toward the bathroom, then pauses and looks back at me. I am lying now on my back, the knee closest to her raised, the other leg stretched out:)

It's such a beautiful angle from here.

MYSELF

What?

BARBARA T.

Your body.

(She goes into the bathroom. When I sit up in the bed I can see my face reflected in the mirror above the hotel vanity table chest of drawers. My eyes are dead, my expression detached. I look away, then look back again. It is the same. There is the sound of a toilet flushing and I get out of bed to join BARBARA T.)

144. INTERIOR: HOTEL BATHROOM.

(BARBARA T. is standing before the sink brushing her hair. I move behind her and, looking at our reflection in the mirror, move my hand up her stomach to her breasts. BARBARA T. turns within my arms until our bellies are together. I hold her tightly, her forehead cradled against my throat. I open my eyes and again see my face in the mirror. BARBARA T. steps slightly back so that she can look at me. One hand rises, her fingers touch my cheek.)

BARBARA T.

I love you. You're so nice. I'm having such a good time. I feel so good.

145. POV BARBARA T.

(Tight close-up of my face, BARBARA T.'s fingers lightly tracing my cheekbone.)

MYSELF

Me, too.

The film sticks in the projector. The single frame depicting Barbara

T.'s caress begins to wilt, bubble, char. My face twists, melts, my eyes are the last to be devoured by the heat, and then the film breaks and the take-up reel snaps up the free end and one hears only the flap-flap-flap-flap of the broken loose end of film.

"I'm having such a good time," Barbara T. had said, and I had responded, "Me, too." It was only half a lie.

I was enjoying Barbara T.'s body, the scent, the touch, the shape of her, the secret that had been withheld for so long. But I was troubled by my distance from it all, the distance from her that I felt. An obvious barrier had been crossed, another reached.

I do not fully understand why she agreed to see me. I think I understood my own motives: curiosity about Barbara T.'s body, her responsiveness in bed. And, certainly there was the viciousness inherent in fucking someone close to Alice, a way of getting back at Alice for all her distance and coldness and hurts. There was no question that Alice was as much a part of my going to bed with Barbara T. as Alice was part of Barbara T.'s going to bed with me. But what I couldn't understand was *why* Barbara T. had wanted to do it, why she had felt free to proceed. Was it because Alice had been unfaithful to me? I wasn't sure. There had been only that hint about "fun" on the Stowe trip. There was nothing tangible. My frustration with Barbara T. always stemmed from my inability really ever to know anything about her for certain. So why should I have expected this time to be any different? Because, goddam it, this time *had been* different. We had made love! And yet her willingness could be interpreted as either an act of confirmation, or betrayal, or both. So I was no closer to her, to understanding her, than I had been before. That is why I felt more than anything else a sadness about what we had done. It hadn't even really been fun. I had thought the challenge of making love to Barbara T. while she was on the phone would have excited me enough to make me come, but it didn't. I had succeeded in breaking through her self-control, but not my own, and I took no pride in any of it. Not in any of it at all.

We had a light dinner in our room and during the meal I attempted to explain some of the frustrations I felt—not with her, but with myself. I could not, I told her, seem to get outside my head—a head, I added, whose perceptions I no longer trusted. It was as if I were viewing life through someone else's lenses; and I was unable to resolve into focus the distortions that resulted. I felt isolated and detached from my actions, controlled by this stranger within my head. Something was going on within me. What it was, I didn't know; I only knew that it was pulling me apart.

On the one hand, I wanted to merge totally with, absorb and be absorbed by, my family, my wife and two children. On the other hand, I wanted to shed them like an old skin. I wanted to get away from them as much, I thought, as they—with the exception of Peter, the youngest— wanted to get away from me. Only then would I have the opportunity, the time, to come to some sort of understanding and peace within myself. And yet, the instant this desire would surface that awful, isolated, other self, the stranger within my head, would emerge to snicker: "Another poor, silly, middle-aged bastard who wants to 'find himself.' "

Barbara T. and I had finished dinner and were sipping coffee now, sitting with legs crossed beside the little table at the foot of our bed. "I keep thinking of a conversation I had with a close friend—it must have been fifteen years ago," I said. "He worked in the sales department of IBM. He said, 'I've got a six-year plan for my customers and about a six-day plan for myself . . .' That's the way I feel, too. I cannot foresee the future at all. I don't seem to be able to imagine what I'll be doing or where I'll be five years from now. I can only plan for the next few hours. The right now."

"And what do you plan?"

"I'm planning on our finishing our coffees and falling back into bed."

When Barbara T. smiled at me it was as if I were watching her smile at some strange man in some strange hotel room. And suddenly, to my astonishment, I was aroused. The idea of watching Barbara T. in a hotel room making love to someone else excited me more than being with her myself! What the hell was going on?

I felt such a rush of guilt and—what? Tenderness, I think. Tenderness and sympathy for Barbara T., who had chosen to spend a night with me. I wanted to give her affection, all that love I could not seem to express, all that bottled-up love I felt for my dead mother and brother, for my children, and Alice, too. I reached across the table to take Barbara T.'s hand, but she lifted my palm to her cheek, pressed it against her mouth, first kissed, then licked it. The hot, sexual wetness of her tongue on my skin was like an electric jolt.

"Jesus," I said.

"I want you," Barbara T. said.

"Me, too."

"Show me."

I pushed back from the table and stood up.

"*Show* me," she said again. A moment later she looked up at me. "Am I doing that to you?"

"Yes."

She leaned forward and took me into her mouth. One part of me wondered why it felt so good; another part wondered why it didn't feel better.

The next morning Barbara T. and I made love again. I tried to make it as good for her as I could, but I did not come this time either. I made some sort of excuse—that because Alice and I made love so seldom I had become accustomed to masturbating and it was difficult for me now to achieve an orgasm any other way. There may have been some truth in that. But the real reason, I think, had more to do with that stranger inside my head, the unconscious desire to hold back. When I looked over some notes I had taken during this period I found a line about "having had great bites taken out of me by women and needing to keep some part of myself."

I did feel that.

Was not coming a form of self-preservation? What a strange medieval interpretation. Did I think by not coming with the women I went to bed with that I was remaining undiluted? Whole? Or wasn't there also the sense of getting even, of not letting them get to me. It is no longer clear to me where this threat was coming from. It is clear only that it wasn't until Alice and I and Arthur and Odette were divorced, and Odette and I were alone together that I began to reach orgasm with any regularity. Not only has the problem now ceased to exist, but also, irony of ironies, I am planning this month to make an appointment for a vasectomy.

None of this, however, does much to explain why so soon after that night spent with Barbara T. in New York I would, along with Alice, make a bid on a new house.

For the past year Alice had been "looking at houses" with Dudley Thompson, our former-airline-pilot-now-real-estate-broker friend. It had seemed a harmless enough diversion, a sort of not-to-be-taken-seriously window-shopping comparison, which, I hoped, could only lead her to becoming more appreciative of the house we had. And yes, I am aware how arrogant such an attitude was. But I loved that house and I could not understand why Alice could not be happy there. She told me, but I didn't want to hear.

There was no privacy in the master bedroom.

There wasn't enough closet and storage space, nor counter space in the kitchen.

There was no place to put the kitty litter box except in the laundry area.

Because of the hot forced air heating system, dust and animal hair were continually being blown about the house.

There was no mud room or coat room or area where the children could remove their wet and muddy clothes without tracking through the kitchen.

There was no shower in the children's bathroom; as a result, they were continually using ours.

Add to these problems the structural flaws, the upkeep problems, and the condition of the furniture—and recognize also that because Alice's housekeeping bordered on the compulsive, she was continually frustrated by her inability to keep ahead of the decay—and I can see now why she was so unhappy with the house. Why couldn't I then?

I didn't *want* to see. Leaving that house would mean more financial worries and suffering yet another emotional loss.

Did I think a new house would keep us from divorce?

I know that that bargain was never actually proposed; it was, however, what I hoped. A new house was a topic that arose between Alice and me about as often as the topic of divorce and I didn't want either of them for much the same reasons: they would both bring too much trouble and be too expensive. I had no cause to believe that I would be any better off—or, if there's a distinction, any *happier*—living either with someone else or in someplace else. After all, Alice and I had been married for ten years and despite our marriage's obvious tensions, it seemed no worse than the marriages we saw around us.

But if my willingness to consider a different house meant less tensions, if it convinced Alice that I was making an effort to pay more attention to her needs and that I was being more responsive to her wants, then so be it. She had, as she had made clear, always hated the house we lived in. If we were to find one she actually *liked*, perhaps she would be happy—or happ*ier*, at least.

Furthermore, I was confident that Alice would never find a house she liked no matter how long she looked. So by humoring her in her house-hunting forays with Dudley Thompson I did not feel I had much to lose. Imagine my surprise, therefore, when I returned from New York and the night with Barbara T. to hear Alice say that she had found a house she thought might be perfect for us.

I had not expected God to punish me quite so soon.

"Where is it?" I asked.

"About eight miles out," she said. "Above Rosemont. The house, in fact, overlooks the town and the land borders the Nature Conservatory. I've made an appointment with Dudley for us both to go look at it tomorrow morning."

"How much are they asking for it?"

"One eighty-five, five," Alice said. "Wait till you see it. It even has a small cottage up in the woods behind it that you could use as an office."

The following morning Dudley Thompson picked us up for the drive out to look at the house. Dudley had been a navy carrier pilot after the Korean War, then worked for Mohawk Airlines out of Boston until Mohawk had merged and he'd been laid off. He moved back to our New Jersey town and entered his uncle's real estate business. Now he lived in a meticulously restored pre-Revolutionary War house on Main Street, drove a Peugeot (as did most of the natives since Peugeot was the only car dealer in town), wore old tweed jackets and Save the Whales ties, and even affected a Down East accent when he thought he could get away with it.

Alice sat in the front with Dudley and I sat in the back. His route took us past Odette's house and out the same road she and I had driven when we had filmed the Rosemont Memorial Day ceremony for ABC News.

I leaned forward and asked Alice, "When do the Villars get back?"

"The end of July," she said. "Why?"

"Just wondering," I said. But I was thinking that I missed not having Odette around. The end of July was still five weeks away. I had a sudden vision of Odette climbing wet and sleek out of the pool in her skintight one-piece burgundy bathing suit. I thought of her hands, the long tapered fingers holding a wineglass. Then I became aware that Dudley had said something to me.

"I'm sorry, Dudley, I didn't hear you," I said.

"I was saying that the house needs work, but the location is magnificent."

"What kind of work?" I asked.

"You'll probably want to insulate it."

"It has no insulation?" I glanced at Alice.

"It can be blown in very easily," Alice said.

"In the new part, yes," Dudley said, then added, "But you'll probably want to use some sort of rigid insulation in the old part."

"How big is the new part?" I asked.

"It's really only the kitchen," Dudley said. "It was added on in the early twenties."

"The seventeen- or eighteen-twenties?" I asked.

"Nineteen-twenty-something," Dudley said with a trace of a smile. He turned off the main road onto a gravel road that swung around the Rosemont Cemetery through woods on either side. "In effect you have about a three-mile private driveway; there are no houses on this road until you come to the one I'm taking you to."

"How much land comes with the house you're showing us?" I asked.

"Three acres. But you can buy more."

"Wait till you see it," Alice said.

"It's perfect for a young couple with growing children," Dudley said.

"How long has it been on the market?"

"Three months. But there's been a lot of interest."

"Crowds of young couples with growing families been passing through?"

"Ay-yuh . . . I've got another showing this afternoon."

"Dudley, if the house is so good why hasn't it sold?"

"It will. Some couples just don't have the imagination to see the possibilities."

"Why is it when you say something like that I get the chills?"

"It doesn't all need to be done at once," Dudley said.

"The kitchen does," Alice said.

"The *kitchen*? I thought that was the 'new' part of the house," I said.

"You may want to update the appliances," Dudley said.

"Jesus," I said.

We passed out of the woods and were in open land now. There were gently rolling fields of tall grasses, some scrub. The river was perhaps thirty feet off to our left, but not visible because of the grasses and the height of the bank. "There it is," Dudley said.

The house lay directly ahead of us at a distance of about a hundred yards. The morning sun slanted down upon it and colored the land a lime green.

I have always been susceptible to first impressions: If I don't like the way something looks right away, I tend to search out the means for justifying the negative opinions. But if something has character or style, I am willing to forgive it almost anything.

The house Dudley and Alice had brought me to see had character. It was also obvious that at one time it had had style. The house had started as a typical unadorned two-story, eighteenth-century center-chimney Colonial with plain wood shingles on its sides and weathered clapboards on the front and rear. The original door was probably quite plain; but the door that now existed, with its carved wooden dummy fanlight, was a country carpenter's version of a late-Georgian doorway, which was further disfigured by an ungainly pillared porch that ran the length of the house. A second, lesser porch ran the length of the small one-story 1920s addition which jutted out of the east side of the house and ended abruptly with a second chimney. A third chimney mysteriously was visible near the northwest corner of the house, beyond the peak of the roof. The house faced south and was situated on a small rise overlooking a curve in the river. Behind the house, beginning about seventy yards to the north, a densely wooded hill rose steeply to a bluff.

"The cottage is up on the bluff; you can't see it from here because of the foliage," Dudley said. We were standing outside the car now; Alice had moved off a little toward the house. "And over there to the west is the cemetery."

"What cemetery?" I asked. "Not the Rosemont Cemetery, is it? I thought we passed that several miles back."

"The Baskin family cemetery," Dudley said. "It's a rather touching story, really. The Baskin daughters died of smallpox."

"What are you two talking about?" Alice asked.

"The family cemetery just over the hill," I said.

Both Dudley and I had unconsciously started walking away from the house toward the cemetery, leaving Alice behind us.

"Aren't you going to look at the house?" Alice called after us.

"In a minute," I said. "I just want to take a look at the cemetery first."

"I'm not sure of the dates exactly," Dudley was saying, "but the daughters died in about 1760. Their father, Jareb Baskin, who lived in the house—"

"The house was here then?"

"Oh yes—at least the main part of the house was. Baskin was a widower. The two daughters' room was on the west side of the house—see the chimney there?" He pointed to that odd third chimney I had noticed when we first got out of the car. "Their bedroom was in a small shedlike structure that evidently came off that side of the house, and a large fireplace opened into it. You can see where it was walled in at a later date."

We had reached the top of the slight rise and were looking down at the cemetery and the town of Rosemont in the distance.

The cemetery was in terrible disrepair, overgrown, with no visible gravestones; were it not for the crumbling fieldstone wall which enclosed it on four sides one would not know what it was.

"How many are buried here?" I asked.

"I have no idea," Dudley said. "I do know the two Baskin girls are here—one of them was Patience, the other Hope, I think."

"Or Charity."

"Perhaps. They both contracted smallpox and died. Jareb survived."

I had stepped across the fallen stone wall and was walking among the weeds when my foot hit a marker. I cleared away the weeds and picked up the fragment of redstone; it read: "—e Baskin" and below it "—ged 19 years." I passed it to Dudley saying, "Well, that rules out Charity as a name." I searched for other pieces of the marker but could find nothing. "Dudley, who's responsible for the upkeep on this graveyard?"

"I'm not sure," he said. "It's not part of the land that goes with the house. It's just the three acres the house sits on, the little rise, and behind it to the foot of the hill."

"And the cottage is on top of the hill?"

"Ay-yuh, and that's not part of the three acres either."

"So if we want the house, the cemetery, and the cottage, how much land are we talking about?"

"I believe nine acres. I'd have to check."

"Maybe we ought to just look at the house," I said. As I turned back I stepped on another stone. It took me a moment to dig it free. The fragment, perhaps nine inches wide at its base and seven or so inches high, was clearly a part of the daughter's stone. When I turned it over I could see that the side that had been half-buried in the ground had been carved. I picked and scrubbed at the caked dirt until it came free, revealing a crudely carved and hideous death's head with angel wings sprouting from its skull.

"What have you got there?" Dudley asked.

"I think it's the top of the Baskin daughter's stone," I said, passing it to him, "unless, of course, it's what we paranoids call a 'bad omen.'"

"Oh my, yes," Dudley said. "This is a very nice one—a very interesting one really. The death's head was a very common image in the mid-eighteenth century. And this one with the eyebrows over the eye sockets, the mouth, *and* the suggestion of a vestigial serrated upper jaw transformed here into a chin . . ."

"Dudley, what the fuck are you talking about?"

"Well, you see, there was a whole change in attitude going on about this time. The earlier markers will have what is clearly a skull, a death's head, on them. But towards the middle of the century, after the middle really, the death's head—symbolic of death triumphant—was gradually supplanted by what were called 'soul effigies,' symbolic of entrance into the new life, the kingdom of God, so to speak."

"Dudley, are you putting me on?"

"No, not at all," he said. "I've always been a history buff, you know that."

"I didn't realize you knew so much about gravestones, though." We were walking back up toward the house, Dudley still carrying the death's head in his hand. We were approaching the house from the west, and one could now see how oddly the chimney seemed placed. "You say there was a shed on this side?"

"Well, it was probably more finished than a shed. More like the sort of lean-two added to the back of a salt-box house. After Jareb Baskin buried his daughters he burned that side of the house off. It wasn't clear whether he did it to isolate the smallpox disease or out of grief. I don't think anyone knows. He died the following summer. Poisoned himself, so the story goes."

"Cheery story," I said, waving to Alice, who was waiting for us at the steps leading up to the porch. "I suppose the house has a curse?"

"The door's open, Alice," Dudley called, ignoring me. "Just go on in." To me he said, "The house hasn't been lived in for a while. Not since Mrs. Deerborn died. Her furniture is still inside."

"Smallpox?"

"No, oddly enough, she choked to death on a piece of turkey last Thanksgiving."

"Are you coming?" Alice called.

"I'll just return this marker to the cemetery while you and Alice go through the house yourselves."

Some people look in other people's medicine cabinets; I look at their books. Mrs. Deerborn's library appeared to have ceased acquiring new volumes in the 1930s. There were sets of James Branch Cabell, Finley Peter Dunne, John Galsworthy, Saki, Walter De la Mare, the Brontë sisters, Edgar Lee Masters, Edward Arlington Robinson, Amy Lowell, and Robert Frost. And stacks of mysteries. A little framed poem hung above a bookshelf:

OLD HOUSE

He who loves an old house
Never loves in vain,
How can an old house
Used to sun and rain,
To lilac and larkspur,
And an elm above,
Ever fail to answer
The heart that gives it love.
ISABEL FISKE CONANT

I pointed out the poem to Alice. "I bet Dudley put it there," I said. "How do you like it?"

"It's terrible—the poem, I mean. I like the house though," I said.

"And it's private. There's no one around for miles. . . . The porches will have to go, first thing, and the kitchen . . ."

"What's the matter with the kitchen?"

"It needs to be redesigned."

"Well, let's take a look."

The house had exposed beamed ceilings throughout, quite good paneling over the keeping room fireplace mantel, chair-rail molding in the library, and half-wainscoted walls in the dining room. The kitchen addition was, as Alice had implied, stupidly laid out, but the dimensions were good, and with the porches gone it would not be so dark.

The second floor was chopped up into four small bedrooms and a bath, and as Alice and I wandered from room to room she said, "If we build an addition on the west side of the house we could have our bedroom on the second floor. Knock a fireplace into the chimney for the bedroom and maybe even one on the other side for our bath. Think of it," Alice said, "a fireplace in the bathroom!"

"You mean where the bedroom now is?"

"What?" she said.

"I'm confused," I said. "I don't know what room you're talking about where."

I suppose I knew Alice and I would make a bid on the house the moment I saw the land and the cemetery. The land was what had drawn me immediately, and the sense of history, the house's roots in the past. And I would have been prepared to forgive the house a great deal because I so liked the view from where it stood. But the house wasn't bad at all. Its handsomest room wasn't even used—it was the attic with its widely spaced heavy principal rafters laid on their broad sides and smaller, lighter common rafters in pairs in between. Connected to the principal rafters by dovetail joints were the attic tie beams, which spanned the attic's width about six and a half feet above the floor. The attic, which ran the entire length and width of the old part of the house, was dominated by the massive stone chimney in the center of the space and the smaller, but still heavy stone chimney in the northwest corner. The old rough-hewn beams were all exposed and there was no roof insulation, of course, but I knew how insulation could be mounted without obscuring the beams. From the small attic windows the view of the village of Rosemont was the best anywhere in the house.

But what dissipated any further reservations I might have had was the cottage high on the hill behind the house. On the walk along the path up to it, I scared up two partridge and a doe. The cottage was made of native fieldstone with a wood shingle roof. It had a stone fireplace at one end, was two stories tall with a fifteen-by-thirty-foot room downstairs, and at the other end there was a small stove, refrigerator, and sink. There were two bedrooms and a bath under the dormer-windowed roof above. It would be perfect as an office and as additional space for the children as they grew older.

Over the next couple of weeks Alice and I returned to the property again and again. I had Burt Taylor take a look at the main house in his professional capacity as an architect. And he did the usual architect's waffling about the wood shingle roof on the big house: it could last another five years or another fifty. Both chimneys would need to be pointed up; if we intended to open up the third chimney, major masonry work would have to be done. The addition Alice and I proposed was feasible, but it would not be cheap; on the other hand, we should expect the same changes to cost 11 percent more the next year and 17 percent more the year after that. The house was basically sound; it had stood for almost two hundred and fifty years, it would certainly hold on for fifty more. What we needed to do was to establish priorities, to repair and restore the important things first.

I had the electrician and plumber I used for the house in town come out to the Baskin house. From the electrician I learned that Mrs. Deerborn's husband had hung himself in the attic, and from the plumber I learned that the basement contained snakes.

"What kind?" I asked.

He was shining his flashlight beam on what looked like a translucent piece of rope hanging from a pipe in the corner behind the furnace. "Black snakes," he said. "That must have been a five-footer when he shed his skin. They bite, but they are not poisonous."

"That's a comfort."

"They like old houses, particularly in this area. They come in to get cool—and to hunt mice. They'll keep the rodent population down in a house."

"How do you keep the snake population down?"

"You could keep hogs in the basement."

"Well . . ." I said, walking carefully up the basement stairs. Alice was in the keeping room talking to the electrician. "There are snakes in the basement," I told her.

"Close the door," she said.

"And Mr. Deerborn hung himself in the attic," I said.

She said, "He must have been very short."

"He was," the electrician said. "He was a tiny man. All the Deerborns were very small."

"Why did he hang himself?" I asked.

"*She* was the one with money in the family," the plumber said. "She never let him have a cent. I think he had had money at one time. He had a small manufacturing company but it went under during the Depression and he never recovered. He used to spend his days in the cottage up in the woods. He was an inventor, but none of his inventions worked out. My father knew him. They went to high school together. And then there was Ralph Deerborn and Parker—Ralph was the first casualty during World War II from this town. He was killed at Wake Island at the beginning of the war. Parker Deerborn, the younger brother, is still here in town."

"Doing what?" I asked.

"He lives off Deerborn Lane. I'm not sure what he does. He rarely leaves the house."

"Where's Deerborn Lane?" Alice asked.

"Off Chimney Hill Road," the electrician said. "It's a new development. Garrison Colonials. All two hundred amp service. Underground cables."

"And Parker Deerborn lives in one of those?" Alice asked. "Why wouldn't he want to live here?"

"Isn't this where he grew up?" I asked.

"I don't think he was very happy here," the plumber said.

"I can see why," I said. "His father hung himself in the attic and the basement's filled with snakes."

That evening back in our library we discussed submitting a bid on the Baskin house. I explained how by taking out seventy-five-thousand-dollar mortgages on both houses—the one we now owned and the Baskin house—we could, with just under thirty thousand in cash, pay for the new house and additional land. Then when we sold the house we were now living in we could pay off its mortgage and pay for the improvements we wanted to make on the Baskin house with what was left. "It could be done," I told Alice, "but you've got to understand that if we buy the Baskin house and sink a lot of money into it, there is no way we can get that money back should we sell it within the next five or even seven years, without taking a terrible loss."

"I know all that," Alice said.

"I'm sure you do, but what I'm saying is, I don't want to buy it and hear you telling me a year, eighteen months from now you hate the house and that you've always hated it. I want you to bear responsibility for the decision, too."

"I've told you I *like* the Baskin house."

"But do you think you will be . . . well, happy there?"

"It isn't only this house that has made me unhappy with you," Alice said.

"I'm aware of that," I said, "but if we get this house do you think you'd be willing to wipe the slate clean? Could you and I make a fresh start?"

She did not answer.

"I just feel there's no point in investing all that money into a big new house if we're going to continue unhappy and angry with each other all the time. If we could just try to show each other a little tenderness, affection . . . otherwise what's the point of being together when there isn't any love?"

"You mean sex," she said.

"That, too."

"Too much has transpired," Alice said. "We've been married too long, been through too much. There are things one doesn't forget."

"I know that, but we can try to forgive each other, can't we? We can try to understand each other, to work together."

"Look, I don't care who you fuck in New York," she said. "You can do whatever you want just so it's out of town and I don't get my nose rubbed in it."

"Jesus, Alice, don't you understand what I'm trying to say to you? I *don't want* to fuck anyone in New York. That's why I'm asking us to make a fresh start. I want to make our marriage work."

"It's working," she said. "We're still married. What do you want me to tell you? I like the house. I'm not going to promise to turn into Snow White just because we get a bigger house. *This* house is too small. If we're going to keep having Joan because Maggie can't cope—"

"—We won't have Joan for at least a year," I said.

"And I won't pretend not to be relieved. But what do you bet Joan will be back in another six weeks? Let's face it, she's a kid who likes her luxury and she knows you can give her a better life materially than her mother. So we'll need a larger house. As for the rest, you do what you want and I'll do what I want."

"What does that mean?"

"Equal freedom," Alice said. "If you are going to fuck other people, then I will, too."

"You don't even *like* to fuck!" I protested, then immediately wished I hadn't. "I'm sorry, Alice," I said. "I didn't mean that. Fucking doesn't have anything to do with what I'm talking about. I'm talking about our being *friends*."

"Oh, I'll be friendly," Alice said.

"Like a roommate?"

"A roommate who does *your* laundry and who cleans up after *your* kids—speaking of which we'll need a new washer and dryer. And I want to talk to Burt Taylor about putting the laundry room upstairs in the Baskin house."

"There's no point in doing that until we've decided we're going to buy it," I said. "And there's no point in buying it until we're sure we want it and we want it for *us*. It means an enormous financial and emotional commitment. Physical commitment, too, working *together*. And I'm willing to do it, if you are. But it's unfair for you to ask me to go into hock up to my ears unless you're as committed to making things work between us as I am."

"What do you expect me to do?"

"I expect you to be willing to try a fresh start."

Alice sat across from me in the library, not speaking. She was looking down at the empty drink in her hand.

"Do you want another drink?" I asked.

"Sure," she said.

I got up and took the glass from her and went out to the kitchen for ice. I was wondering why I was even considering buying this house when our marriage seemed so hopeless. All I could think of was that maybe it didn't need to be so bad. For the first time I had some money. My film was apparently going to be a success and it would lead to other offers, other films. Maybe our lives could straighten out. I had some financial security, a cushion. I would not need to blow it *all* on a new house. And the Baskin house was—or would be—a wonderful house. It would keep Alice busy doing the sorts of things she loved to do: redesigning a kitchen, decorating rooms, picking out paints, slipcovers, new furniture, spending money. Still, why do it?

One side of me said, "Forget Alice! Look out for yourself!" The other side said, "Alice is Peter's mother. You can't forget one without losing the other. You want a home for yourself, your children. You want permanence, stability, roots." And besides, as I told myself, our marriage didn't need to be hopeless.

I still believed that if I just tried harder, showed Alice I cared, loved her enough, gave her enough, then we would be close. Alice would come around in time. She'd be more understanding, loving, *nice*.

And there would be continuity. I would not have to be alone. Terrible was better than nothing.

But what if Alice didn't come around? I would still rather invest the money in a house than lose it and my children in a divorce.

I dropped some ice cubes into Alice's glass and walked back into the library to the liquor cabinet, fixed her a vodka tonic, gave it to her, and sat back down.

"Well, Alice," I said. "What do you think?"

"About what? The house? I told you I like it."

"Do you want us to buy it?"

"It's your money."

"But are you willing to try as hard to make our marriage work as I am?"

"How hard are you trying?"

"At the moment, *very*," I said. "I'm trying very hard to make you understand what buying this house means. It's more than a fresh start. It's a commitment to our marriage, to *us*."

"And you think a new house is going to make everything all right? Look, *this* house doesn't work. The Baskin house might. If we're in a house that makes our life better, then we'll be better off. You're asking me to guarantee that we'll live happily ever after. How can I do that? You have this impossible fantasy that you expect me to live up to. I'm simply not as naïve as you. I don't have your expectations, nor your . . . your power."

"My power?"

"You're laying down a set of rules. You're telling me that if you buy me this house, then I'm to be a good little wife. Those are your terms. I'm to keep doing the work around here, and in return you'll get me an even bigger house with more rooms to clean. I simply don't kid myself, nor do I buy the American Dream about happy wives waiting for their husbands to come home. I'm too *exhausted* to be happy. Why is it . . . for example, why is it that when I went to Puerto Rico and you coped with the children you thought yourself a helluva man for doing so? And yet, when I do it seven days a week the other fifty-one weeks of the year it's only what is expected of me?"

"I always appreciate what you do, Alice," I said. "I've told you that. I've written you that. I've tried to show you that."

"You could show me more by doing more."

"Like what?"

"You could do some of the cleaning. The marketing. The cooking. Moses never came down from the mountain with 'Thou Shalt Not Cook' engraved in stone. If we are going to get this house I'll need you to help."

"I will," I said. "That's what a marriage is all about."

"Helping?"

"Sharing. That's all I'm asking you to do, too."

"I'll start when you start," she said. "For example, I don't suppose you'd consider putting the Baskin house in both our names?"

The bid submitted on the house, its three acres that included the cemetery, the three acres that went up the hill to the cottage on the bluff, and the three-plus acres that the house itself stood on, was for the original asking price on just the house. Within twenty-four hours our bid was accepted; the closing date was set for two weeks. I would then own two houses, but that didn't worry me too much. Dudley Thompson said our house in town would sell soon enough, and we could remain in it while the work was done on the new house.

I lined up carpenters, stone masons, painters, plumbers, electricians, to begin work in August. Burt Taylor, who would serve as general contractor, had come up with preliminary plans for the addition to the west side of the house and had even designed a gazebo that could be built at some later date overlooking the cemetery and the town. I planned to move my office out of the garage to the cottage overlooking the new house. That way I could be nearby while work was being done.

Friday, July 27, the day of the closing, the Villars returned from France.

When Odette called that evening I told her I thought I had just signed my life away.

The following afternoon Alice and I took the Villars, with their children, up to the property to take a look. Peter ran off with Paul and Vanessa to show them the cemetery, while inside the house Arthur and I tagged along behind Alice and Odette as they went from room to room. Alice was excitedly pointing out what walls she would knock out, how the bathroom would be changed, the kitchen redesigned, how and where certain pieces of furniture would be perfectly placed. I was happy that she was happy, that she seemed so pleased with the house.

And later, while Arthur and I were in the basement looking at the furnace and discussing how to rid the place of snakes, Odette was sitting with Alice on the porch.

"You're so lucky, Alice," Odette said.

"Lucky? Why?"

"To have found the house of your dreams. Arthur and I have moved probably a half-dozen times in the last ten years. We've never stayed more than a year and a half in one place. I've never lived in a house I really loved, that I felt a part of. But here . . ." Odette said, looking around her at the house, the view.

"I hate these porches," Alice said. "They'll be among the first to go."

"But that's what I mean, that's why I envy you. You found at last the house of your dreams, a place where you can spend the rest of your life just making it better and better."

"Spend the rest of my life *here?*" Alice said in surprise. "You must be kidding!"

9

When Arthur and I joined Alice and Odette on the porch of the Baskin house Alice asked, "Did you see any snakes?"

"Every pipe, every electrical wire, every piece of hose looked like one to me," I said.

"They're only here now because the house is empty," Arthur said. "Once you move in the snakes will disappear."

I sat down on the porch next to Alice, Arthur next to Odette. We could hear the children playing nearby. I leaned across Alice to ask Odette what she thought of the house.

"I was just telling Alice how much I envied her," Odette said. "It's a dream house, really."

I was surprised by how much Odette's approval meant to me. I wasn't sure whether it was because I admired her taste or because I was so used to Alice's indifference. I asked Odette if she had seen the cottage. "It's up on the hill behind us," I said. "I'm going to turn it into my office. Would you like to take a look?"

Odette turned to Arthur. "Have you seen it?" she asked.

"I want Arthur to look at the attic," Alice said.

During our climb up the hill Odette slipped and I steadied her until she regained her balance. Although I held her for only seconds, I was fully aware of Odette's lightness in my grasp, the swell of her breast against the backs of my fingers where I had seized her arm. I sensed rather than felt her skin, the muscles and bones underneath. I was made suddenly and powerfully conscious of Odette's physical person, her womanliness, her sexuality—how else can I explain the excitement I felt?

I had released Odette the instant I saw she could stand and yet that moment of holding each other so reverberated all about us that we did not speak until we had reached the cottage door.

"Why are you looking at me like that?" she asked.

"Like what?" I asked.

"As if you were going to laugh at me."

While I unlocked the front door Odette stepped back to look at the rough stone cottage, then I stood aside and Odette walked into the large downstairs room. She went directly to the stone fireplace and ran her hand across the hewn-beam mantel, then down the stones.

"It's lovely," Odette said, "it really is."

She walked about touching things, the edge of the small stove, the refrigerator door, the molding on the windowsills. Seeing her, I felt as though I were seeing the cottage for the first time, too, through her eyes.

"You really do like it, don't you," I said.

"Of course I do," she said.

"I'll show you the upstairs."

Sunlight streamed down through the tall trees and in through the dormer windows, flooding the bedrooms in light.

"I would never want to leave here," Odette said.

"I know. I wouldn't mind living here."

"It would be small with Alice and the children," Odette said, "but I could see you living here alone."

"I don't like living alone," I said.

"You could invite friends," she said, walking into the bathroom.

"I could," I said. "Would you come?"

"You've even got an old ball and claw tub!" she said, pretending not to hear me.

When we returned to the Baskin house Arthur and Alice had already departed in our car and taken the children with them, so I drove to our house with Odette. As we got out of the car Alice came to the door. "Arthur's gone to get bathing suits," Alice said. "He and the children are going to take a swim."

"Is he going to pick up my suit, too?" Odette asked.

"He didn't say," Alice replied.

Arthur brought Odette the tight one-piece burgundy Spandex bathing suit I liked. Alice wore the bikini she had worn the afternoon she and Barbara T. had removed their tops. It was so scant that Alice seldom wore it when we had male guests and I remember noting that she had decided to wear it in front of Arthur.

We ended up having hot dogs and baked beans together by the side of the pool and later on, that evening, while we were having coffee the telephone rang and I went into the house to answer it.

It was Maggie. "I just can't handle Joan," she said.

"What do you mean?"

"I mean I can't talk to her. She won't talk to me. She won't help around the house, she won't respond to me at all."

"What do you want me to do?"

"She needs you. She needs a man to keep her in line."

"Joan said she wanted to live with you."

"But that's because she knows she can get away with things here she can't do with you. She just won't do what I ask. I can't control her at all."

"Is she causing trouble?"

"Not the kind you mean. She's a good girl. She just won't do what I ask. All she wants to do is watch TV."

"Be firm, Maggie."

"How? She's already almost as tall as I am. I can't spank her. What am I supposed to do, take away her desserts?"

"She'll have to shape up when she starts school."

"I don't want Joan out here," Maggie said.

"*What?*"

"I told you. I can't handle her. She treats me like a stranger. She's not mine anymore. She's changed."

"Of course she's changed. She's thirteen now, she's not a little girl any longer. You can't just give up. You've only had her for—what? Six weeks? You're her *mother*. You've got to try to—"

"I'm telling you I'm sending Joan back. She's going to have to live with you."

I asked to speak to Joan but Maggie said she was at a friend's house and she'd have Joan call me in the morning.

"Who was that?" Alice asked when I walked back out to the pool.

"Maggie," I said.

"What did *she* want?"

"She wants to send Joan back," I said.

"Swell," Alice said. "I told you so. What reason did she—Maggie," Alice explained, turning to Arthur and Odette, "was his *first* wife. He picked a real winner that time."

"Maggie said she couldn't handle Joan," I said.

"What does *that* mean?" Alice asked.

"That Joan won't pay attention to her."

"So what else is new? What did you tell her?"

"I told Maggie she was Joan's mother, that she had to try."

"And what did she say to that?"

"She said I was Joan's father."

"Well, I'll tell you this," Alice said. "I don't want her here either."

"I know," I said miserably.

"Joan said she wanted to live with her mother. It's up to them to work it out."

"I've asked that Joan call me in the morning. I'll talk to her then and see what's going on."

"You do that," Alice said.

Not surprisingly, the party broke up shortly thereafter.

The following morning I was in my office catching up on some correspondence and bills while waiting for Joan to call. The children used my office as their changing room for the pool and from my desk I could see Vanessa's and Paul's wooden clogs and Peter's rubber flip-flops and their other clothing scattered about. Peter's small blue T-shirt lay on the floor next to Odette's son's red-and-yellow-striped one. Paul, two years younger than Peter, was already the same height and Vanessa, who was Peter's age, towered over him. I folded Peter's T-shirt and shorts and put them on the old office couch, then did the same with Paul's.

Several mornings before, Peter had come out to the office and hung around. Usually he would bop in and out like a beach ball on his way to the pool, but that morning he had wandered instead around the perimeter of my desk, not really bothering me yet not leaving me alone either.

"Something on your mind?" I finally asked.

"Well, sort of," he said. He came over and leaned against my knee.

"You want to talk it over?"

"Daddy, it's just . . . why does everybody tell me I'm so small? Am I always going to be small?"

"Of course not," I said. "The only reason you seem small is because the other children are growing so fast. Every child grows differently. Some stay small until they're thirteen, then sprout, grow very fast like Joan is. Others grow at a very steady pace like Vanessa . . ." I pedaled the office chair over to the center post of the office on which I'd marked off the children's heights. "Look at this. You've already grown over half an inch since the first of the year."

That night instead of reading Peter a bedtime story as I usually did, we sat together on his bed turning the pages of old photograph albums which showed Joan and Peter growing up. I even had photographs of Alice as a little girl; she had been small, too, always the shortest in her class until she was twelve.

The next morning, when Peter came out to the office again, he approached me very seriously and said, "Daddy, I want to thank you for talking to me about being small. I feel much better now." There was about a two-beat pause and then he complained that I had hung his bathing suit on a peg too high for him to reach. I apologized, saying that I didn't think of him as a little boy.

"I'm not a little boy, Dad," he said. "I'm small. That's all."

"Right, kid," I said. "Wanna cigar?"

After I'd folded the children's clothing I sat back down at my desk to wait for Joan's call. I didn't know what I was going to say to her. She was driving her mother crazy in Oregon; she did the same to Alice here in New Jersey. Neither her mother nor stepmother wanted her around. If she stayed with Maggie in Oregon, she'd be going to a local junior high school and from what little Maggie had told me about the schools in her district I was not impressed by the quality of education. I also knew Joan was not the sort to seek a better education on her own. On the other hand, if I brought her back East, although she would be in a decent junior high school, the increased tension her presence would create between Alice and myself would cause an unbearable strain. I wondered if I could get her into a boarding school.

At a boarding school she would be given the best possible education, be kept busy, forced to push herself, and, most important, learn to take responsibility. She would be among kids her own age and in a stable environment away from her parents and their problems. Boarding schools weren't the end of the world. I'd gone to one when I was nine and I'd survived, hadn't I?

Barely. In the first place I never spent any extended time with girls until I was in my twenties. In the second place, since I was seldom home, I had no idea what family life was supposed to be, what a man was expected to do. But the schools—the world—*everything* was different now and Joan was thirteen, which was a lot different from being nine.

The telephone rang. It was Joan calling collect, which put me in a bad mood right away.

"Hullo, Dad," she said.

"Joan, I spoke to your mother last night. What's going on out there?"

"Nothing," she said in a monotone.

"She says you don't pay any attention to her, don't talk to her. All you do is watch TV."

She was silent.

"Why is that?" I asked.

"It's really good TV," she said. "Mom's got the cable."

I had to fight down the impulse to laugh. "The relative merits of cable TV versus our own is not the point. The point is that you told me you wanted to live with your mother and now that you're out there you're driving her crazy."

"She wants to send me back, doesn't she," she said.

"Right now she does, yes," I said, "but maybe if you helped your mother around the house, treated her more like a person instead of your private maid—"

"I wouldn't mind coming back," Joan interrupted.

"If you did, it might be to go to a boarding school."

"A *boarding* school! Why?"

"Because I think it may be what you need."

"Why?"

"For a lot of reasons."

"When would I have to go?"

"I don't know yet," I said. "I'm not even sure this late in the summer I could find one that would take you in—especially with your last year's grades. In the meantime, your job is to do what you can do to help your mother, and I'll see what I can do from here."

After hanging up I immediately called Packy Townsend, a former classmate who was now director of admissions at St. Matthew's, a boarding school I had attended when it had been for boys only. I explained Joan's background to Packy, that I wanted her to be stimulated, excited about learning, that although she was smart I was frustrated by how poorly she did in school. I also told him that if Joan came back to live with Alice and me I didn't know what was going to happen to our marriage.

"Why?" he asked. "Is it in trouble?"

"Isn't everybody's?"

Packy started talking about how competitive St. Matthew's was, that it was a "pressure cooker." He asked more questions about Joan and then told me the school would need transcripts, letters of recommendation, her SSAT scores. He said he'd put the application forms in the mail to me right away and that it was important that we schedule an interview for her at the school as soon as possible.

"When is your daughter coming East?" Packy asked.

"I haven't made any arrangements yet. I wanted to speak with you first."

"Today's July the . . . the thirty-first . . . we should see her no later than the ninth. I have an opening at ten-thirty on Thursday, the ninth."

"Put us down. I'll get Joan there . . . and Packy?"

"Yes?"

"Thanks," I said.

"Don't thank me yet," he said.

I went back outside and pulled up a deck chair next to Alice. Peter was shouting for me to watch him swim.

"Watch, Daddy, *watch!*" Peter yelled.

"I'm watching," I said.

"What are you going to do about Joan?" Alice asked.

"I'm going to try to get her into St. Matthew's."

"And if you can't get her in?"

"I'll try someplace else."

"What if no one will take her?"

"Then she'll have to stay with us. At least in the Baskin house she'll have her own room."

"Then I want my own room, too," Alice said.

During the next couple of days I gathered up Joan's transcripts, found out she had taken her SSATs while I'd been in Leadville, and requested copies of her scores. I bullied my friends into writing letters of recommendation, made airline reservations and appointments with doctors, then called Maggie to say that Joan's flight would leave L.A. at seven on Tuesday morning, the seventh.

"So soon?" Maggie asked.

Three days later I picked Joan up at Newark. "How've you been?"

"Fine, now," she said.

"What do you mean 'now'?"

"I was sick."

"How sick?"

"Pretty sick."

"Jesus Christ!" I exploded. "Tell me what's been going on!"

"Nothing now," she said. Then seeing my impatience building up again, she swiftly added, "I took my temperature Saturday night and it was 104, but it was down to 101 the next morning. It was normal by Monday. I haven't had a temperature since then."

"Good," I said.

"What's for dinner? Will there be meat?"

"Of course there's meat. Why?"

"Good. Mom's a vegetarian now. I've been broccolied to death."

Joan worked all the next morning on her St. Matthew's application forms. She had to fill out a three-part questionnaire designed to let the school know more about what sort of person she was, how she would evaluate herself. The first part was a "Choose One:"

A. Project yourself into the future. Assume, if you can, that you are a grown adult and living a life which pleases you and fulfills your needs. Consider marriage, children, career, any aspect of life that you now think of as a desirable goal. What would you be doing? Who would be with you? What would be the most important characteristics of your life? Tell us about forty-eight hours of your ideal life. Go into as much detail as you can picture in your fantasy—smells, sounds, sights, the weather, if they play a part.

B. Reflect upon the years of your life until now and try to tell us about an experience you had which made you feel worthwhile. Did it involve an activity you were good at? Would you consider it one of the most important events in your life? Was this something you experienced by yourself or with others? Describe this experience briefly and conclude with one of the following statements:

I learned that I . . .

I was surprised that I . . .

I left her alone and went to work outside on the lawn. When I came back in for a glass of water, Joan had moved onto Part Two, designed to explore some of her "interests, likes, dislikes, goals, and aspirations" by having her complete unfinished sentences such as:

The happiest day in my life was . . . ("When I got my braces off," Joan wrote.)

Something I am striving to become or to be, is . . . ("a good friend to those I care about," she answered.)

One success I've had after the age of ten is . . . ("Winning the hundred-meter freestyle in the swimming championship.")

If I had to live my life all over again, I would . . . ("Not have eaten so much fattening foods.")

I get angry when . . . ("I make careless mistakes.")

There were fourteen of them in all.

The final section was, *I feel most successful when I* . . . and the applicant was given choices: . . . *am the smartest in class.*

. . . *have a great many friends.*

. . . *am the best athlete.*

. . . *am drawing or painting or playing music.*

Joan chose having friends.

By the time she was finished and had shown me her application we were both disturbed.

Joan was disturbed because she didn't already know what she was supposed to do with the rest of her life. I was disturbed because I was having her apply to a school that suggested she *ought* to know.

I handed Joan's application paper back to her, and she got up and flicked on the TV.

"No!" I shouted. "Turn that goddam thing off!"

My daughter turned to me in amazement.

"It's not even eleven-thirty in the morning, and you think you're going to watch TV? You're coming outside to work with me on the lawn."

Joan and I worked outside all afternoon and then at four-thirty I quit to shower and dress for the dinner meeting I had to attend in New York for area classmates from college.

Our twentieth reunion was just two months away and the reunion chairman had specifically asked me to come. He wanted me to chair a midlife crisis discussion to be held during the reunion. I liked the reunion chairman and he had never called on me for a favor before, so I agreed. The most memorable moment of that dinner, however, occurred when I first walked into the room. The men gathered there were so wrinkled and paunchy, gray-haired and harried-looking, that I first thought I had entered the wrong private dining room, one reserved not for my classmates, but for a group of men twenty years older.

That night when I returned home I told Alice how startling it had been to be confronted so suddenly and incontrovertibly with such evidence of my own advancing age.

The next morning I drove Joan up to St. Matthew's. During the trip I tried to suggest what she might expect in the interview, how to handle the questions, that she should just try to answer as articulately and openly as possible. I had hoped that by explaining to Joan what was to come I would help her relax. My words had exactly the opposite effect. By the time we passed through the brick gates leading into the school she had slumped down in her seat in apprehension and dread.

A secretary at the admissions desk directed us to Packy Townsend's office. When we entered I saw immediately that Packy, like my college classmates, had aged. He had lost all but a fringe of hair above his ears, wore thick horn-rimmed glasses, and when he rose from his desk to greet us I noticed that he had gained at least thirty pounds.

"You must be Joan," Packy said, turning to my daughter.

"Joan, this is Mr. Townsend," I said. She somewhat tentatively took Packy's hand.

"How do you like your dad's old school?" Packy asked.

Joan shrugged. "It's okay . . . Pretty good, I guess."

"We just drove in," I said. "I haven't had a chance to show her around. She's never seen the school before."

Packy seated us in front of his desk and went to his chair behind it, picked up a pencil and brushed at some dust on a pad. "Joan, do you think you're ready for a boarding school?"

"I dunno," Joan said.

I said, "Joan's thirteen now. She's a pretty independent sort of kid."

"But," Packy asked Joan, "do you want to go away to school?"

"I guess so," Joan said.

I said, "That's a tough question, Packy. How can she know? She's never been away to school before."

"I guess I'd like to," Joan said. "I never really thought about it too much."

I said, "The possibility of sending Joan away to school didn't arise until I called you a little over a week ago."

"Well, Joan," Packy said, "it's not as grim as it sounds. There are movies and dances. The students put on plays. We have a student television station, the students do broadcasts . . ."

"Television?" Joan asked.

"Are you interested in television?"

"She sure is," I said. "Too much, if you ask me."

"I didn't ask you," Packy said. "I'm supposed to be interviewing Joan, not you. You've already been to this school."

"Right," I said. "You're right. Why don't I get some coffee and wait outside."

"That's a good idea," Packy said. "I'll call you when I need you."

Sometimes I behave like such an ass I want to kick myself. I *knew* I was jumping in on every question Packy asked my daughter. I *knew* I wasn't letting Joan speak. But I couldn't stop. I was so worried that she would grunt her way through the interview, and that Packy would turn her down on the spot.

After the interview Joan was given a tour of the school by the seventeen-year-old son of one of the faculty members. He was a senior at St. Matthew's, himself. While the two of them went off I went back inside to talk to Packy, who was still in his office.

"What do you think?" I asked.

"I found it difficult to get her to open up at the interview . . ."

"I was afraid of that."

"Her SSATs are high enough, but these transcripts worry me. Her previous teachers all certainly think she could do the work. Why didn't she?"

"I don't know, Packy," I said. "I have as much trouble getting her to talk as you did."

"She might talk more if you let her."

During the drive back down to our old New Jersey town I asked Joan how she thought the interview had gone.

"Pretty good, I guess," she said.

"What did Mr. Townsend ask you?"

"What I was reading."

"Oh? What are you reading?"

"*Dove.*"

"What's that about?" I asked.

"A boy who sails around the world alone."

"What else were you asked?"

"What sort of things I was interested in," Joan said.

"Yes?"

"I said sports, I guess."

"Are you?"

"Sure," she said, and she turned away from me to look out the window.

"Did he ask you anything else?"

"I don't remember."

"You must have been asked more than what you were reading and what you're interested in."

"Well, sure I was," she said.

"So?"

"I guess he asked me what I thought I could contribute to the St. Matthew's community. I told him I could be on the swimming team."

"Maybe you could," I said. "What were some of the other things you talked about?"

"I don't know," she said. "I just tried to answer the questions the way I thought he wanted."

"The way *he* wanted! Why?"

"So I'd get in."

Barbara T.'s car was parked in our driveway when Joan and I got home. There was no one at the pool and when we went into the house it was empty too. Joan said she thought she'd take a swim and I said I thought I would, too. It was about three-thirty in the afternoon. While Joan went up to her room to change I went upstairs to mine.

I pulled one of my old, ill-fitting bathing suits out of the bottom drawer of my bureau and opened the bathroom door. Barbara T. was standing naked, damp, and pink next to the tub. I'm not sure which of us was the most surprised.

"I was washing my hair," she said.

"I was just going to change into my suit," I said. We had both spoken at exactly the same time.

At that moment Alice pulled into the driveway in her car. By the time she had entered the house and made it upstairs Barbara T. was blow-drying her hair behind the closed bathroom door and I had one leg in and one leg out of my old bathing suit. Without pausing to say a word to me, Alice whirled by me and opened the bathroom door. Barbara T. was standing with a towel around her waist, but her bosom was bare. I had managed to get both legs into my bathing suit but had pulled it only as high up as my knees. I was struggling to slide it the rest of the way when Alice turned from the door and asked me, "Do you have to expose yourself to Barbara T.?"

For one of the few times in our marriage I was at a total loss for what to say.

Work had already started on the new house and after a quick swim I drove out to see how it was going. The last of the porches had finally been torn off and the plain wooden clapboards, newly exposed now that the front of the house had been returned to its simple eighteenth-century facade, were of an entirely different color from the rest. As a result, even though the porches were gone, their ghostly outlines remained. I asked Fred Wright, the carpenter, how long it would take for the exposed clapboards to blend in.

"Hard to tell," he said. "Maybe a year. Maybe never."

"Could they be stained to match?"

"Maybe," he said. "Wood's a funny thing."

As I started to turn away, Fred said, "By the way, I've brought you my first bill."

I took the envelope and put it in my pocket. "I'll give you a check when I come back out tomorrow."

"Appreciate it," he said.

I opened the envelope when I was back in the car. The bill came to just under two thousand dollars, nine hundred and nine of which was for materials, the rest for ten days of labor at twelve dollars an hour. It was, I knew, the first of an avalanche of bills to come. Added to it would be the cost now of a boarding school. I felt the familiar prickles of panic.

That evening the Villars invited us over for drinks after dinner, to meet their friend Philippe, who had just arrived from France.

We sat in the living room and shared a joint while we listened to records. Philippe was saying something about the drug trade in Marseille and Alice said that buying marijuana was the only business I was any good at, that I ought to quit making movies and become a dealer.

"A dealer?" Arthur said. "He's too neurotic to be a dealer."

"All *artistes* are *néurotiques, non?*" Philippe asked.

" 'I praise the Frenchman, his remark was shrewd,' " I quoted, " 'How sweet, how passing sweet, is solitude! / But grant me still,' " I said, turning to Odette, who was seated next to me on the couch, and taking her hand, " 'a friend in my retreat / Whom I may whisper, Solitude is sweet.' "

Odette turned to Alice with a questioning look.

"It's from a poem by William Cowper called 'Retirement,' " I said.

"He always starts quoting poetry when he gets stoned," Barbara T. said, and both Alice and Odette turned to look at her.

Later on that evening while Arthur and Alice and Philippe and Barbara T. were talking together in the living room I was sitting at the kitchen table with Odette. We had been talking about how much more difficult daughters were to raise than sons, that the girls seemed to be in constant conflict with their mothers. "Maggie doesn't want Joan around, Alice doesn't either," I was saying, "and so here I am sending her away to boarding school and I'm sure she feels I'm rejecting her, too."

"But surely Joan recognizes it's for her own good."

"I suspect she thinks it's a punishment."

"Well, you have to admit she is difficult to live with."

"Who isn't?" I asked.

Odette was silent.

"I worry about Peter, too. About how he's going to grow up, how he's going to feel about women. How is he going to learn about love if all he sees is Alice and me?"

"The same way all of us did," Odette said. "Through experience. And he'll make mistakes like we all did but with any luck he'll learn from them."

"It would be so much easier if boys were sent off at a certain age to live with an older woman, someone with the patience and tenderness to teach them and to make them feel like a man."

"Peter's a little young for that, don't you think?"

"He is now," I said, "but ten years from now . . ."

"Ten years from now he'll find a girl his own age to learn with. They'll teach each other."

"In the old days men sent their sons off to their mistresses. I suspect no one does that anymore. But, sometimes I still think it would be nice if a father could send his son off to an older woman friend."

"Who would you send Peter off to?" Odette asked. She paused for a moment, then slyly asked, "Someone like Barbara T.?"

"Someone like you," I replied.

"*Like me?*" Odette asked, flaring up. "I'd want the father, not the son!"

Her sudden vehemence surprised me as much as what she had said. For the second time that day I was at a loss for words. Could Odette want *me?*

"Don't laugh!" she said.

"I'm not," I said. "If I'm smiling it's only because—I only—"

"What?" she asked.

"I thought we were only friends. I didn't think we—"

"We *are* only friends," she said. "We're both too chicken to be anything else."

"Too 'chicken'?"

"Now don't get your male pride all injured. All I mean is that I can desire you a little and you can desire me a little, but we won't do anything about it."

"We won't?"

"Of course not."

"Why?" I asked.

"Because we are too comfortable with what we've got. You've just bought a new house. You have your children. You have . . ." Odette's voice trailed off as Barbara T. entered the kitchen.

"Is there more ice?" Barbara T. asked.

"I'll get it for you," I said, rising.

"She can get it herself," Odette said. "It's in the freezer."

While Barbara T. was emptying the ice tray Arthur came out to the kitchen. "Alice and Philippe would like some coffee," he said, and he put the kettle on the stove. "Would either of you like some?"

I was not alone again with Odette until Alice, Barbara T., and myself were getting ready to leave. We had just an instant together while trying to locate my cigarette lighter. "When you get home tonight," Odette asked me, "are you and Alice going to make love?"

The directness of her question so surprised me that it took me a moment to answer. "The odds are against it," I finally said.

During the short walk back to our house Alice said to Barbara T. about Arthur, "What I admire about him so much is how well he's planning for the future."

Alice *knew* how that would gall me.

I took a deep breath and exhaled it slowly. I knew better than to say anything to Alice about her remark. She would just tell me not to feel threatened. And so we walked the rest of the way in silence.

When we arrived home I saw that Joan had left the half-gallon milk carton on the kitchen counter; the milk was now lukewarm. Her milk glass, unwashed, sat in the sink. There were cookie crumbs on the seat of my chair in the library, a wet-glass ring on the tabletop nearby. While Barbara T. and Alice went upstairs I cleaned up after my daughter. What I really felt like doing was storming up to her bedroom, hauling her out of bed, and bringing her down to clean it up herself. Perhaps I should have.

When I went upstairs Barbara T. was bent over the sink in the guest bathroom brushing her teeth. As I passed she turned her head to look up at me, her lips foaming. She was wearing the same long white nylon nightgown she had worn that evening we had sat together in the library. Because she was still leaning forward the gown had fallen away from her bosom and I could see the soft, rosy curves of her tanned breasts.

"Are you coming to bed?" Alice called.

"G'night, Barbara T.," I said.

And later, lying in bed beside Alice, I was thinking about what Odette had said about wanting me. I was wondering why I had not thought of Odette as a lover before. Had Odette been suggesting we have an affair? Or was I making too much out of what might just have been an angry response to an innocent though, to her, thoughtless remark on my part? And yet there had been Odette's parting question about whether Alice and I were going to make love. It was not the sort of question asked out of curiosity alone. I pictured Odette in her bathing suit, climbing out of the pool, the shimmer of water on her bronze shoulders, her dark hair clinging wetly to her skull. I thought of her long, tanned, perfect legs scissored across my back and found myself becoming aroused. I tried to imagine Odette's expression as we made love, the fullness of her lower lip. Alice's back was to me and I gently touched her hip. She did not jerk away; nor, however, did she encourage me.

She lay on one side, her legs curled up toward her chest. I began to caress her lightly, the backs of her thighs. And when I asked, "Would you like to make love?" she remained on her side and did not answer. But I took her lack of response as tacit approval. I moved closer to her until we were curled together like a pair of spoons, and continued to touch her until it was possible for me to enter her from behind. She still made no sound. I began to move slowly and continued to caress her. In the darkness of our bedroom Alice could have been anyone. I imagined that she was Odette, but the image of Odette would blur, her face would fade and become Barbara T.'s. And then there was Odette and Barbara T.

"It's good," I whispered into the back of Alice's neck. "We haven't made love in a long time. Is it good for you? Do you want me to move faster? More slowly?" No response. I could not tell from Alice's breathing whether she was enjoying it. "It's so nice like this," I said. Alice did not answer. I felt frustrated that she did not respond, but decided we might as well enjoy it. I close my eyes and take my time.

Our bed is making soft, rhythmic squeaks. I wonder if Barbara T. can hear us. I imagine her listening from her room, becoming excited, touching herself until she must slip out of bed and come to our door. She opens it silently and stands there watching us. Her hands glide up her body as she moves slowly toward us until she is standing cupping her breasts and I see her swaying slightly just beyond Alice's shoulder. Barbara T. lets her nightgown slide to the floor. Alice begins to push back against me.

"It feels so good," I say. "Does it feel good to you?"

Alice does not speak.

I close my eyes again. Barbara T. leans forward, edges closer to the bed, then rests one knee on the side of our bed, her hand drops to touch herself, her other hand caresses Alice's breast. Alice gasps. *Yes*, I tell Barbara T., *yes, do it.* Barbara T.'s hand leaves Alice's breast and moves down to where Alice and I are joined. She wants to feel me moving into

Alice. One of Barbara T.'s hands is on herself, the other on me. Alice reaches out for Barbara T. and my orgasm begins.

"Yes," I said. "It's so close now, so close . . ."

My eyes remained tightly closed. I see Barbara T. bending lower, bending until her breast brushes Alice's cheek. Alice and I are still on our sides, Barbara T.'s hand is touching us, caressing me, urging me to fuck Alice harder, deeper. Alice's head is twisting back and forth. Barbara T.'s nipple touches Alice's lips. *Yes, Alice,* Barbara T. is saying, *suck me.* The orgasm takes over and I am slamming into Alice again and again and again, then my body stills. I open my eyes. Alice and I are alone.

"My God," I said, "I haven't come like that in so long!"

Alice did not speak.

"Was it—did you come?" I asked.

Alice still did not answer.

"You were so quiet," I said. "I couldn't tell."

After a while Alice said, "I'm just very passive about sex. I'm not a noise-maker."

"But did you come?"

"What difference does it make?"

"I wanted it to be good for you."

"Look," Alice said, "the reason why you don't turn me on more is that you're too sweet and you talk too much."

The following Thursday, I learned Joan had been accepted at St. Matthew's, and that a vacancy had suddenly opened up in the Communications Department at NYU and the director wanted me to teach this fall term. Then George Mason, my producer, called and said he wanted me to go with him to Chicago, Denver, and Los Angeles on the twenty-seventh of the month through the thirty-first for advanced screenings of our cancer film before medical and special interest groups. We'd be back for Labor Day weekend.

I woke Joan up to tell her about St. Matthew's. "I got in, did I?" she asked. "That's great, I guess."

"You'll need clothes," I said. "Some shirts, sweaters, jackets, loafers . . ."

"*Loafers?*" Joan asked. "Nobody I know wears *loafers* these days."

"Well, whatever it is girls wear," I said.

She was sitting up in bed now rubbing her eyes.

"Get yourself going," I said. "I'll take you into Princeton. We can probably find everything you need at the university store."

Joan looked at me with a rueful smile. "So I'm going to be a *preppy?*"

After I told Alice the news she said, "That job in New York will make it very convenient for you."

"What do you mean?"

"You'll be back with the coeds you like so much."

"Alice, it's one day a week."

"And you'll go in the night before, I bet."

"I don't know," I said. "Since I haven't yet accepted the job I don't know what time the class would be scheduled for. If it's in the early afternoon I can take the train in and back out the same day."

"But you won't," she said. "When are you going west?"

"The week after next. I'd leave Monday the twenty-seventh and return Friday the thirty-first."

Barbara T. came down the stairs and into the kitchen. "I'd better get started on the cake," she said.

"Barbara T. and I are taking a trip too," Alice said.

"You are?" I asked. "When? Where are you going?"

"Tomorrow to Long Island," Alice said.

"Tomorrow's my nephew's birthday," Barbara T. said. "My sister's rented a cottage out in Bridgehampton on the beach."

The telephone rang and Alice answered it. It was Dudley Thompson and she handed the phone to me. Barbara T. went outside to the pool.

"Hello, Dudley, what's up?" I asked.

Joan came down to the kitchen, too, and started making herself a bowl of cereal. Dudley was saying he had some people who wanted to look at our house. "I know I haven't had a chance to draw up the contract yet, but this couple are very eager to see your house and they're leaving town late this afternoon. Can I bring them out?"

"This afternoon?" I asked.

"I don't want anyone coming here today," Alice said. "The house isn't in any shape to be shown."

"Alice says the house isn't in shape," I said.

"Tell her the couple knows it's short notice and they won't mind if the house isn't tidied up," Dudley said.

"You tell her, Dudley," I said, and passed the phone back to Alice. "Hash it out between the two of you. I've got to get Joan into Princeton."

Alice took the phone and said, "No, Dudley. You can't show it today. Tell them to come by tomorrow . . . Well, tell them to spend another night, Dudley, I'm sorry," she said, and hung up.

"You finished, Joan?" I asked. "We've got to go."

Joan put her cereal bowl in the sink.

"Goddam it!" I said. "Rinse your bowl and put it in the dishwasher! I'm willing to be your chauffeur but not your maid, too!"

"*I'm* her maid," Alice said.

As Joan put her bowl in the washer I asked if she'd made her bed. She shook her head, no. "Do it," I said. "I'll wait."

"I thought we were in a hurry to get into Princeton," she said.

"I'll *wait*," I said.

As Joan darted back upstairs Alice said, "Have a good time with her when I'm gone."

On the way to my office to get my checkbook, I stopped by the pool. Barbara T. was doing the New York *Times* crossword puzzle in the sun.

"How are you today?" she asked.

"Fine."

"Really?"

"Really," I said. While shaving that morning I had decided that no matter how I felt I would tell people I was "fine" and that that was all anybody needed to know. "What time tomorrow are you and Alice leaving for Bridgehampton?"

"In the morning. We thought it might be fun. Peter's never met my nephew, who's his age."

"You're taking Peter, too?"

"Didn't Alice tell you?" she asked, and looked back down at her puzzle. " 'Languid,' nine letters ending in 'E,' 'D,' . . . Blank, blank, E, R, blank, blank, blank, E, D."

" 'Enervated,' " I said.

Dudley Thompson was at our house when Joan and I arrived back from shopping. A young couple were in the yard outside. "I called Alice back and she relented," Dudley explained. We were standing in the kitchen. Barbara T.'s freshly baked cake with its Happy Birthday message written on the icing rested on the counter next to the stove. "Who's Andy?" Dudley asked.

"Who?" I asked.

"Happy Birthday Andy," he said, pointing at the cake.

"I guess it's Barbara T.'s nephew."

"Well, whoever it is, it's a nice touch."

"A nice touch?"

"A couple comes to look at a house and it's filled with the scent of a freshly baked cake. . . . It's a nice touch."

"How do they like the house?" I asked.

"They think it's 'utterly divine,' according to the woman. And that you and Alice have 'such good taste.' "

"That's nice," I said. "Where are Alice and Barbara T.?"

"They said they'd be back in a little while."

Much later that afternoon, after Dudley and his couple had departed and after Alice and Barbara T. had returned, Odette came down for a swim. She was sitting on the edge of a deck chair while I stood behind her rubbing some *Bain de Soleil* between her shoulder blades when she said, "Barbara T. and Alice are watching us from the bathroom window."

"I wouldn't be surprised," I said.

"Arthur's going to Chicago for a convention next week. He's leaving Sunday night and will be gone most of the week. Philippe, too. He's going to New York."

"Alice and Barbara T. will be gone, too," I said. "They're leaving for Long Island tomorrow, taking Peter with them."

"So you and Joan will be here alone?"

"Yup," I said. I screwed the cap back on the suntan tube and sat down in the deck chair next to hers. I took my time glancing up at the bathroom window, but no one was there.

"Joan was accepted at St. Matthew's," I said.

"That must be a relief," she said.

"It is. And this morning I was offered a job at NYU to teach a film seminar one day a week."

"Will you take it?"

"I don't know."

"I love New York," Odette said, reaching for a cigarette.

"Do you go into town often?" I asked, passing her my lighter.

"Not often enough." She fumbled with my lighter and it slipped from her hand, bounced once, and disappeared into the pool.

I burst out laughing.

"You're not angry?" she asked.

"Why should I be angry? It was a marvelous shot. I'll get it when we go in for a swim." I stood up. "I've got some matches in the office."

Odette rose, too. "I'll get them. You sit. Just tell me where they are."

"I haven't the foggiest idea," I said. "I'll have to root them out."

We went into the office together and Odette sat on my old, battered couch while I sifted through the debris on my desk.

"What are you working on now?" Odette asked.

"Nothing," I said. "And it's driving me crazy . . . Ah! Here they are." I brought the matches back to the couch and sat next to Odette. When I held the flame to her cigarette Odette's cool fingers lightly touched mine. Her hand trembled slightly and I felt my mouth go dry. It took me two tries to blow out the match. And then, when I took a cigarette out of my case, I saw that my hand was trembling, too. Odette was watching me with a slight smile at the edge of her lips. I leaned forward and gently kissed the corner of her mouth.

"Why did you do that?" she asked.

"I wanted to."

"Do you always do what you want?"

"So I've been told," I said. "I'd like to do it again."

This time when we kissed our lips were not dry. Her lips were so soft, her taste so sweet, that I wanted to kiss her again, but when I had pulled back the expression on Odette's face was one of such tenderness and surprise that I laughed with pure joy.

"You are always laughing at me!" she said.

"Not *at* you, with you."

"But I'm not laughing."

"Inside you are."

"How do you know that?" she asked.

"Because the kiss was as much of a joyful surprise to you as it was to me."

"A surprise?"

"Yes," I said. "Because it was so nice. I have never had a kiss so nice."

She appeared to consider my remark for a moment, then said, "Yes. It was nice."

I struck a match to light a cigarette for myself and the flaming matchhead snapped off and struck my chest. "Ouch! Jesus!" I said, jumping up and beating at the sting on my chest. I knocked the coffee table over in the process spilling the ashtray with Odette's lighted cigarette to the rug.

We were both on our hands and knees cleaning up the mess and Odette had just said, "We make quite a couple," when Alice walked in.

10

"I HOPE I'M NOT interrupting anything?" Alice asked.

Odette and I, still on our hands and knees, looked up at Alice standing over us.

"We're out of milk," Alice said. "I need you to go to the market."

"Right now?" I asked.

"It closes in another half-hour."

Odette stood up. "I'll go with you," she said. "I need some things at the market, too." She dropped several cigarette butts back into the ashtray, dusted off her hands, then walked past Alice to the pool where she had draped her T-shirt dress over the back of a deck chair. I put the overturned coffee table back on its feet and picked up the last cigarette butts feeling Alice's eyes on me all the while.

My eyes were on me, too.

In my mind's eye I saw myself kissing Odette again. If Alice had entered a moment earlier she would have caught us and then all hell would have broken loose! I sat back down on the couch. Why had I taken such a stupid risk? What had I been trying to prove?

I looked beyond Alice to where Odette was slipping into her dress. *We are only friends*, Odette had said. *We're both too chicken to be anything else.* I thought about the gentleness of the kiss, and I thought about how her hand had trembled, how my mouth had gone dry. I thought about Alice's comment of the night before: "The reason why you don't turn me on . . ."

"Well?" Alice said, still looking at me. "Are you going to the market or not?"

Odette reentered the office. "I'm ready," she said. "Shall we go?"

I stood up and put my old khakis and shirt on over my bathing suit. I looked at Alice's sullen face, at Odette's soft brown eyes, her slightly pouty lower lip. I wished at that moment with all my heart that I could pick up the half-gallon of milk with Odette and just keep on going, that I would never have to see Alice again.

The following morning, Friday, Joan and Peter and I were eating breakfast at the kitchen counter. Alice was still upstairs asleep. We could hear water running in the guest bathroom. "Barbara T.'s up," Joan said.

She pushed herself away from the counter, started to walk away, then reconsidered and carried her cereal bowl to the sink.

"Don't just leave it there, Joan," I said.

"Here," Peter said, passing her his bowl. "Rinse mine, too, while you're there."

"Do it yourself," Joan said.

Barbara T. came downstairs wearing a light cotton bathrobe over her nightgown. "Good morning, everybody," she said, and she kissed me lightly on the cheek.

"Morning," I said. "The New York *Times* is on the coffee table."

"I want to take that wicker plant stand I found out to my sister's," Barbara T. said. "Will you help me load it in my car?"

There were moments when I felt more married to Barbara T. than I did to Alice.

I was securing the wicker plant stand to the top of Barbara T.'s Saab when Alice came out and announced that she and Barbara T. had decided to take the Peugeot station wagon instead. "You won't need it," Alice said. Barbara T. appeared with her luggage and told Alice that Peter couldn't find his bathing suit. While Alice went back to help Peter I untied the plant stand, slid it into the Peugeot, then lifted Barbara T.'s suitcases in, too.

She and I were standing by the car waiting for Alice and Peter when Barbara T. asked, "Is Odette your new girl friend?"

"No. She's a friend, sure," I said. "I like her very much. But she's not a 'girl friend,' if I understand your meaning."

Alice came to the back door and called out to me, "The rest of the suitcases are in the kitchen, would you bring them out?"

"Where's Joan? Can't she carry some?"

"She's off somewhere."

I noticed her bike was gone from the garage.

When the car was loaded Peter tilted his head up for a kiss. "'Bye, Daddy," he said.

I kissed Barbara T. and Alice, too; I kissed all three of them on the cheek. It was only after the car had pulled out of the driveway that I realized how ludicrous that scene had been: *Good-bye, dear—and you, too, dear.*

Joan and I finished the lawn by four o'clock and she went off on her bike again. I telephoned Odette and asked if she would like to come down for a swim. She declined, explaining that she and Arthur were off to play tennis.

"Perhaps when you're finished then," I said, "the two of you might like to drop by to cool off."

"I don't think we'll have time. We're going to that new restaurant that opened in New Hope. Why don't you and Alice join us?"

"Alice left this morning for Long Island with Peter and Barbara T."

"I forgot they were leaving today. Are you alone now?"

"I've still got Joan."

"I've got to run," she said. "Perhaps we'll see you later."

"I hope so."

I hung up, disappointed and irritated. Disappointed that I wouldn't see Odette right away and irritated because I was jealous that she was going off with Arthur. "New girl friend" or not, she still did things with her husband. Alice and I did things apart.

I used to blame that on Alice, but I know now it was my own doing. I can understand why Alice would want to get away from me. I tried, as much as possible, to escape me myself.

It wasn't that Alice and I *never* did things together. We went to dinner, to movies, to friends, to auctions and antique shows. But we rarely did anything adventurous and new because I was afraid to depart from my familiar routine and surroundings. "New" was different. I still felt like a swimmer in a darkened ocean on a moonless night: I could not tell how far down the bottom was, nor what beasts might be circling beneath me. My only hope was to keep in sight the one familiar light which told me in what direction lay the shore.

I didn't want to be like that. My impatience with myself was reflected in my impatience with almost everyone else. I couldn't stand being alone and yet I grew quickly bored with company. They all wanted to talk about *things;* I wanted them to talk about *feelings.* They wanted to talk about what they were doing or what they had done; I wanted them to talk about how they felt—about their lives, themselves, their wives, their children—yes, I also wanted them to tell me how they felt about me— not because I wanted to be the center of attention (I did not feel I could withstand too much careful scrutiny), but because through what they said maybe I could gain some idea of who I was and what I had become. I was still desperately trying to understand that stranger inside my head. I knew what was wrong with me, but I no longer had much idea what was right.

Odette, unlike Alice, seemed to think me desirable, amusing, intelligent, sensitive, capable. I needed the uncensorious reflection I saw of myself in her eyes. Odette apparently needed the equally admiring, affectionate, uncritical portrait of herself she saw in mine. I felt unthreatened, safe with her.

This partially explains why Odette and I spent at least part of every day together during the week Alice and Barbara T. and Arthur were away.

We were hungry for the sanctuary of each other's approval.

But I have also come to realize that another reason Odette and I visited one another was because we made no demands, expected nothing of one another, and were sheltered by the protective umbrella of our marriages. Odette and I were free to be friends.

"A friend is a person with whom I may be sincere," Emerson wrote in his essay on love. "Before him I may think aloud."

Odette told me that Arthur used to call her "a stupid bitch." I am ashamed to say I called Alice worse things than that. When Odette and I quarrel now it is because if she is thinking out loud I will sometimes tell her she is wrong instead of letting her tell me whatever it is on her mind. By correcting her I diminish her. I am learning now to let her talk, because what she needs from me is often not advice, agreement, or disagreement, but rather a receptive, compassionate ear. And, most of all, support.

I have learned, too, that once she can articulate her concerns, she can control them. The vast majority of her worries center upon her fear for her future, that if I leave her it will be economically impossible for her to survive in a decent manner. It always comes down to money, doesn't it? Money buys more than freedom, it buys self-respect.

I seem to have strayed again from my story. I was disappointed and irritated by Odette's going off with her husband and the fact that I had no right to feel that way did not lessen my bad mood, nor my impatience with myself. It did, however, make me all the more eager to see her as soon as Arthur had departed for Chicago. I needed to be with a woman who—unlike Alice, and at times, unlike Barbara T., too—helped me feel good about myself.

Odette would drop Paul and Vanessa off at our pool to swim under Joan's supervision. We would explain that we were going up to the Baskin house to check on the workers' progress. And we *would* check. (The foundation had been laid for the addition being built on the west side of the house. The electrician and plumber were knocking holes in floors and walls to run in new wiring and pipes. The interior was a shambles; everything was covered with a fine, powdery layer of plaster dust.) But afterward she and I would walk up the steep hill to the cottage.

At the cottage Odette and I could be alone.

I wanted to move my office up there as soon as possible, so Odette and I would stand in the center of the large downstairs room before the stone fireplace discussing where my office furniture would go. We would measure spaces for rugs, desk, editing table, filing cabinets, the old sofa, shelf space for film cans and books. We drew floor plans and cut out pieces of graph paper representing my furniture to scale, then moved the paper desk and chairs and tables back and forth to see where the pieces would fit best.

Our trips to the cottage contained a certain element of "playing house," but it was harmless, or so we thought. We held hands while we debated what color to paint the walls. Sometimes we kissed, but there was still an innocence to it—our kisses were not so much sexual as they were affectionate, still the sort of embrace shared by friends. I have seen the same tentativeness lately in Joan's relationship with her boyfriend, Barney. They hold hands a lot, stand with their arms around each other's waists. Although they don't kiss in front of us, I imagine their kisses being like those Odette and I then shared: shy, sweet, and somewhat amazing to us both.

Odette and I received such pleasure from each other's company! We let each other *be*. I was never impatient with Odette. She made me laugh. I never knew what she might say next. She was important to me; she made me feel I was important to her. Odette made me feel like someone special and evidently I did the same for her because one afternoon when she and I had gone together up to the cottage she said, "Before I met you I felt I had become a nothing. It was like I was just another piece of furniture Arthur used. I felt taken for granted. You make me feel alive."

Of course I was falling in love with Odette. But the process was so gradual, the affection deepened so slowly, that the intimacy that bonded us was something we recognized more in hindsight. It simply had happened.

Later, Odette and I would descend the hill to the car together feeling free, elated, mellow—the cottage did that to us. Even then it had, in Odette's phrase, a "languidity" that came in part from the quiet isolation of its setting. The pale, translucent green light that filtered down through the tall trees made everything seem easy and peaceful and cool. We always hated to leave.

Friday afternoon Dudley Thompson brought back for a second look the couple who had said our house was "in such good taste," and when the husband asked if he might return a third time with a structural engineer I told him the house had stood for over two hundred years and that I was confident it would still be standing when he was able to come back. There must have been a trace of snarl in my voice because Dudley shot me a warning look.

It was not my impatience with the couple that had made me testy, it was because I knew Arthur was returning from Chicago that evening. Alice, Barbara T., and Peter would be returning from Long Island sometime the next day, Saturday. Odette's and my "vacation" together was over and I did not know when we would have an opportunity to be alone together again.

The afternoon Alice was to return I had taken Joan up to the cottage to help me prepare the walls for painting. She and I got back to the house a little after three. Alice was in the kitchen with Arthur; Odette was at the pool with Philippe, the younger children, and Barbara T. They were all in bathing suits.

"We've decided to have a party," Alice said. "Where have you been?"

"Working up at the cottage," I said.

"Arthur is going to get some steamers, you're to pick up some lobsters at the fish market. I've already called so they know you're coming. Odette's making a fruit salad, and Barbara T. and I will get the place ready and feed the kids."

"When's the party?" I asked.

"Now. Here," Alice laughed, and gave a little toss of her hair. "Arthur and I have already started."

I went back outside to say hello to Odette, Barbara T., and Philippe, conscious that both women were watching me as I approached. Just before I reached the pool deck Barbara T. stood up and came toward me to kiss me on the cheek. "Hi," she said, and touched my arm. "How are you?" She did not pull her hand away.

"Fine," I said. "I like your tan." I continued on to Odette and bent down over her deck chair. I kissed her cheek, then I straightened up.

"You are not going to kiss me, too?" Philippe asked.

I bent forward and we kissed each other on both cheeks.

"Bravo!" Philippe laughed. "We will turn you into a Frenchman yet."

"How was New York?" I asked.

"Very warm, I think."

"I bet it was," I said. I shielded my eyes against the reflected glare of the pool to see the children.

"Daddy! Daddy!" Peter shouted. "Watch me swim." He thrashed across the pool toward me. Paul was hanging by his fingertips to the side of the pool. He looked like one of those Kilroy figures of my childhood, the ones you stuffed in a pocket so that it clung there by its fingers and nose.

I turned back to Odette. "Are you okay?" I asked. "Would you like me to freshen up your drink?"

She patted the empty deck chair next to her. "Why don't you sit with us for a minute and relax?"

Barbara T. held out her glass. "You could put some vodka and tonic and an ice cube or two in mine."

When I took Barbara T.'s glass Odette held hers out to me, too, and said, "Then I'll take the same."

I hesitated for only an instant because of the slight challenge in Odette's tone. If I had to pinpoint exactly where I thought I detected the faint *ting!* of sword tips touching, it was in the "then". I took both of their glasses with me.

Back in the kitchen Alice was holding the freezer door open while Arthur took out the ice tray.

"I need a few cubes, too," I told him.

"You probably ought to get a bag of ice for tonight," he replied.

I asked Alice how her trip was.

"Fine," she said.

I waited for her to say more. She didn't.

"Well," I said, "judging by your tan and Barbara T.'s you had good weather."

"Don't make my drink too strong," she told Arthur.

"How was Chicago?" I asked him.

"Interesting," he said, handing Alice her drink.

"Was it conferences?" I asked.

"That and meetings," he said.

I intercepted the ice tray as he started to put it away.

"How many steamers should we get?" Alice asked him.

"Between four and five pounds," he said.

I dropped ice cubes into Odette's and Barbara T.'s glasses and turned to put the ice tray back into the freezer just as Alice opened the refrigerator door. "You're in the way," she told me. I stepped aside.

"Arthur," she said, "make sure you don't let them load you up with big clams. The little ones are sweeter." Alice turned back to me. "You really are in the way," she said.

"If you'll just let me put this ice back . . ." I put the ice tray in the freezer and moved over to the counter to add the vodka and tonic to Odette's and Barbara T.'s drinks.

"Alice thinks it would be nice if we eat outside tonight," Arthur said. "Do you think there's something in your office we could use as a table?"

"Will you be wanting a table for two?" I asked. "Or will you be inviting the rest of us to join you?"

"Cute," Alice said. "Real cute."

Philippe helped me set up the outdoor table, made from a three-by-six-foot piece of plywood laid across two sawhorses. We found an even piece of ground in the shade of the cherry tree and covered the plywood top with sheets of newspaper. Alice came out with an old but serviceable blue, yellow, and white Marimekko sheet, which we spread on top of the newspapers as a tablecloth. Joan helped me collect enough wrought-iron garden chairs to seat all of the adults at the table, then went with me to pick up the lobsters. By six o'clock everything was organized.

Alice had set the table with the yellow plastic Heller plates and balloon wineglasses. Barbara T. had filled a large vase with brightly colored zinnias and was sitting on the deck outside the house shucking ears of corn. I started the charcoal in the hibachi for the children's hamburgers. Arthur, Philippe, and Odette were expected any minute with buckets of steamers and the fruit salad. Alice had disappeared upstairs to dress. Joan had gone off to the toy store on her bicycle and returned with bubble pipes for the younger children. As I blew on the charcoal to get it going she was patiently showing Vanessa and Paul how the bubble pipes worked. There was a momentary crisis when Paul inhaled some of his soapy mixture and coughed and sputtered and burst into tears. But when he saw Peter and Vanessa blowing streams of bubbles into the soft summer air, his tears ceased and he ran to join them.

I don't think I will ever forget the image of those children on the lawn: the sun lowering behind them, their blond hair glowing like halos about their heads, their tanned, healthy young bodies racing barefoot back and forth across the rich, green lawn, the bubbles floating all about them, the children trying to catch them on their tongues.

And the sounds: the children's laughter, the crickets, the electric carillon bells of the Episcopal church, the sizzle of the hamburgers, a power mower drifting back and forth across a distant neighbor's lawn, blue jays scolding each other from the trees, a motorcyclist speed-shifting past the Turner sisters' house.

By seven the children ,had been fed and were scattered about the house and grounds. Philippe and Arthur had arrived with the steamers. Odette, carrying her huge bowl of fruit salad, looked marvelous. She was wearing a pair of white cotton pants with a drawstring waist and a faded blue-and-white-striped French sailor's shirt, with a light cotton sweater tied around her shoulders. Philippe was proudly wearing a new pair of Levi's and a cowboy shirt he had just bought in New York.

"I am the Frisco Kid, *non?*" he asked me.

"I think it was the Cisco Kid," I told him.

"Crisco," Alice said. "The Crisco Kid." And broke herself up.

"Creesko?" Philippe asked, looking questioningly at Odette.

"It's a cooking fat," Alice said.

Barbara T. passed Odette a joint.

"It's very strong," I warned her.

Odette inhaled the marijuana and passed it to Arthur.

By the time we were all seated at the table Arthur and Odette, unused to marijuana, were ripped. Odette was seated on my right, Barbara T. on my left; Alice who was seated at the opposite end of the table had Arthur on her right, Philippe on her left.

We had finished the steamed clams and were just passing out the lobsters when Odette said, "Got to walk. Got to get up and move." I helped her out of her chair and walked with her outside the gate where we would not be seen. Odette asked me, "Am I going to be sick?"

"No, it will pass."

She sagged against me with her forehead resting on my shoulder. "I do not feel very good," she said.

I hugged her gently and when she lifted her head toward me I kissed her lightly on the lips. "You'll be fine in a few minutes," I said. "We can walk around until you do."

"But your lobster is getting cold."

"I can put it back in the pot." I noted Arthur had not come out to see if his wife was all right. Odette took a deep breath and straightened up. "Walk," she said.

We walked up the driveway to the street, then along the sidewalk to the corner boundary of our property, then back down to the driveway and to the gate that opened between the hedges and the lawn. When we entered we could see that Arthur and Alice were laughing at something and Philippe was worriedly looking up at Odette.

"*Ça va?*" he asked when Odette sat down.

"*Oui*," she said.

I smiled at Alice and she waved back at me with a boiled lobster claw.

By the time we finished dinner it was dark. I had turned the light on beneath the water in the pool and by that light and those from the candles we drank our wine.

"Let's go for a swim," Alice said.

"I didn't bring my suit," said Odette.

"Don't be silly," Alice told her, "we'll all just skinny-dip." She stood up and began to remove her clothes. Arthur too pushed away from the table and began to undress while Odette and Philippe exchanged looks.

"Aren't you going to join us?" Arthur asked us. "Barbara T., how about you?"

Barbara T. shrugged and pushed back from the table. Alice had moved away from the candles so that she could remove the last of her clothing in the dark. She was momentarily silhouetted when she crossed to the lip of the pool and paused, then dove in. Arthur dove in a moment later and I turned toward Barbara T. She was standing not more than three feet away from me unbuttoning her silk blouse. I forced myself to look away. We could hear Arthur and Alice in the water, but because the ground rose between us to the pool we could not see them from where we sat. I glanced over at Philippe, who was transfixed by Barbara T. Odette was looking at me.

"More wine?" I asked her.

She shook her head.

"Coffee?"

There was a rustle of clothing as Barbara T. slipped out of her blue jeans. I did not look, not until she stood at the edge of the pool. I saw her for only an instant, but it was an instant that burned itself in my mind. As she paused at the edge her body, reflected in the glow from the illuminated pool, looked phosphorescent. The blue-green light, broken up by the roiling water, shimmered upon her swollen breasts, her soft belly, her thighs. Her pubic hair appeared thick and dark, as black and feral as a mink. And then she dove into the water, too.

When I turned back to Odette she was talking to Philippe, who was worriedly shaking his head.

"I'm going to make coffee," I said, but neither of them seemed to hear.

I went inside the house and plugged in the coffee machine, then went upstairs to check on the children. Joan had gone up to her room; Peter, Vanessa, and Paul had fallen asleep watching the little portable Sony TV next to Alice's and my bed. I arranged their heads and limbs so they wouldn't hit each other in their sleep, covered them with a light summer blanket, and turned off the TV. I stood next to the bed for a moment listening to their deep breathing, wondering what to do next.

I had not expected the evening to be like this. I didn't know *what* I had expected it to be like, but I knew that it had never occurred to me that Odette's husband would be swimming naked in our pool with a naked Barbara T. and my naked wife. I stepped to the bathroom window and looked outside.

Odette and Philippe had moved to deck chairs next to the pool. Arthur and Alice were standing close together in the shallow end; Barbara T. was alone in the deep end, floating on her back. Odette's head was turned toward her husband and Alice. Philippe was facing away. I looked one more time at Barbara T.'s body, before she let her legs sink in the water and all I could see were her shoulders and the back of her head.

I went back downstairs and set up a tray with mugs, sugar, and cream, and waited until the coffee had perked. Then I carried the coffee out to the pool. As I put down the tray Alice, still standing in the shallow end, shivered and said she was cold. Arthur came up behind her in the water and hugged her against his body. "Here," he said, "this will keep you warm."

"Are there towels out here?" Barbara T. called.

"I'll get some," I said, glad for the excuse to escape the pool again. I could not stand seeing Arthur hugging my wife. I did not know how to deal with it, what to think.

Alice had said she was cold; Arthur was holding her to warm her. Her back was to his front. Her naked back to his naked front. When does a touch become a caress? A feel? A grope?

I looked over at Odette to see how she was responding. Europeans, I knew, were more relaxed about nudity than Americans; they were used to being naked together. Odette's expression as she watched her husband rubbing against my wife was a mixture of aloofness, curiosity, anger. Philippe, I thought, looked a bit dismayed. Odette suddenly leaned toward Philippe and said something to him in French and he responded in French, too. They both spoke too quickly and in too low a voice for me to understand.

"Are there towels?" Barbara T. again called from the deep end.

I went into the house and took my time gathering up the large bath towels.

Alice and Arthur were the first out of the pool. I waited for them by the steps at the shallow end. Arthur took the first towel from me and wrapped it around Alice, then took a second towel for himself.

"Thanks," he said, as if I were a "towel boy" at a Turkish bath.

Barbara T. was climbing the ladder at the deep end, the water shining like oil droplets on her body. She paused midway up, leaned back to shake out her hair, then as I approached holding the third towel open in front of me, she pulled herself the rest of the way up the ladder and out of the pool. She took the towel from me and, holding it lengthwise behind her, stood naked in front of me for just an instant with the towel taut across her back while she watched my eyes upon her body. And when I raised my eyes to meet her look, she smiled slightly, coiled the towel about herself, then walked across the lawn and into the house.

I turned back toward Arthur and Alice, who had seated themselves like bobsledders in the same deck chair chaise-longue. Arthur, behind Alice, had his arm around her waist; his hand was moving slowly back and forth across her towel-covered body just beneath her breasts. Odette was leaning forward toward them, her fingers tightly gripping the arms of her chair.

"Arthur . . ." she said.

Arthur looked over at Odette.

"You can't do that, Arthur," she said in an odd high voice. "I'm *right here*. You're my *hus*band . . . She's his *wife*."

Arthur chose to interpret Odette's protest as a joke since he responded with a smile.

He did not speak. Nor did his hand cease moving upon my wife.

Odette suddenly, obviously angry, thrust herself out of her deck chair and hurried into the house. Philippe, too, rose from his deck chair but instead of following Odette he wandered aimlessly, distractedly, about the lawn midway between the pool and the house just beyond the circle of light. I crossed the lawn toward him, called to him softly, and walked with him into the house. Odette was standing alone at the kitchen counter. "Would you get me something to drink?" she asked.

"What would you like?" I said.

She looked at Philippe. "What would be good?"

"Cognac?" Philippe said.

Odette did not answer. She was looking over my shoulder beyond the back door toward the swimming pool.

"A cognac for each of you," I said.

While I was searching through the bottles in the library liquor cabinet I could hear Philippe and Odette talking together—again in French, again too swiftly for me to be sure I understood much more than that Odette was upset by her husband's behavior with my wife.

I was upset, too, but I felt powerless to act. If I were to object, Arthur and Alice need only deny they were doing anything wrong. They could retreat behind the perfect protective coloration of the setting—a late-night conversation between friends by the pool—ignoring entirely the explosiveness of the situation, the loaded ambiguity of Arthur's touch, the cocked-hammer innocence of Alice's leaning back. Furthermore I, who had spent the last week in gentle flirtation with Odette, did not feel in any moral position to launch a protest—particularly since mine was a position made even less tenable because of my relationship with Barbara T. I could not help but recall Nora's line from Leadville: "I just love knowing I'm fucking both men in this room." It was not a comforting recollection.

As I walked back into the kitchen with the two cognacs Philippe was either telling Odette that *she* was being foolish, or that *they*—Arthur and Alice—were being foolish, or that *it*—presumably the whole situation—was foolish. I wasn't sure which. And I didn't get a chance to ask because Barbara T., wearing a burgundy velour sweater and a long, dark blue skirt came downstairs and joined us.

She had pulled her still-damp hair tightly back into a bun. Philippe, Odette, and I were all looking at her, but none of us spoke.

"What this party needs is some music," Barbara T. finally said.

"I'll put something on," I said. "What would you like to hear?"

"I'll choose something," Barbara T. said. She started toward the library, "But would you fix me a drink?"

"What would you like?" I asked.

"The usual," she said.

Odette glanced up at me and smiled.

When I went to the refrigerator for ice I looked through the back door toward the pool.

"They're still out there," Odette said.

"So I see."

Barbara T. had put the Stevie Wonder album on the stereo and when

I walked into the library with her drink, she took the glass from me, put it down on a table, then held out her arms. "I want to dance with you," she said.

I was very conscious of Barbara T.'s body against mine, of her bosom beneath the velour, her hips as we moved together. If I closed my eyes I could see her body naked and phosphorescent at the edge of the pool, the light reflecting and shimmering upon her breasts, the water glistening upon her shoulders, her thighs, as she climbed out and turned toward me. I pressed her to me with my hand on the small of her back.

"Umm," Barbara T. said just as Philippe and Odette walked in.

Barbara T. and I danced a little longer while Philippe and Odette watched and then Odette and I danced while Philippe watched with Barbara T.

I remember thinking as I held Odette how well she seemed to fit, that she was lighter in my arms than Barbara T. We danced, not speaking, her brow resting lightly against my cheek. I felt *we* were the couple, not Barbara T. and me, not she and Arthur or Alice and me. It was as if what was going on between Arthur and Alice was not in the same league as my relationship with Odette. *Now,* I recognize how schizophrenic I was, but it made perfect sense to me *then.* The "me" who made love to Barbara T. was the same "me" who was married to Alice. It was not at all the "me" who would court Odette, who danced with her that night, who, when Odette finally asked, "Aren't you worried about my husband and your wife?" responded, "Should I be?"

Odette shrugged.

"Are *you* worried?" I asked her.

She shrugged again.

"See?" I said. "Neither of us *really* cares."

"Of course we care," Odette said. "If we didn't it wouldn't have been so much on our minds all night."

A little later I danced with Barbara T. once more and then Arthur and Alice came back inside the house. But when instead of joining us in the library Arthur and Alice only refreshed their drinks and isolated themselves again, this time in the kitchen, Odette asked to be taken home.

Odette and I were discussing that evening not long ago and she said she had been absolutely furious with me. "I thought you were a total bird head," she said.

"A what?"

"Oh, you can smile now," she said, "and I almost can too, but you were so busy being the perfect host, being polite to everyone, fetching

everyone drinks, being busy but never really being with us—being there
but never with us with your head—and when Arthur and Alice came
back into the house you were even polite to *them*. I couldn't believe it!
That's when I went home."

"Didn't Philippe and I go with you?"

"You both carried the children."

"And we had a drink at your house, right?"

"Yes, and afterwards when it was about one o'clock and Arthur still
hadn't arrived you walked back home."

"I remember. He and Alice were still talking in the library. Barbara
T. had gone to bed. He couldn't have stayed much longer though because
Alice came upstairs while I was in the bathroom brushing my teeth. I
remember she seemed very animated, very excited."

"Arthur was too," Odette said. "He came back very cocky, very sure
of himself. As though he were finally playing a game that was really fun.
He had helped create the situation that night, had become master of it,
and he really liked it."

The next morning, Sunday, when I passed the guest room on my way
downstairs for some coffee I saw the door was open. The bed had been
made, the room tidied up, Barbara T.'s luggage was gone. She was not
downstairs and when I looked out toward the driveway I saw her car was
missing. There was always an element of legerdemain to her visits: Now-
you-see-me, now-you-don't.

I spent the morning working outside cleaning up the mess from the
night before; Alice worked inside. We were busy raking, sweeping,
mowing, vacuuming, repairing, as if by pulling our surroundings into
shape, we could do the same for our marriages. Alice and I did not
discuss the previous evening. We chose instead to avoid that subject as
diligently as we avoided each other.

As soon as I could I left for the cottage and I spent the afternoon there
scraping and chipping away at the walls. So lost was I in my own world
up there that I was taken totally by surprise when Arthur and Odette
suddenly showed up with Alice. They had been seeing how the work
was progressing on the Baskin house, they said. I particularly remember
how much I resented Alice's and Arthur's presence in the cottage; it was
as though they carried a corruption with them, a taint left over from the
night before. I kept on working while they watched, then Arthur and
Alice announced they were going for a walk.

"Will you give Odette a ride home?" Arthur asked. "I'll take Alice
back in my car."

"Do you mind staying here with me?" I asked Odette.

"I don't care," she said. And, after Alice and Arthur had closed the door behind them, she added, "Bastard!"

"Who, me?"

"No, *them!*" she said.

I put my arms around her. "Don't let them get to you," I said. "That's why I came up here. To get away."

"To *escape,*" she said, pulling away.

"Are you angry at me, too?"

"I'm angry at all of you—all of us."

"Because of last night?"

"Because of a lot of things."

I picked up the paint scraper and went back to work on the wall.

"You don't want to talk about it?" Odette asked.

"I wouldn't know where to begin."

"Well, what did you think of last night? Why don't you begin there?"

I continued to work on the wall for a moment, then my arm dropped and I turned back to Odette.

"I hated last night," I said.

"I hated it, too." Odette sat cross-legged on the floor behind me.

"And now the two of them have thrown me at you again."

Late that afternoon when I drove Odette back to her house no one was there, so we continued on to my house and found Philippe and Joan sitting by the pool.

"Where is everybody?" I asked.

"Arthur and Alice have taken the children for a bicycle ride," Philippe said. "And they have made a reservation for us at a Chinese restaurant tonight."

"What about the children?" Odette asked.

"I'm baby-sitting," Joan said.

"Is that all right with you?" I asked Odette.

"It's nice of *some*one to ask me," she said.

At that moment we could hear the children on their bicycles turning into the driveway. Paul was the first through the gate onto the lawn. "*Maman! Maman!*" he cried. "We went all the way to the river!" He flung himself at his mother's knees and Odette hugged him tightly.

Alice went directly into the house and Arthur, flushed and smiling, came to us and sat down next to Paul, at our feet. "We rode to the creek," he said, ruffling Paul's hair.

"We went to the *river*, Papa," Paul said.

"No, it's only a creek, a stream," Arthur corrected him. "A river is much larger."

"What does it matter?" Odette asked. "He doesn't care."

"He should know the difference," Arthur said.

Odette shrugged and looked away.

Alice appeared with two vodka tonics, handed one to Arthur and kept the other for herself.

"Odette? Philippe? Would you like something to drink?" I asked.

"*Non, merci,*" Philippe said. "I had enough last night."

"Odette?"

"Could I have a glass of red wine?"

We did go to a Chinese restaurant that Sunday night. Sweet and sour pork would probably provide as adequate a description of our desultory conversation as it would describe what we ate. It was a terrible evening and we were all relieved when it ended.

The next morning George Mason and I flew out of Newark together on the initial leg of our trip to screen the cancer documentary in Chicago, Denver, and Los Angeles.

I had never watched the finished film with people who had not seen it before. And so at the screening that first afternoon in Chicago I was anxious about the response.

The documentary was shown without intermission or interruption. For nearly two hours no one in the screening room moved or spoke. The doctors, the medical researchers and cancer specialists, newspaper editors and TV critics, just sat there in absolute silence. Even when the lights came on no one moved. Only the doctors spoke. The others, the people who had no day-to-day contact with cancer just sat there in absolute silence for about a minute and then, still not speaking, they stood up and began filing out. Nervous, I glanced over at Mason. My producer, surrounded by doctors, was positively beaming. When he saw my look he gave me a thumbs-up sign and mouthed the word "wow." At that moment one of the doctors came up to me. "I want to shake your hand," he said. "Thank you for telling it like it is."

Over the next three days at the other screenings in Chicago and those in Denver and L.A., the response was the same. The doctors expressed their approval of the documentary's accuracy, and those not in the medical profession, were wiped out. It was a success. The documentary was going to be talked about and *seen*.

Mason wanted to stay on in Los Angeles and to continue up to San Francisco for the Labor Day weekend, so I flew back early Friday morning without him and was met at Newark by Barbara T.

She was wearing a washed-out gray skirt and a white cotton tank top that showed off her tan. Barbara T. must have seen me before I saw her because as I entered the main terminal she seemed somehow to simply materialize at my side.

"Hi," she said, and she stood up on her tiptoes to give me a kiss on the cheek.

I looked around. "Did you come alone?"

"Alice is antiquing in New Hope. She'll be back by the time we get home."

"And the kids?"

"They're fine. They're at the pool."

"So that left you to have to meet me?"

"I didn't *have* to, I *wanted* to. I've missed you," Barbara T. said.

I again had the feeling that I was more married to her than I was to Alice.

The moment we stepped outside the air-conditioned terminal the August heat beat at us, bounced off the pavement, pooled about our feet, made the distant buildings dance and shimmer like mirages.

"Jesus!" I said. "A swim will feel good."

"That reminds me," Barbara T. said, "Alice wants you to clean the pool."

In her Saab heading down the New Jersey turnpike Barbara T. pulled her skirt high up on her thighs. When I looked down at her legs, she smiled and said, "It's been so hot this past week that I haven't worn anything but a bathing suit."

"It was hot in L.A., too," I said.

"How did it go with the film?"

"Very, very well, I think."

"Good," she said. "You deserve it." She took one hand off the wheel and laid it on my thigh. I covered her hand with mine. I did like Barbara T. When I was alone with her and she was being nice to me I was almost even in love with her. But, then again, I was almost even in love with Odette, too. It did not seem strange to be almost in love with two so totally different women at the same time, even though it had never happened to me before. I gave Barbara T.'s hand a light squeeze and she returned the pressure on my thigh. I looked down at Barbara T.'s legs again, the pale, fine silver-blond hairs on her tanned thighs, the big thigh muscles flat on the car seat, the way the skirt was gathered about her hips. I thought about the night in the library when I had come home from Leadville. Barbara T. had met me alone at Newark that time, too.

"What?" she asked.

"What do you mean, 'what'?"

"What are you thinking about?"

"Your legs," I said. "I was thinking about that night in the library when you sat opposite me in your nightgown. How you had pulled your nightgown up and I couldn't stop looking at your thighs."

"I know. It was crazy," she said.

"And your mole." I lifted my hand off hers and touched the inside of her right thigh. "I had never seen your mole before." We rode together in silence and then I said, "I wish there were someplace we could go for a couple of hours."

"Alice will be waiting for us," Barbara T. said. "And tonight the Villars have asked us to come by after dinner for coffee."

"How are they?" I asked.

"You mean how is Odette," she said.

"And Arthur and the kids," I said. But I had meant Odette. I was glad we'd been invited there. I was looking forward to seeing Odette. Now that, I thought, *was* strange, that I could be thinking about going to bed with Barbara T. one instant and be missing Odette the next. I had thought a lot about Odette that past week. There had been so many funny moments, scenes I would have liked to have shared with her. Incidents I was looking forward to telling her about. "Did you see much of the Villars this past week?" I asked Barbara T.

"Arthur was around. He was helping Alice fix the dining room chairs."

"Oh? What was the matter with them?"

"They were loose. They needed regluing. Arthur had the right sort of clamps."

"That was nice of him," I said.

Barbara T. shot me a look.

"Really," I said.

She was silent.

"And where was Odette?"

"Mostly with Philippe, I think."

When we arrived home and I got out of the car Alice, to my astonishment, gave me a big kiss. She seemed curiously elated, excited, pleased with herself. I did not have an opportunity to remark on her startling change of mood because Joan and Peter appeared, and stuck with me while I unpacked. Alice remained downstairs.

"Did you meet any movie stars?" Joan asked.

"Not a one."

"Not *one*?" Peter asked.

"One night at a restaurant in Los Angeles I saw Gregory Peck."

"Who's that?" he asked.

"I've seen him on TV," Joan said. "He's old though."

"Who isn't?" I laughed.

Alice called up from the kitchen, "Would you start the charcoal when you have a chance? I thought we'd have hamburgers tonight."

"Did you see the new barbecue?" Peter asked.

"A new barbecue? What happened to the old one?"

"Alice threw it away. She bought a Weber," Joan said.

"Why?"

"Arthur says they're the best," Joan said.

"Alice?" I called.

"What?"

"What time are we expected at the Villars?"

"Anytime after nine. Why?"

"No reason. I wasn't sure what the timing was."

It was probably closer to 10 P.M. when we reached the Villars. Odette opened the door saying, "We were going to sit outside but it's too buggy." Then she stepped aside so that Barbara T. and Alice could enter. "Arthur and Philippe are in the living room," she said as they went past. To me she said, "Hi, welcome home!" She tilted up her face to be kissed. And when I kissed her on one cheek she turned her head so that I would kiss her on the other. "How was your trip?" she asked.

"Fine. I wish you'd been with me," I said.

"And the film went well?"

"I think it's going to be a *triomphe*."

"That would be nice," she said. And in the silence that followed we could hear Alice laughing at something Arthur was saying. There was another murmur of voices and Alice laughed again. "Arthur thinks Alice is wonderful," Odette said. "He can hardly leave her alone."

"Barbara T. told me he reglued our dining room chairs."

"Is that what he was doing?"

She was in a very odd mood that night. "Don't you think Arthur and

Alice look well together?" Odette asked me once within their hearing. Alice responded with a little toss of her head. At another point when Alice came into the kitchen saying, "Arthur asked me to get him a drink, but I told him he had had enough," Odette said, "So have I." And Philippe shot her a questioning look.

Arthur and Alice were obviously enjoying each other's company a good deal. I don't think Alice said more than two words to me once we arrived at the Villars' house. We were always in separate rooms—she with Arthur in the living room, I in the kitchen with Odette—with Philippe and Barbara T. crisscrossing between us.

Toward the end of the evening Barbara T. came to the kitchen table and stood for a moment behind my chair with her hand on my shoulder.

Odette looked at Barbara T.'s hand and said, "Arthur told me I should have as good a friend as Alice has in Barbara T."

Barbara T. squeezed my shoulder. "Alice would like another drink."

"Arthur will make her one," Odette said.

"I'll make it," I said and added, "A short one. We've got to be going pretty soon."

When we returned to our house Alice went upstairs to check on Peter. Joan had left an ice cream carton out of the freezer and it had melted all over the counter. Barbara T. went up to her bedroom to change into a nightgown while I cleaned up Joan's mess. My old cat Tallulah jumped down from a library chair and padded into the kitchen to rub against my legs. I poured myself a glass of milk and carried it into the library, and I stood for a moment just looking at my books all in their shelves, then sat down.

I was still sitting there when Barbara T. came downstairs wearing a pale blue light cotton nightshirt with long sleeves and white cuffs and collar. "Would you like something from the kitchen?" she asked.

"No thanks, I've still got my milk. Do you want something? A drink?"

"Not a drink," she said, "but I'll sit with you after I get myself some milk."

"Where's Alice?"

"She's gone to bed."

A moment later Barbara T. returned milk in hand and sat in the chair opposite me.

"Well, here we are again," I said.

"It's nice to have you back home." She was silent for a moment, looking down into her milk glass, then she looked up directly into my eyes. "I didn't mean to miss you so much," she said.

I felt an immediate tidal surge in my groin. She twisted to put her milk glass down on the table and the nightshirt tautened across her breasts. I looked away. "You would have liked California," I said. "I'm sorry you weren't there."

"I've been there," she said.

"I know. I mean we could have had a good time." It did not occur to me until the words had left my lips that I had said almost the same thing to Odette.

The next morning Alice took Peter and Joan into Princeton to shop. I was in my office in the garage. When I was certain Alice and the car were gone I got up and went into the house. I heard movement upstairs. "Barbara T.?" I called. "Are you up?"

"I'm just getting dressed," she said.

"Do you want some coffee?"

"Sure," she said. "I'll be right down."

"I'll bring it up."

I carried two coffees up to the guest room. Barbara T. was wearing a pair of loose-fitting khaki shorts, cut wide at the leg, and a rust-colored tank top that clung to her breasts. She was rubbing some moisture cream into her skin.

"Good morning," she said, and kissed me on the lips.

"You look marvelous," I said. "Are those new shorts?"

"I got them the other day."

"I like the way they're cut."

"They're like my blue tap panties you like so much."

"Jesus," I said, shaking my head.

"What?" she asked, moving so that we were standing together almost touching.

My nostrils were filled with her scent. "It's not fair the way you turn me on."

"I'm glad you came up," she said. "I was going to come out to the office to get you if I didn't see you soon." She stood resting her forehead on my collarbone. "I've been in a sexual haze ever since you stepped off the plane. I had to do myself last night after we went up to bed. Don't stop, that feels so good."

I was lightly touching her through her tank top. "It does feel good," I said.

"I wasn't going to put any underpants on," she said. "I was going to just put on these shorts and come out to the office and—oh!"

I had pulled up her tank top to bare her breasts. I leaned forward and touched the tip of one nipple with my tongue. The scent of lotion and the warmth of her bosom were delicious. "You taste so good," I said.

"How can I?" she asked. "I just got out of bed."

"I don't suppose you'd like to get back in . . . ?"

"Yes," she said.

Our coffees lay forgotten on her bedside table; I began to unbutton her shorts.

"Oh God," she said. "You. Me. It's so crazy!"

The khaki shorts fell to her ankles and she stepped out of them and stood before me in her cotton panties and the tank top, still rolled above her breasts. She undid the belt on my blue jeans and then the button and zipper and pushed her hand inside. When her fingertips curled beneath the head of my penis I felt my knees shake. A few moments later we lay naked on the unmade bed, my erection trapped between her thighs.

"We don't have to hurry, do we?" Barbara T. asked.

"No one will be home for a couple of hours."

We lay not speaking, just touching one another, and then she asked, "Do you have other lovers?"

"You mean other than you?"

"I mean Odette," she said.

"No. . . . Do you?"

"Yes," she said.

"Anyone I know?"

"No, I don't think so."

"Are you serious about them?" I asked.

"*Them?*" she asked, smiling.

"Him?"

"*Him?*" she giggled.

"Don't tell me you're into women," I said, teasing her.

"Not yet," she said, and she rolled lazily onto her back. "But I think I could be."

I propped myself up on one elbow and cupped her breast. "Do you have someone in mind?"

She hesitated for a moment. "No, not really."

"But you do have someone *sort* of in mind." I slid my hand down her belly.

"It's more a type than an individual." She took my hand and lifted it back to her breast. "Touch me again."

"Like this?"

"Yes . . . Yes, like that. That's nice."

"What sort of woman would you like?" I asked.

"She'd have to be older. Experienced . . . I'd want her to—" She arched her chest toward my fingertips.

"You'd want her to what?" I lowered my lips to her breasts.

"To seduce me."

"How?"

"Oh, dinner . . . a good wine . . . a beautiful room . . ."

"Flowers?" I asked, smiling.

She pushed my head back down to her bosom. "I'd want her to make love to me the way you do . . . Just like that . . . I wouldn't want to have to do anything to her—I don't think I could . . . Not at first, anyway."

I began to kiss my way down her chest to her belly.

"Yes, kiss me there!" Barbara T. said.

I moved until I could kneel between her thighs. "Close your eyes," I said. "Pretend I'm your woman."

Her thighs splayed apart, but her hands came down to cover. "I'm actually *shy*," she said wonderingly.

I kissed her fingers. Nudged them gently apart. Slowly, tentatively her fingers began to slide upward, then her hands were on her belly, her chest; her palms paused for a moment across her breasts, and slid higher until her fingertips lightly touched her nipples, and then she lay with one arm across her eyes, the other at her side.

"Yes," she said. "Just like that . . ."

Two hours later Barbara T. was in her car driving home and I was up at the cottage in the woods priming the walls. I stayed there all afternoon. When I returned to the house the children were back from Princeton, but Alice had gone off again. It had started to rain.

"How was the big city?" I asked Joan.

"Fine."

"We had lunch with Arthur," Peter said.

"Oh? Was Odette there, too?" I asked.

"No," Peter said.

It rained all night and the next day, Sunday, too.

The following Monday morning was Labor Day. I was in the office in the garage behind the house when the telephone rang and Hope Bromley said, "This is your third wife . . . I'm going to be in New York next weekend. I hear you're celebrating your twentieth reunion next month and, well, I was thinking isn't it about time we celebrated our own?" The sun, at that moment, broke through the clouds for the first time and bathed my office in light. I told Hope her timing was perfect, that I had to be in New York that Friday anyway to teach my class.

Two days later, on Wednesday, I drove Joan up to St. Matthew's for her first day at boarding school.

I remembered how, making the same drive with my father, I would feel trapped while he lectured me on responsibility, character, duty, getting ahead. I was determined not to impose that trial upon my daughter and yet . . . and yet, when sending one's child off to her first day at boarding school one does feel compelled to provide some sort of guidance, a bit of advice.

She didn't appear to listen, of course. I started off trying to treat her as an equal, speaking to her as one adult to another to show her that I was prepared to accept her as responsible and mature. But the morning had already been so marked with her mindlessness that I had to fight down my impatience.

I had asked her while we were loading the car if she had remembered her raincoat.

"I can't find it," she said.

"Do you remember where you were the last time you wore it? It rained all this past weekend. Did you wear it into Princeton with Alice?"

"I think it might be at Annie Johnson's house."

"Did you telephone her?"

"No," she said.

"Well, why don't you give her a call," I said. "Ask her if it's there."

"I don't know her number."

I kept my voice calm. "Look it up."

Five minutes later Joan reappeared with some tape cassettes and slid them into the car.

"Did Annie have your raincoat?" I asked.

"I dunno," she said.

"Didn't you ask her?"

"I couldn't find her telephone number. There are seven 'Johnsons' in the book."

"Yes, but they don't all live on Four Yoke Hill."

"Is that where she lives?"

Another ten minutes passed before Joan reappeared.

"Did you get Annie?" I asked.

"Yup," Joan said. "She wished me good luck at St. Matthew's. She even said she'd write."

"Did she have your raincoat?"

"Unk!" Joan said and her face flushed. "I forgot to ask her."

"Call Annie again," I said. "Now watch my lips: Her father's name is Harold. They live on Four Yoke Road. Ask about your *raincoat.*"

The raincoat was not there; it never has been found. Nor have the countless sweaters, gloves, scarves, her bicycle lock, my bicycle lock, her bicycle itself, two Timex watches, library books. If I did not know that I had been mindless at her age, too, I would have savaged her. Instead, I sat quietly in the car next to her as we drove up to St. Matthew's and kept my worries to myself. She was so young. At thirteen could I have been as immature? She is still such an unformed cloud of astral gases that I have never satisfactorily resolved for myself how much of it is my fault.

During the drive up the only advice I urged upon her was that if she didn't understand what the teachers were saying or the lesson itself, she should make it a point to seek out the teachers after class. "If you keep thinking that all you have to do is keep quiet and in a little while longer it will all come clear, that you'll understand it all," I told her, "you won't. You'll just fall farther and farther behind."

"Um," she said.

"Please, Joan, promise me you'll talk to the teachers. I've taught. I *know* teachers want students to see them after class if they don't understand. That's what teachers are there for. And that's what you're there for, too."

"Here," she said.

"What?"

"That's what I'm here for. That's the school up ahead."

As we turned through the brick gates she slumped down in her seat.

"It's going to be fine," I said.

We went through the process of picking up her class schedule, room and mailbox keys, and the forms she would need to fill out, then drove to her dormitory, unpacked the car, and moved her stuff up to her room.

"Do you need any help getting settled?" I asked.

"No, I'll be all right."

I wanted to hug her and started toward her, but the look on her face made me pause. I hugged her anyway. "I don't expect you to get straight A's," I said. "Not at first. But I do expect you to work."

"I will," she said.

For the three and a half hours it took for me to drive from St. Matthew's home, I was entirely alone. I loved it.

The next day, Thursday, September 6, Barbara T. came back to stay with us again. I was in the office when she drove in. I helped her carry her luggage into the house, then left her with Alice and went back to work. Fifteen minutes or so later, Alice drove off. Another three quarters of an hour after that I went back into the house and heard the crash of something breaking in the shower and Barbara T.'s little yelp of pain. When I went upstairs I discovered the soap dish had fallen out of the wall in the shower and she had cut her foot. That was when we made love in the bathroom. "Can you come quickly?" she had asked.

The day after that, on Friday, I met Hope in New York. We spent the night together and I awoke at four in the morning to find her not in the bed. That was when she had told me she wouldn't mind at all if I really were the Angel of Death.

And on the night after that, on Saturday, September 8, the dinner with Philippe and Arthur and Odette and Barbara T. and Alice and myself took place at our house. That was the night Odette knocked the glass of red wine into my lap.

"Odette, Jesus Christ," Arthur had said, "you're such a *klutz!*"

And I, looking down at the red wine stain covering the crotch of my white trousers had quipped, "I think I must have worked that bull a bit too close!"

I went to bed a little after one o'clock that night. Arthur and Alice stayed up talking in the kitchen. Odette was driven back to her house by Philippe. Arthur woke her up when he returned home at six.

Last month, just before Odette returned this past time to France, she and I were talking about that particular evening. That dinner, which took place over a year and a half ago, was the last time Odette, Arthur, Alice, and I ate a meal together. Odette was saying that before she had gone home with Philippe, she had stopped in the kitchen to get Arthur and found him sitting at the counter with Alice. Alice was crying.

"Are you coming home?" Odette had asked.

"No," Arthur had said.

"But, Arthur, you cannot stay here all night. Alice is his wife. We're in their house."

"I'll be home later."

The exchange had stilled Alice's tears and she remained seated next to Arthur watching Odette.

"Then you're not coming home with me?" Odette asked.

"No, I told you. I'll be home later."

Later, as I have mentioned, was 6 A.M.

"Where have you been?" Odette asked as Arthur climbed into bed.

"With Alice."

"What did you do?"

"I just stayed there. The others had all gone to bed."

"But what did you *do?*"

"Nothing. I told you. We sat there and talked."

"Did you fuck her?" Odette asked.

"That's none of your business," Arthur said.

"C'mon, tell me," Odette cajoled him. "Did you?"

"Yes."

"You *did?* Where?"

"In his office behind the house."

"*Under his windows?*" she asked, surprised.

"He was asleep. Everybody was asleep."

"Is she as good as me?"

"I can't tell," Arthur said. "The first time on her husband's couch in his office surrounded by his things . . . She couldn't be herself. It was a little tense."

And then, Odette told me, she and Arthur made love.

"*Why? How could you?*" I asked. Even with all the time that had passed I still felt hurt and betrayed.

"Desperation," she said. "That and the fact that for some reason his admitting he had just come from Alice turned me on. I still wanted him to know he belonged to me. And then, as you remember, Alice came over the next afternoon to talk."

"That was when she said she wished you were old and ugly and fat so she could hate you."

"Yes, and that if I kept my married name there would be a real screw-up on the credit cards."

"What was I doing at this time?" I asked.

"Nothing. You had gone up to check on the big house."

That same Sunday afternoon after Alice and Odette had had their talk, Arthur and Alice went off together. When they still hadn't returned by six, Odette and I took the children to McDonald's for dinner and a seven o'clock showing of *Star Wars*. We had left a note on the kitchen counter of my house saying where we had gone and at about seven forty-five, around halfway through the film, Alice and Arthur entered the movie and slid into seats next to ours.

I was seated on the aisle next to Peter, who was on my left; Vanessa was on Peter's left, then Odette and Paul. Arthur slid in next to Paul and Alice sat at the end. Alice was carrying a vodka tonic in a plastic glass and she passed it across Arthur and Paul to Odette asking, "Would you like a drink?"

"When she handed me that drink," Odette told me during that conversation before she left for France, "I felt like I was taking it from Judas. I could have made a scene. I could have poured the drink on Arthur. Slapped Alice in the face. But I didn't. I didn't want to make a scene at all. I simply drank from the glass and handed it back to show that I wasn't going to act badly. Not at all. I wanted Alice and Arthur to be friends, I wanted them together. I wanted to get out of my marriage . . . You didn't."

"I didn't know *what* I wanted. I just wanted it to stop. I look back on that period as being one big ugly scene."

"Not all of it," Odette said. "You and I had some lovely talks."

"They saved my life," I said. "You saved me. You were the only one of us who made any sense."

"I had my European ethics."

"And I?" I said, smiling, "I had my WASP guilt."

Two evenings later Alice, Peter, and I were having dinner alone at home. I don't know what we had been talking about when Peter suddenly said, "Mommy's in love with Arthur." He said this not looking at either one of us; instead, he delivered his observation as though speaking to his elbow.

"What makes you think that?" I asked.

"She's always kissing him," Peter said.

"Grown-ups are always kissing each other," I said. "There's been an epidemic of kissing lately."

Why did I try to make light of it? At the time I told myself it was because I didn't want Peter to worry, I didn't want him upset. It was enough that his anxieties had surfaced. Now, I know I made light of it for my sake, too. Even then I didn't want to face what lay ahead.

After dinner, after Alice had tucked Peter into bed and I read him a story, I came back downstairs and told Alice it was time we had a talk.

"I don't want to feel guilty if I keep seeing Arthur," Alice said.

"If you're only 'seeing' him why should you feel guilty?"

"You know perfectly well what I mean."

"No, Alice, I'm not sure I do."

"I wouldn't mind if you fucked Odette," she said. "I just don't want you to do it in our bed."

"I haven't fucked Odette, Alice."

"Yet," she said.

The next morning while I was out in the office Odette telephoned. "Has Alice already left?" she asked.

"Left?" I looked out at the driveway. "She must have. I don't see the car."

"She is having lunch with Arthur in Princeton."

"Oh, for Chrissake," I said, "again?"

"She didn't say anything about it to you?"

"No, all she said was that she didn't want to feel guilty if she kept seeing him."

"Why'd she say that?"

"Last night Peter mumbled something about his mother being in love with Arthur, that she was always kissing him."

"What did you say?"

"Something stupid about grown-ups kissing."

"I asked Alice if she were in love with Arthur," Odette said.

"*You* asked her? When was that?"

"Sunday afternoon. Alice came to see me. To talk."

"What did she say?" I asked, but God I didn't want to hear! I could feel the hot band of pressure building up inside my head, a shortness of breath.

"She said she'd never break up her marriage 'for love alone,' those were her words. She said there had to be 'something more. Some security,' she said. 'Some stability.' "

"None of which she's had with me."

"Arthur could give her that," Odette said.

"She said that?"

"No, I did."

"What else did Alice say. Did she say she was in love with Arthur?"

"She said he was the first man who ever excited her."

I did not speak. I felt nauseous. I was thinking, *The reason why you don't turn me on is because—*

"You still there?" Odette asked.

"Yes."

"Well, it was inevitable that this should happen. You know, of course, that they saw each other every day last week while you were gone . . ."

Again I was silent. I was thinking about Barbara T. having been the one who had met my plane at Newark, that Alice was "antiquing in New Hope," how Arthur had "glued the dining room chairs." I was thinking of the way Peter had said "Mommy's in love with Arthur," not looking at us, as if wanting to be told it was not so.

"Oh! There's one other thing," Odette continued. "Something Alice said Sunday that might amuse you." It was then that Odette told me Alice's line, "If you keep your married name it's going to cause a real screw-up on the credit cards."

About twenty minutes after I spoke with Odette, Barbara T. called. "Is Alice there?" she asked.

"She's having lunch with Arthur in Princeton," I said.

"Oh."

"You didn't tell me they were together every day while I was away." Barbara T. was silent.

"Is that why you were so . . . so, affectionate with me? Did you feel sorry for me?"

"Are you crazy?" she asked.

"No crazier than anybody else in this crowd—which is not saying a great deal. I want to get the hell out!"

"Don't," Barbara T. said. "I've tried to kid Alice out of her infatuation. Really, I have, but she won't listen."

"I want to see you," I said. "Will you meet me in New York?"

"When?" she asked.

"*Now!* Well, no, not now. I couldn't do it now. But I've got to be in the city next Tuesday and again on Friday. Could we spend the night together one of these nights?"

"Can I call you Monday and let you know?"

"Sure, Monday would be fine," I said.

And later that afternoon when Alice called to say she and Arthur would be staying in town to have dinner and wouldn't be back until late, I said that would be fine, too.

I didn't care if I never saw her again.

Peter and I ate dinner alone at our house; Odette and her children ate alone at theirs. After dinner, Peter and I played a couple of games of checkers, watched a little television, then I took him upstairs and tucked him into bed.

"What story would you like tonight?" I asked.

"You pick. Read something *you* like."

"I like most of them."

"So do I. I love all the ones you read to me."

"I suppose my favorite is *Stuart Little*," I said.

"That's my favorite, too."

"You're certainly easy to get along with tonight," I said. I pulled E. B. White's *Stuart Little* from Peter's bookcase, then stretched out beside him on the bed. He snuggled up next to me, his head resting against my chest. "Shall we do the Central Park Boat Pond scene with the Lillian B. Womrath?"

"Sure, anything," he said. As I was locating the chapter, Peter asked, "Daddy, when is Mommy coming back?"

"Later on tonight. Probably after you're asleep."

"Will she kiss me good night?"

"She always does."

"Even if I'm asleep?"

"Especially if you're asleep."

Peter was out cold before I finished the chapter. I kept reading it anyway, as much to soothe myself as anything else.

At ten o'clock Odette telephoned. Arthur and Alice had still not returned. "I need you," she said, sounding very upset.

"Do you want to come down here for a drink? Some coffee?"

"Would that be all right?"

"I'll come pick you up."

"No, I'll drive. I'll be there in a few minutes. And I don't want coffee. I'd rather have a drink, I think."

A few minutes later Odette arrived at the door. She came right in and pushed herself into my arms. "*Hold me!*" she said.

I held her to me, neither of us speaking, just holding tight. After a moment Odette's arms loosened around my back and she stepped slightly away, tilted up her head, and kissed me lightly on the lips. "Thank you," she said.

"For what?"

"For being here."

"I wasn't going anywhere," I said. "Except to make us a drink. What would you like?"

"Something strong."

I made drinks, then we sat down opposite each other.

"I'm going to ask Arthur for a divorce," she said.

A surge of panic hit me. "Because of Alice?" I asked.

"Because I cannot stand living like this."

I took a sip of my drink to calm myself. I knew neither of our marriages was any more stable than a house of cards. If Odette pulled out, we would all fall. I was thinking, *Terrible is better than nothing*. I was not thinking of what was best for Odette, I was thinking only of chaos.

"Do you think I'm being foolish?" she asked.

"I don't know. I don't know what your marriage is like. From what I've seen lately . . ." I shook my head. "Does Arthur want a divorce?"

"I don't care what he wants," Odette said. "Do you?"

"Care what he wants?"

"Do *you* want a divorce?" she asked.

"I've been divorced," I said. "No one in their right mind *wants* a divorce."

"So you'd be willing to go on like this?"

"I don't have many illusions about marriage, Odette." Nor did I have any about how much money a divorce would cost. For the first time in years I was getting a financial cushion, a chance to live without money terrors every day. A divorce would take away what little financial stability—among other things—had been achieved. "Alice keeps the house running smoothly," I said. "There's food on the table, the children are clothed, I keep hoping things between us will improve. There's the new house we—"

"You're not describing a marriage!" Odette interrupted angrily. "You're describing having a maid!"

"No, I'm telling you why I'm in no hurry to get a divorce. I'd like to get our life back on some sort of even keel. There are two children to think of. Everyone gets hurt in a divorce. And it's a *dirty* hurt, not the kind you ever entirely recover from. And I'm not sure I want to put the children through a hurt like that. Not now. Not yet anyway."

"Do you think I shouldn't ask for one?"

"You have two children also."

"They're strong. They'd survive."

"You have to be sure," I said.

Odette took a sip of her drink. "I'm sure."

"You don't think this might be a little premature?"

"What do I need to wait for?"

"Maybe if you and Arthur had a talk . . ."

"Have you talked to Alice?"

"One doesn't talk to Alice, one listens."

"I cannot talk to Arthur either. He is like a robot with me." She looked at me for a moment. "You do not want me to do anything, I can tell. You do not want me to make waves. Of course I can understand why you don't feel the need for a divorce," she said. "Why should you? What you're not getting at home, you're getting on the side."

"Yes," I said. There was no point in denying that.

"I'm not," Odette said.

"Is that what you want?"

"No, I don't just want sex. I want a friend, companionship. That's what I need. You'll be my friend, won't you?"

"I *am* your friend," I said, really thinking it was true.

"Then hold me, please?" Odette asked, rising to her feet.

I held Odette and the way she leaned into my chest made me think of Peter curling up against me in his bed. To have someone to snuggle up next to, maybe that's what we all wanted and needed. I stood holding Odette, gently stroking the back of her neck. Slowly, gradually, I became aware that she was crying. "It's all right," I said. "Let yourself go. Cry. You'll feel better."

Odette pushed herself sharply away. "That's such a stupid, *manly* sort of thing to say! You men! Crying isn't going to make me feel better. The only thing that's going to make me feel better is to know a year from now that I'll be all right. When you say something like that it makes me want to go home."

"Home?"

"To France! To my family! My home! I hate this stupid little town. I hate my old house with everything in it going wrong. You don't think I'd want to stay here, do you? Why should I? Who have I got here? My husband is never home. Either he's at his office or off with your wife. And you don't care, you've got your sweet friend Barbara T.! You've got one wife to keep house and another to keep you happy in bed. You've got it made! No wonder you're in no hurry to get a divorce! Why should you? You men are such bastards! All you think of is your bellies and your cocks!"

She was standing less than a foot from me, her face dark with rage. I didn't know what to say, what to do. Suddenly her expression softened to one of utter tenderness and she reached out and gently touched my cheek. "You're so adorable!" she said. "Look at you, you're standing there like a confused little boy. Like Paul when I'm angry and he thinks I'm angry at him." She stepped forward and kissed me again. That was the exact moment that Alice, followed by Arthur, walked in.

My head started to jerk back, but Odette caught the back of my neck and made me finish the kiss. Then she turned and looked at Alice's and Arthur's stunned expressions for a moment and she said to Alice, "Your husband is an adorable man. If I were you I would not try so hard to lose him."

"Take my husband . . . *please*," Alice said as Odette scooped up her cigarettes and walked past Arthur and out the still-open front door.

Alice began sleeping in the guest bedroom that night.

11

It was on a Wednesday evening that Odette told me she was going to ask Arthur for a divorce. That was September twelfth. The next day, Odette took Philippe to JFK International for his flight back to Paris and I borrowed Burt Taylor's pickup truck to begin moving my office up to the cottage in the woods. I did not see Odette until Friday when she came up to the cottage to get away from her house. By then a subtle change had already occurred in our relationship.

I had had time to think.

If I were to try to articulate exactly what this change was, I'm not sure that I could. I know only that from the moment on Wednesday evening when Odette mentioned "divorce," I had realized that a great deal of what was to happen to me in the future was in her hands. I began to become apprehensive about how much power over me Odette held. I was more than apprehensive—Odette's potential for playing havoc with my peace of mind scared the hell out of me.

What sort of peace of mind did I think I had? I know now that it was not unlike that of a survivor of the *Titanic,* one whose immediate past was filled with terror and the awful loss of family and friends, and whose immediate future was confined to the worry that someone might make waves or rock the boat. Odette was threatening both.

That afternoon at the cottage I waited for Odette to say whether she had asked Arthur for a divorce or not. But when she did not say anything I broached the subject myself. She said only that she had thought more about it and decided to wait.

"Good," I said.

Saturday Alice and I worked around the house and did not see the Villars; Sunday I was back at the cottage alone. Late Sunday afternoon when I came back home Alice said she and Arthur were taking the children to McDonald's so Odette and I could have dinner alone.

"When was all this decided?" I asked.

"While you were at the cottage," she said.

"Swell," I said.

"We thought you'd want to have dinner together."

"Do we have any choice?"

"Sure," Alice said. "You can call Odette and tell her to stay home."

"Goddam it, Alice!" I exploded. "I resent your assuming I would want to be with Odette tonight and she with me. Odette and I will see each other at *our* convenience, not *yours!* We don't need you to arrange our social life for us!"

"Fine, then," Alice said. "Don't see her."

But, of course, I did want to see Odette. I just didn't want to be in love with her yet. I didn't like how fast everything was happening. If Odette and I were to fall in love really, I wanted it to be because we chose to have it happen, not because Arthur and Alice did. For the time being I was content to think of Odette as a friend—a friend and ally in an increasingly strange situation. But for as long as the situation did not become too strange, I was comfortable with Odette. And since four days had now passed since I had heard any talk of divorce I was beginning to hope it might all blow over, that the insanity would pass and we could all get along with our lives. So I went ahead with Alice's and Arthur's plan—Odette and I went to a Mexican restaurant and a movie—some mindless comedy, I don't remember which one. We had a relatively peaceful evening, all in all. I should have known that the tranquility was nothing more than the calm that precedes a storm.

The next morning Barbara T. called me on my office phone while I was collecting the last of the furniture and books before leaving for New York. "I don't think I can spend the night with you tomorrow," she said.

"You can't? Why?"

"I just don't think I ought to meet you. I get too crazy. I can't handle it. Not for the night."

"It doesn't have to be for the night," I said. "Even an afternoon together would be nice."

"I don't know . . ."

Barbara T. finally agreed to try to meet me Tuesday afternoon and I hung up relieved. Relieved and ashamed. I had almost begged her to meet me. Why was I putting myself through all this?

Part of the fascination about Barbara T. was that each of us saw in her what we wanted to see.

To Alice, she was the confidante, the best friend, the sister she had never had.

To Odette, she was Alice's "maid" and "baby-sitter" and my "other wife."

To Arthur, she was the sort of friend Odette should have.

To me, she was a sexual maelstrom, she sucked me into her dark orbit. She could seduce me with a look, a smile, a touch. She played me. She made me dance. She was like a drug that promised without ever quite delivering, a sensational high. Her desire for me was like her suitcases that would appear and disappear in the guest room upstairs; her desire could, I knew, just as readily manifest itself in other houses with other men. I never felt possessive of Barbara T.; she never told me enough about herself for me to know what I'd possess. Sometimes I hated Barbara T. for her effect on me. She made me accept her on her own terms.

I drove out to the Baskin house and spent an hour with the carpenter and painters, then continued up the hill to the cottage in the woods. The phone I had ordered had not yet been installed so I was able to work undisturbed. When I came back to the house in town late that afternoon Alice told me she had just spoken with Barbara T. and had decided to drive into New York with me to meet Barbara T. for lunch and a day of shopping. I kept my face clear of any disappointment.

"What time are you going in?" Alice asked.

"I want to arrive around noon."

"What time is your class?"

"It's not a class. It's a faculty meeting at five. My classes are on Fridays."

"Will you be spending the night?"

"Yes," I said. "I've got a room at the Dupont."

I waited for the hassle; but not really to my surprise, there was none.

Barbara T. met Alice and me Tuesday in the hotel lobby. I asked them both if they would care to lunch with me. Alice declined saying she wanted to get out to the stores.

"What are you going to do?" Barbara T. asked me.

"I'm going to do some work in my hotel room, then go down to NYU late this afternoon. But first I've got to check into the hotel."

I walked them both to the door, then registered at the front desk and went up to my room. Not more than fifteen minutes later there was a knock on my door. When I opened it, there stood Barbara T.

"Surprise!" she said, and walked in.

"I thought you were supposed to be shopping with Alice," I said.

"That's what you were supposed to think," she said. "Lock the door."

"Where's Alice?" I asked. Barbara T. was standing next to the bed. She did not reply. "With Arthur?" I asked.

"Hurry," she said as she began to undress. A moment later her dress lay crumpled at her feet and she was reaching behind her to unlatch her bra. In an instant it was on the floor too and her breasts were bare, the

nipples taut, and she was standing before me in the loose-fitting blue
silk tap dance panties she knew I liked. "I had to come see you," she
said. "I couldn't stay away." She hooked her thumbs in the waistband of
her panties and started to push them down.

"No," I said. "Keep them on. Don't take them off yet."

It was later when we were lying next to each other amid the debris of
sheets that she spoke to me about the past couple of weeks of our making
love and how she had "loved the recklessness of it. All the places." And
how that morning after I'd returned from Los Angeles and I had carried
the coffees up to the guest room where we had made love she "must
have come ten times."

When, the following day, Alice started telling me about what she had
done with Barbara T. during their afternoon in New York I did not say
a word. And after dinner when Arthur appeared at our house and said
Odette wanted to speak to me, I don't think I behaved any differently
toward him either.

I telephoned Odette from the library and she asked if I would come
up for a drink.

"I'm really kind of tired," I said. "Can I see you in the morning
instead?"

"Sure," she said. "Tomorrow will be all right."

"I'll see you then." It was only after I'd hung up that I realized there
had been a tremor in her voice I had not heard before. I walked through
the kitchen where Arthur and Alice were talking and continued out to
the office phone. I called Odette back. "I'm sorry," I said. "That was
very selfish of me. Is there something wrong?"

"I've asked Arthur for a divorce," she said.

"I'll be right up."

Odette met me at the door wearing a cotton bathrobe over her
nightgown; her eyes were puffy from crying. "Thank you," she said,
"thank you for coming."

"I'm sorry I didn't come right away. I didn't know."

"Am I terrible? For saying that I want a divorce?"

"Not if you do."

"I do," she said. "Will you sit with me for a while?"

"Of course."

"I can't go on living this way, with a husband who comes home, eats,
and then goes to see another woman every night. He won't talk to me
about it. First, I asked for a six months' trial separation, to give us time

to straighten our feelings out, to give us time to think and he said, 'No way. I don't want a trial separation. I want a divorce. And if you won't ask for one I will.' And so what could I say? He is pushing me out. What am I to do?"

"What do you want to do?"

"I don't *know!* I just don't want to live this way! Did Alice say anything to you about wanting a divorce?"

"Not yet," I said, shaking my head.

"I don't want to go on this way and yet, and yet—I'm panicked about what a divorce means. I don't even know what one has to do, what is involved in a divorce in this state."

"New Jersey is a no-fault state, but I don't really know the legalities involved. I can find out."

"You think I'm wrong, don't you? To divorce Arthur?"

"No, not wrong, Odette."

"Then what?"

"I don't know. I think it's all going too fast."

"But what is my choice? To be patient? How long can you expect me to be patient in this situation? I feel helpless. Arthur didn't come home until three o'clock last night and would not say where he had been. He sleeps in the guest room. Gets up in the morning and leaves without a word to the children or me. I can't stand living like this. When I try to talk to him about it"—she shook her head—"he turns to stone. Keeps everything inside. I know he's hurting, that he's hurting as much as I. When I told him I wanted a separation I gave him a chance to protest, but all he said was that he wanted a divorce and that he'd move out as soon as he could find a place."

"Do you think he really wants one?"

"Yes! I told you, he said if I didn't ask for one, he would."

"Ah, Jesus," I said sadly.

Odette and I sat talking until two in the morning and I spent the last hour in her bedroom rubbing her back. Sitting on the edge of her bed, my hands moving on her shoulders, I spoke about my confusion, that I didn't know whether my unwillingness to press for a divorce stemmed from weakness or strength, that I was used to Alice. We were like roommates assigned to each other who had adapted to one another's quirks—or had until now. And that even though at times I had thought that might be enough I had always known how vulnerable I was to signs of affection or tenderness from another woman.

"I'll soon be forty-three," I said, "and I've never yet had a truly loving relationship with a woman. I want one. I want to feel close to a woman."

"How much of this is your own fault?" she asked.

"All of it, I suppose."

"Do you believe that? Or are you just saying that?"

"I don't know. I don't know what I believe anymore. I've always kept the wall up, pretty much kept my feelings to myself. But whether that was out of choice or because I had no one to share those feelings with I don't know."

"Do you think you could share those feelings with me?"

"Some of them, some of the time. Yes."

"Do," she said, twisting on the bed to look at me.

"Okay." I pushed her head back down on the pillow. "I will as soon as I know what I think. Now close your eyes. Enough's been said today. For the time being there's nothing any of us can do but try to take each day as it comes."

"You don't want to talk?" She sounded half-asleep already.

"Shhh," I said. "Later."

I continued to rub her back until I heard the front door open. Arthur was back. I kissed Odette lightly on the cheek and went downstairs to meet him.

"Arthur," I said, "we'd better talk."

"Not now," he said, weaving past me. "Tomorrow. Tomorrow. We'll all talk tomorrow. Got plenty of time," he said, and he continued on up the stairs. It was only then that I noticed he had no shoes on his feet.

I found his shoes when I looked in on Alice. They were on the floor in the guest room, neatly aligned with the side of the bed in which Alice lay asleep.

I closed her door and continued on into the bedroom, which was now mine alone. I sat down on the side of the bed and smoked a cigarette. I thought about sharing my feelings then, with Odette; but they were probably not feelings she would want to hear. In fact, I realized I was perfectly willing for Arthur to take Alice off my hands, but not if it meant I would be taking responsibility for his two children and Odette. I liked Paul and Vanessa, and I liked Odette, but if he thought we were simply going to trade wives and families he was out of his mind. That's what I had wanted to talk to him about that night. It could, however, wait.

By tomorrow I would have found out what one did about a New Jersey divorce.

The next morning I asked Alice if she were aware that Odette had asked Arthur for a separation.

"We talked about it," Alice said.

"How do you feel about it?"

"I want a separation, too," she said.

I just stood there looking at her.

"How do you feel about *that?*" she asked.

"A little sick to my stomach, to tell you the truth."

"Well, don't you want a separation, too?"

"If *you* get one it's a separation from *me*. So I don't see that I have much choice."

"So you'll move out?"

"Why should *I* move out? You're the one who wants the separation."

"I knew you'd be difficult," she said.

"That's up to you, Alice," I said. "I can be more than 'difficult.' With any encouragement at all I can be a real sonuvabitch."

"Are you threatening me?"

"No. I'm just telling you how I intend to play this game."

Later that morning I visited Parker Dudley, a lawyer in the firm of Dudley, Benton & Quinn.

Parker had handled the closing on the Baskin house and was about my age. He had been recommended by Dudley Thompson, my real estate agent friend. Parker Dudley was related to Dudley Thompson by marriage.

Parker Dudley rose from behind his desk when I entered and gestured to the leather chair across the way. We sat for a moment looking each other over, then he asked, "What can I do for you?"

"I want to find out what the procedures are for getting a divorce in this state."

"You thinking of getting one?"

"Not yet, but there's been enough talk for me to feel it's prudent to find out what's involved."

"Time," Parker said. "Time and money."

"How much time?"

"You're not worried about the money?"

"I can guess how much money," I said. "I've been divorced before. New Jersey has 'no-fault divorce,' doesn't it?"

"Yes. But in order to qualify for it one has to have been physically separated, living in different habitations, for eighteen months."

"Eighteen months! My God, isn't there some way—aren't there other grounds that would be faster?"

"There are other grounds, certainly," Parker said. "Extreme cruelty, adultery, habitual drunkenness, desertion, imprisonment. But to file on those grounds would not necessarily bring any faster action."

"Why not?"

"Because of the backlog of cases. There are only two judges in each county assigned to hear matrimonial matters. There are between a million and five hundred thousand people living in each county. You asked what was involved in a divorce and I told you. Time and money. Time first of all. It's not uncommon for a divorce to take two years. That is why no matter what grounds parties may initially file their divorce claim upon, they usually amend their grounds to uncontested divorce."

"All right then, how does one go about getting a divorce here? What is the first step?"

"The first step is to retain an attorney. Your attorney writes a letter to your spouse indicating that there are certain matrimonial difficulties and that he has been hired to represent you. This letter is simply to see if something can be worked out—if not, you then file a complaint detailing the charges and your wish to dissolve the marriage based on these grounds. The complaint is then sent to a sheriff for service on the other party's attorney. Once the other party has received the complaint, he or she has twenty days in which to answer it. Normally within twenty days the other party will file an answer. It's basically a denial of the charges made in the complaint, but it may include a counterclaim of that party's charges, the grounds the other party possesses for divorce . . ."

Parker then went into detail on "conducting discoveries," the interrogatory process designed to elicit details on the income and assets of the divorcing spouses, and the *pendente lite* motions used to resolve the temporary support question while awaiting final outcome of the case.

"What about custody and property settlements?" I asked.

"They're decided at the final hearings," he said.

"Parker, should the need arise, would you be willing to represent me?"

"Of course," he said. He thought for a moment, then asked, "Whose names are your houses in?"

"Mine," I said.

"Both of them?"

"Yes."

"What do you plan to do with the big new one?"

"I don't know yet."

"You'd better give it some thought. You can be damn sure your wife's lawyer will put a lien on both your properties. Do you know who might be representing your wife?"

"I don't think she has a lawyer yet."

"I hope she gets a smart one," Parker said. "I love a good fight."

I stopped off at Odette's and told her what I had learned. She was as upset by the two years it took to get a divorce in New Jersey as I was. I asked if she had contacted a lawyer yet.

"No, who should I get?"

"Do you and Arthur have any lawyer friends you trust?"

She shook her head. "No."

"I can call Parker and see who he might recommend."

"No, don't," she said. "I'll get one on my own."

"Well, let me know if you need help. When will Arthur be home? It's time we all had a talk."

"He's meeting Alice in town for dinner."

"So they won't be back until late."

"If at all."

Odette, the children, and I went out for dinner that night. We were all somewhat subdued. The children picked at their food; Odette and I lapsed into long silences. After dinner I dropped the Villars back at their house and went straight home with Peter. I still didn't feel much of anything at all. As I sat in the bathroom watching Peter brush his teeth I made mindless conversation with him about how lucky I felt Odette's children were to be raised bilingual in English and French and that I hoped they would be able to keep it up.

"Daddy," Peter interrupted, "do you like living with Mommy?"

"Not as much as I used to. Why?"

"I don't want to talk about it now."

"I know. Why don't we finish up in here and get to bed?"

"Will you read me a story?"

"Which one would you like?"

"*Good Night Moon*," he said.

"*Good Night Moon?* Aren't you a little old for that book now?"

"I still like it," he said.

"So do I." I pulled out the book and lay down on the bed next to him. It was the story I had read to my son night after night several years before. I knew why he wanted to hear it again: it made him feel safe.

Alice woke me up several hours later—I had fallen asleep next to Peter on his bed.

Alice was furious: "You're such a *sneak!* That's what really pisses me off about you," she said. "Why didn't you tell me you went to see a lawyer today?"

"I didn't sneak off, Alice," I said. "It seemed to me since everyone was tossing around words like divorce I'd find out what was involved."

"And did you?"

"Yes," I said. "Time and money."

The telephone had been installed in the cottage by now, but in the beginning I rarely got any calls. That was why when the telephone rang early the following afternoon while I was getting myself some coffee, it scared me so badly I dropped and smashed the cup. Arthur was calling from his Princeton office: "I think we ought to talk about what's happening," he said.

"What *is* happening?"

"You've upset Alice terribly with your threats."

"Arthur, I haven't *made* any threats."

"According to Alice you plan to make it very difficult."

"I told her that it was entirely up to her. I certainly don't plan to make it easy."

"Why can't it be? I'm willing to assume financial responsibility for Alice, to live with her and take care of her, if you'll do the same for Odette."

I thought about that for a moment. How could he be so sure Odette and I *wanted* to live together?

"Have you spoken to Odette about this?"

"Not in any great detail."

"Don't you think you ought to talk to her first?"

"Of course I'll talk to her. But I thought I'd sound out your feelings."

"You've spoken to Alice, I assume."

"Certainly."

"And she'd be willing to go along with such an arrangement?"

"In principle, yes."

I felt sick to my stomach again.

"So what do you think?" Arthur asked. "Obviously you and Alice have no real marriage to speak of. Haven't for years. And—"

"Do tell, Arthur."

"There's no need to get passive aggressive with me. Odette's and my marriage, as I'm sure she's told you, has not been good for some time. It seems only sensible, under the circumstances, that we—"

"Arthur," I interrupted, "I don't want to discuss this without Odette and Alice being present."

"Fine," he said. "Then the four of us will meet at your house tonight."

"Let's do just that," I said. After I hung up the telephone I found myself shivering. It must have been seventy degrees in the cottage, but still I felt cold. I sat hugging myself in my office swivel chair and gently rocking back and forth.

Fear began hammering at me again. Fear and loneliness and despair. On the one hand I felt torn by the desire to be utterly free of Alice and all the resentment and guilt, anger and bitterness she felt toward me; but on the other hand, I was anxious about having to start all over again facing the future alone. I didn't want to be divorced—I just didn't want to be married to Alice.

I liked having a wife, a family. I loved the familiarity of a home. I was afraid of all the anguish the divorce would bring. I wanted to stop what was happening to us. But I did not know how. I had been waiting for us all to somehow miraculously come to our senses, to realize we had been behaving irresponsibly, to pull ourselves back from this brink before it was too late. But it was too late already. And that is why I felt so cold.

I tried to reach Alice to tell her about the meeting that night, but the phone was busy. I telephoned Odette. "I've just spoken to Arthur," I said. "There's to be a meeting at our house tonight."

Odette did not speak.

"He suggested he and I simply take over responsibility for each other's wives. I told him I wouldn't discuss it without your being present."

She was still silent.

"Are you there?" I asked.

"What about the children?"

"You should get a baby-sitter, I guess."

"I'm not talking about tonight!"

"I'm sure you would have custody."

"Of course I would have custody, but does it occur to him that there are children involved?" When I didn't answer Odette sighed and said, "Oh well. What time do we meet?"

"He didn't say."

"He and Alice will decide," Odette said. "They seem to make all the plans for everybody."

"I'll talk to you later, just as soon as I know."

"All right, fine," she said, and abruptly hung up.

I tried telephoning Alice again. The phone was still busy. I continued to try for the next half-hour until finally I got through and Alice answered.

"Arthur called," I said. "He wants us all to talk tonight at our house."

"I know," she said. "It's set for nine o'clock after the children are in bed."

"Okay," I said. "I'll be coming back from here about five-thirty then."

"I don't care when you come back. The only thing I care about is when are you moving out?"

"When am I moving out?" I asked. "I'm not moving anywhere."

Alice hung up. And when I tried telephoning Odette to give her the time, there was no answer.

Our house in town was empty when I came back down from the woods. I was still alone when I finished a shower and, wrapping a towel around my waist, I went into the bedroom to telephone Odette. I sat on the edge of the bed listening to her phone ring. There was still no answer. It was about 6 P.M. and I tried every fifteen minutes or so until after eight. By that time I had fed Tallulah, fed myself, and washed the dishes. I tried calling Odette one more time, but there was still no answer and no sign of Alice and Peter. I went into the library and turned on the TV.

At eight-thirty the back door opened and the cast began to assemble for the scene . . .

FADE IN:

214. INTERIOR: OLD NEW ENGLAND SALT-BOX LIBRARY. 8:31 P.M., FRIDAY, SEPTEMBER 21, 1979.
I am sitting in my usual chair, Tallulah, the CAT, on the chair opposite me. The television set is showing a movie, but the sound is off. A book lies open in my lap. We hear a door open behind me and then the voices of ALICE and PETER as they enter the kitchen. I twist in my chair to look. PETER enters the library, comes to the side of my chair, and throws himself on its arm like a gymnast balancing across the beam. Both of PETER's feet are off the ground, his head is in my lap, his face turned toward the television set. HE rocks back until his weight is on his feet. ALICE remains in the kitchen.

PETER

Hi, Dad. Whatcha watching?

MYSELF

Some movie.

PETER

What's it about?

MYSELF

I don't really know.

ALICE

(Calling from kitchen:)
PETER! It's your bedtime!

PETER

(Ignores mother:)
Is it a good movie?

MYSELF

I don't really know that either. I haven't been paying much attention.

ALICE

(Impatiently:)
PETER!
(ALICE comes to the doorway and stands there.)

MYSELF

You'd better do as your mother says, pal. Go brush your teeth and get ready for bed. I'll be up in a minute.

PETER

Will you read me a story?

MYSELF

If there's time.
(PETER slowly and deliberately turns away from me, one hand drifting down the arm of the chair.)

ALICE

And I want you to really brush your teeth, not just slosh water around your mouth.

PETER

(With infinite resignation:)
I will.
(ALICE watches PETER until he disappears up the stairs, then ALICE comes into the library, pushes the CAT out of the chair opposite me, and sits down. Just as ALICE seats herself, we hear PETER coming back downstairs. ALICE waits for PETER to reappear in the doorway before asking:)

ALICE

What now?

PETER

Are you and Daddy going to sleep together again after you get over your cold?

ALICE

I don't know . . . Go brush your teeth.

PETER

In a couple of weeks maybe?

ALICE

I don't know.

PETER

(To me:)

Do you like sleeping alone?

MYSELF

Sometimes. You have your own room and you like that, don't you?

PETER

I like sleeping with you, too.

ALICE

Quit stalling and go to bed now, Peter.

PETER

I want you to be together.

(In the silence that follows PETER looks from his mother to me and back to his mother again. The silence grows deafening.)

ALICE

It's too late for that.

PETER

(Turns to me desperately seeking a denial. His eyes fill with tears.)

Daddy?

(I pick up PETER and sit him back down in my lap. I cannot bear to look at ALICE. I cannot bear to look at PETER either. My eyes, too, are filled with tears. ALICE stands up and I see there are tears in her eyes as well. SHE moves toward PETER and MYSELF, hesitates for a moment, then swerves away to the liquor cabinet and pours herself a drink. I stand up, still holding PETER, and carry him upstairs. The camera remains behind with ALICE, who is fighting hard not to cry.)

CUT TO:

215. INTERIOR: MASTER BEDROOM. A FEW MINUTES LATER.

The camera tracks as I carry PETER past our bed and into the master bathroom.

CUT TO:

216. *INTERIOR: MASTER BATHROOM.*

We have seen the bathroom before. It was in this bathroom that Barbara
T. cut her foot. It was from the bathroom window that I watched Barbara
T. and Alice and Arthur naked in the pool. The walls are stark white.
All the fixtures are porcelain, the counters are white, too. There are
double sinks. One is obviously ALICE's, the other mine. ALICE's has
a china mannequin's hand with her rings on its fingers and beside the
hand various jars of beauty products have been neatly aligned. My sink
has next to it an antique shaving mug and brush. There are a few well-
kept plants, a seashell or two, and on the wall above the roll of toilet
paper there is the antique china plate with a Cyclopean eye centered
within the legend "Thou God See'st Me." I enter still carrying PETER
and lower him gently to the floor and almost immediately leave.

MYSELF

I'm getting your pajamas, be right back.

PETER

(Stands there entirely alone not moving, then slowly, resignedly, he
begins to undress button by button. He does not look up when I return
carrying his pajamas, his toothbrush, and a small stool for him to stand
on to reach the sink. I sit on the toilet seat to keep him company as he
undresses. It is obvious from PETER's posture how tired and dejected
he is. When he stands for a moment naked and is looking around for his
pajamas I am struck by his vulnerability, his fragility.)

MYSELF

(Holding out my arms to him:)
    Come here, Peter.
PETER, still naked, walks to me and fits between my legs. As I hug
him the camera holds at an angle that reveals over my shoulder the
"Thou God See'st Me" plate. It is the exact same angle and almost the
same scene as when I was kneeling between Barbara T.'s naked thighs.
My hands caress PETER's back, his shoulders, just as Barbara T.'s hands
had caressed mine.)

PETER

Are you and Mommy going to get a divorce?

MYSELF

I don't know.

PETER

Do you hope not?

MYSELF

(After a moment's hesitation:)
     I don't know that either . . . Now brush your teeth, put on your
pajamas, and get into bed.
                                                              CUT TO:
217. *INTERIOR: PETER'S BEDROOM. ABOUT TEN MINUTES LATER.*
I am lying next to PETER on his bed, just closing the book in my lap. I
read:
                                    MYSELF
     "And they lived happily ever after . . ."
                                    PETER
Did they?
                                    MYSELF
Says here in this book they did.
                                    PETER
Do you love Mommy?
                                    MYSELF
I guess I do.
                                    PETER
Then why can't—
                                    MYSELF
(Quickly:)
Because it's not the kind of love that makes things work out.
                                    PETER
But if you *love* Mommy, can't you just try?
                                    MYSELF
     Like your mother said, Peter, it's late. It's time to go to sleep.
(I lean forward and kiss PETER, then stand up and adjust the covers
around the child, who lies there on his back in bed:)
     G'night, sleep well.
(PETER follows me with his eyes, but does not move his head. I am
tense and distracted and it shows. I force myself to calm down. I lean
forward and kiss PETER again on the cheek. It is a longer, more attentive
kiss. I turn out his bedside light and walk to the door, pause, and turn
back to say:)
     Sweet dreams . . .
(PETER nods but neither looks at me, nor responds. My last view of
him lying there is of his eyes wide open staring up at the ceiling.)
                                                              CUT TO:
218. *INTERIOR: LIBRARY. SEVERAL HOURS LATER.*

It is obvious from the filled ashtrays, the collection of glasses, the plates with partially eaten canapés, the disheveled and angry appearance of ARTHUR, ODETTE, ALICE, and MYSELF that we have been at it for some time. I am sitting in my usual chair; ODETTE is in the chair opposite mine. ARTHUR and ALICE are at two smaller chairs on the other side of the small room.

ARTHUR

But I don't see why it's essential for us at this stage to have lawyers, who will only demand more of our money. Why can't we behave like adults about this and work the details out among ourselves?

MYSELF

Because we cannot behave like adults about this. There are too many details to work out—*responsibilities*.

ODETTE

The proof that we need lawyers is that we've been at it all night and we haven't agreed on a thing!

MYSELF

Who's going to decide on alimony? Child support? The division of property? What I think might be fair will probably not seem fair to Alice.

ALICE

I agree we need lawyers—especially since you have one already.

ARTHUR

But can't we at least agree to keep their participation to a minimum?

MYSELF

That's up to you, Arthur. But I plan to have a lawyer advising me every step of the way . . .

(Turns to ODETTE:)

. . . and I would urge you to do the same.

ODETTE

I have. I got myself a lawyer today. He told me not to agree to anything until I had covered it all with him, spoken to him. He said—

ARTHUR

—Of course that's what he wants! It means more money for him.

ODETTE

It means better protection for me. *And*, I might add, the children.

ARTHUR

All I'm saying is that we need to keep communicating with each other.

ALICE

Arthur's only trying to keep our legal fees to a minimum.

MYSELF

We can if we can agree, but what happens when both of us want the same thing?

ALICE

We talk it over. And if we can't agree we trade off.

MYSELF

I'm not talking about furniture, Alice. Jesus Christ, I'm talking about Peter. What if I were to ask for custody of Peter?

ALICE

No! Peter's the only good thing I ever got out of this marriage.

MYSELF

You'd better get a lawyer.

ARTHUR

He's bluffing, Alice. He doesn't want custody.

MYSELF

Speak for yourself, Arthur.

ALICE

He *can't* have Peter!

ARTHUR

He'd never get it. After all, look how he's handled Joan.

MYSELF

Oh, fuck off, Arthur, will you? You really piss me off.

ARTHUR

That's very healthy. And now, if you're prepared to *listen* to me, all I'm saying, *suggesting* really, is that if we can try to talk things over, try to resolve our differences among ourselves, then, perhaps, we can at least agree upon what we disagree upon. *That's* when to bring in the lawyers.

ODETTE

The only thing we seem to agree upon so far, Arthur, except for you, is that we need lawyers.

ALICE

What about our houses?

ARTHUR

That's a good point. I've thought that over.

(He turns to ODETTE:)

Odette can sell our house.

(To me:)

You can stay here.

(To ALICE:)

Alice and I will find a place of our own.

ODETTE

And where am I and the children to move to after I sell our home? Are we supposed to live in the street? Are we no longer your concern? Is the omniscient doctor just going to stamp our file "Closed" and forget about us?

ARTHUR

Don't pull that passive aggressive shit with me, Odette.

ODETTE

Then don't you be so almighty godlike with my life, Arthur.

MYSELF

(To ARTHUR:)

Here's a better idea. Why don't you buy Odette's share of your house from her and buy this house from me, and Odette and I will move into the Baskin house when it's done.

ALICE

(Outraged at me:)

No! You can't have that house! That was to be my house! I designed it for me!

(She bursts into tears:)

I don't want *them* living in my house. I don't want—I don't want *her* using my things!

ODETTE

In the first place, lady, *you're* using my husband. In the second place, I and only I will decide where I live and you can be sure it won't be in anything of yours!

ARTHUR

(Standing up:)

Come on, Alice, it's time for us to get out of here. There's no point in talking when Odette gets like this . . .

ODETTE

Fine, Arthur, *do* leave. Run off with your lady friend as usual—and such a lady, too. *Cette conne!*

ALICE

What do you mean by that? What does that mean?

ODETTE

You know exactly what I mean.

ARTHUR

(Crosses to ALICE and takes her arm:)
    Come on, Alice.

ALICE

(Not moving:)
    I want to know what she said!

ARTHUR

(He pulls ALICE up from her chair:)
    It doesn't matter. Let's go.
(I remain seated in my chair and barely look up as ARTHUR and ALICE
leave. When the door closes behind them ODETTE rises and comes
over to my chair. There is a moment of silence and then I look up at
ODETTE and ask:)

MYSELF

    What does "*Cette conne*" mean?

ODETTE

    It means "that cunt."
(I laugh and after a slight pause ODETTE laughs with me. I pull her
down onto my lap and hug her.)

MYSELF

    You are a hell of a woman!
(I hold ODETTE and gently caress her shoulder:)
    Are you all right? How do you feel?

ODETTE

    I feel . . . I don't know, numb. You?

MYSELF

    I guess numb, too. Even relieved. Do you think you'd like a drink?

ODETTE

(Looks at watch:)
    It's almost eleven-thirty. I'm exhausted. I'd better be going home.
    The baby-sitter . . .

MYSELF

    I'll walk you back.

ODETTE

(She rises from my lap:)
    You don't have to.

MYSELF

    I want to. I think we could both use some fresh air.
(I push myself up:)

Just let me check on Peter, first, okay? I want to be sure he's asleep.

CUT TO:

219. *INTERIOR: PETER'S BEDROOM. A MOMENT LATER.*

The camera shows me standing in the doorway looking down at PETER, who is lying exactly as I had left him hours before, his eyes still wide open. He is staring at the ceiling.

MYSELF

Couldn't sleep?

(PETER shakes his head "no" but does not speak.)

I'm going to walk Odette home, then I'll be right back.

PETER

Is Mommy here?

MYSELF

She went out with Arthur to have a drink. Why don't you climb into my bed and you and I can sleep together tonight. Would you like that?

(PETER nods "yes" and I pull back his covers and scoop him out of bed. The camera follows as I carry PETER out his door.)

220. *INTERIOR: MASTER BEDROOM. SAME TIME.*

The camera picks me up as I carry PETER to my bed and tuck him in. I lean forward to kiss his forehead:

MYSELF

I'll be back in about fifteen minutes. You okay now?

(PETER nods "yes.":)

Okay, pal, I'll be back in just a little while.

CUT TO:

221. *EXTERIOR: SIDEWALK OUTSIDE HOUSE. A FEW MINUTES LATER.*

We see ODETTE and me walking along the darkened sidewalk. ODETTE shivers slightly and I put my arm around her and pull her to me for warmth.

ODETTE

Are we going to be all right?

MYSELF

You and me?

ODETTE

I mean all of us?

MYSELF

We're going to live happily ever after.

ODETTE

(Not unkindly:)
    Liar.

MYSELF

Not anymore.

CUT TO:

222. *INTERIOR: MASTER BEDROOM. A HALF-HOUR LATER.*
I am in my pajamas in bed. PETER is asleep next to me, curled up in
my arms. My eyes are wide open. I am staring up at the ceiling.

FADE TO BLACK

12

By the time the twentieth reunion of my college class was held that first week in October both couples had separated and filed for divorce. I had put the Baskin house and my house in town on the market. Alice and Peter were living in the old house; the carpenters and painters were still working on the new. Odette had remained in the gray Federal up the street with Vanessa and Paul. Arthur had taken an apartment in Princeton near the university and I had moved with my ancient cat Tallulah into the cottage in the woods.

Snow fell November eighth and melted the day after. Two more storms hit toward the end of the month and another heavy snow fell the second week in December. The accumulation from this, the fourth storm of that beautiful, awful winter remained on the ground through Christmas, the first "white Christmas" we had had in years.

I described that first winter of our separations as beautiful and awful because it was beautiful up in the cottage with the deer drifting like smoke through the snowy woods. I, however, was awful, especially to Odette. I would drive down from the woods to have dinner with her after an afternoon spent in bed with somebody else. I would see Arthur's car parked in the driveway of my former house and I'd feel a surge of rage and betrayal at the two of them being together, blame them for the mess our lives were in. And then I'd continue on past to Odette's, where in the middle of dinner I would suddenly look up at her and her two children as if they were strangers and wonder what I was doing there. But in the next instant I would feel engulfed by love and gratitude for this woman and her family who had taken me in. During this period I felt buffeted by the most intense emotional confusion I have ever encountered.

I did not feel only confused!

I felt ashamed and guilty, lonely and anxious; resentful and angry when I saw Alice, saddened and apologetic when I saw Peter; and constantly uncertain and apprehensive about where we were heading and what I was going to become.

I was especially bewildered by the ambivalence of my feelings toward Odette and Alice. I had hoped and intended that by moving out of the house my marital relationship with Alice would be ended. In fact, the marital relationship was, but the emotional relationship intensified. I

ricocheted between nostalgia and fury, remorse and pain. I made excuses
to return to the old house—I needed a heavy sweater, a specific book,
a pot or pan. (My cooking for myself, what little I did, was still terrible;
but it was an improvement, at least, on my former TV dinners or canned
beef stews.) I would turn into the drive and see the house and remember
little vignettes of happiness, scenes of laughter and good times that we
had enjoyed there; but then I would see Alice and she would say
something hurtful and I would be overwhelmed by an anger I could
not—or would not—express.

During that snowstorm in December I had returned to the house
ostensibly to pick up a pair of winter boots. Alice met me at the door.
"Have you still got both houses on the market?" she asked.

"Yes, of course. Why?"

"I can't find a decent house anywhere," she said. "Nothing you'd want
Peter to grow up in. Everything's either in a development or a raised
ranch in the middle of nowhere."

"You can't expect to retain the same lifestyle after a divorce."

"*You* are," she said.

"I'm living in a cottage one fifth the size of this house and one tenth
the size of the Baskin house you wanted so badly and into which I'm still
pouring money."

"You've got Odette's house."

"*I* don't have Odette's house! *Odette* has Odette's house—that is, what
little of it isn't owned by the bank."

"Arthur isn't trying to evict Odette. Why are you trying to throw Peter
and me out?"

"Alice, the two houses are on the market at *your* lawyer's insistence.
He's put a lien on both properties and I have to sell them to raise the
sizable cash settlement you and your lawyer are demanding. If you'd be
willing to settle for this house and a substantially smaller cash settlement,
I'm sure someth—"

"Why are you being so cold?" she interrupted. "I don't understand
how you can be so cold to me. You'd think after twelve years of marriage—"

"—Actually it was closer to ten," I said.

"—some sort of relationship would still exist between us. But I don't
know what's left to believe in. We must have had some good times
together, didn't we? All those years couldn't have been entirely bad."

I stood there in the kitchen, the snow covering the hemlocks we had
planted, the lawn we had so carefully nurtured. I looked around the

kitchen at the beams we had scraped together, the library with all our books resting on their freshly painted shelves. I looked at Alice and remembered the tenant farmhouse we had shared in Nebraska, our excitement over our first furniture purchases, our laughter, our friends. I remembered the soft, sweet exhaustion on her face after Peter's birth. Where had all that softness, that sweetness gone? What had this marriage—what had *I* done to her? I saw that Alice had bought a Christmas tree. The tattered angel ornament my mother had had from her childhood Alice had put on top. I felt as though we were forfeiting our entire past and I stood there feeling sorry for Alice, for Peter, for Joan, for us all. I felt inundated with a sense of loss.

"Well?" Alice said.

"Well, what?" I stalled.

"Were all those times so bad?"

I struggled to pull myself together. "It's difficult under the circumstances to remember the good times," I told her. "We must have had some."

"Are you happy now?"

"Happy? What does that have to do with anything?"

"I just hope at least one of us feels better off as a result of all this."

I could feel the anger rise up in me, give me strength, anger at Alice for trying to lay that guilt on me, anger at myself for weakening enough to feel sorry for her.

"Peter misses you terribly," she said.

"I miss him, too."

"He's taking this very hard."

"So are Vanessa and Paul."

"I don't care about *them!*" she said.

"They also love their father very much. I'll see Peter this weekend. Is Arthur going to see his kids?"

"How should I know."

"I thought he might have mentioned something to you. You *do* see him, don't you?"

"Jesus, you're so *cold!* Why are you so cold to me?"

"Alice, I've got things to do. I'll just pick up my boots and get going if you don't mind."

I had treated Alice coldly, I knew, but it was the only way I could cope. The death of the marriage was more difficult for me to handle than the deaths of either my brother or mother. Death ended relationships cleanly; Alice's and my divorce only dirtied the relationship more. Because I would never see my mother and brother again, the connection was broken; but I had to keep seeing Alice whether I wanted to or not. And despite the very real sympathy I felt for Alice I had only to look at Odette's life to see how much better off Alice was.

The moment Arthur had left home, he had turned his back on Odette as though she had ceased to exist. Because he had closed out their joint checking account she had to count on temporary support to feed herself and her kids. She had taken a position as a secretary for a local architect, but the job was only from nine to two, three days a week, while the children were in school. It paid so poorly that Odette was forced to waitress on weekends in a French restaurant in New Hope, an hour and a half away. It was grueling, exhausting work, but waitressing was the only job a woman with no specific skills could do that would earn her a decent amount of money and still allow her time to be with her children.

Alice did not work; she did not need to. I kept her charge accounts open, paid her bills, saw that she had adequate money.

Looking back on that first winter I am astonished at how *strong* Odette was. She was really the only one of us who made it entirely on her own. I am also ashamed of how unaware I was of the difficulties I created for her myself.

These difficulties existed because there was a vast difference between what I thought I was doing and what was actually taking place. I would tell Odette that I believed in equality between the sexes and yet I let her do all the cooking and cleaning, the "woman's work." I was not even good company. I was constantly talking about my problems and worries, myself. When Odette would try to talk about her difficulties, I would become restless and distracted. I would not want to hear about them because I believed I already knew what they were. Her problems, I thought, were the sort that either we could easily take care of, or the sort that would iron themselves out given enough time. It pains me when I see how selfish I was.

What were happy, humming little scenes of domesticity to me were, I now recognize, an unfair, thoughtless burden upon her. I would come down from the cottage, build a fire, mix her a drink, sit and chat with her while she cooked. Oh, I would do the dishes (rinse and stack them in the dishwasher), but I'd leave the pans to soak. When the ashes built up in the fireplace, Odette would clean them out. Inevitably Odette grew impatient with me and tense.

"Dinner was delicious," I told her one of those winter evenings as I brought us our cups of coffee.

"Thank you," Odette replied.

"Thank *you*," I insisted.

"Stop treating me like someone you just met!"

"Am I? I don't mean to be."

"Well, you are."

"I'm sorry," I said. "This whole situation is so crazy. It's making me a little crazy, too."

"You're just using being crazy as an excuse. Don't you think I feel crazy at times, too? Put yourself in my shoes. I have no husband, two children, two jobs, this house which is falling apart all around me—over there, look," Odette said, pointing to an area of water-stained and loose plaster in a corner. "And here, too," she added, indicating another stain. "At the windowsill. The water pours in every time it rains. I have to deal with this all by myself. I have no one to fix it, to take care of it for me."

"I'll call a carpenter," I said. "It's probably only a loose clapboard by the sill. It may just only need caulking."

"And when the carpenter comes, how will I pay him?" she asked. "You don't seem to understand! Yesterday Paul came to me saying he needed a new pair of shoes for school, that the pair he's been wearing are too small and hurt his feet. I screamed at him! I *screamed* at him! I told him I couldn't afford a new pair of shoes this month . . . Three days ago I bought sandwich meats for their school lunches. The meat was to last all week. Last night when I went to make their lunches, the meat was gone. They'd eaten it for snacks. I screamed at them again! Vanessa wanted a school folder to keep her papers in, something that would look nice. I told her to ask her father. It's these little things day after day that grind me down—the children take forever in the shower, use up the hot water, I get a higher bill. I'm yelling all the time and it isn't fair to them. They're always eating, always growing out of their clothes, needing new shoes. I don't have the money to pay for it all and you want me to hire a carpenter?"

"I'll pay the carpenter."

"Why should you?"

"Why not?" I said, and shrugged. "What with the work still going on in the Baskin house I'm paying every other goddam carpenter in town."

"No, I'll fix it myself," Odette said wearily. "Just like I fixed the sink when it leaked and replastered the bedroom upst—"

"You should have let me help you."

"No one was preventing you."

"But you always fixed these things while I was working. In the evenings I could have—"

"They have to be done."

"I could have plastered. I'm not much of a plumber though, beyond fixing a stuck toilet . . ."

Odette laughed and I felt vaguely irritated.

"Why are you laughing at me?" I asked.

"Because you seem to assume I know how to fix these things better than you. I don't. I've just had to teach myself like everybody else."

"All right, tomorrow in the daylight I'll take a close look at the clapboards. Maybe I'll be able to locate the leak. I'll come down from the cottage early in the afternoon."

"If you like."

We were both silent. I got up to put another log on the fire.

"No, don't," Odette said. "It will burn too long. I don't want to have to stay up to watch over it—*you* can stay if you want, but I'm going to bed."

"Do you want me to stay?" I asked.

"Why not?" she said. "Everybody thinks we're living together anyway. They see your car in front of the house all the time."

"Not in the morning."

"I'm too exhausted to care."

I followed Odette upstairs, gave her a backrub, and when she had fallen asleep I went back up to the cottage and my own bed.

Why didn't I stay with Odette?

A half-dozen of that period's rationalizations spring to mind: I was reluctant then to get that involved; I didn't want her to know I couldn't come; I needed time alone; I didn't want Arthur and Alice to assume I was living with Odette; I didn't want Arthur's and Alice's lawyers to have that sort of ammunition against us . . .

I told Odette I wanted a mature relationship with her, but what I really wanted was an approximation of family life, a sense of continuity, stability, structure that I knew to be artificial even then; but still, it helped me contain my anxiety in the face of the irretrievable loss of my former paternal and marital roles.

I would eat with Odette, but I had no appetite. I would then return to the cottage exhausted, but I could not sleep. I had an unshakable cough, headaches all the time. Odette, too, was always exhausted—but with better reason than I. She, too, had headaches. Instead of coughing, she felt nauseous and many nights she would leave her bed to throw up. The next morning she would get up with her children, then leave for her own job after seeing them off to school. And still, *and still* she would treat me with humor and gentleness, thoughtfulness, too. She would not only feed *me* dinner, but when Joan came back from St. Matthew's prior to heading west for Christmas with her mother, Odette even fed her, too.

Why did Odette put up with me?

God only knows.

She says it's because she saw something good in me. There were not many available men in our little town. She was lonely. She was sure she could make me happy, that I was basically a decent and generous man, that I would let the barriers down, become more trusting and giving, capable and willing to love. Until that time came she had resolved to be patient and to *faire le poing dans sa poche*, one of her wonderful French expressions meaning, literally, "to make the fist in one's pocket."

That whole December I was restless, distracted, quick to withdraw. I was torn by wanting to take care of Odette and leery of my ability to assume the responsibility. I was torn, too, by wanting to love Odette and my fears about such a commitment.

I had quit seeing almost all of my local friends—divorced them, too, in a sense. I would complain that they were avoiding me, and yet make excuses for not seeing them when they called. I felt lonely, but shunned parties where I might see someone who had known Alice and me together. If asked out by people I did not know, I went and tried on "new personalities" like clothes. Sometimes I took Odette, but not always. Sometimes I went alone because I had arranged to meet some other woman there.

There was Didi, the disgruntled wife of a Princeton professor whom I'd encountered at one of the few parties I'd attended. There was Margaret, who had called me after the reunion. I met her only once in New York; she scared me more than I scared myself. There was Louise, who had opened (and six months later closed) our town's only health food store. There was Marge, a real estate lady I first saw when I shifted both houses to multiple listings. And there was a NYU graduate student I'd come in contact with while teaching. None of these affairs was satisfying. I was too manic to be a good lover. As a result, it was rather lonely for us all. I owe them an apology. I would not let these women get close to me. I wanted them to think me wonderful; I did not want them to see me as I really was. The moment the woman guessed that I was not what I pretended to be, I would flee. It was an approach that guaranteed no attachments. It also led inevitably to the woman's anger at me. To be close meant being open, vulnerable, risking more pain. I would break off before I'd let that happen to me again.

Of all these women only Didi was around for any length of time. Like Alice she had no illusions about closeness. In fact Didi once made a comment that reminded me so strongly of Alice it put me off for a while: "I didn't come up here for you to 'make love' to me," Didi said one afternoon at the cottage, "I came here to 'get done.' "

Didi could be vicious about her husband and told me far more about him than I wanted to know.

"He has trouble getting it up," she said. "And when he does get it up he doesn't know what to do with it. But when I try to guide him, tell him what I want, he tells me I'm a 'ball-buster,' that I'm too aggressive about sex."

Didi and I were on my bed when this conversation took place. She had climbed on top of me and was kneeling over me as I lay on my back.

"Do you think I'm too aggressive?" she asked as she sank down on me.

I laughed. I couldn't help myself.

"Bastard!" she said. "Play with my breasts before I punch you." But she was laughing, too, by then.

Didi didn't mind my not coming. She said she liked the fact that I stayed hard longer.

Notable by her absence from this list is Barbara T. I still saw her every now and then on those weekends when I stopped by the house in town to pick Peter up. Once she was sewing buttons on one of Peter's shirts, another time she was ironing a pair of Alice's jeans. When on those few occasions she and I were left alone while Alice was upstairs gathering Peter's overnight bag, Barbara T. seemed nervous, hesitant to talk or even look at me.

I had telephoned her once very soon after I had moved up to the cottage to suggest we meet again in New York. She was very distant and made it clear that she and I, too, were getting a divorce.

Perhaps I should have anticipated that, but I hadn't. My disappointment was tempered somewhat by my relief at having one more link to Alice broken.

I spent that Christmas Eve with Odette and her children. We had trimmed the tree together in the afternoon and after dinner I had tried reading to them from Dylan Thomas' "A Child's Christmas in Wales," but Paul and Vanessa were too tired and restless, and probably too young, to pay much attention, so I put the book away and Odette sent them up to bed. Afterward Odette and I wrapped presents and Odette discovered the mini-garage and filling station set she had bought as Paul's big present needed to be assembled.

"I'll do it," I said.

"No, we can do it tomorrow," she said. "It's late."

"Let me do it. It should be ready for him under the tree. It shouldn't take too long."

It shouldn't have, but it did.

There was an odd, dreamlike quality to that whole evening: the drinks, the fatigue, the loaded emotions, the feeling of displacement, Odette's children missing their father, me missing my kids. Odette was disappointed that she had had to spend most of her Christmas money on necessities like clothes and could not afford more frivolous gifts. She was worried that when the children unwrapped their presents and discovered they were getting underwear and socks and a new sweater each that they would be upset.

I told her I thought the children understood how difficult these times were for her, that they saw how hard she worked, that they loved her and were proud of her no matter what.

When I was finally able to get the filling station grease-rack lift to work properly it was after two o'clock in the morning. I slid Paul's present under the tree and shakily stood up. "Don't sleep at the cottage tonight," Odette said. "You're too exhausted to drive."

"I can make it," I said.

"Why should you? Stay here."

What was fatigue on my part Odette mistook for hesitation and she added, "You don't have to sleep with me. I'll take Paul into my bed and you can have—"

I silenced her with a kiss. "No," I said. "I'm going back to the cottage. When the time comes that we do go to bed together, I want it to be right."

As I've said, there was an odd, dreamlike quality to that evening. What memory I have of it seems fuzzy, the way food tastes and voices sound when one has a terrible head cold. But I do clearly remember not

wanting to go to bed with Odette while I felt so tired, so passionless, so
. . . *ordinary,* I suppose. I wanted more than that for us.

Early the next morning, when I returned, the children opened the
door for me shouting, "Merry Christmas! Merry Christmas!" They seemed
not in the least bit surprised to find me there. Odette, wearing a wool
bathrobe over a flannel nightgown, said "Merry Christmas!" and we
kissed. Vanessa and Paul stood on tiptoes and I kissed them, too.

"Did you open your stocking presents?" Odette asked them.

"Stocking presents?" Paul asked. "Where are they?"

"Wherever Santa left them," I said.

"There isn't any such thing as Santa Claus," he said. "*Maman* and
Papa are Santa Claus. And you, too, now."

"I thought I put your stockings at the foot of your beds," Odette said.

"We forgot to bring them up," I said. "I think they're still here,
somewhere." I began to search under the tree.

"Let the children find them. They can open them now," Odette said.

"Then I'll get us some coffee," I said.

Later as we sat on the floor with the children by the Christmas tree
and watched them unwrap their presents Odette passed me a large box.
"This is for you."

I felt the weight of the box, shook it, turned it over. "What is it?" I
asked. "I have no idea what it can be."

"Open it," she said.

I undid the wrapping paper carefully, wanting the moment to last.

"I could not afford to get you anything extravagant," she said.

"You should not have gotten me anything at all!" I undid the last
corner of the paper and slid out a deep-red Saks Fifth Avenue box. "You
say you weren't extravagant?" I asked.

"It is an old box I had saved," she said. "I just put your present in it
. . . I hope you won't be disappointed," she said.

"Disappointed?" Inside the box I found a soft, thick, natural woolen
sweater Odette had knit me herself!

"My God!" I said.

I lifted the sweater out of the box and laid it in my lap. I was stunned
by the effort, thoughtfulness, kindness, and unselfishness of Odette's
gift. I saw the thousands of stitches, imagined the knitting needles in
Odette's thin fingers, the ball of yarn unraveling at her feet. "It's so
beautiful! When did you find time to knit it?"

"Nights," Odette said. "When the children were asleep."

"He's *crying!*" Paul said.

I hugged Odette and thanked her and hugged her again. I could not believe she had knit me a sweater, as exhausted as she was and as tiresome as I had been. "No one's ever knit me a sweater before," I said, holding it up against my chest.

"Alice never knit you one?"

"Are you kidding?" I laughed.

"I hope it's large enough," she said. "I wasn't sure how long to make the sleeves."

I pulled the sweater over my head and Odette plucked at the shoulders and chest until it hung right. "Damn," she said. "I made the sleeves too long!"

"I like long sleeves. I hate cold wrists."

"Yes, but these go to your fingertips."

"I'll roll the cuffs back." I smoothed the sweater down over my chest. "It's beautiful. I love it. It's a perfect fit."

"Do you like it, really?" she asked.

I looked at Odette kneeling opposite me and felt such love for her I could only nod "yes," I could not speak. I had always envied schoolmates of mine whose mothers or girl friends had knit them sweaters, socks, scarves. And during my adult years I had seen my contemporaries wearing sweaters knit by their wives. I envied these men being with women who cared enough for them to knit.

"*Maman*," Vanessa said, "there's something here for you." She slid a smaller box toward her mother. Odette picked up the present and looked at me. "It's from you?" she asked.

"Yes."

When Odette undid the wrapping paper she saw that my gift to her was also in a red Saks Fifth Avenue box. "Did you knit me a sweater, too?" she asked.

"Not yet," I laughed.

Odette lifted the lid and pulled from its bed of tissue paper a long white silk nightgown. She ran her fingertips across the gown's French lace border, squeezed the silk between her fingertips, then looked questioningly up at me. "But we haven't, we don't—"

"We will," I said, and she *blushed!* "Ah, God, you're adorable!" I said, and hugged her again.

"It's beautiful," she said.

"I wanted to get you something you would never get for yourself," I said. "It's for morale purposes because—I'm not saying this right."

"You don't have to explain."

"I want to. I got it because I know how tired you are, how much you look forward to going to bed, that it's the only time you have to yourself, and I wanted you to have something beautiful and soft and warm like you are to go to bed in."

"You don't like my old flannel nightgowns?"

"I wanted you to have an alternative—actually, what I really wanted was to get you something tiny and silky and black with lots of lace and I didn't have the nerve to get it without you there."

"Was it very embarrassing for you to buy this?" she asked.

"I was a little uncomfortable," I said. "But when we go into New York together we can pick a different one out."

"It's almost eleven-thirty," Vanessa said. "When is Papa coming?"

By prior agreement Arthur was to come to Odette's house at eleven-thirty to be with his children and I was to stop by to pick up Peter. Alice had not offered me the chance to spend any time with Peter at the house and I had not requested any since I felt it would be more comfortable for both Peter and me to be alone. I had simply given her the majority of my presents for Peter to put under the tree.

When I arrived to pick up Peter, Alice met me at the back door. "Merry Christmas," I said. Alice eyed the sweater Odette had knit me without saying a word.

"Joan called here this morning," Alice said. "Evidently she had tried to reach you at the cottage."

"I must have been at Odette's," I said.

"I guess you must have been," Alice said, giving me the look.

"Hi, Dad! Merry Christmas!" Peter said. I knelt at the back door to hug him and saw Arthur, still in his bathrobe, pour himself a fresh cup of coffee. I thought for a moment of Odette, Paul, and Vanessa still waiting for him up the street. He caught my look and gave me a little wave.

During the drive up to the cottage Peter sat next to me holding a brightly wrapped, oddly shaped gift in his lap.

"Are you having a nice Christmas?" I asked.

"It's okay, I guess."

"Well, that's about as much as we could hope for," I said.

He did not speak.

Tallulah met us when we entered the cottage and circled in and out between my feet until she'd been fed. Peter was looking around the cottage. "Didn't you put up a Christmas tree?" he asked.

"No, I didn't see much point in it. You have one with your mother and there's one at Odette's."

Peter was kneeling by the coffee table. There were only three presents on it and one of them was a catnip mouse for Tallulah.

"I want you to open my present first," he said. "I made it in shop."

"What is it?" I asked as I undid the paper.

"You'll see."

It was a wooden duck with a clothespin bill.

"It's for you to stick your papers in," he explained.

"I'll keep it right here on my desk," I said. "I'll use it for important notes."

"And bills," he said.

I wondered what made him think like that.

My two presents to Peter were good editions of *Treasure Island* and *Wind in the Willows.*

"Oh, wow!" he said. "Terrific!" and he meant it. I loved the pleasure he got from books. "Will you read them with me?" he asked.

"Sure, but you're old enough to read them yourself now."

"I know," he said, "but I like reading with you. I think I'd like to leave one of them here so we'll have something to look at together when I spend the night."

"That's a fine idea," I said.

"What time is it?" he asked.

"About twelve-thirty, why?"

"Mom wanted me to tell you that I have to be back by one."

"Why so soon?"

"She didn't say."

I ran my hand over the sweater Odette had knit me. It felt warm and comforting and soft.

While Peter tied a red ribbon around Tallulah's neck I telephoned Joan in Oregon and wished her a Merry Christmas. Most of the presents I had mailed her had arrived, fortunately, but a heavy parka I had sent was evidently too small. Peter was looking at the illustrations in his copy of *Treasure Island,* Tallulah was on her belly twitching and purring as she attacked her catnip mouse. The bow Peter had tied around her neck had slipped beneath her chin.

Thirty minutes later, after I had dropped Peter off at his mother's, I returned to Odette's house and found her sitting alone at the kitchen

table in tears. The moment she saw me she stood up and flung herself
into my arms. "Oh, that son of a bitch!" she cried. "In front of the
children! In front of the children the things he called me!"

"What did he say?"

"That I was out to get him, that I was a stupid bitch, that I was turning
the children against him, that he was going to get custody of the kids—"

"He'd never get it," I said.

"I wish he would. I told him to go ahead. To take them if he wanted
them so much."

"You don't mean that," I said. "It would kill you if Arthur took the
children and they wouldn't want to go. They adore you, Odette, and
they know you adore them."

"Sometimes I think they would be better off with Arthur. They wouldn't
be screamed at so much."

"Maybe not by you, but if he brought them to live with Alice . . ."

"I don't want them to live with her!"

"You can be damned sure she doesn't either."

"It's not fair," Odette said. She dried her eyes with a paper napkin,
and looked up at me with her sad, brown eyes. "I see how you take care
of Alice, pay her bills, dote on Peter, and how Arthur takes care of her,
too . . . and I feel so *alone!*"

"It's because it's Christmas," I said. "The suicide rate always takes a
leap this time of year. It's Christmas and the divorces."

"It's more than *that!*" Odette said.

"I know." I wanted to tell her that she wasn't alone, that she had me.
But, of course, she *didn't* have me. I hadn't let her have me. The moment
I realized this a minor epiphany occurred as though up to that point I
had been viewing our life together through the eyepiece of one of my
cameras and suddenly I put the camera down. Reality crashed in upon
me. No longer could I deliberately limit my field of vision, focus only
on what I wanted to see. I had to see what was taking place between us
from her point of view as well. And what I saw was that Odette had
merely traded the security of one unhappy relationship with her husband
for the insecurity of an unhappy relationship with me. And to see, to
understand that meant admitting culpability, accepting responsibility for
the loneliness of this woman I so inadequately cared for. I had to
acknowledge the inescapable fact that by my actions—or lack of them—
I had helped bring this feeling of abandonment upon Odette myself.

"You probably want some coffee," Odette said, pushing herself away
from me. "I'll put the water on."

"No," I said. "You sit down. Let me make it."

"I'll get it," Odette said.

"No, please," I insisted. I took her by the shoulders and guided her into a chair. "Sit. Please. Let *me* do something for *you*."

The following morning when I was up at the cottage an old friend telephoned to invite me to a New Year's Eve party in New York. "Bring Alice, too," he said.

"Alice and I have separated," I said.

"Then bring a friend," he said.

That evening I asked Odette if she would like to go to the party and spend the night in the city. New Year's Eve that year fell on a Monday, but I knew the French restaurant at which Odette worked on weekends had called to ask if she could work Monday night because they were expecting a crowd. "Would it be possible for you to get out of going to the restaurant New Year's Eve?"

"I don't know. I can try," she said, but I knew Odette was thinking of the wages and tips she would miss.

"I'll make it up to you for the money you'd lose," I said.

I saw from her expression that I'd said the wrong thing. If I could make it up to her for one night, then why was she working so hard all the other nights? If it was so easy for me to cover the financial loss she would suffer, why didn't I help her out more?

"It's not just the money I'd lose," Odette said. "It could cost me my job if I did it too often."

"It would be only for one night. Monday," I said. "They really only hired you to work weekends."

We were sitting at the kitchen table. We had finished dinner—a dinner that, for once, I had prepared.

"Call them," I said.

"No, I'll see them Friday night. I can tell them then."

"Then I'll make the hotel reservations. We can stay at the Dupont—no," I said. "Let's stay at the Warren House. Have you ever been there?"

Odette shook her head, "No. But I've heard good things about it."

"I haven't stayed there either. I'd sort of like to try a hotel neither of us have been to before."

Odette was silent.

"And you can wear your new nightgown," I said.

Odette got up from the table and stood with her back to me looking out the kitchen window.

"What is it?" I asked. "Did I say something wrong?"

"I don't want—I don't *need* a 'quicky,' " Odette said as she turned to face me. "I don't want to get involved in an affair that's going to end. I don't want the children to see another man just disappear."

"I don't want a 'quicky' either. And I'm not going to disappear."

"Then I want you to understand this," she said. "If we do spend the night together, it also means you've decided to quit fucking around."

I responded with a nervous laugh.

"I'm serious," she said.

"I know."

I knew, too, that asking Odette to spend the night with me in New York was a big step. But I wanted to take it. Immediately after Alice and I had separated I had felt as if a great weight of chains had fallen from me. I was *free!* I could go to bed with anyone I wanted—and pretty much did. So why wasn't I having any fun? Because I didn't want to just fuck, I wanted to make love.

I wanted romance, the silly excitement of courtship: candlelight dinners, holding hands, sending flowers. I wanted a woman who was feminine, not just female. I wanted her in soft clothes. I wanted to admire her ankles, her calves, the way her skirt fell across her thighs. When she undressed I wanted to hear the light rustle of clothing, not the heavy metallic *clunk* of the belt buckle from her blue jeans hitting the floor. I wanted to hold the woman I was with, to feel the small of her back beneath my hand, the smooth curve of her forehead against my cheek. I wanted to inhale the faint scent of her perfume, taste her skin. I wanted to love the woman I took to bed. I wanted a woman who felt that way about me.

I suspected Odette might be that woman and that it was nobody's fault but my own if I lost her. She had been waiting for me to grow up, to risk being in love. I suspected, too, that she would not wait much longer, that her patience and interest in me were running out. My apprehension lay in my uncertainty over whether I was capable of being the man she and I both wanted me to be.

What if I disappointed her? What if I couldn't please her? What if by the time we went to bed I was tired? What if I was impotent? What if I couldn't come? What if because of our night together in New York she decided she never wanted to see me again? What if I lost Odette, too?

"There's another thing you should think about if we do spend the night together," Odette was saying. "Arthur and Alice."

"They won't be in New York."

"But they'll find out."

"So what?" I said. "They don't seem the least bit concerned that we know they're spending nights together. It seems silly for us to keep worrying about them, still."

"We'll have to make some arrangements about the children . . ."

I stood up and walked over to Odette. "Maybe Arthur and Alice would take them Monday night. Or we can get a sitter." I took her in my arms. "We can work it out." She was tense at first, a bit rigid in our embrace. "I want to be alone with you, to go someplace where there's just the two of us. The party's just an excuse to be in New York. I want to . . . to court you. I want to spend the night with you. And I want us to start out right."

I felt Odette relax.

"Will you come to New York with me?" I asked.

Odette looked at me searchingly, then she rested her brow against my cheek. "Yes," she said.

Odette called Arthur to ask if he would take the children over New Year's and I asked Alice if she would keep Peter. Instead of giving us the expected hassle they said they were planning to spend the holiday quietly and it wouldn't be any problem if the children spent Monday night with them. I told Alice we would be back late Tuesday afternoon and she said, "Do what you want. You always do."

And so it was settled. Odette and I would spend New Year's Eve in New York. I felt both anxious and pleased.

Later that night after I had returned to the cottage the telephone rang. "Where have you been?" Didi asked when I answered the phone.

"Out," I said.

"With Odette?"

"Yes."

"Harry's going to some conference. He's leaving tomorrow and he'll be gone over the whole New Year's holiday. We could spend the night together," she said. "Ring in the New Year."

"I'll be in New York New Year's Eve," I said.

"I could meet you there."

"I don't think—"

"I need to see you," Didi interrupted.

"That's not possible."

"When will I see you again?"

"We'll have to play it by ear."

"You don't sound very eager."

"I'm sorry," I said. Why, I wondered, was I always apologizing to women? Why couldn't I just tell Didi the truth?

"You're always distant after you've been with Odette."

"Am I?"

"You're in love with her, aren't you." It was not a question.

"Jesus, Didi," I said impatiently.

"I only want to know when I'll see you again."

"I don't know."

"Are you going to be home tomorrow night?"

"Why?"

"Don't panic. I'm not going to drop in on you. I just thought I might telephone you again."

"If I'm here, I'm here," I said.

"I can't talk to you when you are like this!" she said. "I'm hanging up."

I held the dead telephone in my hand and felt relieved, realizing that my need for company was different from what I thought. I really didn't just want to be with some woman; I wanted to be with Odette. I also knew that I did not have an infinite number of opportunities with women left, that the passage of time itself reduced the options. I was struck by an odd childhood memory: I always used to save the icing on a cake for last, but by the time I got to it I was too full to enjoy its taste.

Odette and I had our children for the weekend and on Monday morning we drove together to Princeton Junction and boarded an eleven o'clock train for New York.

I had never seen Odette so happy. Throughout the train trip she hugged my arm and chattered away. Every now and then she would interrupt herself to squeeze my hand and say, "I'm free! I can't believe it, I'm really free!" Our trip to New York was the first real escape Odette had had since she and Arthur had separated over three months before.

I, too, felt the excitement grow. With every mile added to the distance between Arthur and Alice and the two of us, I felt emotionally lighter, closer to Odette. Still, it was not until we had been in New York for several hours that I think Odette and I were really able to see each other without the shadows of our former mates falling across our faces.

We checked into the Warren House, a small hotel on Forty-eighth Street off Madison Avenue, and I saw we had been given a room with a single king-sized bed. Odette glanced at the bed when she entered the room, then looked away—though not too quickly, I thought.

"What time is it? I'm starving!" she said.

"Nearly two."

"Can we get something to eat?"

"Do you want room service? Or do you want to go out?"

"Let's go out. I want to be in the city. I want to walk."

"You don't want to unpack, hang up your clothes or anything first?"

"No, let's go out right now!"

We stepped out of the hotel onto Forty-eighth Street and turned toward Madison Avenue. We held hands as we walked. "I have missed New York so much!" Odette was saying. "I can't remember the last time I was in the city. It's been close to six months at least."

I had not spent a night in the city since I had stayed at the Dupont with Barbara T.

We passed three coffee shops that were closed for the holiday before we found a hamburger and English muffin café that was open. We sat across the counter from a woman in her thirties who appeared so obviously suicidal that I was alarmed. The woman was mumbling and fretting, twisting her napkin between her fingers until little bits of shredded paper fell. I looked away from her to Odette, who from the moment we had boarded the train had been so marvelously light and gay. "I'm so happy to be here with you!" I said.

Odette had just taken a bite of hamburger and she gestured that I should wait until she had swallowed. Then she wiped her lips and kissed me on the cheek. The woman opposite us burst into tears.

Saks Fifth Avenue was open and I took Odette's arm and pulled her into the store.

"What are you doing?" Odette asked.

"We are going to look at something in silk."

"What?" she asked.

"For you."

"But you're not going to get me . . ." Odette said, then paused.

"What?"

"Something short and slinky and black? What was it you said Christmas morning?"

"Something silky—though slinky would be nice, too," I said. We were walking between the display counters toward the elevator bank at the back of the store. "But, no, I'm only going to try to get you something you want."

"I don't want *anything*," Odette said. "You've already given me that beautiful nightgown."

"But I wanted to get you something else, a silk blouse or something like that, but I didn't know your size."

"Then let's!" she said.

We rode the elevator to the fifth floor, which was almost deserted except for several salesladies talking together by the counter. Odette and I walked toward them and one of the ladies came to meet us. "May I help you?" she asked.

"We'd like to look at silk blouses," I said.

"Something light and very simple," Odette said. "Light-colored."

"Yes, this way. They're all over here." We followed the saleslady to a rack of designer blouses, and she let Odette search through them. Every now and then Odette would pause, lift out a blouse, turn it back and forth in the light, take a close look at the stitching, the buttons, and the finishing of the seams. Within a few minutes she had four different creamy or white silk blouses on hangers in her hand. The saleslady took the blouses and led the way to a dressing room with Odette following her and with me following Odette. The saleslady opened the dressing room's louvered door, hung the blouses Odette had selected on a hook, then stepped aside so Odette could enter and I started to follow her right on in.

"You can't come in here!" Odette said, smiling.

"Oh, it's all right," the saleslady said. "Go right in, sir." And so I did.

The changing room was the size of a small closet. There was a bench against one wall, and the wall opposite the bench was covered with a mirror. I squeezed onto the bench, stuffed my heavy overcoat onto the floor, and ducked as Odette removed her ankle-length khaki down coat. She then stood before me in a calf-length burgundy-colored tweed skirt, boots, a rose-colored crew-neck sweater and a muted pink silk blouse.

"You look wonderful," I said.

She looked at herself in the mirror and laughed. "It's ironic, isn't it? Here I am, shopping at Saks, wearing silk and cashmere, a diamond on my hand . . . and I'm broke!"

"It's the American way," I said.

"It's the remnants of the past." There was just an instant of sadness in her expression, then she ran her fingers across the silk blouses she had selected. "Which one shall we try on first?"

"Try the one on top. . . . Are you sure you wouldn't like more room?" I asked. "I could wait outside."

"No, stay," she said, and smiled at me. She pulled the sweater over her head and turned to face the mirror as she began to unbutton the blouse.

"Not fair," I said. "I can't even see your reflection."

She hesitated, her fingers poised on a button midway down the blouse, then she turned toward me and undid the button, still holding the material pinched closed.

She was standing so close to me I could smell her perfume. The material parted and I saw the front clasp of her brassiere. Odette undid the last buttons of her blouse, shrugged out of it, and reached across me to hang it on a hook. The thin nylon covering her bosom grazed my nose. I had to touch her. I could not help myself. My hands rose to her naked waist and held her as I leaned forward to kiss the small hollow between her breasts. Odette's hands fell to my shoulders and pushed lightly against me, not thrusting me away exactly, but not pulling me to her either. We remained like that for only a few seconds but it was time enough for me to inhale her body, feel her velvety warmth, my own rising excitement.

"Take off your bra," I whispered.

"No!" she said. When my fingers moved to the clasp her fingers covered mine as the catch came undone and the bra slid away. We were both trembling slightly. Her bosom filled my hands.

Odette leaned into me. "Oh God," she said. "We can't, not here."

"You're beautiful," I said. Odette slowly lowered her arms. I removed her bra entirely and gently kissed her breast. Odette's hands cradled my head and she held me against her until we heard a woman enter the next booth, the rattle of coat hangers, a light grunt as the woman struggled into clothes.

Odette pulled away. "I'll try on another blouse."

For the next few minutes Odette and I were very businesslike together. She was buttoning a blouse, looking at her reflection in the mirror. The blouse was an egg-shell white, too hard and bright for Odette's complexion. I wanted her in something softer. The blouse also had ruffles at the throat. When Odette saw my expression she laughed and said, "I don't like it either," and quickly removed it and leaned across me for the next.

It was hot and close in the changing room; there was a light sheen of perspiration between her breasts. When I raised my head to again inhale her body she laughed and twisted away.

Facing the mirror, Odette buttoned up the second blouse, but she stood slightly to one side so she could see my eyes.

"You prefer a more classic silk blouse, don't you?" she said.

"Yes, one that isn't so . . ."

"Busy," Odette finished for me. "I know." She lifted the remaining two blouses on their hangers off the hook and held them for me to see.

"The one on the right," I said. "I like its color. It's more like antique silk."

"That's the one I like, too," Odette said. She undid the button at the side of her skirt and pulled up the bottom of the blouse. She had only unbuttoned the bottom two buttons of the blouse when her skirt fell to her ankles and she was standing in front of me in cream-colored silk tap pants and boots.

"*Jesus*," I said, riveted by her near-naked body.

"I can't stand pantyhose," Odette said. "They itch my thighs."

I reached up and unbuttoned the blouse the rest of the way, then slid it off her shoulders. Odette's hands fluttered here and there about her body as if not sure what to cover and what to expose. I hugged her to me, one hand around her silken bottom, the other at her back. I pressed my mouth to her bosom, the nipple was already hard. She sagged against me, pulling my head into her breast. I don't know how long we remained like that—two seconds? Two minutes? Odette looked down at me, her face flushed, a dozen different questions flickering in her eyes.

"You're delicious," I said.

She did not speak, instead she continued to look at me.

"And I love your boots. You've caught me between two fantasies. Your costume is half Jeanne Moreau and half dominatrix."

"Which do you prefer?" Odette teasingly asked.

Before I could answer there was a light knock on our dressing room door and the saleslady asked, "Do you need any help?"

Odette, at least, had the presence of mind to say, "Thank you, no. We're okay."

I lifted the fallen blouse from the floor and replaced it on its hanger, while Odette tried on the cream-colored blouse we both had liked. But when she had it buttoned and bent forward to pull up her skirt, her hip was opposite my nose and I lifted the loose leg of her silk tap pants and licked her thigh. Odette straightened up as though she'd been shot, tripped because of the skirt still wrapped around her knees, and fell onto me with such force my back crushed into the wall with a resounding thump. She and I froze. Odette was half-sitting, half-lying across my lap, both of us giggling and certain the saleslady would come back to check.

But as the seconds ticked on and no one appeared I could not resist touching Odette's thighs, her hip, her back naked beneath the blouse.

"I want you," I said.

"Yes," Odette said. She twisted in my arms so that we could hold each other and kiss.

"You're delicious," Odette said.

"You take my breath away."

"Am I crushing you?" Odette started to pull away.

"No, no, it's an expression, a figure of speech . . ." I helped Odette to her feet and she pulled her skirt up over her hips and tucked in her blouse, then looked at herself in the mirror.

"We'll take it," I said.

She turned to face me. "Do you like it?"

"It's perfect on you."

Odette looked at herself in the mirror again. "I love it," she said. She twisted back and forth, seeing how the blouse hung on her body. "I'll wear it to the party tonight."

Fifteen minutes later Odette and I were walking arm in arm on Fifth Avenue, her new blouse in a shopping bag in my hand. We picked up a cold bottle of champagne at a liquor store on Madison Avenue and some plastic glasses at a drugstore near the hotel. There was never any discussion of where we were going, both of us knew we were on our way to bed.

I opened the champagne in our hotel room and poured us each a glass while Odette hung her new silk blouse in the closet. It was such a homey gesture that suddenly the room no longer seemed a hotel room, it had become our room. As if reading my thoughts Odette at that moment turned away from the closet saying, "I love this room."

I looked around the room as if seeing it for the first time. It was comfortable, with two stuffed chairs that were soft, broken-in, covered with the same clean, deep blue- and yellow-flowered chintz used on the heavy curtains in front of the three tall, narrow windows looking out upon the street.

Odette lifted her champagne glass. "Santé," she said.

"Santé." We each took a sip, then I put down my glass and helped Odette lift her sweater over her head. I next unbuttoned her blouse and slipped it off.

"Wait," she said. She sat down on the edge of the bed and I pulled off her boots. She removed her socks, then stood up again. When she reached for the buttons at the side of her tweed skirt I brushed her fingers away saying, "No, let me. I want to undress you."

In a minute she was standing before me in only her tap pants and bra. When I undid her bra and slid it off she covered her breasts with her hands. "Suddenly I'm *shy!*" she protested.

"Don't be," I said. "You're beautiful." As I reached for the waistband of her tap pants she twisted away to the bedside table and picked up her champagne glass.

"I want to take a bath," she said. "We don't have to rush, do we?"

"We have all the time in the world."

"Oh God," she said, "I'm so glad to be here!" She carried her champagne into the bathroom and a moment later I heard the bath water running. Odette reappeared wrapped in a towel and walked over to where I was sitting on the side of the bed. She bent forward to kiss me. "I'll only be a minute," she said.

"I'm excited just thinking about it. I want you so much!"

"I know," she said. "It's going to feel so good."

I was still smiling when Odette climbed into her bath. It *was* going to feel good. I didn't feel squashed, sat upon, tense the way I did with other women, with Alice. I felt only a marvelous sexual desire different from any I had felt before. As I began to slowly undress I tried to figure out what made it so different. It came to me in a flash: I was *happy* for once.

I could hear Odette splashing about. "How's your bath?" I called.

"Marvelous!" she replied. "Why don't you join me?"

When I walked naked into the bathroom she looked at me in surprise. I looked down at myself, then back at Odette. "I can't help it," I said.

Odette laughed. "That's one helluva rubber duck!"

And after our bath we dried each other quickly, suddenly in too much of a hurry to do a good job. I jerked back the bedspread and we fell onto the sheets in a damp jumble of thighs, feet, arms, hands, bellies, lips touching, tasting, feeling, testing, learning about each other's bodies for the first time. We could not be still; we were always in motion. There was a fluidity to our movements, like swimmers underwater, like warm-bodied seals cavorting. Several times we both laughed aloud with pleasure and surprise at how good it was, how well our bodies fit, the way there didn't seem to be any sharp edges where our bodies met.

She was delicious; there was a little taste of soap, a touch of milk and honey, a scent of herbs and spices, cool and fresh and clean. I wanted more. Odette's body stretched beyond me, she was supporting herself on her elbows, her head was arched back, her breasts tilted up. Her taut dancer's body was coiled like a spring. She gave into me with a mixture of shyness and abandon I had never encountered before; and I responded with a tenderness I was surprised to discover I still had within me.

And during our lovemaking Odette's expression contained everything I had ever wanted to see, everything I was feeling myself: excitement, ardor, understanding, happiness, an awareness of the rarity of the moment, the need to seize as much pleasure and freedom and joy out of our special time together as we could.

Afterward, when we were just lying in bed, holding each other, kissing sleepily, lightly touching each other's skin, neither of us spoke. Although I had not had an orgasm, Odette did not mention it and so I did not feel anything but awe at how good it had been. In fact, I remember thinking afterward only what I had thought that afternoon more than twenty years before at college after Hope and I had made love the first time: why had we waited so long?

Odette stretched, and I could feel our naked bodies touching the entire length of our thighs, our hips, our bellies, our chests. And later, when I pulled the sheet up to cover us, Odette's feet curled between mine.

We took a taxi downtown to La Buena Mesa, a small Lexington Avenue restaurant, and walked inside where a Spanish guitarist was trying to make himself heard over the pre-New Year's Eve celebration din. I was guiding Odette between the crowded tables to the smaller, quieter dining room upstairs when I heard my name called and turned and recognized a woman I had known some fifteen years before. She had been, at that time, married to the writer-in-residence at a midwestern university I was teaching film at. When Odette and I stopped at her table and I introduced Odette to her, the woman said, "You heard about Jim, didn't you?"

Jim had been her husband.

"He killed himself," she said.

"I'm sorry," I said. "I didn't know that."

"We were divorced by then."

I did not know what to say.

"Do you remember that endless novel he'd been working on, the one about five generations of a family who had emigrated from Ireland?"

"I remember a reading he gave from it."

"He put ten years into that book and finally finished it. The manuscript was accepted for publication when the publishing house was bought by some conglomerate. Jim's book was delayed and delayed again, then finally dropped from their list. He couldn't take it. You know, of course, he was drinking heavily. We were divorced and he'd married one of his students—perhaps you remember her? Gail Thompson?"

"The one who wrote *Matricide?*" I asked, surprised. It had been a very big novel about eight years ago, one of the first very successful "women's novels" of the 1970s.

"He couldn't take her success," she said. "Jim never had much in the way of balls." She looked directly up at Odette and asked me, "Are you still married to what's-her-name?"

"Alice and I are separated," I said.

"Oh?" she said, swiveling her head to look at me again. "Do you come into New York often?"

"Occasionally," I said.

"Call me," she said. "I'm in the book. Under my initials 'M.K.'—M. K. Turner on Ninety-third Street off Second Avenue. *Do* call me." She looked back at Odette again. "It was nice to meet you, Ondine," she said.

Odette just ignored all this until we were on our way up the stairs, when she said, "I mean, *really!* I have never seen such nerve. She all but asked you to bed right in front of me!"

A waiter led us to a small table overlooking Lexington Avenue, then brought us two glasses of sherry. Odette was still angry and upset over the woman downstairs.

"Are you going to call her?" Odette asked.

"No, of course not."

"Maybe she could please you in bed better than I."

I looked at her with surprise. "Why do you say something like that?"

"I'm too inhibited. Unpolished."

"You were marvelous," I said.

"But I didn't please you," she said. "You didn't come."

I looked down at my knife and fork. "It had nothing to do with you. It's not you. Please don't think it's you." I looked up at her. "You were wonderful."

"I could be better," she said, searching my face.

"We both will be."

"But with other women . . . ?"

"Shh," I said, taking her hand.

Odette shook her head. "We shouldn't have made love," she said. "I feel you withdrawing, pulling back from me."

"No, I'm not," I said. I stroked her hand. "It's just that I'm embarrassed because of my not coming. I just don't seem to, to come anymore, not unless I'm alone." I found myself telling Odette about masturbating alone at night in the bathroom while Alice slept and how it had become my only release. I had never admitted this to anyone before but I knew with Odette I had to explain, to talk it all out. Odette responded that she thought I was probably worrying too much about not coming. She mentioned the Kinsey and Masters and Johnson reports and all the others that said there was no physical reason for nonorgasmic women existing, that there was no such thing as a frigid woman, there were only inept men.

"My not coming has nothing to do with the ineptness of—of you," I told her. "It's all inside my head."

The waiter brought gazpacho soup and I was grateful for the interruption. After the waiter departed Odette said, "We are alike, you and I. We are always asking questions of ourselves. You spend too much time inside your head. You must learn to listen to your heart."

"If I were not listening to my heart, I could not talk to you about this."

"When I first got to know you, you reminded me of an adolescent who had grown too fast: a little awkward, a little helpless, a little unsure of yourself—"

"A *lot* unsure of myself," I interrupted.

"You had these sad, understanding eyes. I looked into them and saw me, my other half. I was getting from Arthur the opaque curtain, the rudeness, the sinking feeling in the groin. But then you lifted the curtain just by being there. You were my friend. And when my marriage broke up, when *I* broke up my marriage, you . . . you suddenly weren't there any longer."

I took Odette's hand. "You scared me," I said. "You were a threat. I thought you were going to destroy my world. Instead, I saw my world, such as it was, collapse in on itself—not because of you, but because it was so precarious to begin with. Only I didn't see that right away. I think I did blame you."

"But it *was* my fault," Odette said. "If I hadn't asked Arthur for a divorce, if we hadn't moved up the street . . ."

"If you hadn't been born . . . It's silly to play these 'if' games because where do they begin?" I lightly touched Odette's wrist. "Alice and I would not have stayed married long in any case."

"But if Arthur and I had not—"

"I would not have met you."

Odette took a sip of her soup, then put her spoon down carefully. "You cannot understand how you hurt me," she said.

"Yes, I can," I said.

"No," she shook her head.

I started to protest but she stopped me with a finger to my lips. "The mere sight of you," she said. "Your smile. Your voice. Your body, the way you move. Your one-hundred-thousand-volt mind. I knew you were the right man for me immediately." Odette's eyes filled with tears.

I felt miserable, too. I could not stand to see Odette cry. I wanted to tell her I would love her forever, that I wanted to spend the rest of my life with her, that I would protect and take care of her until the end of time. I wanted to tell her that I knew she was the right woman for me. But I *didn't* know that. I knew only that I loved our day together and that I didn't want to lie to her anymore.

The waiter came carrying the fondue pot and set the pot on the table between us so that I had to lift my hand off Odette's. "Careful," the waiter said. "This oil is hot." A nearby table of revelers burst into song: "Oh, Gloria's divine, she's got hair on her chest, but how is her old wazoo-ooo . . ."

The party to which Odette and I had been invited was being given by Harry Parkinson, an old friend of mine. We arrived at the Parkinsons a little after eleven. Harry met us at the door and was immediately smitten by Odette. Nicky held up her cheek to be kissed, then twisted her head at the last minute and kissed me on the lips. Odette saw that and wiggled her eyebrows at me before allowing herself to be led away by Harry.

I was left in the narrow, crowded hallway with Nicky as I watched Odette disappear. "It's a big party!" I said to Nicky.

"It's Harry's party," she said. "I'm just a guest."

I really did not want to know why she'd say such a thing. I looked around for Odette. "Maybe I should try to find Odette," I said, "get her a drink. You, too, Nicky. You don't have a glass."

"I have the flu," she said, then added, "But so do half the people here."

Despite the large number of people at the Parkinsons' party, there did not seem to be much conversation. Harry had the old Red Nichols and his Five Pennies album with the jazz version of "The Battle Hymn of the Republic" playing, and people were slumped in couches and chairs half-listening to it. When I found Odette she turned to me with an expression of such relief I felt my stomach turn inside me. I hugged her to me and kissed her ear. "I missed you," I said.

"Me, too."

"Are you okay? More champagne?"

"I'm fine," she said. "Everyone here looks so unhealthy. Why does everyone look sick? Is it the city?"

"I think it's the flu. Nicky says everyone has it."

"You'll probably get it, too, then. Serves you right for kissing her on the lips."

Someone had turned on the television set and we could see crowds milling about Times Square. I looked away and then I heard someone say, "Jesus, look at that girl!"

I turned back to the television set and there was Nora standing underneath the waterfall in Hawaii, followed by the night-surfing sequence and other bits and pieces of the airline promo I had filmed only a year and a half before. I say *only* because it seemed to have taken place a lifetime ago. The commercial ended with a stock shot of a 747 jumbo jet climbing above a vivid sunset.

"It almost makes you want to go there," Odette said.

"Almost," I said. The action was live again. The cameras were cutting back and forth between couples dancing at the Roosevelt Hotel and the crowds in the street looking up at the ball atop the Times Tower. Someone began counting, "Ten . . . nine . . . eight . . ." and others joined in. The couples in the deep couches pushed themselves forward to watch— it appeared to take an enormous effort on their part. Odette and I turned to watch the TV. "Four . . . three . . . two . . ."

A friend of the Parkinsons' came out of the bathroom wearing a diaper with "1980" printed on a card pinned to his rear. His head, bald but for a fringe above his ears, and the soft, gelatinous flabbiness of his body did make him look like an overgrown baby. His entrance was met by a ratchety burst of noisemakers from the hallway. A couple on the couch made mournful tooting sounds with tin horns before falling back.

"Happy New Year," I said to Odette.

"You, too," she said, and we kissed.

"It can't help but be better than the last."

"For you, maybe," Odette said.

"For us both," I said. "We're in this together."

Odette did not speak.

"Let's get out of here," I said. "This party depresses me."

"It's not only the party," she said.

A brutally cold wind struck us the moment we stepped out onto the sidewalk. I put my arm around Odette and she huddled against me for warmth. The Parkinsons' apartment was only a few blocks from Elaine's Restaurant and we decided the cold air might refresh us, so we walked there. Balloons had been tied to the wall-lighting sconces, a balalaika band had been imported for the occasion, the floor was littered with streamers. We stayed until four in the morning at a table with Linda and Tony Murphy. I had first met the Murphys when I was married to Maggie. Even back then I had envied them.

The Murphys were *happily married* and had been for *years!* And that night with Odette at Elaine's I could not help but notice the hundred little touches, looks, smiles, intimacies, that passed so unself-consciously, so effortlessly between them. They were a *couple*.

I wanted to be part of a couple, too. I looked over at Odette and took her hand. She met my look and smiled. Her eyes told me that it might just be possible for me not to always feel so alone.

We had to ring for the night man to let us into the hotel, and a few minutes later Odette and I were in our room. I was standing in front of the mirror removing my tie when I saw Odette, reflected behind me, cautiously lower herself to sit on the corner of the bed. What happened next seemed to be occurring in slow motion: her torso and head sank, disappeared from the lower-right hand corner of the mirror like a submarine's conning tower gliding beneath the unruffled surface of the sea. There was a gentle bumping sound, a little sigh, and then to my astonishment one of Odette's feet rose, like a periscope, and appeared reflected in the corner of the mirror where moments before her head had been. I turned to see how this could have been done. Odette had simply slid off the corner of the bed and was lying now on her back on the rug, one leg sticking straight up in the air.

"Are you all right?" I asked, as I helped her back up onto the bed.

She smiled a bit shyly. "I think I am a little *dronk*."

And later, when we were in bed together, we were both suddenly overcome with a wonderful, boozy passion. But then the last wires gave way, the muscles relaxed, and she just lay there with one leg thrown over my hip, her nose buried in my neck. "Champagne," she mumbled.

"What?" I asked.

"Champagne and strawberries. I want champagne and strawberries for breakfast."

"Then you shall have them!"

She nudged my neck in assent. "Um-hum," she said.

I held her in my arms and lightly caressed the back of her head. "I love you," I whispered.

"No, you don't, not yet, not completely," she answered drowsily. "Not really. But guess what? You will."

I was still trying to frame a response to that when I noticed her breathing had changed, deepened. She was asleep.

13

I THOUGHT I DID LOVE Odette. But I also knew that in previous years, and with other women, what I had mistaken for love had been nothing but a strong physical attraction, or the need for approval, or the anguish at being alone . . . at one time or another, all three.

And so, that January, Odette and I saw each other every day and spent nights together either at the cottage or her house in town. And although I would tell her that I loved her, there remained an off-again, on-again quality to that love. I would feel totally in love with her one moment, out of love the next. There did not seem to be any middle ground— though, of course, there was.

When Odette insisted during moments of anger and frustration that she didn't need me, that her life would be easier if I were not around, I knew she was right. I had always known she had the strength to take care of herself, to be fine whether I was with her or not.

My work was going badly. I had applied to the New Jersey State Council on the Humanities for a grant to do a film on the assimilation of large groups of Puerto Ricans by small New Jersey towns. I was turned down. They did not give a reason; but then, they did not need to give one. A different film idea submitted to a Boston station had become obsolete by the time they got around to rejecting it. I had sent an outline and proposal for a film on Agent Orange and cancer links to WNET but had heard nothing from them yet. I was getting desperate. I needed to keep calm. But serenity, after Odette's and my New Year's Eve in New York, was hard to find.

Both of us were suffering from reimmersion into the grinding realities of our daily lives, realities which consisted of Alice's unrelenting hostility, my worries about work and money, Arthur's distance from and detachment about Odette's financial plight, the children's confusion and unhappiness with our divorces, and Odette's exhaustion from holding down two jobs in addition to raising two children and taking care of her house. Conscious of the strain upon her, I had begun to help more. But I think the only thing that saved our sanity was being able to escape to the cottage.

Lights, please . . .

FADE IN

417. EXTERIOR: MY COTTAGE. FRIDAY, FEBRUARY 1, MID-AFTERNOON.

The scene appears at first to have been filmed in black and white. A light snow is falling from an opaque sky. The trees are bare, their trunks and limbs a dull gray. In the middle distance we can see my small, two-story, gray fieldstone cottage with its weathered-now-to-near-black wood shingle roof. My Peugeot station wagon, its paint dulled with dirt and age, is parked to one side.

Off-camera right we hear children's voices, laughter. The sound is faint at first, but grows louder as the children come closer, giving us time to absorb the visual details of the scene.

The CHILDREN then appear at right.

VANESSA is wearing a bright red snowsuit. SHE is pulling a toboggan upon which PETER in a blue snowsuit sits with PAUL, who is wearing yellow. The primary colors of their snowsuits are almost shocking against the winter grays.

Camera point of view (POV) remains fixed as CHILDREN cross from right to left. Just as VANESSA departs scene at left, I appear at right. I am wearing corduroys tucked inside the tops of rubber boots, an old, ill-fitting overcoat on top of the sweater knit for me by Odette—the sweater's sleeves are so long they have been rolled back over the overcoat's cuffs. I am also wearing a battered old felt hat.

As I reach center we hear ODETTE's whistle—an immediately recognizable "family signal" sort of whistle, and I stop and turn toward the sound. ODETTE remains off-camera. As I turn, I have to twist and duck the snowball flung at me. The snowball strikes my shoulder and ODETTE rushes toward me from off-right and we embrace laughing, then follow the CHILDREN off-camera left.

418. EXTERIOR: SAME SCENE. LATER THAT AFTERNOON.

It is still snowing and we can see by the increased accumulation upon the Peugeot's and cottage's roofs how much time has passed. Off-camera voices of the CHILDREN are again heard approaching now from left. ODETTE and I appear pulling toboggan upon which all three CHILDREN sit. When we reach front door of cottage, ODETTE and I lift toboggan and dump CHILDREN out.

There follows a series of quick cuts depicting scenes of domesticity from both inside and outside the cottage as late afternoon progresses through to late evening.

CUT TO:

419. EXTERIOR: COTTAGE. DUSK.

Warm lights glow from within the cottage through snow as ODETTE passes in front of a window.

CUT TO:

420. *INTERIOR: COTTAGE. DOWNSTAIRS. 6:00 P.M.*
ODETTE is setting the table for dinner. I am at the stove preparing spaghetti.

CUT TO:

421. *INTERIOR: COTTAGE. UPSTAIRS BEDROOM. A MOMENT LATER.*
The CHILDREN are lounging on my bed playing cards while the television shows an evening news program that is going unwatched. Their small overnight bags and unrolled sleeping bags are piled on the floor.

CUT TO:

422. *INTERIOR: COTTAGE. DOWNSTAIRS. 6:20 P.M.*
My hamburger and tomato spaghetti sauce is bubbling and splattering the stove top. ODETTE comes up behind me, turns down the burner heat, and places a grease screen on top of the saucepan. I look at her gratefully and she shrugs and kisses me on the cheek.

CUT TO:

423. *INTERIOR: COTTAGE. DOWNSTAIRS. TEN MINUTES LATER.*
The CHILDREN are sitting around the table. I am serving the spaghetti. It is obvious I have misjudged the amount and made far too much. As ODETTE pours the CHILDREN's milk, I remove garlic loaf from the oven. It is hideously burned. The CHILDREN eye it warily and ODETTE laughs as I drop it into the garbage can.

CUT TO:

424. *EXTERIOR: COTTAGE THROUGH SNOWFALL.*
Through the windows one can see ALL of us at the table, eating happily.

CUT TO:

425. *INTERIOR: COTTAGE. DOWNSTAIRS. 7:20 P.M.*
The CHILDREN clear the table and stack the dishes in the sink while ODETTE and MYSELF have a cigarette and finish our wine.

CUT TO:

426. *INTERIOR: COTTAGE. DOWNSTAIRS. TEN MINUTES LATER.*
I am doing the dishes at the sink while ODETTE herds the CHILDREN upstairs.

CUT TO:

427. *EXTERIOR: COTTAGE. SAME TIME.*
The snowfall continues, big fat clumps spiraling down through the lights of the cottage windows. ODETTE appears in the illuminated bathroom

window upstairs while the heads of the smaller CHILDREN swirl about her. I am visible downstairs, too, still at the sink.

CUT TO:

428. *INTERIOR: COTTAGE. DOWNSTAIRS. 8:00 P.M.*

I am finishing the pots and pans as ODETTE prepares two cups of coffee for us. SHE carries the coffee to the chairs by the fireplace and adds another log to the fire.

CUT TO:

429. *INTERIOR: COTTAGE. UPSTAIRS. A MOMENT LATER.*

The CHILDREN are on my bed in pajamas watching television.

CUT TO:

430. *EXTERIOR: COTTAGE. 9:00 P.M.*

The snow is still falling. The cottage with its lights on seems cozy, warm. Smoke is rising from the chimney. ODETTE and I are visible sitting with our coffee by the fireplace. We are both reading magazines. I put my magazine aside and rise and cross to ODETTE to massage the back of her neck.

CUT TO:

431. *EXTERIOR: COTTAGE. LATER THAT SAME EVENING.*

The lights are out downstairs. We can see ODETTE at the upstairs bathroom window removing her makeup. The telephone rings. It is a sharp, shrill sound, the first real noise we have heard and it disturbs the quiet of this snowy, woodland night. The telephone rings again.

CUT TO:

432. *INTERIOR: COTTAGE. UPSTAIRS BEDROOM. 10:30 P.M.*

I am sitting on the side of the bed, the telephone to my ear. The three CHILDREN are asleep in sleeping bags on the floor. ODETTE emerges from the bathroom wearing only my pajama tops. She is brushing her hair back from her temples, five quick strokes on either side. I look up at her, the telephone still to my ear, and shrug helplessly. ODETTE continues to my bureau, picks up my wristwatch and glances at it, puts it back down. ODETTE then stands in front of the mirror above my bureau and resumes brushing her hair.

MYSELF

(*Into telephone:*)

Alice, we've talked about all this before. I'm not trying to evict you.
I'm perfectly willing—

(One can hear ALICE interrupting, her angry voice, but cannot quite distinguish what she is saying. I am watching the way the pajama top rises up ODETTE's right thigh when with her right hand she brushes her hair back from her left temple. ODETTE repeats the pattern of five brisk brushstrokes counting softly in French:)

> ODETTE

(*Whispering:*)

> *Quatre-vingt-trois, quatre-vingt-quatre, quatre-vingt-cinq* . . .

(ODETTE switches sides and the pajama top drops. I cup my hand over the telephone mouthpiece and tell ODETTE:)

> MYSELF

> It's that business about selling the house again. I've told her she's welcome to stay in the house until it's sold, but then she has to find a place of her own.

(ODETTE nods and continues to brush her hair. I uncover mouthpiece and say to Alice:)

> Alice, it should be obvious to you—it is, God knows, to your lawyer— that there is no way for me to come up with the kind of settlement you're asking for without selling both houses. And this is what I intend to do . . .

(ODETTE goes to the window and looks out.)

433. *EXTERIOR: COTTAGE. A MOMENT LATER:*

We see ODETTE silhouetted in the cottage window as a snowplow, its blade rasping against the road surface, churns by. As we watch the snowplow's progress we hear the telephone conversation voice-over throughout.

> ALICE

> I'm not asking for much, considering I could *cream* you. Take *all* your money. But I have no ax to grind. I only want what's fair for Peter and me.

> MYSELF

> How could you cream me?

> ALICE

> I could subpoena Odette and your "Go-Go" dancer of the year before. And your friend Malone's wife—

> MYSELF

> Karen? We never had an affair.

> ALICE

> Don't tell me you're still denying it! How do you think I could have found out about it then?

> MYSELF

> Woodward and Bernstein?

ALICE

Funny. Very funny. Maybe you won't think it so amusing when I bring your little "Go-Go" dancer in to testify—

CUT TO:

434. INTERIOR: COTTAGE. UPSTAIRS BEDROOM. SAME TIME:

ODETTE turns away from the window and, as the conversation continues, she picks up an old *Penthouse* magazine and lies down on the bed beside me. During this I am saying:

MYSELF

The "Go-Go" dancer wasn't so little. She was about five feet ten and weighed at least one hundred and forty pounds.

ALICE

And you loved her for her mind.

MYSELF

Among other things.

ALICE

Barbara T. is willing to testify against you, too.

MYSELF

To say what? That could be risky for you. She could then be asked about all your skiing companions when I wasn't with you.

ALICE

You don't have any names. I do.

MYSELF

I don't need any names. They're all called things like Jean-Claude, Spider, Billy the Kid, for Chrissake. We could have a sensational divorce, Alice. We could have the waiting room catered for all our subpoenaed witnesses.

ALICE

Well, that's not what I'm calling about. We've had eleven years together, so we can say we know each other pretty well. Believe me, I have no ax to grind. I hope you and Odette will be very happy. I really do.

MYSELF

Odette will be very pleased to hear that.

(At the mention of her name ODETTE looks up from the magazine. She turns to me, a trace of anger and apprehension in her eyes. I shake my head and gesture that she is not to worry. ODETTE looks back down at the magazine opened now to a photograph covering both pages. It shows a woman wearing one shiny black patent leather high-heel shoe and nothing else; the model is holding the other spiked heel to her pursed lips. ALICE is still talking:)

ALICE

Aren't you interested in what Barbara T. might testify?

MYSELF

No, I don't think so.

ALICE

She's willing to testify that you admitted to her last summer you were having an affair with Odette. . . . Well, aren't you going to say anything?

MYSELF

Yes. Good night, Alice.

ALICE

I'm only trying to warn you. If you think you've got such a good deal with Odette, all you have to do is ask Arthur. He's right here. I'll put him on the phone.

MYSELF

I don't want to talk to Arthur, Alice. I just want to go to bed.

ALICE

Arthur? . . . He's coming.

MYSELF

No, Alice, I don't want to talk to him.

(ODETTE reaches across me to break the telephone connection. When she releases the button the screen goes blank and the only sound we hear is a faintly ominous *buzzzzzz.*)

GO TO BLACK

"I mean, *really!*" Odette said. "How long were you going to talk to her?"

"I couldn't get off the phone."

"Of course you could have. All you had to do was hang up!"

"That would have pissed Alice off even more and then she would have hassled me about Peter and it wouldn't have been worth it."

"So you instead let her ruin our peace and quiet on the first weekend I haven't had to work. . . . Goddam that woman!" Odette was saying. "I resent her calling at all hours of the night!"

"She doesn't often call at night."

"Why do you *defend* her?"

"I'm not defending her. I was only saying she doesn't do it often."

"Well, I think it was rude," Odette said. "Milacious."

"*Milacious?*"

"Yes, milacious. What is that word? Deliberate?"
"You mean 'malicious.' It comes from 'malice' as in . . . as in Alice."
"*Malice!*" Odette giggled. "Perfect!"

The next morning I awoke with the children and while I fed them breakfast I could hear Odette running herself a bath. By the time I had zipped them all into their snowsuits and sent them out with their toboggan Odette was soaking in my bathtub, one elegant, long-muscled leg draped along the tub's ancient porcelain edge.

I went back downstairs, fixed us two coffees, and carried them up to the bathroom. The white walls, the enamel of the sink, the tub, were dappled with the pale, misty-yellow morning light of the sun filtered through the naked branches of the tall oaks and maples surrounding the cottage. I sat on the toilet seat cover in my aged, threadbare dark-blue terrycloth bathrobe watching Odette bathe. An ashtray was balanced on my knee; Odette was smoking. I steadied the ashtray while she stubbed out her cigarette. When I twisted to lift the ashtray to the windowsill she brushed aside my bathrobe with her fingertips to touch my naked knee, then her hand slid back into the tub.

"You have the body of a fifteen-year-old," I said.

"Only the body?" she teased. Her accent was soft, delicious. "Do you think I need a facelift?" She touched the light web of wrinkles at the corners of her eyes, then slid her fingers down her cheekbones to pull taut the skin around her jaw and throat.

"No, not yet," I said. "Though maybe the nose could use some work."

"*Dégeulasse!*" she said, and laughed.

"I'd keep the ears . . ."

"They are like little shells," she said. She brushed her dark hair aside and cocked her head slightly toward me. "See how beautiful they are?"

"It's a crime to hide them."

A crow called from the woods; after a moment, another crow answered. I turned to listen. Every motion seemed languid, easy. Odette slowly pushed herself up in the tub and, taking my can of shaving cream, began to lather her leg.

When she asked me which of my razors she might use, my voice was suddenly ragged, as if I were emerging from a deep and dreamy sleep. "It does not—" I cleared my throat. "It doesn't matter," I said, and smiled.

"I love your smile," she said.

"My smile? Even with my old and battered teeth?"

"I like your teeth, but I love your smile. It is a very gentle smile and shy, a shyness that erupts at the oddest times."

"You make me smile," I said.

She was waiting, one foamy leg lifted above the water. "The razor?"

"Oh yes," I said, rising abruptly and knocking the ashtray off the windowsill with my elbow. Dead ashes and cigarettes sprinkled the floor. Odette laughed at my clumsiness and, after the slightest of pauses, I laughed, too, handed her the razor, then squatted down to clean up the debris at my feet.

"I heard you get up early this morning," she said. "Long before the children."

"I tried not to wake you."

"Was it the 'crazies' again?"

I nodded.

"Were they bad?"

"Not as bad as usual," I said. "I'm all right now. The morning sun, having you here . . ." I paused, hearing the telephone ring.

"Telephone," Odette said, but I was already rising. I gathered up my cigarettes and walked into the bedroom. When I sat on the edge of the bed, Odette's scent rose from the pillow. The telephone was still ringing and I lifted the receiver before it could ring again.

"I want to speak to Peter," Alice said.

"He's outside playing," I answered.

"Will you get him for me, then?"

"He's gone off with Vanessa and Paul. They went tobogganing. I don't know where they went."

"In other words you're not watching them?" she asked.

"In other words they're perfectly safe and can perfectly well take care of themselves. I can ask him to call you when he comes back."

"I wanted to tell him that he's been invited to a birthday party this afternoon, that you're to drive him to it at two."

"Today?" I asked. "This is his weekend with me."

"He seems to be spending it outside, away from you."

"He's playing, Alice. He's having fun."

"By the way, he won't be able to see you the weekend after next."

"Why not?"

"I'm taking him with me to New York. But you can see him Thursday."

"I have a library board meeting that Thursday from eight to about ten-thirty."

"You could skip the meeting."

"No, I can't, Alice. It's an important one."

"More important than seeing your son?" she asked, and hung up.

I sat holding the dead telephone until the rush of pure rage had passed, then I replaced the receiver gently on its cradle and walked back into the bathroom. I stood in the doorway watching Odette soap her bosom. She looked up at me and gracefully covered her small breasts with her hands, then dropped her hands and smiled.

"That was Malice," I said. "She told me she wanted me to drive Peter to a birthday party this afternoon. I told her this was his weekend with me. Then she decided I shouldn't have him the weekend after next, that she'd take him into New York instead."

"I could hear you talking."

"Until she hung up on me as usual."

"So you don't know when you'll see Peter next?"

"I don't think that was ever decided." I remained standing in the doorway.

"Call her back," Odette said. "I know you too well to think you'd be happy not knowing when you'll be seeing him. But before you go, could you pass me my coffee?"

Less than two minutes later I returned to Odette, my face tense. When I tried to smile, the smile would not hold. I sat back down on the toilet seat. "I called. I was nice. I said, 'Hello, Alice, can't we straighten this out?' And she said, 'I don't want to talk to you. You only see Peter at your convenience, when it doesn't interfere with your social life. I include Peter in my social life,' she said. 'Peter *is* my social life,' she said. 'Here along with all the disappointments, the humiliations you've caused me, I never thought I'd be disappointed in you as a father. But, no, you don't care about anybody but yourself. It doesn't bother me that you don't want to make the time to see Peter, but it hurts him terribly and so I'm through talking to you,' she said and 'click' before I could even get a word in, she'd hung up on me again."

"So you still don't know when you'll see him next?"

I shook my head. "Sometime during that week, probably," I said, and stood up. "More coffee?"

"Sit. Relax," she said.

"I can't help it," I said. "She still gets to me." My hands fluttered in my lap. "How is it possible that Alice changes all the plans I have to see Peter and *I* still end up feeling guilty and a bad father?"

"You're a good father," Odette said. "You know that and, damn it all, so does Alice. She knows you will always take care of Peter no matter what. That all she has to do is pick up a telephone and call you. She can see how you've taken care of Joan, always been responsible. Alice knows she can count on you—which is more than I can say about Arthur. His children seem no longer to exist as far as he's concerned. And Vanessa can't understand why. When she walks back from school and sees her father's car parked next to Alice's house, she doesn't understand why her father is too busy to call her and yet has all the time in the world for Alice."

"Better him than me," I said. I saw Odette had nicked her leg just below her knee; a thin, vermilion trickle of blood drifted down from the razor cut, staining the water. "You cut yourself."

"Did I?" she asked, twisting her leg to look.

"It will attract the sharks."

"Sharks?"

"*Les requins*. You mustn't panic. I know what I'm talking about. And for God's sake, don't thrash. You must simply rise slowly and smoothly out of the tub and into my arms."

"I see you're feeling better," she said. And when she smiled, her sweetness physically assaulted me.

"God, I love you," I said. I leaned forward and kissed her shoulder. Her skin was wet and tasted slightly of bath oil and soap.

"Would you care to join me?" she asked.

I stood up, letting my bathrobe fall, and Odette twisted about in the bathtub so that her back was against the sharp faucet.

"I would have taken that end," I said.

"I know."

I stepped gingerly into the tub and lowered myself into the water. When I was seated, Odette lifted her legs over mine so that her calves rested on my thighs.

"Does it bother you, loving me?" she asked.

"It makes me wish for a somewhat larger tub."

We shifted about until we were more comfortable and then Odette asked, "Can you still reach my cigarettes?"

Her cigarettes were on the edge of the sink. "Do you want one now?" I asked.

"No, lie back," she said, and picked up a washcloth and began lathering my chest.

"I really do love you, you know."

"But I'm the wrong woman for you. You should find yourself someone rich. Some middle-aged divorcée with grown children."

I smiled. "Why does she have to be middle-aged and divorced? If I'm going to have to look for someone rich, why can't she be young, with no children at all?"

"Because you're too old, decrepid, and shaky for one of the young girls." She was not smiling.

"You're not kidding, are you?" I said.

"Were you kidding about wanting a young girl?"

"Of course I was kidding," I said.

She began soaping me again. "But I was not," Odette said. "I was being serious. I really do think you should find yourself a rich woman."

"I love *you*," I protested.

"You won't."

"Why do you *say* such a thing?" I reached over and took a cigarette from the edge of the sink. I lit it, then asked, "Why do you think I won't love you, Odette?"

"Because we have too many problems. The children. Yours. Mine. I will never have any money, only what Arthur gives me in alimony and child support, plus what little I can earn from my jobs. And you will get tired of me and my moods. And you'll probably stick around too long because you won't want to hurt my feelings. If you're going to leave me, I'd rather you do it now."

"I don't *want* to leave you."

"If you did, I'd survive." Odette began telling me about the conversation she had had at a dinner given by a woman friend. The woman, a widow, had decided to invite only her female friends; no men were present by design. None of the women had met before, they had only their friendship with their hostess in common. "And yet," Odette explained, "we all immediately felt like friends. There is a comfort when a woman meets another woman whom she knows has experienced similar things. We recognize each other," Odette said. "There is a frankness, a freedom women have with each other that men cannot possibly attain. 'I'm here tonight,' one of the women said, 'because my lover is with another woman.' And immediately another woman said, 'I know my husband is seeing someone else tonight, too.'"

Odette paused for a moment. "How did I get on this subject? What were we talking about before?"

"That if I were to leave you, you'd—"

"Oh yes," Odette interrupted, "that I'd rather you do it now. We all agreed that night that when a man leaves a woman he always thinks that the woman might kill herself. But when a woman leaves a man, she doesn't think that way about him at all. She thinks only that the man will soon find himself another woman."

"Isn't the woman going to find herself another man, too?" I asked.

"Not right away. She's going to hurt, *souffrir*, for a while." Odette leaned forward to take a puff on my cigarette. "But she certainly isn't going to kill herself! . . . There are two kinds of women," she continued. "Either a woman will walk around like someone in widowhood—suffering good and strong, but with her eyes open to others and without trying to recapture the man she has lost—because you can't, you know, build on ashes. You can't. Not after a real break." And Odette paused here for a moment. I wondered whether she was thinking about Arthur. "And then there is the second kind," Odette said. "She will try to get back what she has lost at all costs. And in the process, I think she . . . No," she said abruptly. "Once it's over, it's over. It would never be any good."

As Odette told me more about the women's conversations that night, I realized that Alice had never shared with me what she and her friends discussed, what they truly felt. And Alice had not seemed all that different from many of the other women I had met in recent years, women in their mid-thirties and forties teaching at universities, or wives of friends, women encountered at parties who were so swift to withdraw into the exclusivity of their sex.

Whenever I had wandered in from the office to find Alice and her friends sitting around the living room, vodka tonics in hand, I had felt myself an intruder. Their voices would still as they watched me pass and as soon as I was in another room, I would hear their voices, their hard laughter again. Could it all have been paranoia? Or wasn't there after all some reason to feel they saw me as the enemy?

If it was true, as Alice had said, that I didn't like women, it seemed equally apparent during that period that she and her friends didn't like men. Come to think of it, during that period, I probably *hadn't* liked women very much. Lying in the tub with Odette, I realized until I had met her, it had been a long time since I had gone to bed with a woman out of anything more than sex or curiosity or revenge.

"If you left me now, Odette," I said, "I don't think I would want to live."

"Yes, you would," she said. "You would find yourself another woman, or another woman would find you. In fact, at that dinner, a couple of the women asked about you."

"Asked what?"

"If you were a good lover."

"Dear God," I said. I remembered the conversation she had had with Arthur, who had asked of me, "Is he a better lover than I am?" "To me, he is," Odette had replied. "Have you learned new things?" he asked. "Yes," she had said. "You *have?*" Arthur asked, unable to conceal his surprise. "What?"

Odette had not answered, she had only smiled. When she had repeated this conversation to me, I had felt a twinge of sympathy for Arthur, a twinge tempered by a sense of triumph, too. Odette had always told me that Arthur had been a very good lover, and her loyalty to Arthur had both angered and pleased me. I had had to respect her honesty. Her response to Arthur's question, "Is he a better lover?" had been only the slightest bit unkind, far more merciful, I suspected, than Alice would have been to me.

"Don't you want to know what I told the women?" Odette asked.

"You know I do."

"I said you were very good for me."

My expression must have revealed my disappointment that she had not waxed more rhapsodic.

"Oh-h-h, men's egos!" she cried. "If I had told them the truth they would never have left you alone." She touched my cheek.

I brushed her hand away in mock impatience. "You play me like a trout," I said, but I could not disguise my pleasure. "Which of the women asked?"

She laughed at me. "I am not so much a fool that I would tell you that!"

I was silent for a moment.

"What?" she asked.

"I was thinking that one man doesn't ask another if his woman is good in bed. Not if the first man knows the second man really cares for the woman."

"Women generally don't ask either," Odette said. "They can usually just look at a man and know."

"How?"

"By the size of his thumb."

"Be serious."

"If a man comes on strong about sex, he's a turn-off. So is a man who makes an off-color joke at a woman's expense. They both bore women or, or *anger* them. Women are turned on by someone like R——" (and here she mentioned a musician whom I had met and admired and instantly liked) "—He is quiet and sensitive," she said. "He looks at a woman and we guess."

"What do you guess?"

"We think. We imagine. We guess right. We know he is good."

"Just by the way he looks at you?"

"It's in the man's eye," she said. "And his mouth. His hands. The way the man moves. The little gestures. The *nuance*. The way he helps the woman into her coat, looks at her, touches her. Looking at him, we know he must be good. Women are turned on by men who treat women with respect. When men are being tender, they think they are being less of a man. Women think the opposite. We think he is *more* of a man."

I touched the soft undersides of Odette's knees beneath the water. "It is very hard to be a man to a woman these days . . . To know what a man, what being a man even means."

"You don't doubt yourself, do you?"

"Constantly," I said. "As you know."

"Oh-h-h, your *smile!* When you smile like that I could eat your lips! Now listen to me, you must stop questioning yourself so much. You are more of a man than anyone I know."

"I can't help it. Malice was an expert. She never left any marks that showed, but under the skin . . ."

Odette took my hand. "She will never know how much I envied her. I have told you how when I would walk by your house I would think of the two of you in there. I had been so lonely that winter. And then last May when we would talk—"

"—about films," I said. "I loved talking to you about what you had seen."

"And you would get so nervous, do you remember? You'd come in for a cup of coffee with me and flee after five minutes."

"I'm not proud of how I behaved."

"I know how much I hurt Arthur. I used to talk about you all the time. I would tell him how funny you were, how interesting—you were the first interesting person I had met in this town, the only one I could talk to."

"Alice could talk to Arthur, too," I said. "That's when phrases like 'passive aggressive' and 'predictable behavior patterns' began popping up in her conversations."

"I would like to have a child with you," Odette suddenly said. "If I knew you were going to leave me, that I was never going to see you again, I would let myself become pregnant and not tell you."

"Not tell me?" I asked, a little angry and surprised. "Why?"

"You would think I was trying to hold you. I wouldn't want you to feel responsible, which is what you would feel if you knew."

"Jesus!"

"You would think I was trying to trick you into—"

"I would think you were being very cruel to both the child and me."

"Well, don't worry," she said. "I'm not going to do it."

I was silent.

"What?" Odette asked.

"I was thinking if you became pregnant now I would be sixty-five when our child graduated from college—that is, if I could afford to send him or her there."

Odette's face was suddenly overwhelmed with such sadness that I sat forward in alarm. "What is it?" I asked. "What did I say?"

She shook her head. "Nothing." A tear that had formed in her eye jarred loose and tumbled down her cheek.

"Odette, what is it?"

"It's the beginning of the end for me."

I cradled her face in my hands. "What are you talking about?"

"I'm talking about reality," she said. "You *do* need someone rich. It all comes down to money. I have two children. You have two. We will never be able to afford to live together, to marry."

"I'll earn money again," I said. "Maybe not a lot, but it will come. I'll sell these houses, pay off Alice, do a new film . . . Besides it doesn't *all* come down to money."

"Yes, it does," she said. "If I were younger I'd probably ask what does money matter, but I'm thirty-four with two children and money means their skiing lessons and clothes, and college educations and security. It means if the dishwasher breaks down it can be repaired. Or if the car—"

I kissed her on the lips. "We'll do the dishes by hand. You can have my car. I *love* you. Things will work out."

"But you need someone rich."

"Not as much as I need someone loving. Dear God, Odette, what do you think a man wants from a woman? He wants tenderness, understanding, companionship, support . . . sanctuary."

"Not big breasts?" she asked, looking down at her own. "I would like mine to be bigger for you."

"Yours are *huge!*" I protested. "They just start deeper in your chest, that's all. They're like icebergs. Only the tips show."

She smiled, pleased with my image. "They *are* huge," she said, cupping her breasts as if they were alive. "You're laughing at me," she said. "Why are you laughing at me?"

"You reminded me of an old joke," I said. "A woman at the seashore loses the top of her bikini in the surf and comes running up out of the ocean covering herself as best she can. A little boy on the beach sees her and as she passes he calls out, 'Hey, lady, if you're going to drown those puppies, may I have the one with the pink nose?' "

Odette looked down at her breasts. "My puppies," she said.

"Switch ends with me," I said. "You've spent enough time with that faucet in your back."

"No," she said, rising to her knees. "I'm going to wash your hair." She attached the rubber hose with the shower head to the bathtub spigot and fussed with the water controls until the temperature was just right. "Put your head back," she said.

I was thinking about what she had said about needing somebody rich and was suddenly seized by a terrible thought. "Odette, is it that *you* want to leave *me* for someone rich?"

"Put your head back," she said again.

"*Do you?*"

The hot water coursed down on my head, my face, warming my shoulders and back, but I could only think that she hadn't answered. As her fingers kneaded the shampoo into my scalp, I wanted to surrender to the massage, but I was worried that I had discovered what she had been trying to tell me all along and I felt nothing but dread. I saw I had begun to lose her, that part of her must have left me already and I hadn't even known. It is the beginning of the end, she had said. I could not bear that thought.

"How can you think—" she said. "Put your head forward now. How can you *think* I'd leave you for someone else? How many times have I told you I've been looking for you all my life?" She rinsed off the shampoo. When it was safe for me to open my eyes, I saw through the curtain of water cascading off my forehead the soft, familiar curves of her bosom, the sparkle of water droplets on her skin, and I leaned forward to rest my brow against her body. I was so stunned by my reprieve and my love for this woman that, to my astonishment, I began to cry. At first I did not think Odette was aware, but when she gently lowered the shower attachment and cradled my head against her, I was not in the least ashamed to give into my tears and the relief they brought.

"Sweet man," she said. "My dear, sweet man."

Odette and I had just come back into the cottage later that same afternoon after taking a walk with the children when the telephone rang. It was the restaurant calling for Odette. She had not had to work the last night because February was always slow, but reservations had picked up unexpectedly and they needed her to waitress that night. I saw Odette's face fall and heard her say, "All right, I'll be there at five-thirty." When she turned to me she looked so miserable and disappointed I wanted to tell her not to go, that it wasn't fair, they had told her earlier that they wouldn't be needing her this weekend at all. But I kept my mouth shut. I had no right to interfere.

I hated Odette's job. I hated the men who would make passes at her, the women who would be so artfully condescending, the bartender who would try to cheat her out of her rightful share of tips. I hated that Odette never had a Friday or Saturday night free to have dinner or go to a party with our friends. I hated the bone-weary exhaustion waitressing caused and how tense and angry she would often be when she returned.

"I need the money," she always said. "I have to go."

And the money was very good. Odette made close to a hundred and fifty dollars on a weekend night, over a thousand dollars a month. What money she had not needed to spend on daily living expenses she had been putting aside so that when nine days from now Paul and Vanessa's spring vacation began on February 11, she would be able to take them back to Europe to spend two weeks with their French grandparents.

Odette did not return from waitressing that night until close to two in the morning.

I was waiting for her downstairs and when her car headlights flashed across the cottage windows I threw down my book and rushed to the door.

"I was so worried!" I told her. "You've never come back this late."

"The roads were terrible," she said. "I was afraid to go fast."

I helped her off with her coat. "Was it bad at the restaurant, too?"

"A party of eight arrived just as the kitchen was closing," she said, and sagged onto the couch. She was wearing the calf-length black skirt and white blouse she always wore to work. "It was a group of those immaculate WASPs—you know the type, Cartier tank watches, Tiffany scallop-shell gold earrings, monogrammed sweaters, Barbados tans . . ."

I knelt before her to pull off her boots.

". . . I knew the moment they came in that they were lousy tippers," Odette continued. "That type always is. They make some comment about every price, the women are loud and bossy, patronizing to the waitresses and their husbands. They ask the same questions over and over again. The men are always trying to sneak a look down my blouse when I serve them—if they weren't with their wives, they'd make a pass—and the wives feel that and take it out on me. The women always ask to see the bill, always check my addition, then get involved in deciding my tip— *ow!*" she cried. I was massaging her calves. "My legs ache so much I want to cry!"

"Come to bed," I said. "I'll give you a back rub."

"Not yet," she said, "I need to rest here for a while." Odette opened up her purse and spilled out the money she had made in tips. "Give me the 'blue-collar' crowd any time," she was saying. "They're honest! They put on their Sunday best because it's obviously a treat for them to eat out. They don't bitch about the prices. They're at a restaurant to enjoy themselves. They work *hard* for their money and they tip well because they know what it's like to work hard for a living. . . . But those goddam WASPs! They tip as if you were serving them at a lunch counter! If a tip should have been fifteen dollars, I'm lucky to get five." Odette brushed her coins into a little pile. "Do we have any milk left or did the children drink it all? How were they, by the way?"

"No trouble." I crossed to the refrigerator. "They watched TV until ten and then I put them in the other bedroom so they wouldn't wake us up in the morning." I poured Odette and myself each a glass of milk and started back to where she was sitting.

"And my cigarettes? And an ashtray? No, never mind," she said. "It's too much to carry. You'll spill."

Later, when we are in bed, I light candles and massage her neck, her shoulders, her back. I knead the muscles in her calves and thighs. Odette lies stiffly beneath my hands, her nightgown gathered over her shoulders.

"Are you warm enough?" I ask.

"It's delicious."

I sit on the side of the bed looking down at her body, her long back, her taut, round buttocks, her perfect thighs rosy in the candlelight. I press with my thumbs the base of her spine and as I slowly, evenly, work my way up her back to her neck I can feel the tension rise from her body like morning mist from a valley.

I put some oil on my hands and begin gently kneading the small of her back, working the oil into her firm buttocks, the tops of her thighs, the backs of her knees, her calves, the heel tendons, her feet. I continue to massage her, her thigh between my hands until my fingers are brushing against the soft curls of her pubic hair. When I push Odette's thighs wider apart she moans softly.

I look up at her. One of her hands is gripping the pillow; her eyes are squeezed tightly shut. When my hands return to the insides of her thighs, her fingers crush the pillowcase. I feel the heat growing within me as I continue to caress her thighs.

"I want you," I say.

Odette says, "Me, too," and twists in the bed until she is on her side and pulls me down next to her.

Odette's mouth is soft, her breath so sweet. A tendril of hair falls across her eyes and I brush it away.

"I love your mouth," she says. "Give me your lips."

Time stops for only an instant as I feel Odette's hand searching for me, and then she is holding me as I roll over her and we are moving together. Her eyes are open watching me. I feel her hands on my hips, they slide up my rib cage to my chest. When she sees the pleasure she is giving me we both laugh at how good it feels. Her breath is hot against my cheek. "So good!" she is saying.

"It *is* good," I say.

"Yes." I hear the rush of her breath. "Oh yes," she is saying. *"Don't stop!"*

I have a moment of wonder at how easy this all is and then I realize I could not stop even if I wanted to. "Oh yes," Odette is saying and I can hear myself say, "Oh, Jesus!" I am worried that I am hurting her, but I cannot stop. Not until it is all over and I am holding Odette in my arms, the blood still pulsing and pounding in my ears, my breath still ragged, do I become aware that Odette is crying and I think, *Oh my God*, I hurt her. And I pull away to ask if she is all right.

"Oh yes," she says.

"But you're crying!"

"I'm happy," she says and kisses me.

"Happy?"

"You came," she says.

"I love you," I say.

And Odette says, "I love you, too."

I think we did love each other. That is why I find it so hard to explain what happened between us beginning with late the following Wednesday morning when I heard a car turn in and stop at the cottage and saw Barbara T. climbing out of her Saab.

"Hi!" she said, when I opened the cottage door.

"Hello," I said.

"I was on my way back to New York, but I had something I wanted to stop by to give you first." She was holding a small box in her hand. "May I come in?"

"Sure," I said. "Why not?"

I was not really very surprised to see Barbara T. It was typical of her now-you-see-me, now-you-don't style. Barbara T. entered the cottage, stamping the snow from her boots. "I'm sorry to drop in like this without calling, but it was sort of a spur of the moment thing." She handed me the box and I put it aside on my desk while I helped her out of her coat and hung it on a hook. She was wearing blue jeans and a soft flannel shirt,˙ its top three buttons undone. When Barbara T. bent forward to pull off her boots her breasts were loose beneath her shirt. I could not look away in time. When Barbara T. saw where I had been looking she said, "I've missed you."

I thought of her nervousness, her silence when I'd pick up Peter. "I've been right here," I said.

"It's been difficult. I couldn't—because of you and Alice—I couldn't be myself."

"Whatever that is."

"Don't be mean," she said. "You were never mean to me before."

"You weren't going to testify against me in court before." I looked at Barbara T.'s expression. She seemed honestly surprised. "Alice told me," I said.

"Told you what?"

"Over this past weekend she told me you were willing to testify against me. Testify that I had admitted to you last summer that I was having an affair with Odette."

"You were, weren't you?"

"No. Not last summer."

"But you are now."

"Yes."

"So what difference does it make?"

"The difference is that now Alice and I are separated. I didn't sleep with Odette before! Jesus, Barbara T., how could you think testifying against me wouldn't make a difference?"

"I wasn't going to testify," she said.

"You wouldn't have the choice," I told her. "You'd be subpoenaed."

She turned away from me to look around the cottage. "It's nice here," she said. "You've really made it look very nice." When I didn't answer she said, "Don't be angry with me. I would never testify against you, you must know that. If I were subpoenaed I'd simply say that I was mistaken. That I'd misunderstood you. And besides, I won't be around. I'm going back to California to live."

"When?"

"In a month or so. That's why I stopped in. I wanted to see you before I go. I've been thinking of going back for quite a while." She crossed the living room to the kitchen. "Is that coffee hot?" she asked.

"I can heat it up." I lit the burner and while the coffee warmed Barbara T. continued to stroll around, picking up books, reading the jacket flaps, putting them back down. She lifted a photograph of Odette off a table. "This is nice," she said. "Where did you take it?"

"In the woods here behind the cottage."

"It's nice," she said again. "I like the frame." She replaced the photograph and asked, "Does Odette know about us?"

"Yes."

"Do you think she'd tell Alice?"

"I don't know."

"You never said anything, did you?"

"What do you think?"

"I don't know," she said. "You, Alice, this divorce, Arthur, Odette . . . Anything's possible."

"Well, I haven't. Would it worry you if I had?"

"Alice is my *friend*," she said.

I pulled two coffee mugs down from the cupboard.

"May I see the upstairs?" Barbara T. asked.

"Sure. Help yourself."

I could hear Barbara T. walking back and forth in the bedroom and then her footsteps halted and I heard the squeak of bedsprings as she sat down on my bed. I poured two mugs of coffee and waited a few moments for Barbara T. to come back downstairs, but when she didn't reappear I carried the coffee up. Barbara T. was still sitting on the side of the bed and I sat down next to her.

"I was thinking about that night we had together in New York," she said. "It was nice."

"Yes."

"Why are the men I like always married?"

"There are probably a half-dozen good reasons," I said. "But maybe it's just that you only see married people. Who are you seeing now?"

"A man in New York."

"And he's married?"

Barbara T. nodded. "He has three children. He's afraid to leave his wife. She's an alcoholic."

"Do you know that for a fact, or is that just what he tells you?"

"I believe him," she said.

"And you're in love with him."

"Sometimes I think so."

"Is he in love with you?"

"He tells me he is."

"But there doesn't seem to be any future?"

"That's why I'm going to California." Barbara T. was silent for a moment and then she said, "You know, after you and Alice separated I thought maybe you and I . . ." She paused, then said, "But it would never have worked. You and I were too much . . ." She paused again. "When you called me after the separation and asked me to meet you in New York I knew it was only for sex and I don't know why I felt so hurt, but I did."

"I'm sorry," I said.

"Don't be. We had wonderful sex."

"Yes."

"Do you come with Odette?"

Her question was so startlingly direct that I answered without thinking. "I've started to," I said.

"I thought you would. You're in love with Odette, aren't you." It was not a question.

"Yes."

"Good. I'm happy for you." Barbara T. stood up suddenly. "I've got to be going. I told my sister I'd meet her at her apartment at six."

I stood up with her, then followed her back downstairs.

After I had helped Barbara T. into her coat she turned to me. We stood just looking at each other for a moment and then she kissed me gently, tenderly, on the cheek. "Good-bye," she said.

"Take care of yourself, Barbara T."

And then she was gone and I went back to my desk to the outline I had been working on for a documentary on the apparent link between Agent Orange, the chemical defoliant used in Vietnam, and cancer. It was then that I saw the present Barbara T. had brought me and which I had entirely forgotten about.

The package contained a small, beautiful antique cut-crystal vase. The card read, "Love, Barbara T." An hour or so later a florist delivered a little bouquet of yellow roses.

At dusk, when I left the cottage and drove to Odette's, her house was empty and dark. I waited for about fifteen minutes, then left her a note asking her to call me when she got back.

I returned to the cottage, made myself dinner and waited, but there was no call. I thought maybe my note had fallen off the door or blown away, so I telephoned. I kept calling Odette every half-hour until after midnight. No one answered. No one was home. I called the local police to ask if there had been any reported accidents. There had been none. I telephoned again at one. Still no answer, nor was there any at eight, nine, or ten o'clock the next morning.

The following afternoon I spotted Odette getting into her car in the parking lot behind the hardware store. I pulled in next to her and got out. "Where have you been?" I asked. "I've been so worried. I've been calling you constantly. Are you all right?"

"I was in New York," she said.

"*New York?*" I asked, surprised. "What were you doing there?"

"Did you enjoy your afternoon?" she asked.

"It was all right," I said. "I got quite a lot of work done."

"You're such a goddam *liar!*" she said. "I drove up to the cottage yesterday to surprise you with some lunch and I saw Barbara T.'s car. It was hers, wasn't it? You were humping her all afternoon! *Admit* it!"

"I *wasn't!*" I protested. "She stopped by on her—"

"—So I figured what's good for you is good for me and I went into New York."

I felt the blood drain from my face. "Did you . . . ?" I could not even express what I feared.

"Yes, I did," she said. "With a beautiful young man I'd met at the restaurant several times who's been asking me to go out with him. He's a lawyer and he's young and he's rich and he knows how to treat a woman!"

The cry sprang from my lips, "You *fucked* him?"

"What do *you* think?"

I wanted to kill her. I wanted to reach through Odette's car window and grab her by the throat! How could she have done such a thing? I could not look at her. "How *could* you?" I asked.

"How could *you?*" she replied.

"But I *didn't!*" I said. "We just talked."

"You're such a liar! Why should I believe you?"

"Why shouldn't you?"

"God," she said, "I can't wait to get out of this place! Thank God I'm leaving for France. There's no life for me here."

"What do you mean?"

"I've invested eight months in our relationship with nothing in return but hurt and disappointment. You make me feel so empty I ache! Your lies are hurting me, destroying me. What am I supposed to do, cook your dinner, do your laundry, ask you how your afternoon fuck was with a smile on my face? You're treating me like you treated your ex-wives and I'm not going to put up with it. I'm *not!* When I leave Monday I don't think I'll come back."

"You won't come back?"

"I'm going to investigate the possibility of staying there."

"But *why?*"

"Why not?" she said as she started her car. "There's nothing for me here." She put her car in reverse. "I'm not going to waste my time any further with an incurable loser like you!" Then she drove off.

Well, fuck you, lady, I said to myself as I got back into my car, slammed the door, and pulled away. *An incurable loser? Thanks a lot!*

I parked the Peugeot outside the cottage and walked into the woods. My mind was filled with images of that other man, that sonuvabitch who had been to bed with Odette. *How could she do such a thing? He's probably one of those furry bastards, with great clumps of curly black hair all over his back and his hands!*

"GODDAM YOU, ODETTE!" I yelled, scattering doves into the naked trees.

I stumbled along through the snow, slipping on the icy buried rocks and roots. *Why couldn't Odette just believe me? Why did she automatically assume the worst? What hypocrites women are, taking everything a man is able to give, but never giving a man the benefit of the doubt! How could she do that to me?*

I was surprised to discover myself on the dirt road that led to the cornfields where, during the fall, I had heard the pheasants calling to each other. Snowmobiles had packed down the snow and it was easier now to walk.

It had turned very cold. An icy wind cut through my sweater and overcoat. I continued along the road until I came to the cornfield with its cut stalks poking up through the snow like the stubble of a wino's beard. The field was empty, bleak, ringed on all sides by woods. A crow

called from one edge of the field, nothing answered. There were deer
and rabbit tracks, tiny field mice prints in the snow. I followed the
snowmobile tracks into the center of the field and stood there. I had
never felt so alone.

The familiar panic was rushing in. Without Odette there was no one
left who cared. Didn't she understand what she meant to me? I felt like
weeping, but could not.

How could I have made such a mess of my life?

I sank to my knees in the snow and prayed. I prayed to God, to my
mother and brother, deceased uncles and friends, my father, my grandparents. I asked them all to give me courage. To make me strong. I
asked them to help me learn how to love and to be loved, to help me
understand Odette and what she needed from me. I asked them to teach
me to *see*.

The wind stopped. The air was absolutely still and then, suddenly,
out of nowhere came a warm breeze. *A warm breeze!* I could not believe
it! *My God, they're trying to tell me I'll be all right!* The air moved
softly, tenderly about me like a caress. Tears sprang to my eyes and I
raised my head. "Oh God," I whispered, "or whoever you are, thank
you!"

The breeze swirled once more about me and was gone. For an instant
I regretted not having also asked for help on the new film and then,
inside my head, I heard, "God helps him who helps himself, pal." It had
been my brother's voice.

I returned to the cottage determined to make up with Odette. I
telephoned her house and she answered on the second ring.

"I'd like to see you," I said.

"Why?"

"To talk."

She was silent.

"Can we have dinner together?" I asked. "We could go out."

"Tonight?"

"Tonight. Any time. As soon as we can."

"I can't tonight," she said.

"Tomorrow?" I asked. "You told the restaurant you wouldn't be
working."

"I don't know," Odette said. "We'll have to see."

She was silent.

"How are the children?" I didn't want to hang up.

"Fine."

"Give them my love."

"I will."

". . . Odette? I'm sorry about today."

"Me, too."

"I had no right to get angry like that."

"No, you didn't," she said.

I felt a flash of anger. *Why couldn't she at least give an inch.* "Well, I apologize." There was another silence and I added, "But I was jealous. I was angry. . . . Are you going to see him again?"

"He's asked me to."

"I'm sure he has," I said. "He's a lawyer?"

"Yes. With CBS in New York."

"What was he doing in your restaurant in New Hope?"

"Having dinner."

"Asshole," I mumbled.

"What?"

"I said, 'asshole.' Not you, *him.*"

"He's not. He's a very warmhearted, giving man—"

"Why are you defending him?" I cried.

"Because he's a friend."

"And I'm *not?*" I rubbed my brow.

She was silent for a moment and then she said, "If you were my friend, you wouldn't treat me the way you do. Would you want your daughter to be treated by a man the way you treat me?"

"Hell, yes!" I said. "I think she'd be very lucky to find a man as basically decent as I am."

There was a moment of silence and then Odette asked, "Even if she knew he was sleeping around?"

"I'm *not* sleeping around!" I said. "Barbara T., as I told you, only stopped by to say good-bye."

Odette was silent.

"Are you going to see that lawyer again?"

"I don't know," she said.

"Then you're not seeing him tonight?"

"No."

"Well, thank God at least for that."

"He asked me to go to the theater with him tomorrow night."

"In New York?"

"Yes."

"And you said what?"

"I said I'd let him know."

"You're going to *call* him? You're going to speak to that hairy bastard *again?*"

"He's not hairy and he called already tonight. I said I'd let him know."

"Don't go," I said.

"Why not?"

"Because it hurts me."

"Then you know how I feel when you see Barbara T. and all those others."

"But I don't see any others. And Barbara T.'s arrival was a surprise. I didn't invite her. She just came to say she was leaving for California. And as I've told you, all we did was talk. So will you please not see that lawyer again in New York?"

Odette was silent and then she said, "Maybe we shouldn't see each other quite so much."

"*What? Why?*" I asked. "I *need* to see you. I *want* to see you."

"Not tonight. I'm too tired. I need some space."

"How about Friday?" I asked, knowing it was her theater evening in New York.

"Maybe."

"That is, if you can't see me tonight."

"Not tonight. I'm too tired."

"Then I'll see you tomorrow and Saturday too."

"Call me tomorrow," she said.

"I will." I was encouraged she had not ruled out Friday night entirely. "And Odette?"

"Yes?"

"I love you. I do."

"Are you trying to convince me, or yourself?"

Odette and I did have dinner together Friday and Saturday nights. We spent that entire weekend before she left for France together. The first thing Odette noticed when she came into the cottage was the cut-crystal vase filled with now fading yellow roses and she asked me where it had come from.

"Barbara T. gave it to me," I said. "It was her going-away present."

"Are you sure she's going?"

"As sure as I can be based on what she said."

"And she's not coming back?"

"Probably not," I said. "I wouldn't be seeing her any more even if she did."

"Do you mean that?" she asked.

"Yes."

"Then you won't miss this," Odette said, and deliberately dropped the vase on the floor. The glass shattered with a terrible crash into hundreds of pieces. Water splashed everywhere, the flowers were scattered about. I just stood there too astonished to protest and then I began to laugh.

"You're *laughing?*" Odette asked.

"You are one hell of a woman," I said.

"Yes," she said.

On Monday morning when I stood in Odette's kitchen surrounded by all her suitcases and her children, I found myself close to tears again. She left on a midafternoon flight to France. And neither of us was sure she would come back.

14

I SAW ODETTE AND HER two children off on the plane and during the long drive back from JFK International I kept waiting to feel that sense of freedom I usually felt at being separated from the woman I was living with. I was alone. I no longer had any woman whose moods I had to respond to, whose tensions I had to cope with. But instead of feeling relieved, I felt empty, and a sharp, awful, familiar ache of loss, a loneliness that intensified as I passed Odette's house, darkened now but for the security light in her bedroom. I continued down the street by my former house in which, I knew, Alice and Peter were having dinner and probably Arthur, too, although I did not see his car. And then I drove on out of town to the turnoff before Rosemont and the road up to the woods.

When I reached my cottage I turned on every light upstairs and downstairs and the radio, too. Tallulah swirled around my legs until I fed her, then even she withdrew, leaving me as alone as ever I had been. I lifted the telephone receiver to make sure that there was a dial tone, that the phone would be working should anyone (anyone at all) want to call. I was about to step into the tub when the telephone rang.

I froze in panic. I suddenly knew without even having to answer the telephone that Air France was calling to say Odette's plane was down in the North Atlantic. Hadn't I learned about my mother's death through a telephone call just after I returned from the airport?

The phone rang again. It couldn't be Air France, I told myself. They didn't have my number. I next thought it might be Didi, or a male friend (Burt Taylor? Dudley Thompson?) wanting me to go to a movie. But when I answered the phone it was Alice. "Are you busy?" she asked. She obviously had a cold. "Arthur and I are leaving for a week in Jamaica on Wednesday—" (Alice, I recalled, always got a cold before a trip) "—and I wanted to know how you felt about that."

"Envious," I said.

"Are you going to cause trouble?"

"What do you mean?"

"I mean use it against me in court."

"Alice, I don't want a messy divorce. I just want a divorce."

"So you wouldn't use it?"

"Of course not."

"Do you want to keep Peter while I'm gone?"

"Sure, he can stay at the cottage with me."

"You could use this house," she said. "It might be easier. All of Peter's—and incidentally, half of *your* stuff—is here."

"Well, I don't know . . ."

"It would be nice for Peter," she said, then added, "And it will make it easier for you to keep an eye on Odette's house while she's away."

"I'll be doing that anyway," I said.

An hour after dinner Alice called again.

"The trip's off," she said.

"Oh?"

"All my friends say I'm hanging myself."

"Why?"

"For taking off with Arthur while we're getting a divorce."

"I told you, Alice, I wouldn't use it against you. But if you're so worried about taking the trip maybe Arthur will take me. I'd love to go to Jamaica."

"That would be ducky," Alice said. (Actually, because of her cold, I thought at first she had said, "Thad wood be duggy.")

"Well, I wouldn't cancel the trip just because of your friends."

"You *want* me to go?"

"All I'm saying is I won't use it in court against you."

"And you'll take Peter?" she asked.

"Yes."

"Arthur wants to talk to you," she said.

There was a slight pause, then Arthur came on the phone. "I think you're being very decent about our trip," he said.

"We'd all be better off if we got a little break."

"It looks as if we might go then," he said. "The issue arose simply because when I called Odette this morning to talk to the children she began singing the blues to me about money, that she didn't know whether she could afford to live in this country anymore and might instead have to move back to France. There was a lot of resentment, aggression, in her tone and we could not communicate at all. Alice—"

"Did you tell Odette this morning you were planning this trip?"

"I couldn't tell Odette *anything*," Arthur said. "Alice said that one gets divorced the way one gets married. That you and she had never been able to communicate and that all your troubles had been over that."

"I'm not sure I would agree," I said, "but go on."

"Well, Alice was nervous about taking this trip, naturally, because of

the divorce. She's feeling a bit anxious—that's why she has this cold—"
(I could hear Alice protest in the background) "—and she feels a little
guilty about leaving Peter alone."

"Peter won't be alone," I said. "He'll be with me."

"Yes, that's what I tried to tell her."

"Maybe you and I should do the 'communicating.'"

"We do okay, don't we?" Arthur said.

"Just let me know when you're leaving so I can make arrangements
about Peter."

I hung up the telephone feeling confused. When Arthur said he thought
I was being decent was that his way of saying I was weak? Should I have
been upset? Protested? Confronted them with a loaded revolver? Alice
was hardly Evelyn Nesbit; Arthur and I were not Stanford White and
Harry K. Thaw. The fact was I rather liked the idea of their trip, of their
being out of town. Alice wouldn't be around to hassle me. I could lead
a semi-normal life with Peter. All in all I wished Arthur and Alice *bon
voyage.*

And when they got to Jamaica, perhaps, rain.

What they got, as it turned out, was a three-hour head start out of
New York before we were struck by what newscasters referred to as "the
worst snowstorm New Jersey has suffered since the 1700s." A light snow
had dusted the roof of the cottage by eight-thirty the morning Arthur
and Alice were taking off. By ten o'clock Peter's school called me to say
he would have only a half day. By noon it was snowing heavily, great
thick clumps that did not melt on the ground. Radio programs were
giving storm-watch bulletins every half-hour. The blizzard moved in so
hurriedly that I packed up the clothes I would need, scooped up Tallulah,
picked up Peter at his school, and headed for the house in town.

It snowed for the next thirty-six hours, but the accumulation, less than
thirty inches, was not the problem. The difficulty came from the
accompanying high winds, which created enormous drifts. The governor
prohibited all road traffic except for four-wheel drive and emergency
vehicles. Schools were shut. The New Jersey Turnpike was closed down.
And so I was stuck inside a house filled with the scent and spoor of my
former life.

In the evening Peter and I would play checkers or watch TV. It was
almost possible to pretend being there together was the same as it had
always been, but then I'd see Arthur's squash racquet in the umbrella

stand, his overcoat hanging now from my hook in the hall closet, his electric razor in the upstairs bathroom on my side of the double sink.

"Do you like living here again, Daddy?" Peter asked.

"I like being with you."

I had difficulty looking Peter in the eye. It hurt me to look at him. Looking at him only reminded me of how much of him I had lost, of how much I had hurt him, too.

The following Monday when Peter's school reopened I moved us both back up to the cottage. I didn't want to stay in that other house one extra day. By then Odette had been gone a week, Arthur and Alice for five days. I had written Odette a half-dozen letters but nothing had reached me from her yet. I had no idea how long a letter took to arrive from France. I did know, however, that due to the storm all of the Europe-bound mail was being diverted to Dulles Airport outside of Washington because JFK International was running on only a limited schedule and Boston was still closed.

While waiting for the mailman, I wandered outside where the blue jays scolded me for having let the feeders get so low. Snow had drifted halfway up the cottage's north wall and there were deer tracks all around the salt lick I had put out. When the mailman finally did arrive all he brought was bills. I went back inside and wrote another letter to Odette.

I pictured her in the Alps leaning back against the wooden railing of a restaurant halfway up some mountain, her face turned to the sun, her lips smeared with cream. I imagined her with her ski boots unbuckled, legs crossed at the ankle, chattering away in French.

I missed the wrinkles at the corners of her eyes when she smiled, the way she'd touch my shoulder, lean her forehead against my collarbone, sag against me when she laughed. I missed our walks in the woods together, her hand holding mine, our strides evenly matched until we'd have to stop and embrace, hug each other, and then, with our arms still about each other and hips touching, walk on.

I missed watching her undress in front of the bathroom's electric heater, the deliberate bawdiness of the way she would step out of her panties and toss away her bra. I missed the way she would lift her nightgown over her head, then let it fall like a theater curtain about her body. I missed the way she counted as she brushed her hair *vingt-et-un*, *vingt-deux*, *vingt-trois* . . .

I hated the emptiness of my bed at night. I missed not having Odette's body curled around mine, our legs "entwingled" (Odette's invented word). I missed all her smells: The shampoo and conditioner scent of her hair, the mixture of perfume and soap, smoke and skin, that deep, wonderful musky scent of her throat. I missed feeling her rolling over next to me at night, the way she would spoon, fit her bottom against my belly.

I missed sitting across the table from her in her kitchen, sipping wine, talking while Paul and Vanessa busied themselves about us. Every day there had been a dozen little things I would have liked to talk to her about, show her, share with her. I missed her tenderness, her caring what happened. Why did I always have to lose people before I knew how much they meant to me?

On Wednesday I received my first letter from Odette:

"Blue skies, parents eagerly awaiting, children 'at home' at once. Amazing. Coffee, croissants, and a talk with *maman* for *seven hours!* I am dry-mouthed, jet-lagged, feeling puffy around the eyes. Off to a restaurant tonight. Phone calls from other members of the family and friends. My parents had open ears and good words and seem resigned now to the divorce. Naturally they are disappointed and sad. My father looks very tired, and old. I think of you all the time. Too numb and fatigued for it to be acute yet, but I miss you. You are on my mind and I do not fight it.

"(Later). We went to a discothéque after dinner. The band was fabulous and I lost liters of water. The people are all 'beautiful' and love to dance. I envied the couples I saw whispering and hugging. I have an enormous craving for you and keep counting six hours backward—or is it seven?— and wonder what you are doing, where, and *with whom!!!*

"I feel this trans-Atlantic umbilical cord to you, which surprises me. My earlier trips have always come as such a relief, but now I think only of my separation from you. I miss you so much it alarms me. My eyes are getting soft and I must tuck myself into bed. I want to bury my nose in your neck, see you walk, hear your voice. I miss sleeping with you. *Bonne nuit,* my sweet . . ."

Just holding her letter in my hand provided comfort.

Peter got out of school at two-thirty and I picked him up and brought him back to the cottage. Alice would not be back from Jamaica until late afternoon so I suggested to Peter that we take a walk.

We walked along in silence for the most part, every now and then I pointed out deer tracks or birds and he made an effort to look interested.

"Something on your mind?" I asked.

"Daddy, when you and Mommy are divorced is Joan still going to be my sister?"

"Of course she is," I said. "Divorces don't change that."

"But will I see her?"

"Sure. She gets out for vacation next Monday and she'll stay with me here at the cottage. You'll see her then."

"Are you going to marry Odette?"

"None of us is even divorced yet."

"Sometimes I wish Arthur and Odette had never moved here."

"That wouldn't have made any difference," I said. "Your mother and I would still be getting a divorce."

"I wish this was all a bad dream and I'd wake up and discover everything was like it was before."

When we returned to the cottage the phone was ringing.

"Where have you been?" Alice asked. She still had her cold.

"Peter and I were taking a walk."

"Well, I'm back."

"Good. How was your trip?"

"Terrible. It rained the whole time."

"That's too bad," I said. But there must have been something not quite right in my voice because Alice responded, "You really are a sonuvabitch, you know?"

There was no letter from Odette Thursday or Friday. Saturday a postcard came saying, "This first week has been super. Know I could live here again, and well. Met a *promoteur* who offered me a job selling chalets to foreigners. Off to the mountains tomorrow. Six feet of fresh snow. *Je t'embrasse*. Odette."

I received no comfort from that one. I was glad her week had been "super," but I was worried about what followed—her even considering living there, the *promoteur*, was she going to the mountains to look at chalets with him? And what mountains? Where? I had no address. The umbilical cord seemed to be unraveling fast.

Joan's spring vacation began Monday, twenty-fifth of February, and lasted beyond all endurance. I drove to St. Matthew's to pick her up and she told me she had been studying for her French exam and had not gone to bed at all the night before. As a result she fell asleep immediately upon entering the car and remained asleep the whole trip home.

At dinner that night in the cottage I tried to get her to talk about school but all I got were monosyllabic answers except when she spoke about volleyball, which she seemed to like better than anything else she did.

"What about your teachers?" I asked. "Are there any you particularly like?"

"No," she said.

Her first morning Joan slept until eleven-thirty, then came downstairs yawning and scratching, spilled orange juice on the floor, followed it with sugar and cold cereal, then stepped in both spills as she carried her cereal to the low table near my desk, where she slopped milk over the side of her bowl onto my outgoing mail, and dropped more cornflakes on the rug. When she had finished, she dumped her empty cereal bowl into the sink on top of the orange juice glass, breaking it, mumbled "shit," and headed back upstairs as if she had lead weights attached to her feet. She had climbed but four steps before I exploded.

There was no mail from Odette that day.

The second morning Joan only spilled the sugar, and although she again needed to be reminded to wash her cereal bowl, she did not break anything. The third morning she suffered a relapse and after I made her clean up the kitchen, her bedroom, and the bathroom sink filled with dried toothpaste and hair I told her to go outside.

"*Outside?*" she protested. "It's freezing!"

"Put on the down jacket I bought you last Christmas."

"I left it at school."

"Then borrow mine."

"But what can I do?"

"Take a walk. Look for deer. Count the birds. See a friend. Hitch a ride to Milwaukee. I don't care what you do," I said, "just so long as I can work undisturbed until three o'clock."

"Three o'clock! I'll be frozen to death by then."

Joan stayed outside for less than an hour, then came in with the mail. There was still nothing from Odette. I had received only the one letter and that postcard saying she was off to the mountains. Why hadn't she written? I was crazy with worry. Had she fallen in love with another man? Had she been lost in an avalanche? *Why hadn't she written?* She had been gone now two weeks.

That afternoon when I returned from the market Joan said, "Odette called."

"She *did?* When?"

"About a half-hour ago."

"Where is she? What did she say?"

"She sounded far away. She wants you to call her."

"Did she give you the number?"

"I wrote it down on the back of an envelope," Joan said. She began sifting through the papers on my desk. "It's here somewhere." I watched her search. With maddening slowness she would pick up one envelope, turn it over, put it aside, and go on to the next. "Maybe it wasn't an envelope," she said.

"Find it," I told her through clenched teeth.

Ten minutes later I was speaking with Odette.

Her father had died suddenly. A stroke. It was a terrible shock, totally unexpected; he had seemed tired lately, but certainly not ill. She would have to stay with her mother in France at least until June. She had enrolled Vanessa and Paul in an American school nearby. She loved me. She missed me. But what else could she do?

I told her how sorry I was, that of course I understood why she needed and wanted to stay. I told her that if I could get Alice to keep Joan for me I would fly out the next day to be with her, to help.

"No," Odette said. "There's nothing you can do. It's all been taken care of."

"I could take care of you."

"No, really, I'm all right," she said. "Anyway it would only be more confusing to my mother. She's barely had time to get used to Arthur and my getting a divorce. Meeting a new man would only make things more difficult for her."

"Are you *sure?*" I asked. "I don't want you to be alone at a time like this."

"I'm not alone. The family has been wonderful. My uncles and aunts have been here. Everything's under control. There really isn't anything you could do."

"I miss you so much!"

"Good!" Odette laughed. "Keep missing me. I thought you'd forgotten all about me."

"Forgotten you? How could you—why did you think that?"

"Because I didn't get any mail from you. Not until today then suddenly three letters arrived."

BEAUTIFUL WOMEN; UGLY SCENES

"But I've written you at least *ten* letters! I thought you'd ditched *me!* I've only gotten one letter and a postcard from you. It must be the storm. I was so worried! I thought you'd run off with that *promoteur* or some Olympic skier, some blond guy with lots of muscles and white teeth."

"I loved your letters. They have been so marvelous, so sharing, so full of confidence in us, in me."

"I *love* you."

"Me, too. I have never felt with anyone what I feel with you—and even now without you. It must be love. I am not disturbed at all by your 'crazies.' You are getting so much better now. You know that, too. As you wrote me, once you start getting healthy, you never let yourself get that low again. I crave you. It's a fantastic sensation knowing we have only opened the door between us a little way."

"I want to open it all the way."

"We will. In June," she said.

"But June is so far off! Three months is a long time," I protested.

"We'll be all right. You'll see."

"I know . . ."

"Listen, I've got to go. You'll keep writing me, will you?"

"You know I will."

"And we'll be all right."

"Yes," I said. "And maybe I can fly over and see you at some point."

"I'd love that," Odette said.

After I'd hung up I sat for a moment looking out at the snowy woods surrounding me and waiting for the old familiar feelings of abandonment to strike. But they didn't. I wasn't in Leadville anymore. My winter sojourn in the cottage wasn't an "exile." I wasn't alone. I had Joan. Peter was coming for the weekend.'Odette loved and missed me. The more I thought about it, the more I realized my life didn't resemble Leadville at all. I was no longer "coming unglued." The "crazies" were subsiding. I no longer woke up *every* morning at four. I wasn't always depressed. I was optimistic about my work. I was in love.

The proposal and outline I had submitted to WNET on the apparent link between Agent Orange and cancer had been received enthusiastically. In fact, WNET indicated an eagerness to expand the documentary to cover ten other chemicals used during the Vietnam war plus the unresponsiveness of the Veteran's Administration and the Pentagon to the resulting problems.

I had contacted a former student who had written me that her husband had been exposed to Agent Orange while a Green Beret and who had now learned he had cancer. (Their four-year-old son had been born without a forearm and with a hole in his heart.) She had replied immediately that they were very eager to cooperate with me. I knew the most effective way of telling this story would be by playing that family's personal trauma against the bureaucracy's insensitivity to their plight.

I never did get to France.

A New York couple to whom Dudley Thompson had shown my former house had offered a bid nine thousand dollars below my asking price. Dudley telephoned to give me the news.

"Do you think we can bump them up a bit?" I asked.

"I don't know. But another couple looked at it yesterday and they seemed very interested in it, too. They were asking mortgage rates so I think they might make an offer."

"Then tell the first couple my asking price is firm."

"You're sure you want to do that?"

"Yes."

"I'll let the other couple know a bid is in, maybe it will make them move. Has Alice found a house yet?"

"No."

"So you don't have an occupancy date?"

"No, Dudley, but I think it should be after school lets out. Some time in June. Have you been showing her anything?"

"Nothing she's liked."

"When is this second couple coming back for a look at the house?"

"They said this afternoon. Will you be around?"

"I'll make it a point to be," I said.

At about five-thirty that afternoon Dudley called back to say the second couple to whom he had shown the house had offered exactly what I was asking for. "Before you decide to take it, let me get in touch with the New York couple and tell them of the new bid."

Two hours later Dudley called again. "Are you sitting down?" he asked. "Do you have a drink? I've been back and forth between the two couples ever since I spoke to you last. The New York couple have offered twenty-three thousand over your asking price, with a closing date of June 30. Shall we accept?"

"Good God, yes!" I said.

I wouldn't see any of that money, of course. What would be left after paying off the mortgage and agent's commission would be held in escrow for Alice as part of the settlement. But we were making progress, at least.

When I told Alice about the sale she said, "If you insist that Peter and I move, something radical is going to happen."

"What does that mean?" I asked.

"You'll see," she said, and hung up on me as usual.

We were all still, in Odette's phrase, "pregnant with divorce": swollen and tense with the weight of decisions on proposals and counterproposals and simultaneously anxious for and apprehensive about the resolution of this machinery we had put into motion and over which we no longer felt we had full control. The negotiations were dragging on and on and dragging us down with them. The summer months with all the children home loomed ominously ahead. I would have Joan for the summer, Peter for July and alternate weekends in August. Odette would be returning in June with her two children and had written that since she anticipated going back to her two jobs, her children would be alone and she would have to hire someone to be with them. That letter arrived the same day in April that I was offered a job by a British tourist agency to film a promo on the British Virgin Islands. I could shoot the film in under five weeks and clear eight thousand dollars. I wrote Odette back that same day suggesting she and I rent a summer cottage together at Bradley Beach on the ocean, big enough for all our children and ourselves. "You have had a rough enough time so far," I wrote her, "without making it even tougher on yourself by coming back to jobs that would only exhaust you more and which would pay only enough to pay someone else to look after your children. I will have the money to rent the cottage and am confident that additional funds will come in for me to do the Agent Orange film. Think my proposal over and let me know as soon as possible so I can locate a suitable place. If we are ever able to make it together as a couple we might as well find out now. Please say yes . . ."

Eight days later Odette sent me a cable: YES. YES. YES. DO YOU HEAR ME. YES. That was April 9. April 11, I signed a lease on a beach cottage.

The rest of that month and the first week in May I was on Tortola with side trips to some of the other British Virgins—Jost Van Dyke, Peter Island, Virgin Gorda, and Salt Island (for the wreck of the *Rhone*).

Shortly after I returned I received what I had come to refer to as a "screamer" telephone call from Alice. This one started with how could I use that Jamaica trip against her, that if I wanted to fight dirty she had plenty to go on and would subpoena Odette. "But what really burns my ass," she continued, "is how you can spend four thousand dollars on a beach cottage—"

"—It's nowhere near that much," I said.

"—for the summer while at the same time you are having your son and me evicted."

I told Alice that I knew nothing about the Jamaican trip being used against her, that I had just gotten back and it was the first I had heard of it, and that I would not let it happen. "As for the beach cottage," I said, "I cannot keep Joan and Peter in this small place all summer and since there would also be Odette's two children in addition to Odette and myself, the beach seemed like the best answer."

"You could stay in the Baskin house."

"I don't want us in there. I want to keep it untouched for prospective buyers and, in case you need a temporary place to live, a place for you."

"I don't want to live there, not after what you've done to it. I want to stay here."

"You can't, Alice. The house has been sold. You have to move out by June 15."

"We'll see."

"I'll take Peter the whole summer if it would make it any easier for you to find a house."

There was no answer. Alice had hung up again.

On June 14, the day before Odette and her children returned and the day before Alice moved into the Baskin house, I dusted and aired Odette's house, mowed the lawn, trimmed the hedge, ordered flowers—a large arrangement for the kitchen table, which she would see immediately upon entering, and three smaller bouquets for the bedrooms, one for Vanessa, one for Paul, and one for Odette's bedroom.

The following day after helping Alice move I picked up the flowers and returned with them to Odette's house. I went from room to room turning on a light here and there so that her house would look warm and inviting when we drove in, picked up some milk, breakfast cereals, eggs, and orange juice at the market, gave the house one final check, and left for the airport.

I arrived at the International Arrivals building with forty-five minutes to spare. I felt alternately panicked and excited. What if Odette had changed? What if she took one look at me and decided she had made a terrible mistake and wanted only to return immediately to France? I was acting like a teenager on the afternoon before the big prom; I half expected to break out in zits. When Alice had gone off on a trip I had always dreaded her reappearance.

It took Odette and her children about thirty minutes to clear customs and then I saw Paul and Vanessa running toward me and I hugged them just as I spotted Odette walking beside a porter with a cart filled with their luggage. She stumbled slightly, then regained her balance and hurried to me. I could hear the blood whistling in my ears while I searched her expression, and then we were together, hugging each other, laughing, kissing, pulling away to look into each other's faces, then hugging again.

Odette's eyes were wet, mine were, too. I must have been saying something to her, God knows what, probably "Hello, hello, hello, hello," over and over again. I hugged her to me, inhaled her skin. Her hands touched my face, my lips. She was back, we were really together. I was so happy, so totally in love, so relieved she had made it safely.

The children were swirling about our legs. "Vanessa," Odette said, "see where the porter puts our luggage."

"I'll do that," I said.

"No," Odette said, holding me to her. "Don't go away from me."

On the drive back to our old New Jersey town Odette sat almost in my lap. Our fingers interlaced, or caressed each other's thighs. We touched each other constantly as if to confirm our presences. Odette would lean into my shoulder, kiss my cheek. When she would pull away I would feel the absence of her skin until she would bury her nose in my neck again.

When two pieces of a jigsaw puzzle fit together, shouldn't one be able to hear their sigh of relief?

Two weeks later I was working up at the cottage when Alice called. Ever since the fifteenth we had been neighbors—"we" being Alice and Peter and Arthur and myself. "I hate this house," she said. "You've ruined it."

"Ruined it? How?"

"By painting over the paneling."

"Alice, the paneling was crap. It was South Carolina knotty pine put there in the 1920s. It was so dark with grease and smoke it made the house look like a cave."

"Well, you've ruined it. You tried to make this house elegant and instead you spoiled it for good. No one's going to want to buy it now. I feel sorry for the house, for what you did to it. It's a crime."

"Alice, is this what you've called me about?"

"No. I'm calling to tell you the screens in the kitchen don't fit properly, the door to the bathroom doesn't have a lock, the water pressure's too low to take a decent shower. And why wasn't the washer-dryer installed? How am I supposed to wash my clothes?"

"Take them down to the river and beat them with rocks."

"Very funny. There was supposed to be a washer-dryer when I moved in."

"I'm not going to buy a new washer-dryer for someone else. Whoever buys the house can put their own in."

"There's no water."

"What do you mean?"

"I mean there's no water. The pump's stopped."

"It's probably lost its prime."

"Well, I want you to fix it."

"I'm busy right now, Alice. I'll come down later."

Later, when I was walking down the hill toward the big house, I saw Arthur and Alice having a picnic beneath a giant oak by the cemetery. Just the tops of their heads were visible directly beneath one of the oak's oldest and heaviest dead limbs. I halted on the path and studied where the thick limb joined the massive tree trunk not more than a dozen feet over their heads. If that limb were to fall I would be widowed not divorced.

Concentrate, I told myself. *Concentrate on that limb. If there is ever going to be anything to this Angel of Death business let it be now.* I fixed the image of that dead limb in my mind, then closed my eyes and focused with all my attention upon its weakest spot and *willed* the limb to drop.

"Hey, *Daddy!*" Peter shouted. "Hey! Hi!"

I opened my eyes. Peter was running up the slight rise toward me. He had been sitting under the dead limb, too. "Hi!" he called. "I didn't see you!"

"I didn't see you either," I said. But the dead limb had held firm.

Two days later, on the first of July, Odette and I and all our children (plus Tallulah) were on our way to our rented Bradley Beach summer cottage at 28 Birdsong Lane.

Bradley Beach was about fifty miles from our town, not quite an hour and fifteen minutes by car, an hour and forty-five minutes counting our lunch stop at a McDonald's. Odette drove the two boys and two girls in her car and I took Tallulah and, with the back seat folded down, most of the luggage, an inflatable raft, my old black and white TV set, a hibachi, my typewriter and notes, folding deck chairs, beach towels, bicycles, a cooler, and a cardboard carton containing sand castle molds, a trench shovel, and various other items added by Peter and Paul at the last minute. The goddam cat screamed at me the entire trip and, just before we reached the beach cottage, within sight of it, in fact, threw up on the front passenger seat and gearshift lever. When Odette pulled into the parking space beside me she found me with my head hanging out of the window, gasping for air.

The smaller children immediately rushed out of Odette's car—Joan, with studied nonchalance, hung slightly behind and disappeared down to the beach.

"HEY!" I shouted after them. "How 'bout grabbing some of the luggage?"

Odette came to my side of the car and ran her fingers through my hair. "Relax, we'll get it later," she said. "Let's take a look at the house."

Our cottage was one of a dozen two-story sagging-roofed and crumbling-porched gray-shingled summer bungalows built in the 1930s next to each other along a straight stretch of beach. If one stood ankle-deep in the water and faced the row of cottages, ours was the one with the barn-red trim, fifth from the right. The beach cottage to our immediate left was owned by a Baptist congregation from Trenton whose members took turns coming down for a week or a weekend by the sea. Their cottage had once been a Baptist youth camp and many of the men and women, now in their fifties and sixties, who were sitting on the aluminum and plastic tubing rocking chairs on the deep, shaded porch, had come first to the cottage as children. Sometimes, at night, they would turn on huge floodlights mounted on their cottage roof to illuminate the surf. Strangers walking along the beach would stop in thinking it was a restaurant. At the foot of the stairs leading up to their cottage from the beach was a carefully lettered sign:

We like to see you

In a Bathing Suit

—— BUT ——
NOT ON THE PORCH

To our cottage's immediate right was a narrow strip of sand less than
thirty feet across, which belonged to the association of cottages behind
us. It was used as their private beach and was already packed with small
children and baby-sitters.

As Odette and I walked past our cottage and down to the water where
our children were standing I noticed one fifteen-year-old baby-sitter in
a black Spandex bathing suit who was especially lovely. I was thinking
how there is something so beautiful and sweet about certain teen-aged
girls' bodies. It isn't just sex, it's the promise, the new leaf, the uncoiling
fern of spring. There is a magic to witnessingwhat had been all bones
and big feet beginning to fill out, the metamorphosing of a young girl
into a young woman. Joan, fourteen that summer, had suddenly become
very tall, taller than her mother, almost as tall as Odette. She had become
more solid, too, with wide shoulders and strong legs. At times I would
find myself gazing at her with wonder. It was as though she had pulled
on a woman's body like a pair of blue jeans; from the waist down she
already had a woman's curves. And yet there was no femininity to her
yet; she still behaved like an overgrown and clumsy fourteen-year-old
boy. I worried that she'd never change, that instead she represented a
new wave of warrior women, self-sufficient, combat-booted, clenched-
fisted, and Amazonian.

"Hey, *Dad!*" she called to me as Odette and I approached. "They got
a volleyball net up at the cottage next door!"

"Good," I answered. "Maybe they'll invite you to play."

"Yeah," she said, leaping into the air to smash an imaginary ball.

"Relax!" Odette told me when she saw the look on my face. "It's just
a phase. At fifteen or sixteen it will begin to pass."

"You honestly think so?" I asked, but I couldn't help noticing that
Odette had felt compelled to start her first two sentences to me with the
word "relax."

I wanted these two summer months to be fun. I had visions of us all
tanned and healthy, relaxed and happy, smiling all the time. I had
anticipated a certain amount of resistance from the children at being
thrown together, but I did not expect the resistance to crop up immediately. Within minutes of our entering the house arguments broke out
about who would sleep where and with whom. Paul wanted to sleep with

Vanessa; Vanessa wanted to sleep with Joan; Peter wanted to sleep with Joan, too; Joan wanted to sleep alone.

"Why don't you draw lots to see who sleeps where?" I suggested. "Then switch off at the end of each week."

"Why don't you just let them settle it all among themselves?" Odette asked.

"What's for dinner?" Peter wanted to know.

"I'm bored," Joan said. "There's nothing to do."

Odette led me into our bedroom and closed the door. "This is summer vacation," she said. "Not just *their* vacation, it's *ours*. They can get their bags out of the car. Their bicycles. If they're hungry they can fix their own sandwiches." She pushed me backward until I sat on the bed.

There seemed to be a lot of muttering coming from the other side of our door and then the heavy clomp of feet going down the stairs, the scream-*slam* of the screen door, and a few moments later an argument out by the Peugeot.

Our bedroom's walls, like the rest of the house, were finished in what I have always known as "stable-board," those thin vertical tongue and groove strips of wood. And although the walls had been painted white, no matter what light fell upon the wood, it always seemed a cool, cucumber green. With just Odette and me in there and the door closed, it was peaceful.

"It's not such a bad place, is it?" I said. I began to relax.

All that first week the children were complaining: the beach was too rocky, there were too many jelly fish, there was sand in their beds. "Paul spilled my milk!" "Peter used my towel!" "Joan won't let me in the bathroom!" "Vanessa called me a swear!" "Joan keeps bumping into me!" "They never let me use the raft!" "No one will play with me!" Someone was always being picked on, put down, laughed at, made fun of, pushed away.

No one cleaned anything up. The sand they tracked in from the beach remained on the floor. Dried-out milk glasses, crumpled napkins, jelly-smeared crusts of bread on sticky plates were left behind on the porch. Beds went unmade, damp towels were simply dumped on the floor; wet bathing suits left in chairs.

"It isn't *my* mess!" someone would say.

For a while Odette and I cleaned up, but one afternoon shortly after the first week while I was upstairs working and Odette was sweeping the living room, Joan simply tramped in with her sandy feet, dropped her wet towel at the foot of the stairs, and continued up to her room.

Odette exploded. When I peeked out to see what was the matter I found her raging by herself in the empty room. "I've had it!" she shouted at me as I came down the stairs. "I'm not going to be these children's goddam maid. It's bad enough picking up after my kids but when that great *slug* of a daughter of yours treats me like some-some-some goddam *maid!* I've had it!" She flung down the broom. "*Enough!*" she cried. "No more! I've tried to be nice to them but they're ungrateful, lazy, spoiled brats! *Brats!* And I'm not going to stand for it!"

"Good," I said.

"What do you mean, 'good'?" she asked, surprised.

"I mean take a towel, go out to the beach, and lie in the sun." I went to the porch and called the children in. When they had assembled I compiled a list of chores that needed to be done and told the children that each one of them was being assigned specific jobs and it was that person's responsibility to see that his or her job was taken care of properly. "For the past week Odette has been cleaning up after you while you've done nothing."

"*We've* helped," Vanessa protested.

"Cool it," I told her. "As of this moment Odette's summer vacation has started. She is *not,* repeat, *not* going to pick up after you anymore. There will be no need to pick up after you anymore, because *you* are going to pick up after *yourselves.*"

This, of course, led to: "Daddy! Paul won't sweep the porch!"

Tears. "I was going to, but Joan won't give me the broom."

"I'm *using* it!"

"Odette!" (Peter this time.) "Vanessa won't help me put the dishes away."

Vanessa: "It's Peter's turn."

Peter: "But I can't reach the top shelf!"

Odette's solution: "Climb on a chair."

The children would nit-pick at each other all day long and yet, at 5 P.M. on the dot, they would be silently mesmerized by "The Brady Bunch" on TV. Joan would pretend the program was ridiculously juvenile; but while it was on, she watched it.

Odette and I would take our drinks out to the porch. In the background we'd hear the theme of the show: "This is the story, of a lovely lady . . ." and exchange glances.

It *was* Odette's summer vacation. She had agreed to take July and August off, but intended to go back to work in the fall—doing what, she did not yet know. She knew she never wanted to waitress again, that she wanted something with a future so that she would not have to be financially dependent upon anyone anymore. Odette had an interpreter's degree from the University of Grenoble and I asked whether there wasn't some way she could take advantage of her languages. Odette felt that that time had passed; New York was filled with foreigners who spoke English and Americans who spoke French. She did not think she had the patience to teach, the effort was not worth the pay, and besides, to teach in the public school systems she'd need a teaching certificate.

The children knew this time on the porch at the end of the day was our time to be together and prudently left us alone. Odette and I would sit next to each other, sometimes hold hands, sometimes just touch each other as if to reassure ourselves that we were together still. We would watch fishermen casting into the surf or a sailboat with its bright red-and-white-striped spinnaker moving slowly across the horizon. We would sip our drinks and talk about her opening a store with her own clothing designs, or an exercise spa for both men and women, or a small restaurant and inn; but we did not have the seed money for any of these possibilities. We talked about real estate, interior decorating, social work, travel agenting, catering; but none of these ideas really appealed to her. I wondered aloud whether because of her interest in finances there might not be some way for her to become a brokerage house trainee. That idea interested her, so I wrote some friends in the business to find out what could be done. Their answers were not encouraging. One of them wrote back, "Our interest in Odette would be directly proportional to the size and number of accounts she could bring in." I told Odette not to be depressed, that I was sure something would turn up. But it was depressing. Frustrating, too. Late one afternoon while we were watching a tanker pass slowly by Odette said, "Well, I could always go back to waitressing, again."

"Over my dead body," I said.

"I may have to. You could die tomorrow, you know."

As a result of that remark I got in touch with my life insurance agent and my lawyer to make sure that if I did "die tomorrow" not just my children but Odette would be taken care of, too.

Perhaps it was because we were living next to the ocean, or maybe it was because of all those days we spent working out the appropriate measures to ensure coverage of Odette in the event of my sudden, unexpected death, or it could even have been only the passage of the requisite amount of time. In any case I found myself thinking about my brother a great deal and I tried talking about Carter with Odette. What I was attempting to explain to her was how men's awareness of each other changes through the years and how, I felt, those changes were initiated and complicated by the love-hate relationship that exists between brothers.

Because Carter had been five years older than I, our childhood relationship had been determined largely by the difference in our ages. As we grew older I wanted to change this "big brother/little brother" association into a relationship between equals. It was not until I had been struggling for several minutes to express my resentment at how my brother had treated me—with affection certainly, but always with a bit of patronizing disdain as well—that Odette pointed out to me that most of my difficulties with women, with *her*, came when I treated them the same way.

"You think I patronize you?" I asked. "That I treat you with disdain?"

"Sometimes," she said.

"When?"

"The other day when I blew up at Joan, at the children leaving everything for me to pick up. You just dismissed my anger, sent me out to the beach like a little girl, then like a 'Daddy' drew up a work list. It was all so condescending I wanted to hit you."

"I didn't mean to be," I said.

"Maybe your brother didn't mean to be either."

It must have been about this time that the movie *Jaws* played at a local theater. Odette and I had never seen it and Joan wanted to see it again. We did not take the other children because we felt they were too young. I should not have seen it either, not while I was thinking so much about my brother, and his death.

I had already started having nightmares about Carter's drowning. I would see the sudden gust of wind sharply tipping the Hobie Cat, my brother falling out of the boat.

There was nothing I could do but watch. I would see the storm waves buffeting my brother, the heavy ocean spray hitting his face, Carter's first spasms of coughing as the water entered his lungs.

And then he would slide under.

I would descend with him, the opalescent green light growing dimmer as his body sank. I would see the bubbles escaping from his lips, the convulsions and then the slackness as he spiraled down toward me, his arms and legs outstretched like a sky diver in free-fall.

After *Jaws*, in my nightmares my brother would also be hit by a shark. Sometimes the shark would take him as he sank; but more often, I would not see the shark, only my brother's face: his eyes wide with fright at the shark's first bump, then the terror, the *horror*, as the shark came back and jerked him under.

Several times Odette had to shake me awake and I'd lie there sweating and gasping, my legs swallowed by the twisted sheet. Gently, soothingly, she would talk me back to the here and now.

But now when the children went into the water, I could not work. I would watch them, standing guard from the beach. And I would not let them swim at night. I was as afraid for myself as I was for them, that I would have to go out into that black ocean to save them, the black water that had taken my brother down.

It must also have been about this time that Andy Perlmutter and his parents came to stay at the Baptist cottage. The first time I saw Andy I felt the blood drain from my face. He was Joan's age; I didn't say anything about Andy to her or to any of the other children, I was curious to see if they noticed anything themselves. They didn't, but Odette did.

"That boy looks like you," she said.

"I know. He looks more like me than *I* did when I was his age!"

The resemblance was uncanny! Andy Perlmutter had the same stooped posture I had had, the forward tilt of the neck that tall boys often acquired from trying not to look so much taller than their contemporaries. He had the same shaped head, his glasses (clear plastic frames that had yellowed with time) were the same I had then worn and they slid down his thin nose, too. He had the same skinny chest, the drooping bathing trunks— Carter's nickname for me when I was six had been "Droopy Drawers." His cheekbones were a bit more pronounced than mine had been at his age, but our profiles were so similar it was eerie. I could not look at Andy without seeing myself as a child.

Curiously enough, Andy's parents were both short—neither of them more than five feet five. Mrs. Perlmutter had pink cheeks, huge, pendulous breasts, and a warm, quick, bubbly laugh. Her German accent was less marked than Andy's father's. Mr. Perlmutter, who owned a Buick agency in Trenton, had broad shoulders, a large belly, and surprisingly spindly legs.

The first time Odette and I met the Perlmutters and introduced ourselves Mr. Perlmutter had asked, "Are you married?" The question had taken us both by surprise and before we had had a chance to say anything he had said, "No, mien wife and I thought not. The others"— he indicated the Baptists with a nod of his head—"the others think you are. Ve vill not tell them. They see you embracing and they make clucking sounds. Vhat's wrong with two young people being in love?" He paused, then asked, "You are in love, aren't you?"

"Yes," we said.

"And young," he said.

"*She* is," I laughed, touching Odette.

"Und you?" he said, turning to me, his eyebrows dancing. "You are a Methuselah?"

"He's more a '*meshugga*,' " Odette laughed.

Andy seemed incredibly happy. In the mornings he would be up early raking the beach in front of their cottage or sweeping the porch. He would play cards with the older people, ask if they minded his calling them "Grandma" or "Grandpa." I'd overhear him tell them in the middle of a hand, "Hey, you're really very clever, aren't you, Grandma! You're really trying to take advantage of a young kid." The older Baptists loved it, loved *him*. He would sit and talk to them for hours. I could not help but compare him with my own daughter, who talked to no one. I would watch Andy bantering effortlessly with the Baptists, see him being helpful, carrying towels, bringing them beach chairs or drinks. I would watch him swimming with his parents, splashing his father, kidding his mother about her old-fashioned sidestroke. When old Mr. Massey lost his dentures in the shallow water it was Andy who searched for them for over an hour—and then, when he found them, joked he had been bit.

Several times Andy hesitantly approached our cottage as if wanting to talk to Joan. Joan would pointedly look the other way.

"Why don't you speak to him?" I asked. "Toss a frisbee, take a swim. Maybe you could be friends."

"That's just what we need around here," Joan said. "Another kid."

Andy wasn't just "another kid," damn it. Not to me.

I was upstairs in the bedroom working when the rain began. It was gentle at first, but then it fell harder and the cottage began to be lashed by winds. A nor'easter was blowing up and as the afternoon progressed the sky grew darker and the surf became rougher. The children came inside the cottage to play cards; I could hear them arguing.

At about five, when Odette came back from marketing, I heard Joan say, "Here comes Queen Odette."

It was not the first such remark from one of my children. Joan had called Odette "that shit" in front of Vanessa when Odette had made Joan clean a spaghetti pot a second time. Vanessa had reported Joan's comment to her mother and Odette had repeated it to me adding, "And Peter told Alice that I don't do anything here. I just sit around."

"How'd you hear that?" I asked.

"Arthur told me. And you know Peter would never have made such a remark without the backing of Joan."

"I'll have a talk with them," I said.

"No, don't. If it happens again I'll talk to them myself."

"I want them to stop. I'm sick of their complaining and competition. The summer's halfway over. I wanted it to have been *fun!*"

"It *has* been fun."

"For us, yes. But it hasn't been the way I wanted it to be for us as a family."

"It couldn't have been," Odette said. "You had this cozy little image of us all together like 'The Brady Bunch.' And that sort of life doesn't just happen. Everybody has to be pulling together."

The howl of the wind was matched by a howl from Peter. "I was *not* cheating! I *did* play the three!"

That evening Odette made a pasta primavera for us as a special treat. She had bought all the little carrots, broccoli, Chinese peapods, baby peas, and tomatoes at a local farmers' market. Even the pasta was fresh. Afterward, when I asked Joan how she had liked it, she shrugged and said, "It was okay, I guess."

Odette, seeing the look on my face, swiftly interceded. "Your children aren't used to food like this," she said. "They were brought up like you on meat and potatoes."

Joan glanced at her gratefully.

Five minutes later, Odette and I had just settled down with our coffees on the porch when the argument in the kitchen broke out.

"Where are you going?" she asked.

"To quell the savages."

"Let them be."

"No," I said. "It would be nice to have a *quiet* cup together."

When I entered the kitchen I found Vanessa and Peter washing the dishes, Joan was not doing a thing. Paul had disappeared. "What's the trouble?" I asked.

"Joan won't help," Vanessa said.

"I'm waiting for the sink to be free so I can do the pots and pans," Joan said.

"That sounds fair," I said.

The telephone rang and Odette called, "I'll get it."

"It *isn't* fair," Vanessa protested. "I already did the big pot, there's only the frying pan to do."

"Why did *you* do the pot?" I asked her. I was listening with one ear to Odette on the phone. She sounded very excited about something.

"I did the pot," Vanessa was saying, "because it took up all the room in the sink and Joan wouldn't do it. She said I was the only one who could do a spaghetti pot really well."

"Oh, for Chrissake, Joan!" I said.

"You said you wanted everyone to clean up and I was waiting for both Villars kids to join us."

"Where is Paul?" I asked.

"He said he didn't want to help," Peter said.

"He was too tired," Vanessa explained.

"Then let him go to bed," I said. "The rest of you have to work it out among yourselves. Why do you have to fight all the time?"

No one spoke. In the silence I could hear Odette say something about taking an early train to New York. The children were facing each other like border guards. "Like it or not," I said, "you're all going to be seeing a lot of each other, so you might just as well try to get along." I looked at my daughter's stony expression and added, "And you, Joan, I'm sick of seeing you looking so miserable all the time."

"What do you want me to do?" she asked.

"I'd like to see you smile once in a while."

"I'm not a 'smiler,' " she said.

"Perhaps you could try to look a little less depressed?" I said. "And you could also help by pulling your weight."

Her face turned dark with anger. "Vanessa and Peter weren't doing anything either until they heard you coming."

"That's not true!" Peter protested. "I was waiting for Vanessa to pass me something to dry."

"Well, just finish the dishes, then you can do anything you want. I would like a few moments of peace with Odette."

As I was leaving the kitchen I heard Joan say something and Vanessa's angry reply, "She does *not!*"

I turned back. "What now?"

"I'm sick of hearing Joan and Peter say mean things about my mother!" Vanessa said.

"I didn't say anything!" Peter said.

"Not this time," Vanessa answered. "But you and Joan are always calling her names and saying she doesn't do anything."

"Who did the marketing and made the dinner tonight?" I asked.

"My mother!" Vanessa said.

"Any questions?" I asked.

No one spoke. Odette came into the kitchen carrying our coffees. "They were getting cold," she said. She looked from me to the children and back at me again. "Am I interrupting something?"

"We were having a little talk," I explained.

"Where's Paul?" Odette asked. "He was supposed to help."

"He's in his room," Vanessa said. "He was tired."

"Tired?" Odette said. "Is he feeling all right?" Odette departed to check on her son and Vanessa went with her, leaving me temporarily alone with my two children.

"I'm only going to say this once to the two of you," I told them. "I love Odette. I need her. I want to spend the rest of my life with her. I'm not going to stand for anyone preventing me from doing that. You have two choices: either try to get along with Odette and me, or leave us alone. I'm asking you to help. It's a difficult enough period for us all without your fighting all the time."

"It's not only the two of us," Joan said.

At that moment Odette appeared with her two children and their sleeping bags.

"Where are you going?" I asked.

"Back to our house. I have to go into New York early tomorrow and I need some clothes."

"To New York? Why?"

"That was S—— on the phone," she said, naming the CBS lawyer whom she had gone to see in New York the afternoon she thought I'd been in bed up at the cottage with Barbara T. "He wants to talk to me about a job."

"How did he know you were here?" I asked.

"I wrote him. He called to say his firm was looking for a part-time para-legal something or other and he thought of me. I'm going into New York to meet him for lunch."

"You're going to *meet* him?" I cried.

"Don't worry," she said. "We're just going to talk."

"Yes, well, that's what I did with Barbara T. and look what happened. Don't you think we ought to discuss this a little before you run off?"

"If I'm going to get these children to bed at a decent hour I've got to run."

"Let them stay," I said. "Put them to bed here early and you and I can talk."

"No, I think we could all do with a break tonight." She turned to her children. "Come along," she said, and led them down the back steps to her car.

I followed her out. The wind had suddenly come up again and with it a fresh spray of rain. "You're just going to leave?" I asked.

"I've got to," Odette said as she climbed into her car. "We talked it all over, you and I. We agreed I should get a job, didn't we?"

"Yes," I said, "but not with *him!*"

"I love your jealousy," she said. "I'll be back tomorrow night, really. Relax. You have nothing to worry about."

"That's easy for you to say."

Odette laughed and I felt the rain cold against my back. "Go on inside," she said. "You're getting soaked." She started her car and backed up away from me. As she headed out the road I looked up at the beach cottage. Both of my children were gathered at the back door watching. I walked back up to the cottage, entered the kitchen, picked up my cold cup of coffee, and continued past the children and out to the porch and sat down. From where I sat I could see Andy in the living room of the Baptist cottage playing cards with the older members.

I had been sitting there for about ten minutes worrying about Odette meeting that man in New York when Joan came out with a fresh cup of coffee. "Odette said the one you have is cold," she explained.

"Thanks," I said.

Joan sat down next to me. "Are you angry with us?"

"Angry?" I thought for a moment. "Yes. I'm disappointed, too. In all of you."

"Because Odette left?"

"Odette left because she has to catch an early train into New York."

"But she said everyone could do with a break. Did she mean from us?"

"We're all fed up with the bickering and name-calling that's been going on."

"What name-calling?"

"You must have said something to get Vanessa upset. And I heard you myself this afternoon refer to Odette as 'Queen Odette.' "

"That was a *joke*."

"It's not funny."

Joan's expression became distant. "Well, I can't help that."

"The hell you can't."

"Why do you always blame me?"

"Who is to blame is beside the point. The point is all this, this petty meanness has got to stop! It's hard on everybody."

"It's hard on me, too!" she said, suddenly bursting into tears. "You've *changed!* I don't understand you anymore. You act as though you have no time for me. You make me feel as if I don't even belong with you, that you don't like me as much as, as Peter and the others and Odette." She sat beside me with tears streaming down her cheeks.

"Oh, Joanie, how could you *think* such a thing? Of course you belong! Of *course* I like you. I *love* you!"

"But you never talk to me. The only one you talk to is Odette."

"I talk so much with Odette because we have to build *our* relationship, work hard on staying together because in not too many more years you and all the other children are going to want to leave home. You're all going to want to lead your own lives. And once you leave Odette and I will only have each other. I'm not going to spend all these years with Odette raising you only to find that she and I are strangers to each other when you're gone. Maybe now you think Odette is taking me away. That because I love her you think I don't love you—Jesus, sometimes I wish Arthur were here. A psychiatrist could explain all this so much better— but you've got to understand that I'm this way while you're with me so that it will be easier for you to say 'So long, Dad' when the time comes. It will be easier because you can leave free of worrying that you're abandoning a lonely old man and feeling guilty about it. Instead you'll know I have a woman, I'm not lonely, and that you've helped to contribute to that happiness and are free to pursue your own happiness."

I handed Joan my pocket bandanna and she blew her nose with a loud, manly *honk* that startled me.

"Sorry," she said, and smiled a little shyly.

"All right, to bring this lecture to a close I'll say only we *all* have to pull together for *all* our sakes. That is why if I see you behaving like a spoiled, lazy brat I'm going to kick ass."

She leaned away from me and burst out laughing.

"What?" I asked.

"You're beautiful when you're mad."

I kissed her on her forehead. "That's my girl!"

It began to rain hard an hour later and I telephoned Odette to see if she had reached home all right. She told me she was fine and that the children were already in bed. "I'm sorry I had to leave in such a hurry," she said.

"I understood."

"I know. And you're also being very nice about my going to New York."

"I'm working hard at it," I laughed.

"Don't worry."

"I don't want to lose you."

"You couldn't even if you wanted to."

"What kind of job was he talking about? What did he say?"

For the next several minutes Odette told me how para-legalism was a relatively recent field, that it covered a broad area, how nowadays almost anyone in a law firm who wasn't a secretary or a lawyer was a para-legal. She had no idea what she would be doing, that it could be anything that didn't require a law degree.

"Why did you write him?" I asked.

"What?"

"You said he knew to call you here because you'd written him. Why did you write him?"

"To ask if he had any ideas about a job. I wrote him when you were writing all your brokerage house friends. And I told him about us. On the phone he was very friendly, but businesslike, and he said he had this opening and thought of me."

I was silent for a moment and then I said, "I'm going to be very mature about this. You'll be surprised."

"I wouldn't be surprised."

"Well, I would," I said, and laughed. "I want to kill the bastard. Just tell me one thing, will you? I have only one personal question, okay? . . . Is he covered with hair?"

"*What?*" Odette laughed.

"You heard me."

"How would I know?" Odette asked, and laughed again.

"Jesus, you're quick."

"I have to be to keep up with you."

When I was silent, Odette asked, "Is everything all right there with you?"

I told her of Joan's and my conversation.

"Don't be too hard on Joan," Odette said. "We knew it wasn't going to be easy. We're not, as I've pointed out, 'The Brady Bunch.' It's important only that the children understand that we have a right to be happy, too. But it's hard because we're all still so afraid and worried and down about the divorces that none of us acts or reacts normally to anything at the moment."

"Come back as soon as you can tomorrow."

"Maybe you should spend more time alone with your kids."

"I'm alone with them now. I need *you*."

"Me, too," she said. "I hate not sleeping with you."

"I know. I dread sleeping alone tonight." There was a sudden brilliant flash of lightning and a crash of thunder so loud even Odette heard it in her telephone. "Jesus!" I said in alarm.

Odette laughed. "You don't want to sleep alone because you're frightened by the storm!"

"I admit it. But I still wish you were here."

"Why?"

"Because if you were here and we were alone in bed I'd . . ." I whispered what I'd do to her and I knew she was smiling when she hung up.

The storm raged all night with great gusts of wind driving sheets of rain against the beach cottage's windows. The next morning, although the wind had died down, the sky remained overcast and there were occasional short bursts of rain. A little after one o'clock the wind began to pick up again and with it came more rain. The foul weather matched my mood.

I imagined Odette at lunch with that lawyer. I saw him lean toward her, touch her hand for emphasis. I recalled Odette's angry, "He's young and he's rich and he knows how to treat a woman!" Well, I was not young and I wasn't rich; but damn it all, I was finally learning how to treat a woman, too.

I wanted Odette to get this job because it would put her bad marriage behind her. She would be her own woman, in control of her life and free. What did it matter if she worked for *him?* The world was filled with "hims." It was up to me to prevent her from being susceptible, vulnerable to the blandishments of another man. And if I lost Odette, if she decided she wanted someone else, then I knew I would hurt, "*souffrir*" as she would say, but I also knew I would survive.

Had I not—had we *all* not made it this far?

We were all like survivors of a war—Odette, myself, Arthur, Alice, our children, our friends—survivors of the war between men and women. It had been a long war, one with atrocities on both sides. And although there has never been an unconditional surrender or a negotiated peace, both sides seem to have agreed to a truce. There were still tensions, God knows, occasional incidents, terrorist acts. But the worst was over. The women I saw around now seemed, for the most part, more relaxed. There was a softness in their eyes and at the corners of their mouths.

I was beginning to relax, too. I trusted Odette. I believed her when she said I was not to worry. And I tried not to. But when by six o'clock Odette had still not telephoned, I could not prevent myself from feeling almost physically ill.

Odette finally called at six-thirty. "We didn't finish lunch until nearly three," she said, "and then I did some shopping in New York. Listen, I think I have the job."

"You do? That's wonderful!"

"And I won't have to start until September when the kids are back in school. The hours are very flexible. I could even do some work at home."

Odette was so enthusiastic and excited I was almost able to forget with whom she'd be working. "Oh, and guess what?" she was saying. "He said if I worked full-time, my salary would be between sixty and seventy-percent of what a starting lawyer gets. I'd be earning good money. And they have a lot of contract work with European television and so my languages are useful."

"It sounds perfect, Odette," I said. "It really does."

"It is. I really think it is." She was silent for a moment. "You wouldn't be upset if I took this job?"

"Not if it's what you want."

"I do want it."

"Then it's settled," I said. We were both silent until I said, "Oh, Christ!"

"What?"

"I can't help it. I hate myself. I have to ask. Did he try to kiss you?"

"No!" Odette laughed. "No, we shook hands. He was very businesslike. He was friendly, but it was all business."

"Well, then it *is* all wonderful news," I said. "When am I going to see you?"

"The children are still with Arthur. He's taken them to dinner, so they won't be back until nine or so."

"Not until then?"

"It would be too exhausting to drive to the beach tonight. And besides we haven't been in this house at all and there's a lot of catching up I have to do."

"I know. You're right."

"We'll drive out first thing in the morning."

"I hope the weather will be better by then."

Overnight the wind shifted direction and blew the storm out to sea. By ten-thirty there was blue sky, but as an aftermath of the winds, the surf was still high. The children changed into their bathing suits and headed for the beach. I saw Joan tuck the raft under her arm and called out to her to be careful. "And you, Peter," I said, "I want you to stay out of the water."

"Oh, *Dad!*" he protested.

"I'll join you in a little while. But I don't want you going into the water unless I'm watching you."

"Hurry up then. I want to go in."

"I will," I said. At that moment Odette's car pulled up to the back of the cottage and I went out to meet her.

She climbed out of her car and hugged me. "I missed you," she said.

"Me, too."

The children came out with paper bags. "We brought fresh corn!" Paul said.

"And tomatoes," Vanessa said.

"Where's Peter?" Paul asked.

"He and Joan have gone down the beach."

"Oh, can I go, too?" Paul asked his mother.

"Sure," Odette said. "You and Vanessa can go together."

"The surf's much rougher than usual," I warned. "So be very careful. Wait for us."

The children were already running to change.

"And tell Joan to keep an eye on you!" I shouted.

"I don't think they heard you," Odette said.

We gathered up the children's sleeping bags, overnight bags, and the groceries and carried them inside the cottage. Odette put the groceries on the kitchen table and we turned to look at each other.

"Congratulations again about the job," I said. "I really do think it's wonderful news."

She hugged me and said, "Thank you. Thank you for understanding me and . . . and for your trust."

"If we can't trust each other, who can we trust?"

"You've come a long way, baby," she said and smiled.

"Not as far as I'd like."

"Farther than you think." She kissed me on the cheek. "Come on, I want to see the ocean."

I followed her through the living room and onto the porch. I quickly counted the children. Paul was already in the water up to his knees. Joan was resting on the raft about fifteen yards out. Peter was digging in the sand. Vanessa was doing cartwheels on the beach. I glanced over at the Baptist cottage. Their beach was empty, the rocking chairs on the porch unoccupied. They were all inside.

"I've never seen the surf this rough," Odette said. "It's a little scary."

Joan was paddling the raft toward the beach. We could hear her laughter over the crash of the surf. "I'd better start the charcoal," I said.

"*Paul!*" Odette called. He was wading deeper into the waves. "PAUL!" She shouted louder this time.

"He can't hear you," I said.

"He has absolutely no fear," she said. "I don't want him to go out too far."

"He won't. He has more sense than that," I said. I turned back to get the charcoal and did not see the wave that hit Paul and knocked him down. All I saw out of the corner of my eye was Odette quickly dart toward the ocean, and I ran, too. Paul's head was under water and we could see him clawing at the sand as the undertow dragged him out. Suddenly, as if out of nowhere, Joan was next to Paul, grabbing his arm, and she pulled him gasping and sputtering to the surface.

Odette and I reached Paul at the same time. His cheek was bleeding slightly where his face had scraped across a shell. He was not crying, but he would not let go of Joan until Odette's arms were around him. It wasn't until Odette had carried Paul back up the beach that the little boy began to cry.

"Is he all right?" Vanessa asked.

"He's fine," I said. "Just still very scared."

"What happened?" Vanessa asked.

"He got hit by a wave," I said. "Knocked down."

"Joan saved him," Odette said.

My daughter was standing with us. "I had a feeling that was going to happen," she said. "I don't think Paul realized how rough the water was—is."

I picked up a beach towel and wrapped it around Paul's thin shoulders, then I reached out and touched Joan's arm. "You did fine," I said.

"I don't know why," she said, "I just had a feeling. I'm glad I was there."

"Me, too," Paul said.

Peter arrived at that moment and saw us all gathered around Paul. "What happened?" he asked, he was towing Joan's raft by its rope.

"Paul swallowed a fish," Joan said.

"What?" Peter asked.

Joan snatched the raft from Peter and ran with it back out to the water.

A couple of hours later, although the surf was still higher than usual, the wind had stopped and the sea was calming down. The older Baptists had returned to their rocking chairs on the porch to watch the setting sun. We were sitting at our picnic table. We had finished our dinners and Odette and I were drinking coffee and watching Andy and his parents setting up the volleyball net on the beach in front of their cottage. When they had finished they came over to us to ask if we wanted to play.

"Can we, Daddy?" Joan asked.

I glanced over at Odette. "Would you like to?"

"Sure," she said.

Mr. Perlmutter said, "Mien son and I and my good wife here and we will get two of the young girls from the kitchen to join us and we will have five on our team."

"We have six," I said.

Mr. Perlmutter smiled at Paul and Peter. "We will count the two little ones as one big one."

"What shall we name the teams?" Andy asked.

"We could make it the Baptists versus the Episco—"

"*Mein Gott*, no!" Mr. Perlmutter interrupted, eyeing me with true alarm. "There are two things one can never make light of: religion and politics."

"Three things," I said. "War."

"Four," Odette added. "One should never make light of love."

Mr. Perlmutter responded with a series of elegant Old World gestures all implying agreement. "Vy don't ve call the teams Cottage One and Cottage Two. Ve shall be Cottage Two," he said, "because ve try harder."

Mrs. Perlmutter's bubbly laughter followed. "*Ja! Ja!*"

Because he was the smallest, Peter was given three attempts to serve over the net. Throughout the first thirty minutes of the game he succeeded in getting only one serve in. The ball would rocket off his fist sideways, roll down the beach and into the ocean. Joan would roll her eyes in dismay. Peter would serve again and the ball would dribble out of his palm and he would end up swinging at empty air.

"Strike *two!*" Andy would whoop.

When I was up at the net opposite Andy, he would say, "Oh-oh, here's trouble. We've got the mean one up front." I would feel strangely flattered, cheered; I wanted to make a good shot.

Midway through the game with the score tied at eight all, Odette's shoulder strap broke. She had changed before dinner into a light summery white cotton dress held up by two thin straps. When her strap snapped, she continued to play holding the broken strap up with one hand until an elderly Baptist lady came down from the porch murmuring sympathetically and safety-pinned Odette's strap back together. The sun had already set by then; it was growing dark.

"Okay, let's get this game *going,*" Joan said. "It's Vanessa's serve. Just get it in."

Vanessa's serve bounced into the net. "Oh, come on!" Joan said, exasperated. Neither side could accumulate the two-point lead needed to win. The game went on and on.

Mrs. Perlmutter's serve soared high over our heads and out of bounds.

"Aw, Mom!" Andy said, shaking his head like an old man. "C'mon, Mom, you've got to get your act together."

"I'm not a volleyball player," Mrs. Perlmutter said with a shrug.

"*I'll* say!" Andy laughed.

We rotated positions and it was Odette's turn to serve. She hit a gentle blooper over the net that Mrs. Perlmutter managed to deflect backward over her head and out.

"Eighteen–seventeen!" Joan shouted. "Match point!"

"Look out," Andy said, laughing at his mother, "they've found our weak spot."

Andy and I were directly opposite each other at the net again. Looking at him was like seeing myself across the net from my father thirty years before.

"Match point! Match point!" Joan was saying. "If we get this point, we win!"

Odette's serve was returned by one of the kitchen girls. Her shot looped high over the moonlit net toward me, a perfect ball for me to spike, to hit back down at Andy. I glanced quickly to see where Andy was, heard the boy say, "He's gonna *kill* me!" I saw Andy's expression: half-terror and half-ecstatic anticipation. I took two steps backward to get into position and Joan slammed into me shouting, "I've got it! I've got it!" and the two of us fell in a tangle of arms and legs; the ball bounced away and down the incline of the beach toward the sea.

"Oh, *Joan!*" Vanessa said, mimicking Joan's accent exactly.

Paul retrieved the ball and rolled it under the net to Cottage Two. Joan had quickly gotten to her feet and was busy pretending the collision had never occurred. "Okay, Cottage One," she said. "We can get the serve back. Let's get it back."

Andy's serve passed high over my head and bounced at Vanessa's feet. Joan looked at her with utter incredulity.

"I couldn't see it!" Vanessa said, looking defiantly at Joan. "Well, I *couldn't!* It's dark and I couldn't see around your father."

"Eighteen all!" Andy called. "Just two more serves to win. We've got them now."

"C'mon, Cottage One!" Joan yelled. "We've got no *discipline!*"

Joan hit Andy's next serve back into the net.

"Nineteen–eighteen," Andy said. "Match point."

"Match point!" Joan cried. "We've got to get this one. We'll get it. Okay, Cottage One, settle down . . . Keep your eyes on the ball, Vanessa. You, too, Peter, Paul." She passed among us like a team captain, stopping here and there for an encouraging word. "If the ball comes to you, just get it up in the air, let Daddy or Odette set it up for me."

"You guys ready?" Andy called.

"As ready as we'll ever be," I said.

Andy served the ball directly to Odette, who hit it with a great swinging roundhouse punch that sent the ball glancing off her fist at right angles to the volleyball court. It cleared the surf and bobbed in the ocean just beyond the breaking waves.

"Game?" Andy said quietly, almost questioningly. He looked at Joan, who was looking at me, and then we were all looking soundlessly at Odette, who was as astonished by her shot as the rest of us.

Mrs. Perlmutter's bubbly laughter broke the silence and Odette laughed, too. I looked away from her to where the white ball floated in the water; the slight wind, the falling tide were carrying it further out. My bewilderment must have shown on my face, for she looked at me and her smile died on her lips.

"I didn't *mean* to do it," she said, then she squared her shoulders, walked down to the edge of the surf, and, standing with her back to us, slid smoothly out of her white cotton dress—she wore no bra—and in only her translucent bikini panties began wading out through the surf toward the ball.

"Odette, no! *Wait!*" I called out to her, but she did not listen or could not hear. I turned toward Mr. and Mrs. Perlmutter, who were worriedly talking to one another and, looking back at Odette, saw she was already in the black water up to her breasts.

"ODETTE!" I yelled. "*Leave* the ball! *Forget* it!"

No response. The ball had already floated thirty yards out.

"*We can get another!*" I shouted. "*Don't go for it! It's too dark! The tide's going out!*"

The children, sensing the worry in my voice anxiously gathered at the edge of the water.

Although Odette could swim, she was not a strong swimmer and I was afraid the tidal current would carry her out. I couldn't understand why she would plunge into the dark ocean after a stupid volleyball. I was frightened for her—for myself, too, since I would have to go into the ocean after her. I hated the ocean at night. My imagination was too fierce.

"Is *Maman* going to be all right?" Paul asked.

"Of course she is," I said.

"I can't *see* her anymore," Vanessa said. "*I can't see her!*"

I had removed my shirt and was unbuttoning my pants. Joan, who was standing between Paul and Vanessa said, "I can see your mother. She's about fifty feet out."

"Is she going to be all right?" Paul asked again. He was on the verge of tears.

I left my pants next to Odette's discarded dress. The water was cold, but not unbearable. The first wave hit my thighs, the water splashing like icy needles against my groin. The second wave struck me in the chest knocking me backward a step. I waded out farther and dove into the third wave before it broke and then I started to swim.

Almost immediately I could feel the current pulling me out and I tried to gauge how strong it would be pushing against us when we swam back in. I would take about five strokes then lift myself as high out of the water as I could to locate Odette. She was about twenty yards ahead of me, the ball perhaps another fifteen yards in front of her. I put my head down and swam.

I was furious and frightened. I kept thinking I saw large gray shapes in the choppy water about me, or that something had just lightly brushed my leg. I imagined the bottom endlessly deep beneath me, the sharks curling and rolling up toward us. I was afraid that a wave would break over me as I breathed in and, like my brother, water would rush into my lungs and I would drown before ever reaching Odette, and without Odette even knowing I was sinking. Or I imagined that Odette would be unable to find the ball, that she would swim past it in the dark, and keep swimming further out until, too tired to return, she would give in and let herself be carried out to sea.

I swam harder—still as much out of anger as fear. Odette and I were going to drown because of a stupid goddam volleyball. Because the tide was going out. Because she had overestimated her strength. When I lifted myself up on a wave to look for Odette she was gone.

She was gone!

I swam until I felt the next swell lift me and again I searched the black water ahead. The waves were running about three feet high and as I would be carried up on one, I could not see into the troughs behind the others.

"*Odette!*" I shouted. "ODETTE!"

There was no answer. There was only the gurgle of the water. *Oh God*, I thought, *She's gone under! I've lost her!* Three more strokes and I felt the next wave lift me. Again I shouted, "ODETTE!"

Someone back at the Baptist cottage turned on the rooftop floodlights and just before I slid into the trough between the swells I thought I saw a faint sparkle of water spray ahead of me. It could have been Odette's kick as she swam. When the next wave lifted me I shouted again. I saw nothing and there was no response. I swam another ten strokes and let myself be lifted by the wave. "ODETTE!" I yelled.

"*Here!*" She was just ahead of me, the volleyball in her arms.

"Thank God," I said, and swam to her side.

"Are you all right?" she asked.

"Am *I* all right?" I panted. "I was worried about *you!* I thought *you* had drowned."

"I'm fine," she said. "I've got the ball." I noticed she didn't sound winded at all! "Were you really afraid I might drown?" she asked.

"We still might," I said. "The tide's taking us out." I took the ball from her. "Swim for the lights. If you get tired, let me know and we'll rest."

"If *you* get tired, let *me* know," Odette said.

"I *am* tired."

The wave lifted us and we were facing the Baptist cottage lights. "It looks like someone's making a movie, doesn't it?" Odette asked.

"If we don't start swimming back it could turn into a sequel to *Jaws!*"

Odette struck out for the beach and I followed after her. I tried tucking the volleyball under my arm and doing a sidestroke, but the ball kept squirting out. I then tried floating on my back, holding the ball against my chest and kicking in; but the waves kept breaking across my face and I would cough and cough.

I was becoming increasingly nervous. I could feel the tide pulling against me. When I stopped to cough, I could feel myself being carried back out. I floated in the darkness thinking *I am going to drown.*

I tucked the ball back under my arm and swam. I could not tell how far away we were from the beach or how far I was from Odette. I took several strokes and then something huge and cold and hard bumped my arm, struck my thigh. "JESUS!" I shouted in panic. The ball squirted away from me as I spun in the water and flailed out against the shark.

"*Ouch! Hey!*" Odette yelled. "It's me! Are you crazy?"

"Am *I* crazy?" I answered. "Was I the one who swam out here after a goddam volleyball?"

"Are you angry with me?"

"I'm too scared to be angry," I said. But I *was* angry. So angry as Odette began again to swim toward the beach that I felt like throwing the ball at the back of her head. *Throwing the ball?* Why hadn't I thought of that?

All I had to do was throw the ball ahead of me, swim up to it, and toss it ahead of me again. I could repeat that all the way into the beach and have both arms free to swim. I waited until the next wave lifted me up, then threw the ball as hard as I could toward the Baptist cottage's lights.

Odette and I were less than ten yards from the beach when I realized she would be walking out of the ocean wearing now-transparent panties and no bra. The floodlights, which so brightly illuminated the surf would, of course, illuminate Odette as well.

I caught up with Odette and we swam in together until we were just behind the breaking surf. I threw the volleyball over the breakers and saw someone dash forward to catch it as it washed up on the beach.

The lights seemed blinding. I could make out clumps of people standing at the edge of the water, their bodies silhouetted blackly in front of the glare. I touched Odette's arm. "Let me get out ahead of you," I said. "If you keep behind me, no one will see you when you get out."

"Who cares?" she asked.

"*I* do!" I cried. "Those are *our* breasts. I don't want them being ogled by everybody else!"

She just laughed.

"Jesus Christ!" I exploded. "Have you lost your senses? *First,* you punch the ball into the goddam ocean. *Next* we almost drown. And now, and *now,* you're going to rise up out of the ocean in front of the assembled Trenton Baptist congregation like . . . like some goddam Botticelli's *Venus* and you—"

"You adore me, don't you?" she said.

"Of course I do, but I—"

"And you'll never love another woman the way you love me, will you?"

"No, you're right, I won't. But I—"

"You swam out to save me, didn't you?" None of these had been questions, really. "Put your feet down," she said. "We can stand here."

Cautiously I lowered my legs and found myself standing facing the Baptist cottage in water up to my chest. Odette threw her arms around me and kissed me on the lips. "Don't be angry with me," she said. "I didn't mean to hit the ball into the ocean."

"I know you didn't."

"And I'm sorry we lost. But it *was* only a game."

"It was only a volleyball, too," I said. "Hardly worth the two of us drowning for."

"I would have saved you."

"*You* would have saved *me?*"

"Of course," she said. "Or are women not allowed to save men?"

"I think, under the circumstances," I said, somewhat stiffly, "when one is drowning, one tends not to be especially sexist."

" 'One tends not to be especially sexist,' " Odette laughed, mimicking my accent. "I *adore* you." She was standing in front of me in the water, the surf still breaking just ahead of us. "Well, we didn't drown, did we? And now you know something that you didn't know before."

"What?"

"That you really love me."

"Of course I *really* love you," I said. "I didn't have to nearly drown out there to know that!"

"No, you didn't," Odette said. "But you were willing to risk your life for me." She touched my cheek with her fingertips. "All of them know that now," she said, and she turned away from me to wade through the surf toward the beach.

"*Odette!*" I cried. "Your *breasts!*"

"I know!" she laughed, and turning back to face me, she cupped them in her palms. "Aren't they beautiful?"

"Yes," I said. "Especially the one with the pink nose."

By then, of course, I was laughing, too. Odette and I stood there hugging each other as the surf crashed about us and diamond flares of spray sparkled about our heads. I looked past Odette's shoulder to the beach.

The lights were so bright it was difficult, at first, to distinguish the silhouettes of the Baptists from those of our children, but then I was able to make out the little figures of Peter and Paul off to one side and next to them, Vanessa and Joan. The girls appeared to be standing like Romans holding up long, rectangular shields.

As Odette and I waded in Vanessa and Joan advanced toward us. For a moment I thought they wanted us to go back into the sea. It wasn't until we were a few yards from them, the surf tugging at our ankles, that I saw that the large "shields" they had been holding up were beach towels, to cover and warm us.

"We thought you might want these," Joan said, as she wrapped her towel around Odette.

Vanessa handed me her towel saying, "You'd both better come inside and warm up."

They were speaking to us as if we were their children. In an instant Peter and Paul were beside us, their arms filled with our clothes. "Are you all right?" Peter asked.

"We're fine," Odette said.

"Were you scared?" Paul asked.

"*I* was," I said. "Your mother seemed to have everything under control."

The six of us turned to walk back up the sand to our cottage. Someone in the Baptist cottage switched off the floodlights and, as the beach faded to black, we could hear Paul start to sing. As I listened to his sweet, incredibly beautiful boy-soprano, I could feel my heart swell with love for them all. And then suddenly I realized that Paul was singing the theme from "The Brady Bunch."

"Oh, *ick!*" Joan said.

Odette glanced over at me. Because of the soft light coming from our cottage I could see her smile.